The
MURDERS
at FLEAT
HOUSE

Also by Lucinda Riley

The Hothouse Flower
The Girl on the Cliff
The Light Behind the Window
The Midnight Rose
The Italian Girl
The Angel Tree
The Olive Tree
The Love Letter
The Butterfly Room

The Seven Sisters Series
The Seven Sisters
The Storm Sister
The Shadow Sister
The Pearl Sister
The Moon Sister
The Sun Sister
The Missing Sister

The
MURDERS
at FLEAT
HOUSE

By Lucinda Riley

BLUE
BOX
PRESS

The Murders at Fleat House
By Lucinda Riley

Copyright 2022 Lucinda Riley
ISBN: 978-1-952457-82-1

Published by Blue Box Press, an imprint of Evil Eye Concepts, Incorporated

This is a work of fiction. Names, places, characters and incidents are the product of the author's imagination and are fictitious. Any resemblance to actual persons, living or dead, events or establishments is solely coincidental.

Dedication

This novel is dedicated to all those who dream. Never give up and never give in—Lucinda didn't.
—Lucinda's family

Glossary of terms

AA: Alcoholics Anonymous, an organization that helps alcoholics achieve sobriety.

ASBO: An antisocial behaviour order given out by a court to stop a person behaving in a certain way.

CID: Criminal Investigation Department; the branch of a police force to which most detectives belong.

CPS: The Crown Prosecution Service.

PM: A post-mortem examination; an autopsy.

San: Short for 'sanatorium'. Some boarding schools have these as a sick bay for pupils.

SOCO: A scene of crime officer. Their job is to recover and record evidence, such as fingerprints and DNA samples, from a crime scene.

Foreword

Dear reader,

I hope you are as excited as I am to be turning the pages of a brand-new Lucinda Riley novel. Perhaps you are an avid fan of The Seven Sisters series, and are eagerly waiting for Lucinda to transport you to a new and vivid realm. Maybe, though, you are new to her writing, intrigued by the promise of this fresh and compelling crime novel. In this case, very sadly, I must start at the end, to contextualise the pages you are about to devour. For those not aware, Lucinda—Mum—died on 11 June 2021, following an oesophageal cancer diagnosis in 2017. I am Lucinda's eldest son and co-author (not of this project, I hasten to add). Together, we created the Guardian Angels series for children, and I am tasked with fulfilling her enormous literary legacy, by completing the eighth and final novel in The Seven Sisters series.

For this reason, I wish to tell you how *The Murders at Fleat House* came to be. Firstly, although it has never seen the light of day, it was written in 2006. Once her youngest children had started school, Lucinda penned three novels without a publisher, two of which have subsequently been released to great acclaim—*The Olive Tree* (also called *Helena's Secret*) and *The Butterfly Room*. It was always her plan to publish the third of these novels, which you currently hold in your hands, after the conclusion of The Seven Sisters series.

In the case of *The Olive Tree* and *The Butterfly Room*, Lucinda undertook extensive rewrites (as any author revisiting a project after a decade would wish to). Mum has not had that opportunity in the case of *The Murders at Fleat House*. As such, I faced a quandary when taking the decision to release this book. Was it my responsibility to edit, adapt and update the text, as she would have wished to? After much contemplation, I felt that preserving Mum's voice should take precedence. With this in mind, only the bare minimum editorial work has been undertaken.

All that you will read, therefore, is Lucinda's work from 2006.

Mum was hugely proud of this project. It is the only crime novel she ever wrote, but loyal readers will instantly recognise her unrivalled ability to capture a sense of place. I'm sure it will interest you to know that, at the time of writing, my family lived in the vast, mysterious landscape in which the story is set. What's more, the Norfolk school featured in the book was heavily inspired by the one which we, her own children, attended. Thankfully, I can confirm that nothing so dramatic actually took place in the corridors of the boarding houses.

As you might expect, hidden secrets from the past strongly influence present-day events, and we are treated to some typically superb characterisation in the form of DI Jazz Hunter, who I'm sure you'll agree has the potential to anchor a series of her own.

Perhaps she would have, in another life.

Harry Whittaker, 2021

Prologue

St Stephen's School, Norfolk
January 2005

As the figure took the stairs leading to the sixth-form corridor—a maze of shoebox-sized studies, one per boy—the only sounds were the clanking and stirring coming from the antiquated radiators, inefficient cast-iron sentinels that had struggled to warm Fleat House and the boys within it for the past fifty years.

One of the eight boarding houses that made up St Stephen's School, Fleat House had taken its name from the headmaster at the time it was built a hundred and fifty years ago. Known as 'Fleapit' by its current inhabitants, the ugly red-brick Victorian building had been converted into student accommodation just after the war.

It was also the last house to benefit from much-needed refurbishments. Within six months, the corridors, stairs, dormitories and common rooms would be stripped bare of the torn, black linoleum that covered the floors; the yellowing walls would be re-papered and freshened with magnolia and the archaic shower blocks would be re-equipped with glistening stainless-steel fitments and glossy white tiles. This, to appease today's demanding parents who insisted their children live and learn in comfort akin to a hotel, not a hovel.

Outside Study Number Seven, the figure paused for a moment, listening. Being a Friday, the eight boys on this floor would have signed out and walked to the pub in the nearby market town of Foltesham, but it was as well to be sure. Hearing nothing, the figure turned the handle and went in.

Closing the door quietly and switching on the light, the figure was aware almost immediately of the ingrained, musty smell of teenager: a mixture of unwashed socks, sweat and raging hormones which had, over the years, permeated every nook and cranny of Fleat House.

Shuddering, the smell triggering painful memories, the figure nearly stumbled on a pile of underwear thrown carelessly onto the floor. Then, reaching for the two white tablets placed on the boy's locker every night and replacing them with identical ones, the figure turned, switched off the light and left the room.

On the nearby staircase, a small figure in pyjamas froze as he heard approaching footsteps. In a panic, he dived into the small alcove under the stairs on the landing below, merging with the shadows. Being caught out of bed at ten o'clock would get him punished and he couldn't take any more of that tonight.

Rigid in the darkness, his heart hammering, eyes squeezed tightly shut as if this would somehow help, he listened, breathless, as the footsteps climbed the stairs inches above his head, passed him, then mercifully retreated into the distance. Shaking with relief, he crept out from his hiding place and hurried along the corridor to his dormitory. Climbing into bed and checking the time on his alarm clock, knowing there was an hour before he could allow himself the sanctuary of sleep, he pulled the blankets up over his head and, finally, let the tears come.

Approximately one hour later, Charlie Cavendish entered Study Number Seven and flung himself onto his bed.

Eighteen years old, eleven o'clock on a Friday night and he was gated like a child in this crap-heap of a rabbit hutch.

And he had to be up for bloody chapel at seven tomorrow. He'd missed it twice so far this term and couldn't afford to do so again. He'd already been hauled into Jones's office over that stupid thing with Millar. Jones had made noises about expulsion if he didn't mend his ways but it galled Charlie to have to keep his nose clean. His father had made it clear he wouldn't fund his gap year without a decent set of A level results and a school report to match.

Which would be a goddamned bloody disaster.

His father didn't approve of a gap year in any case. Hedonism was anathema to him and the thought of his son lolling on some Thai beach, probably high on drugs, was not what he had in mind, especially if he was the one paying for it.

They'd had an almighty row about Charlie's future just before the beginning of term. His father, William Cavendish, was a high-flying barrister in London and it had always been assumed that Charlie would follow in his footsteps. Growing up, Charlie had never given it much thought.

Then, as he headed into his late teens, it had slowly dawned on him what was expected, seemingly without regard for his own wishes.

Charlie was a wheeler-dealer, an adrenalin merchant; that's how he saw himself. He enjoyed living on the edge. The thought of a life stuck in the hierarchical, stuffy atmosphere of Inner Temple turned his stomach.

Besides, his father's idea of 'getting on' was completely outdated. It was all different these days; you could do what you wanted. All that respectability bollocks belonged to his parents' generation.

Charlie wanted to be a DJ and watch beautiful, half-naked women prancing around a dance floor in Ibiza. Yeah. That was more like it! And…you could make *loads* being a DJ.

Not that money was ever going to be a serious issue. Unless his unmarried, fifty-seven-year-old uncle suddenly decided to start having kids, Charlie was going to inherit the family estate with thousands of acres of farmland.

He had plans for that too. All he had to do was sell off a few acres with planning permission to a developer and he'd make a bloody fortune!

No, it wasn't his *future* finances; it was the fact that his tight-arsed father held fiscal dominion over him *now*.

He was young. He wanted to have some fun.

These were the thoughts cascading through Charlie Cavendish's mind as, absent-mindedly, he reached for the two tablets he had taken every night since the age of five and picked up the glass of water left there for him by Matron.

Placing the tablets on his tongue, he took a generous swig of water to wash them down before replacing the glass on his bedside locker.

For a full minute, nothing happened and Charlie, sighing, continued to ruminate on the unfairness of his situation. But then, almost imperceptibly, he felt his body begin to shake.

'What the hell...?!'

The shaking intensified, becoming uncontrollable, and suddenly Charlie felt his throat constricting. Panicking now, uncomprehending and gasping for breath, he managed to stagger the few steps to the door. He grasped the handle but in his increasing terror, he fumbled with it, unable to turn it before collapsing semi-conscious, one hand at his throat, his mouth foaming. Deprived of oxygen, the lethal toxins coursing through him, his vital organs gradually shut down. Then his bowels relaxed and, little by little, the young man who had once been Charlie Cavendish simply ceased to exist.

Chapter One

Robert Jones, headmaster of St Stephen's School, stood with his hands in his pockets—a habit he constantly chastised his charges for—and stared out of his study window.

Below him, he saw pupils crossing Chapel Lawn on their way to and from lessons. His hands were damp with sweat, his heart still racing from the adrenalin, as it had done constantly since the accident.

He left the window and went to sit behind his desk. There was a mounting pile of paperwork that remained untouched and a list of telephone messages he had yet to reply to.

Taking out his handkerchief, he wiped the top of his bald head, then sighed heavily.

There were any number of potentially nightmarish situations facing a headmaster in charge of hundreds of teenage boys and girls: drugs, bullies and, in these days of mixed-gender boarding schools, the unstoppable phantom that was sex.

During his fourteen years as headmaster of St Stephen's, Robert had dealt, to some degree, with them all.

But all these crises had paled in comparison to what had happened last Friday. This was the ultimate head's nightmare: the death of a pupil in his care.

If there was a way to leave a school's reputation in tatters, this was it. The details of *how* the boy had died were almost irrelevant. Robert could visualise hordes of parents currently shopping for boarding schools crossing St Stephen's off their lists.

Yet, Robert sought comfort in the fact that the school had survived for more than four hundred years—and looking through the records, he saw this kind of tragedy had occurred before. Perhaps the numbers would fall short term, but as time passed, surely what had happened last Friday would eventually be forgotten.

The last schoolboy death had been back in 1979. A boy had been found dead in the trunk room in the cellar. He'd hanged himself with a piece of cord tied to a hook on the ceiling. The incident had become part of school folklore. The kids loved to perpetrate the myth that the boy's spirit haunted Fleat House.

Young Rory Millar had looked like a ghost himself when he'd been found hammering on the door, having spent the night locked in there.

Charlie Cavendish, without question the perpetrator, had denied everything as usual and, worse, found it funny… Robert Jones shivered uncomfortably, wishing he could find it in him to mourn the loss of his young life and finding he couldn't.

That boy had been trouble from the moment he'd set foot in the school. And, thanks to his death, Robert's future was now in question. At fifty-six years of age, he'd been looking forward to retiring in four years on a full pension. If he was forced to resign, there would be little hope of getting a position elsewhere.

At the emergency meeting of the board of governors last night, he'd offered his resignation. The governors, however, had stood by their headmaster.

Cavendish's death was an *accident*…natural causes. He'd died of an epileptic fit.

This was Robert's one ray of hope. As long as the coroner returned a verdict of death by natural causes and media coverage was kept to a minimum, it was possible the damage could be limited.

But until this was confirmed, his reputation and future were hanging by a tenuous thread. They had promised to call this morning.

The telephone rang shrilly on his desk. He pressed the speakerphone. 'Yes, Jenny?'

'It's the coroner's office for you.'

'Put them through.'

'Mr Jones?'

'Yes, speaking.'

'It's Malcolm Glenister here, the local coroner. I wanted to discuss the results of the post-mortem conducted yesterday on Charlie Cavendish.'

Robert swallowed hard. 'Of course. Fire away.'

'The pathologist has concluded that Charlie did not die of an epileptic fit. He died of anaphylactic shock.'

'I see.' Robert swallowed again, trying to clear his throat. 'And…what was the cause?'

'Well, as you must know, his medical records show he was violently allergic to aspirin. Six hundred milligrams of it were found in his bloodstream, which would correspond to two over-the-counter tablets.'

Robert couldn't reply, his throat now too dry to speak.

'Other than traces of the drug Epilim, which Charlie took every day to control his epilepsy, and minimal alcohol levels, the pathologist found nothing else. He was perfectly healthy.'

Robert found his voice. 'If he'd been found sooner, might he have survived?'

'If he'd been given treatment immediately, then yes, almost certainly. However, the likelihood of him being able to call for help in the couple of minutes before falling unconscious were slim. It's understandable no one found him until next morning.'

Robert paused, feeling a small trickle of relief enter his veins. 'So, what happens next?' he asked.

'Well, we know *how* he died. The question is, why? His parents have confirmed Charlie *knew* he was allergic to aspirin; he'd always known.'

'He must have swallowed the tablets by mistake. There's no other explanation, is there?'

'It's not my job to speculate without the full facts, Headmaster, but there are one or two unanswered questions. And I'm afraid there's going to be a police investigation.'

Robert felt the blood drain from his face. 'I see,' he said quietly. 'How will that affect the day-to-day running of the school?'

'You'll have to discuss it with the detective in charge.'

'When will the police come?'

'Sharpish, I would think. They'll be in touch with you shortly to make the arrangements. Goodbye now.'

'Goodbye.'

Robert switched the speakerphone off, feeling dizzy. He took three or four long, deep breaths.

A police investigation… He shook his head. It was the worst possible news.

And then it struck him: for the past few days, all he'd been able to think about was the school's reputation. But if the police were involved, then the coroner must have doubts about Cavendish taking the aspirin by mistake.

'Jesus Christ.' Surely they couldn't think it was murder?

Robert shook his head again. No, it was probably just a formality.

In fact, come to think of it, Charlie's father would have the clout to insist on it. He thought back to the number of times Cavendish had stood in front of his desk, gazing down at him insouciantly as he was reprimanded. It was always the same routine: Robert would remind him that the ancient pastime of using the boys as servants had ended years ago and that he was not to bully them into subservience if they didn't co-operate. Charlie would accept his punishment, then carry on as if nothing had happened.

Charlie, originally down for Eton, had failed the entrance exam. From the day he'd arrived at St Stephen's he'd made it clear he considered the school, its headmaster and his fellow pupils beneath him. His arrogance had been breathtaking.

In search of inspiration, Robert stared at the painting of Lord Grenville Dudley, the sixteenth-century founder of the school, then, looking at his watch, realised it was almost lunchtime. He jabbed at the intercom button.

'Yes, Mr Jones?'

'Jenny, could you come through, please?'

The comforting form of Jenny Colman appeared through his door a few seconds later. She'd worked at the school for the past thirty years, initially as a dinner lady, then, after a secretarial course, as an admin assistant in the bursar's office. When Robert had arrived fourteen years ago and found his secretary about to retire, he'd chosen Jenny as her replacement.

She'd been far from the most sophisticated candidate, but Robert liked her calm, unflappable style and her knowledge of the school had been invaluable as he'd settled into his headship.

Everyone loved Jenny, from the cleaners to the governors. She knew each child by name and her loyalty to the school was beyond question. Three years older than Robert, she was further down the road to retirement and Robert had often wondered how he would cope when she left. Now, he realised miserably, he'd probably be leaving before her.

Jenny had been absent all of last term, due to a hip operation. Her replacement had been competent, and probably far more up to speed on office technology, but Robert had missed Jenny's motherly demeanour and was glad to see her back again. At the ready with her notebook and pen, Jenny settled her rotund frame into a chair in front of the desk, a look of deep concern on her face.

'You're a right funny colour, Mr Jones. Can I get you a glass of water?' She spoke with a Norfolk burr.

Robert had a sudden urge to put his head against Jenny's ample bosom, to feel her maternal arms wrap around him and find comfort in them.

'That was the coroner's office,' he said, dismissing the thought. 'It's not good news. There's going to be a police investigation.'

Jenny raised her bushy eyebrows. 'No! Surely not.'

'Let's just hope they get it over with quickly. It's going to be disruptive and destabilising for everyone having the police snooping around.'

'I'll say,' agreed Jenny. 'Do you think we'll all have to be interviewed?'

'No idea, but we'll obviously have to alert everyone. Apparently, a detective is phoning me any minute. I'll know more when I've spoken to him. But perhaps it might be best to call a school assembly in Main Hall tomorrow morning, warn everyone of what's going to happen. That means *all* staff, too, from the kitchen porters up. Can you organise that for me?'

'Of course, Mr Jones. I'll do it now.'

'Thanks, Jenny.'

She stood up, then said, 'Have you called David Millar back yet? He's rung again three times this morning.'

The last thing Robert needed was a deranged alcoholic parent panicking about his son.

'No, I haven't.'

'Well, he rang several times yesterday evening and left messages, something about Rory being upset on the phone.'

'I know, you said. He'll just have to wait. I've got more important things on my mind at the moment.'

'How about some tea? You look as though your sugar levels could do with a boost. It's ever so good for shock.'

'Thank you, that would be nice.' He nodded gratefully.

The telephone rang on his desk. Jenny got there first and picked it up.

'Headmaster's office.'

She listened for a moment, then shielded the receiver with the palm of her hand and whispered, 'It's a Commissioner Norton to speak to you.'

'Thanks.' Robert took the receiver and waited until Jenny had bustled out of the door. 'Headmaster speaking.'

'Headmaster, Assistant Commissioner Norton from the CID here. I presume you know what this call is regarding.'

'Yes.'

'I thought I should alert you to the fact that I'm sending a couple of detectives in to investigate the death of Charlie Cavendish.'

'Right, yes. Yes.' Robert Jones did not know what else to say.

'They'll be descending on you tomorrow morning.'

'From where?'

'London.'

'London?'

'Yes. The case has been passed to us at CID Special Ops. We'll be working in conjunction with the North Norfolk Constabulary.'

'I appreciate you must do your job, Commissioner, but I'm obviously concerned about the disruption to the school, not to mention the panic factor.'

'My colleagues are very experienced in dealing with cases like this, Headmaster. I'm sure they'll handle the situation sensitively, and advise you on how to handle the staff and pupils.'

'Yes. I was going to call a full school assembly tomorrow anyway.'

'Excellent idea. That will give my team an opportunity to brief the school, and perhaps stem some nerves about our presence amongst them.'

'I'll do that, then.'

'Right.'

'Can you give me the names of the detectives you'll be sending in?'

There was a slight pause on the line, before the commissioner said, 'Not sure yet, but I'll call you to confirm by the end of the day. Thank you for your time.'

'Thank you, Commissioner. Goodbye.'

Thank you for what? Robert Jones asked himself as he replaced the receiver. He put his head in his hands. 'Oh God,' he mumbled.

These police guys would be probing into everyone's background...their private lives... You never knew what they might drag up. He *himself* might become a suspect...

Numbers had been down for the past three years. There was so much competition these days. This was the last thing the school needed. Or, more selfishly, he thought, as he picked up the receiver to call the head of the governors, the last thing he needed.

Chapter Two

Jazmine Hunter-Coughlin—Jazz to her friends, Detective Inspector Hunter to her former work colleagues—drew back the curtains and glanced out of her small bedroom window. The view was limited, the condensation blurring the landscape of the Salthouse Marshes and the dour North Sea beyond. Automatically drawing her initials on the glass, the way she had done as a child, she studied the *JHC* for a moment, then smudged out the *C* with a determined swipe.

She glanced at the numerous cardboard boxes littering the floor of her bedroom. She'd moved in three days ago, but apart from unearthing essentials such as her pyjamas, the kettle and some soap, she had left the rest untouched.

This tiny cottage was the polar opposite of the white-walled, minimalist Docklands apartment she had shared with her ex-husband. And she loved it. Usually pathologically tidy, her unwillingness to unpack stemmed from the fact that the cottage would have to endure invasive renovations in the coming weeks. The plumber was booked for a week's time to put in the central heating, the joiner was calling tomorrow to measure up for the kitchen units, and she'd left messages with a couple of local decorators.

Jazz hoped that in a couple of months Marsh Cottage would look as picturesque on the inside as it promised from without.

It was brighter outside today, and Jazz decided to go for a morning stomp across the marshes to the sea. She put on boots and a Barbour, opened the front door and stepped outside, breathing in the rejuvenating fresh sea air.

Her cottage was situated on the coast road that separated the village from the marshes and the sea. In the summer, the road became congested with tourists using it to gain access to the beaches and coastal villages of North Norfolk, but today, at the end of January, it was deserted.

Jazz felt a small glimmer of contentment as she studied the view. Its flatness and lack of trees presented a bleak, unwelcoming picture, but Jazz coveted its rawness. There was nothing pretty about the landscape, nothing to break up the starkness of a horizon that stretched for miles on either side. The simple elegance of the land's distant curvature with the sea and the sheer vastness of the vista appealed to her unfussy nature.

As she crossed the road, she caught sight of a man coming out of the post office out of the corner of her eye, fifty or so yards away. Continuing across the road and onto the rough, marshy grass, she was focused on the comforting squelch of water underfoot when she thought she heard someone calling her name.

Dismissing it as the screeches of curlews that had gathered in a circle to the right of her, she continued up the incline, the only protection the cottage had from flooding—a moot point when she had been trying to secure a mortgage.

'Jazmine! DI Hunter! Please, wait a second!'

This time there was no mistaking it. She stopped and turned to look back at the road.

Christ! What the hell's he *doing here?* Jazz was appalled as she retraced her footsteps. She stopped a few yards away, offering him a small smile that didn't reach her eyes.

'Hello, DI Hunter.'

'Why are you here, Sir?'

'Nice to see you too,' said Norton, offering his hand.

'I'm sorry,' she sighed, finally, walking towards him and taking it, 'I wasn't expecting you, that's all.'

'It's quite all right. Now, are you going to invite me in before I freeze to death in this flimsy suit?'

'Yes, of course. Come in.'

Once inside, Jazz settled Norton on the sofa and stoked up the fire. She made them coffee, then perched on a wooden dining chair.

'Nice little place,' he said. 'Cosy.'

'Thanks,' she said, 'I like it.'

There was an awkward pause.

'So, Jazmine, how are you?'

It was odd hearing Norton call her by her first name. It underlined the extent to which her life had changed over the past months, but it also felt patronising.

'I'm fine,' she said.

'You look…better. Got a bit more colour since I last saw you.'

'Yes, it's warm in Italy, even in winter.' Another pause and Jazz wished he'd get to the point. 'How did you know I was here?' she asked finally, not ready to start the ball rolling herself. 'I only moved in three days ago.'

Norton chuckled. 'I'm surprised you need to ask, having worked at the Yard, although even *our* computer could only manage Twenty-Nine Salthouse Road. When I got here and couldn't find any numbers on the doors, I asked at the post office.'

'Ah,' said Jazz.

'Why here?' he asked.

'Childhood holidays, I suppose. I've always loved Norfolk and it seemed as good as anywhere. Near my parents, too.'

'Yes. Of course.'

Another pause.

'So,' said Norton, suddenly businesslike, sensing her impatience, 'you want to know why I drove more than a hundred miles to see you first thing on a frosty January morning. I did try your mobile, but apparently you've cancelled it.'

'I left it behind when I went to Italy. And when I got back I decided I didn't really need it.'

Norton nodded. 'Not much point in North Norfolk, anyway. Mine hasn't had a signal since Norwich. Anyway, the reason I'm here…is because I want you to come back to work.'

Jazz was silent for a moment. 'I thought I'd made things pretty clear,' she said quietly.

'You did. But that was seven months ago. You've had a sabbatical, got your divorce, found somewhere to live—'

'Which I've no intention of leaving to go back to London,' Jazz interjected sharply.

'I'm sure you haven't.' Norton seemed unfazed.

'Besides, how could I *possibly* come back? What makes you think I'd *want* to come back?'

'Jazmine, if you'd just stop the defensive routine for a minute and hear me out.' There was a sudden hard timbre in his voice.

'Sorry, *Sir*,' she said, 'but you'll forgive me if I'm not that keen to revisit the past.' Jazz knew she was being hostile but she couldn't help it.

'Yes, I can see...' He looked up at her. 'What I want to know, though, is why you're so angry with *me*? *I* didn't cheat on you.'

'That's a low blow, Sir.'

'Well'—Norton studied his immaculately manicured nails—'perhaps you felt I did.'

'Sir, I accept you could do nothing about my husband. I was already disillusioned by that time anyway and—'

'That was the straw that broke the proverbial camel's back.' Norton sipped his coffee and looked at her. 'Jazmine, do you know how much it costs to recruit and train a DI?'

'No, I don't.'

'Well, if I said a ball-park figure would buy you another cottage...'

'Are you trying to make me feel guilty?'

'If it works, yes.' Norton managed a half-smile. 'You didn't even give me a chance to talk things through with you. One week you were at your desk, the next you'd hotfooted it off to Italy.'

'I had no choice.'

'So you say. I'd have hoped that the good working relationship we'd forged would have meant you felt you could come to me and discuss it, that's all. If we'd agreed your resignation was the only alternative, I wouldn't have stood in your way. Instead of which, you just...ran off, no debriefing, nothing!'

Jazz's face was impassive. 'Oh. So, that's why you're here, is it? To debrief me?'

Norton gave a small sigh of frustration. 'Come now, I'm doing my best here. You're acting like a truculent teenager. The fact is, technically, you're still employed by us.' He pulled an envelope out of his inner breast pocket and pushed it towards her.

'What's this?' she murmured, frowning. Inside were payslips, correspondence relating to the account she'd shared with Patrick, the monthly statements which had continued to be sent to her old home and which, obviously, she hadn't seen. Also in the envelope was the resignation letter she'd hurriedly scribbled at the airport and posted before she got on the plane to Pisa.

'Not a very...professional departure, was it?'

'No, I suppose it wasn't, though I can't see that it matters now.' Jazz tucked the letter back into the envelope and offered it to him. 'There you are, Sir. I'm handing this to you officially. I resign. Will that do?'

'Yes, if that's the way you want it. Look, Jazmine, I do understand; I know you felt let down and demoralised and your personal life was in ruins. You probably needed some time to think things through…'

'Yup! That just about covers it, Sir.' She nodded vehemently.

'And because you were angry and bitter, you acted on your instincts and, at the time, your instincts told you to run. But you were also blinded by them. Can't you see that?'

Jazz didn't say anything.

'And,' Norton continued, '*because* you were blinded you made a spur of the moment decision, which, in addition to ruining a promising career, lost me one of my best officers. Look,' he smiled gently, 'I'm not an idiot. I knew what was going on. Finding out about your husband, especially if you were practically the last to know about it, must have been awful.'

Silence.

Norton sighed. 'It all comes back to the same thing: relationships at work are dangerous, especially doing what *we* do. I told DCI Coughlin that when he told me you two wanted to get married.'

Jazz looked up. 'Did he? Patrick told me you'd given us your blessing.'

'I actually suggested that one of you transfer to another division so that at least you wouldn't be tripping over each other. He begged me to let you stay where you were. So rather than lose both of you I decided to give it a try, against my better judgement, I might add.'

'Er, Sir, did you say DCI?'

'Yes. Your ex-husband has recently been promoted.'

'Don't bother to send him my congratulations.'

'Rest assured, I won't.'

Looking at him, Jazz thought how out of place Norton seemed in his Savile Row suit, his long legs bent almost up to his chest on the low sofa.

'Did you know, Sir? About Patrick and…*her*?'

'I'd heard a rumour, but I couldn't interfere. If it makes you feel any better, she put in for a transfer to Paddington Green a couple of weeks after you left. She knew she couldn't hope to compete with you. Everyone in the team cold-shouldered her with a vengeance. You were very popular, you know. They all miss you.'

Norton smiled broadly, showing a good strong set of white teeth. Jazz couldn't help thinking, with his thick black hair greying at the temples, his reading glasses perched on the end of his nose, how growing older was only enhancing his physical gravitas.

'Well, that's nice to know, I suppose. Anyway, what Patrick and his pet DC do now is up to them. I'm not interested any more. Mind you,' Jazz quipped, 'you might warn her that at the first sniff of competition, she'll get a knife in her back.'

'I don't doubt it. Your ex is a talented officer, but he's also ruthlessly ambitious. The one thing he couldn't deal with was a wife who was potentially better than he was. I knew what he was up to, undermining you, constantly putting you down, but because you never came to me, I couldn't do anything about it.'

'I was in an impossible situation. He was my husband.'

'I accept that. Anyway, as long as he learns to keep his trousers zipped I daresay he'll get what he's after, in the end.'

'He can screw the entire department if he wants. I really don't care.'

'That's the spirit,' Norton replied cheerily. 'So, are you sure you want me to take this letter back? It'll make it official, you know.' He waved the envelope at her.

'Yes, I do.'

'Okay, DI Hunter,' Norton said, suddenly formal, 'having had the opportunity to discuss the situation with you, you've made it clear you are determined to leave the force. I will take this letter and return to London with my tail firmly between my legs and not mention the other options I had in mind.'

The image of Norton with his tail between his legs made Jazz smile. She raised her eyebrows and sighed. 'Go on then, you might as well tell me, as you've come such a long way.'

'Believe it or not, there *are* other CID divisions. I might have suggested you transfer to one of those.'

'Paddington Green perhaps? Then I could share cosy *tête-à-têtes* with my ex-husband's lover.'

'I'm going to ignore that childish remark. But it does bring me to the point rather neatly. The question is, did you resign because of the situation *vis-à-vis* Patrick? Or because you no longer wanted to be part of the force?'

'Both,' Jazz answered honestly.

'All right, let me put it another way: here you are, thirty-four years of age, a highly trained CID officer, living in a Norfolk backwater like an old spinster. What on earth are you going to do with yourself?'

'I'm going to paint.'

Norton raised his eyebrows. 'Paint? I see. What, professionally, you mean?'

'God knows. If I hadn't joined the force, I was going to the Royal College of Art, once I'd got my degree at Cambridge. I had a place on the foundation course.'

'Really?' Norton looked surprised. 'Well, perhaps that's where you get your eye for detail.'

'Maybe, but anyway, that's the plan. I'm going to convert the outhouse into a studio. I've got enough left over from the sale of our old apartment to see me through for a while. Plus, there's a course at UEA I might apply for next year.'

'Admittedly, this isn't a bad place to rediscover your creativity,' agreed Norton.

'*Re*discovering is right, Sir,' Jazz said vehemently. 'The force took me over. I'd lost sight of the person I used to be.'

'Hmm.' Norton nodded. 'I understand that, but strikes me you've found her again. Your fighting spirit certainly seems to have made a return.'

'It has.'

'Look.' He sighed, serious again. 'How long are you going to keep on running? I don't think it was the force that got you down, but a man who was determined to undermine you and your confidence at every turn. I've watched you, Jazmine. You thrive on the adrenalin. You're an exceptional detective. And I'm not the only one who thinks so.'

'That's...kind of you, Sir.'

'I deal in facts, not kindness. It just galls me to watch someone of your ability throwing in the towel purely because her marriage didn't work out. I've seen you fighting against male chauvinism day in, day out, over the years. Are you really going to let Patrick win?'

Jazz remained silent and studied the carpet intently.

'Now, listen,' he said. 'Cutting to the chase, something's come up. What if I said I had a case only a few miles down the road from here?'

'A case here in Norfolk? How come?'

'There's been an incident at the local boarding school just outside Foltesham. A pupil was found dead in his study last Saturday morning. I was called because he's the son of a lawyer who's just managed to get a couple of major terrorists extradited to the UK. I've been asked to send some people along and double-check there's no foul play.'

Norton looked into Jazmine's clear green eyes and registered the small flicker of excitement.

'By the father?'

'The call *came* from the commissioner actually. As you know, the Met wouldn't usually be involved with something like this but—'

'What it is to have friends in high places.' Jazz smiled as she finished the sentence for him.

'Quite.'

'So how did the boy die?'

'He was an epileptic. The paramedics who arrived at the scene said the body presented all the hallmarks of a fit. However, his father rightly insisted on a post-mortem. The coroner contacted me this morning and it looks as if there might be more to it than meets the eye.'

'Such as?'

'I can't say any more until you've told me whether you're interested or not.'

They both knew she was.

'Maybe, as long as I can be home in time to paint the next *Mona Lisa*,' Jazz replied casually.

'*And* I'll send DS Miles down to give you a hand.' Norton's eyes were twinkling now.

'Give me a day to think about it, will you, Sir?'

'No time, I'm afraid. I need you on the case as of now. You're booked to see the boy's mother at two this afternoon. She lives a good hour and a half's drive from here. That means'—Norton checked his watch—'you have approximately one hour to make up your mind. Otherwise I must send someone else in. Here's the file.'

Norton handed Jazz a thick brown envelope.

She looked at him helplessly.

'An hour?'

'Yes. Seems like you're going to have to make another one of your famous spur of the moment decisions, DI Hunter. Looking back on your career, I'd say they've never served you wrong—apart from your decision to up and leave, of course.' Norton checked his watch. 'I must make a move. Said I'd be back in town for a meeting at two and these country roads are a nightmare.'

He stood up and, taller than Jazz at six foot two, brushed the top of his head against the ceiling.

'If I say no, what do I do with this?' She indicated the file.

'Burn it on that rather sad fire of yours. Looks as if it could do with some kindling. Right, I'll be off then.' Norton shook her hand. 'Thanks for the coffee.' He walked towards the door, then turned and faced her. 'I wouldn't come chasing all the way to Norfolk for just anyone, DI Hunter. And I promise you, I won't go down on bended knee again. Call me by noon. Goodbye.'

'Bye, Sir,' Jazz said. 'And thanks...I think,' she muttered, as an afterthought.

Chapter Three

David Millar paced up and down the small, untidy kitchen. Then, in a blaze of fury, he grabbed a milk bottle and hurled it against the far wall as hard as he could. It bounced off and fell with a clatter onto the linoleum-covered floor, but, infuriatingly, didn't break.

'Christ!' he screamed, then crouched where he was, head in his hands. Tears pricked under his eyelids, his breathing heavy and ragged.

'What the hell did I *do*?' he moaned, staggering to his feet, walking through the arched alcove and throwing himself onto the sofa.

In desperation, he tried practising the exercises the therapist had given him. Breathing slowly, concentrating on each breath, his anger gradually subsided. Opening his eyes, he found himself staring at the photograph of himself with Angelina and Rory, the smiling, happy family of three years ago.

He remembered the day it had been taken. A hot July afternoon, the sun gently baking the Norfolk countryside whilst they'd sat in the garden, eating lunch from the smoking barbecue nearby.

Everything had been perfect then, hadn't it? Everything. A beautiful wife, a gorgeous son, a new life. What he'd always dreamed of.

David had been born here, spent the first five years of his life in a small village outside Aylsham, and thereafter enjoyed childhood holidays on the coast. So when he and Angelina had talked seriously of escaping London, Norfolk had seemed the natural choice.

They'd bought a pretty farmhouse five miles from Foltesham and put a huge amount of time, effort and money into renovating it. Angelina had been in her element, choosing wallpaper and curtains; she'd been happy. She'd *seemed* happy, anyway. Rory had settled in at St Stephen's Prep, a far cry from the confined city school with its two feet of playground and choking London air. That had been fantastic, watching his son starting to embrace country life, his cheeks growing pinker, his thin frame filling out.

The only downside to it all, of course, was the long, daily commute David had to endure to his desk in the City, but he didn't even mind that. He would have done anything to keep Angelina and Rory happy.

Angelina, too, had blossomed, throwing herself into her new life, making new friends from the group of mothers she met in the school car park. Many of them had similarly escaped the London drudge, seeking a better life in the country.

She had never been busier. Book clubs, the PTA, ladies' lunches and tennis lessons filled the long days while David was at work. She invited like-minded couples round for supper, who then returned the favour, and gradually their social life became more and more active.

Going to dinner parties, David was aware that their new friends' houses tended to be grander than their own. The women talked a lot about designer clothes, designer shoes and holidays in Mauritius or the Caribbean; the men boasted of their wine cellars and the 'pair of Purdeys' they'd bought for the season's shoot.

He felt no envy. Coming from relatively humble beginnings, David felt he'd achieved a lot. He was perfectly happy in his comfortable house with his wife and son. At the time he'd believed Angelina was, too.

Looking back, he probably should have realised. Should have sensed what was going on from Angelina's wistful remarks: 'Oh darling, Nicole's husband's just bought her *the* most wonderful new four-wheel-drive Mercedes!' And, 'Everyone seems to have rented villas in Tuscany for the summer; wouldn't it be gorgeous if we could too?'

She began saving the property pages from the local paper, placing them discreetly on his knee to point out a particular house that had recently come onto the market. Before long David began to realise that Angelina was firmly hinting their lifestyle should match that of their smart, moneyed friends by taking a step up the property ladder themselves.

Considering Angelina had been a beauty therapist living in a terraced house in Penge when he'd met her, David felt, justifiably, that he'd already raised her some considerable distance.

But Angelina's need to keep up with the Joneses had become insatiable. David finally gave in on the car, buying her the four-wheel-drive she so desperately craved, and which she doted on like a second child. The pleasure it gave her driving each day into the school car park made David smile. He enjoyed making her happy, but the fact she was so obviously preoccupied with social status troubled him more and more.

David was a successful broker in the City, trading in foreign currency for a steady list of clients. He had a solid reputation as a safe pair of hands but wasn't considered a high flyer. He didn't take risks which could result in the kind of rewards that a small handful of City boys were famous for receiving, but he also avoided the equally publicised losses that came hand in hand with those risks. He was sensible with money, insisting they live on his salary, any bonuses being lodged safely in the bank for the future. Aware that his City career could not last forever, he was determined to make sure he had a comfortable amount of cash in reserve for any enforced early retirement.

Angelina had known the money was there, but she couldn't understand why David refused to touch it.

'Darling, we're still young,' she'd complained. 'Surely this is the moment we should be shooting for the moon? Your career's on the up and up; I can't think why we have to keep saving for a rainy day that may never come. We don't want to be seventy and sitting on a wad of cash! We'll be too old to enjoy it. Think about it, we could have the house of our dreams!'

David remembered murmuring that he thought they already *had* the house of their dreams, but Angelina wouldn't let up.

Eventually, against his better judgement, he'd given in and Angelina had immediately set off with a girlfriend to see a house on the edge of Foltesham. It was an impressive if unmodernised Georgian rectory set in five acres, far too big for a family of three, but as Angelina coyly said as she and David later wandered through the eight bedrooms, maybe that number was set to grow.

'Darling'—she had thrown her arms around his shoulders as they entered yet another bedroom with a sagging ceiling—'wouldn't this make the most divine nursery?'

'Angie, are you serious?'

She'd nodded, her eyes shining. 'Absolutely. I think another child is just what we need to make this house feel like a home.'

That had been the clincher. David had always wanted a second child, but until now, Angie had been adamant that she couldn't go through the horrors of pregnancy again.

'Not to mention the havoc it played with my body,' she'd said, one morning, smoothing her skirt over her hard-won, taut stomach. 'It took me a year to get my figure back. Imagine how much longer it would take second time around!'

With Rory nearly twelve, David had given up hope. He took Angelina's change of heart on trust and put in an offer on the house.

Eighteen months later, having secured it with a huge mortgage, not to mention undertaking a programme of works that had wound up costing three times what he'd originally planned, David's reserves of cash had all but dried up and there was still no sign of a baby.

Then the economy began to falter. All around him in City bars, the talk was not of how many bottles of Krug one could down in a night, but of a bear market and which firm would be next to wield the redundancy axe.

And still Angelina wanted more. The money she spent on soft furnishings began to resemble the GDP of a small Third World country and they absolutely *had* to put a pool in the walled garden so Rory could bring his friends round to swim.

After increasingly stomach-churning days in the office, David dreaded getting on the train to go home to a house that had become symbolic of the fact he was out of control, as well as to a wife who seemed discontented whatever he gave her.

So, rather than facing reality, he had taken to drowning his sorrows in bars after work. With five or six pints inside him followed by a whisky chaser or two, listening to Angelina's demands and giving in to them became less painful. He took out a bank loan to cover the swimming pool, then another to cover the costs of resurfacing the tennis court and landscaping the garden.

With the added pressure, his work had suffered. His usual, careful eye was not so firmly placed on the ball as it had once been, and David had made the odd mistake. Nothing serious enough to get him sacked, but with things as tough as they currently were, it was enough for him to be surplus to requirements when the firm decided to downsize.

His boss had finally called him in and told David they were letting him go. He was unemployed as of that moment. He'd get a year's salary but had to clear his desk and leave immediately.

David had spent a long, long evening in his favourite bar, just managing to catch the last train home.

When he'd got back, Angelina was already in bed. David had staggered into the kitchen, head already pounding, poured himself a large glass of tap water, then went to the cupboard in the pantry, where Angelina kept her first aid box, to find some painkillers.

He lifted the box out, then managed to drop the contents on the floor. Falling to his knees, he began putting the assorted creams, plasters and pills back again. One box, however, caught his eye. It contained the contraceptive pills that Angelina had taken before they'd started trying for a baby.

Then, heart racing, he saw the date they'd been dispensed: two weeks previously. David had opened the box and seen that half the blisters were empty.

In a fury, he'd stormed upstairs to their bedroom.

Angelina was propped up in bed reading her book.

'Darling, I've been so worried. Where have you bee—'

Before she could finish, David had gripped her by her forearms and lifted her bodily out of bed. He began to shake her like a doll.

'What the hell are you playing at?' he'd screamed at her. 'How dare you lie to me! How DARE you!' Then he'd slapped her hard across the face and she'd crumpled to the floor.

He'd sunk down onto the edge of the bed, his head in his hands, weeping. 'Why did you lie to me? Why? You never had *any* intention of us having another child, did you?'

When he'd opened his eyes again, Angelina had disappeared. He'd discovered her downstairs; she'd locked herself in the drawing room and dialled 999. When the police had arrived a few minutes later, they'd found him banging on the door demanding she let him in so he could explain.

Next morning, having spent the night in a police cell, he'd been charged with common assault. Angelina had been taken to the hospital to be checked out, but was back home again, shocked but unhurt.

Horrified at what he'd done, David had tried to explain to the police what had happened to him, and because he had no previous record of domestic violence, he'd been released.

Full of remorse, he'd walked the short distance home to find the house locked up like a fortress. He'd rung from a telephone box, but Angelina was not answering, so he'd gone back to the house, banged on the door and then tried to break in.

The police had arrived again, just as he'd smashed a windowpane with a large stone from the garden.

Angelina's lawyer had immediately obtained a restraining order, forbidding him to go near the house, his wife and beloved son for the foreseeable future.

The following weeks were an alcohol-fuelled nightmare, from which David could not seem to wake.

Then finally, he'd woken up in the nasty cottage he'd rented out of desperation, and switched on the television.

On a morning chat show they were interviewing a reformed alcoholic and as David listened to the story of the man's fall from grace, tears fell down his cheeks. It mirrored his own demise.

That night, David took himself off to an AA meeting.

And that was the beginning of his journey back to sobriety.

It had been hell, to begin with. Far more difficult than David could ever have imagined. But as the weeks went by and he was still sober, his vision had begun to clear.

He'd consulted a lawyer in Foltesham, a woman called Diana Price, who'd remarked that the speed with which Angelina had obtained the restraining order was distinctly odd.

'Your wife wasn't actually admitted to hospital,' she'd said, 'even though she spent some time in Casualty. And, of course, you should be seeing your son, even if it has to be under supervision.'

'And what about money?' David had asked. 'I don't know what my wife's living on; our joint account's practically dried up.'

'What about your redundancy?' Diana had asked.

'That went into my building society account; she can't touch it.'

'Well, that's something, I suppose.'

'Yes, I know, but that's all I've got. I'm unemployed and whatever happens, we're going to have to sell the house. I can't possibly service the mortgage or the loans. Angie still won't talk to me and I could do with having some of my things. I've literally only got the clothes I'm standing in.'

'Look, let me write to her lawyer and we'll see where things stand,' Diana had said. 'You're due in court on the sixth of next month, but I need to ask you, were you and your wife having any marital problems *before* the night of the assault?'

David had tried to think back. He'd been so involved with his financial worries he'd lost track of the actual state of their marriage in those past few months. There hadn't been a lot of sex, but then again, he'd been coming in so late...

'I suppose there was a kind of breakdown in communication,'

David replied, 'but we didn't really argue, and apart from that one time I would never have dreamed of hurting her.'

'It's just that...' Diana shook her head. 'Usually the wife would at least give the husband a chance to explain himself. I'm not trying to excuse your behaviour, but surely, if she loves you, she'd look at the circumstances and at least *try* to understand why you behaved as you did?'

'Maybe she's frightened of me.'

'Maybe she is, but don't forget, she knows she lied to you about wanting a baby. I would have thought she'd want to try and sort things out, if only for Rory's sake. It seems very odd to me. Anyway, I'll write and we'll see what happens.'

David had spent the next few days pacing up and down the small cottage kitchen in an agony of suspense. Finally, a week later, Diana had called him into her office.

'What does she say?' he'd asked.

'Well, I'm afraid there's good and bad news,' Diana had replied gently. 'Your wife is prepared to drop the assault charge and lift the restraining order.'

David felt his heart surge with hope.

'But,' she added, 'in return, she wants a quickie divorce. She'll base her petition on unreasonable behaviour and leave it at that, as long as you don't contest it.'

'What?' David was stunned.

'In addition, Rory will continue living with her in the family home.'

David was beginning to feel sick. His hands shook.

'But why does she want a divorce? We haven't discussed *anything*. She probably doesn't even realise I've lost my job. If she did, she'd know we have to sell the house.'

'From what her lawyer says, that's irrelevant,' said Diana. 'Your wife says she wants to buy you out.'

'Buy me out? How the hell's she going to do that?'

'The house is jointly owned. Your wife will receive her share of what's left after the mortgage is paid off, and you will receive yours. What she's suggesting is that she stays in the house, takes on the mortgage and pays you your slice of the equity. That way, she'll own it outright.'

'But that's crazy! Angie's got nothing—no income and certainly no savings. Where on earth would she find the money to pay the mortgage, let alone buy me out?'

Diana had shrugged. 'I've no idea, but that's what she wants to do. Look, David, you've had a lot to take in. Why don't you take this letter, go home and have a think about it? Then let me know what you'd like me to do.

'What are my options?'

'Well, you can call her bluff and let her take you to court for assault. But just remember, it's her word against yours. You can fight for custody to have Rory live with you, but the court usually rules in favour of the mother, especially when there's been some form of violence at home. You can make the divorce as long and as drawn out as you want, but I wouldn't advise that either.'

'So, you're saying she has me over a barrel, then?'

'I'm saying you have to make a decision. It's bound to be painful, but at least this way you won't have a criminal record, your divorce will be cheap, clean and quick and, most important of all, you'll be able to see Rory.'

'That's great!' he replied sarcastically. 'One day, I can see my son whenever I want, make him breakfast, play football with him; the next, my wife tells me I can only see him a few times a year!'

'It won't be as bad as that. Now Rory's a weekly boarder at the senior school, we'll ask that you can have him every other weekend and half the holidays. I'm sure she'll agree.'

'Well, how gracious of her! Christ! What have I ever done but love him? For that matter, what have I ever done to my wife, except provide her with the life she told me she wanted?'

David felt the familiar white-hot anger welling inside him once more. 'Thanks, Diana. I'll be in touch.'

That had been four months ago. The financial arrangements were now being finalised and even though David had expressed grave doubts over Angelina's ability to raise the cash to buy him out, he'd had a letter from Diana telling him to expect a cheque within a few days.

The amount would cover the bank loans, leaving some left over to help him begin again—probably in a one-bedroomed bungalow if he was lucky, David thought bitterly. Actually, he was past caring about money. The only thing he really cared about now was Rory.

He lived for his son's fortnightly visits, and even though Rory was a much quieter child these days, David was determined to rebuild the relationship they'd once had.

But—and this was the reason he was in a state this morning—something was wrong with Rory.

Sebastian Frederiks, Rory's housemaster at St Stephen's, had called him several days ago, saying he wanted to chat through a few 'issues'. Apparently, Rory was becoming more and more withdrawn, and Frederiks was concerned about him.

'But I won't see him until the weekend after next. He has choir tour on Saturday, Mr Frederiks. Could I come in to the school and see him?'

'Well, how about I get him to give you a call and take it from there? The last thing we want is Rory to feel pressurised and clam up.'

'If that's what you think is best. And please, take care of him.'

'Of course, Mr Millar. Goodbye.'

David had put down the phone, feeling frustrated and desperate to see his son. The long day stretched in front of him and David had found his thoughts turning to alcohol.

That evening, drunk for the first time in months, David had driven to the school, determined to see Rory, whatever Frederiks might say. His boy was in trouble, David knew it.

That had been four days ago. The night he'd gone to the school was now a blur. He remembered entering Fleat House, searching the deserted corridors for Rory, banging on study doors, but the place had been empty and his search for his son fruitless.

He couldn't remember driving home.

Since then, he'd left various messages with Frederiks and the headmaster. Neither had returned his calls.

His mobile phone rang. He snatched it up.

'David Millar.'

'Dad, it's me.' Rory sounded breathless.

'Rory, oh God! At last! How are you?'

'Dad...I...' Rory let out a strangled sob. 'I'm so scared.'

'Of what?'

'I...who'll be there to protect me now?'

'Rory, what are you talking about? Tell me.'

'I can't. You can't help me, no one can.'

The line went dead.

David redialled the number. The line rang and rang. Realising it must be the pupil's payphone in Fleat House, he dialled the headmaster's secretary.

'Yes, it's David Millar here. I need to speak to the head, now! My son, Rory, has just rung and he sounded very distressed.'

'I'll pass on the message, Mr Millar, and make sure he calls you back.'

'No! I need to speak to him now!'

'That's not possible, he's in a class, but I will pass on your message.'

'Then get him out! My son is in trouble, I know he is.'

'I will ask Mr Jones to ring you back as soon as possible, Mr Millar. He really is very...busy at present, but he does know you've been calling.'

'I asked you to do that yesterday and you didn't! Tell him it's urgent, will you?' David implored.

'Yes, I will, but please try not to worry. Rory's probably homesick. It's the first few weeks of his second term, always a difficult moment. I can try putting you through to Mr Frederiks in Fleat House, if you like.'

'Yes, would you do that, please?'

'Hold on one moment, then.'

David paced up and down the tiny sitting room as he waited to be put through.

There were a couple of clicks and the housemaster's voicemail came on. In frustration, David left a message.

Half an hour later, with no call from the head or the housemaster, David was frantic.

He'd go to the school now and see his son. Picking up his car keys, David left the cottage and climbed into the ancient Renault he'd bought a few weeks back. He turned the engine over a few times, but nothing happened.

'Dammit!' David thumped the wheel in frustration as he saw the headlamp switch was on. Which meant the battery was almost certainly flat.

He had no near neighbours to provide him with jump leads. He'd have to phone the garage in the morning to come out to him.

David wandered back inside, his agitation uncontrollable.

He went to the cupboard in the kitchen and pulled out a bottle of whisky.

Chapter Four

Jazz pulled the car away from the kerb in front of her cottage and began her journey west towards Peterborough.

'The bottom line is to find out whether Charlie Cavendish took the aspirin by mistake or not. First port of call is the parents, to get some background information on their son. Adele Cavendish, his mother, is expecting you. Good luck, Inspector Hunter. I'm pleased to welcome you back on the team. Let us both hope you came to the right decision.'

'Thank you, Sir. I hope so too.'

As she put a Macy Gray tape into the cassette machine, Jazz doubted whether Charlie's mother would be expecting a detective inspector from the CID to turn up in a fifteen-year-old orange Mini. DS Miles was driving down tomorrow with her staff car, but for today, this would have to do.

She wouldn't dwell on the fact that the last thing in the world she had been expecting to do this afternoon was interview the mother of a dead child… As her father always said, life was too short. And all you could do was to follow your instincts. If it didn't work out…hell, she'd resign properly at the end of the case.

An hour later, Jazz arrived in Rutland. Having only ever passed through on the A1 heading north, she was surprised how pretty it was here, similar to the Cotswolds, with its soft yellow sandstone buildings and gently rolling countryside.

After a couple of wrong turns, Jazz drove up a winding drive to the Cavendish house. She parked her Mini between an old Land Rover and a mud-spattered Mercedes estate to one side of the imposing Queen Anne house.

Walking up the steps to the impressive entrance, Jazz took in the horses grazing in a field next to the house and the magnificent views beyond it onto open countryside. It was an idyllic setting, even on a cold winter's day.

Jazz pressed the bell to the side of the heavy double doors. She could hear footsteps approaching, followed by the sound of a key being turned, then bolts sliding back. Finally, the door opened to reveal a woman the same height as Jazz, slim and immaculately dressed in a striped shirt, cashmere cardigan, dark trousers and a pair of blue leather slip-ons. Her thick brown hair was short and well cut, the touch of make-up on the eyes and lips complementing the perfectly groomed—if old-fashioned—appearance.

'So sorry,' the woman said, 'we hardly ever use the front door. Everyone usually goes round the back.' She put out a hand. 'Adele Cavendish. You must be Inspector Hunter.'

'Yes,' said Jazz, 'thank you for seeing me.' Jazz shook the outstretched hand.

'Please,' Adele said, 'come through.'

She led Jazz across the elegant entrance hall, with its spectacular curving staircase, and into an ornate drawing room with French windows opening onto the terrace beyond. The room was filled with antique furniture, the windows draped with heavy floral curtains, family photos atop a bureau and china figurines on the mantelpiece.

'Please, sit down.' Adele indicated one of the heavily stuffed chintz sofas. 'Can I get you anything? Tea? Coffee?'

'No, thank you, I'm fine.' Jazz reached inside her briefcase for a notepad and pen. 'I'm sorry to intrude on what must be a dreadful time for you and your family.'

Adele folded her arms and walked across to the French windows, her back to Jazz.

'To be honest, it hasn't sunk in yet. I can't believe Charlie's gone.' She turned round, and Jazz saw the pain in her eyes. 'And now, to know that his death might have been avoided, that it wasn't his epilepsy, I...' Adele shook her head. Looking desolate, she walked to the sofa opposite Jazz, perched on the edge of it, arms hugging her body. 'Forgive me. How can I help?'

'Is your husband here? It might be easier if you were able to speak to me together. I'm going to have to ask you some questions you might find distressing.'

'He's not here.' Adele shrugged. 'He's at the flat in London. I did tell him you were coming but he has a big case on at the moment, which apparently takes precedence over the death of our son.' She gave a pained smile tinged with bitterness. 'Anyway, he said he wanted the best people on the case to try and establish what did happen to Charlie. What makes it so awful is that we can't do anything until the coroner has decided on a verdict. How can I begin to move on when my son is still lying in a mortuary?'

'Mrs Cavendish, I realise this must be the last thing you need at the moment, but I'm sure you must want to know how and why Charlie died.'

Adele's face softened and she nodded. 'You're right. Of course I do. So, please, fire away. Let's get it over with.'

As Adele talked, a picture of a privileged and rather spoilt teenager began to emerge.

'I couldn't have any more children so I suppose in a way it's natural we overindulged him.'

'Did he and his father see eye to eye?'

'William was disappointed Charlie never shone academically. Not getting into Eton was a big blow. He always thought Charlie was just lazy.' Adele sighed. 'Perhaps he was. Charlie managed to get by on charm. He loved sport and channelled his energy into his social life and having a good time. In a way, I'm glad he did now.'

'So, there was some tension between Charlie and his father?'

'Charlie wanted to go to Marlborough, where many of his prep-school chums were going, but William refused. He felt it was too progressive. If you want the truth, I rather think William sent him to St Stephen's as a punishment for not getting into Eton. I was happy enough; I was born and brought up in Norfolk. It's a decent enough school, but I accept it's not in the same league as some of the others.'

'Do you think Charlie was happy there?' asked Jazz.

'Not particularly, no.' Adele sighed. 'He felt like a failure from the moment he got there. When he came home for Christmas—the last time I saw him—he told me he couldn't wait to leave.'

'Was he going to try for university?'

'Yes, although...' Adele put her hand to her brow. 'God, this is difficult. William and Charlie had a blow-up just before he went back to school for the Lent term. Charlie wanted to take a gap year, like everyone does these days, and because he wasn't sure exactly what he wanted to do, he thought he might delay his applications for a year until he came back.'

'Until he'd some idea of a career path?' Jazz prompted.

'Exactly. William saw red and accused Charlie of being a layabout. He'd always assumed Charlie would follow him into the law, but Charlie was having none of it.'

'And was the argument resolved before Charlie went back to school, three weeks ago?'

'No.' Adele shook her head. 'I'm afraid it wasn't. William insisted he wouldn't pay for a gap year if Charlie didn't get a place at a university before he left. I took Charlie back to school at the beginning of January.' Adele studied her hands. 'His father hasn't spoken to him since.'

'Your husband must be very upset, under the circumstances?'

'I'm sure he is; not that you'd know it.' Adele looked up at Jazz. 'Stiff upper lip and all that. But, underneath it all, I know he loved Charlie to bits. They were very similar: strong willed and single-minded. That's probably why they fought so much.'

'And when you took Charlie back to school, how did he seem?'

'Quieter than usual, naturally.'

'Mrs Cavendish, this is a horrible question to have to ask...' Jazz spoke slowly. 'But given the argument between father and son, plus the fact you say Charlie felt like a failure, in your opinion, is there any chance that Charlie might have deliberately taken his own life?'

Adele looked at Jazz in horror. 'You're asking me if Charlie committed suicide because he'd had an argument with his father? Never! Never!' Adele shook her head fiercely. 'If you'd met Charlie, you'd understand. His problem with his father stemmed from his zest for life, not his *fear* of it. He was the most vibrant person I know!'

The last shreds of reserve fell away and Adele Cavendish burst into tears. She pulled a handkerchief from her cardigan pocket and blew her nose. 'I'm sorry, but just the thought of Charlie taking his own life, it's...just too much.'

'I'm sorry, Mrs Cavendish. I had to ask,' Jazz replied gently. 'I believe the coroner has spoken with you and told you Charlie died of anaphylactic shock, brought on by an allergic reaction to aspirin?'

'Yes. He called William last night.'

'So...' Jazz paused. 'It is just possible that suicide might be one explanation, don't you think?'

'No! Absolutely not! Charlie wouldn't do that. He *must* have taken them by mistake.' There was another pause as Adele blew her nose once more and pushed the handkerchief back in her pocket.

'Charlie definitely *knew* he was allergic to aspirin, didn't he?'

'Of course he did. We drummed it into him. We found out when he was five. He'd had a temperature and I gave him some aspirin-based suspension. A few minutes later, he started to choke and fit; it was terrifying. Fortunately the ambulance arrived just in time to revive him, but it was a very close call. It was that which triggered the epilepsy—it's quite common apparently—and from then on, Charlie had to take pills every morning and evening to control the fits, and steer well clear of aspirin.'

'A dose corresponding to two aspirin tablets was found in Charlie's bloodstream. There was no sign of a struggle, so we can discard the theory that he was forced to take them.'

'Had he been drinking?' Adele asked.

'The alcohol found in his bloodstream only amounted to consuming one pint of beer, so he wasn't drunk.'

'I almost wish he had been,' mused Adele. 'God knows what he must have gone through in his last moments. It's the most awful way to die. And alone...'

Jazz waited until Adele had collected herself again before asking, 'Mrs Cavendish, do you know if your son had any enemies, anyone who disliked him? Did he ever mention a particular boy at school, or a teacher, for instance?'

Adele paused before she answered. 'I'm sure there were those who disliked Charlie. Strong personalities always tend to create enmity in others, don't you think?'

Jazz nodded.

'But if you're asking me whether someone murdered Charlie...well, no, it's ridiculous!'

'Did Charlie ever mention having a girlfriend?'

Adele managed a weak smile. 'Oh, Charlie had lots of girlfriends. But they came and went regularly, as they do when you're eighteen and as handsome as he was. It was about the only thing he liked at St Stephen's, the fact it was co-ed.'

Jazz put her notepad and pen in her briefcase. 'Well, I think that's all for the moment. Thank you for your help, Mrs Cavendish. I promise I'll do everything to find out what happened to Charlie.'

'It's William who wants answers. I just want my son back.' Adele stood up. 'I need a drink,' she added, almost to herself.

Jazz followed her to the door of the drawing room. 'Would you mind if I took a look at Charlie's bedroom? It might help me get a feel for him.'

'Of course not. It's this way.'

'This is a beautiful house, Mrs Cavendish,' said Jazz as she walked with Adele up the spectacular oak staircase.

'Thank you. I wanted Charlie to grow up in the country like I did.' She paused at the top of the stairs and turned to Jazz. 'We moved here so William could commute. It's only an hour on the train from Peterborough, but William soon found it a chore and rented a flat in town. He never was one for the country, anyway.' Adele turned abruptly before Jazz could reply and walked along a corridor.

'This is Charlie's room.' She hovered outside the door. 'Would you mind if I left you to it? Can't face seeing all his things just yet.'

'Of course. And do you have any of the tablets Charlie took to control his epilepsy?'

'I'll go and find them for you.' Adele folded her arms around herself and walked back down the corridor.

Charlie's room had the usual teenage hallmarks: posters hung askew on the walls, rugby team photos arranged on a unit next to a television and a hi-fi, piles of books and magazines stacked up untidily on a bookshelf.

Jazz walked over to the bed and picked up a furless teddy lying on the pillow.

She'd been on a bereavement counselling course a few years ago and learned that no parent ever got over the loss of a child. Often, couples drifted apart, unable to come together in grief, feeling bereft and isolated. From what she'd seen and heard, Adele Cavendish would take little comfort from her husband.

Jazz leaned nearer to take a look at the photograph on Charlie's bedside table. Father and son in ski gear at the top of a mountain. They were broad-shouldered and heavy set, fair in colouring, both with the same blue eyes.

Jazz surveyed the room, looking for anything that might provide a clue to who Charlie had been. She pulled open the desk drawers, leafed through some rugby magazines, opened a couple of letters from friends and, finding nothing of interest, left and walked back down the stairs.

Mrs Cavendish was sitting on the bottom step, nursing a glass.

Jazz sat down beside her.

'Did you find anything?'

'No, not really,' Jazz replied truthfully.

'Here are the tablets.' Adele pulled a packet out of her cardigan pocket. 'You might as well take the lot. He…won't need them any more.'

'No.' Jazz took the packet, paused and then asked, 'Did Charlie have a computer?'

'Of course, who doesn't these days? But it's at school.' Adele took a sip of her gin. 'I suppose I'll have to think about collecting his things.'

'Well, if you'd rather, once we've had a look through them, we could have them sent on to you.'

'Would you?' Adele's face relaxed a little. 'Call me a coward, but the thought of setting foot anywhere near that place and having to suffer the false look of sympathy on that bumptious headmaster's face fills me with horror.'

'You're not a coward, Mrs Cavendish. People grieve in different ways.' Instinctively, Jazz put her arm on Adele's shoulder.

'It's the endless stream of visitors and the sympathy cards. I can't even bring myself to open them.' Adele indicated a stack of envelopes lying on the hall table. 'I know people are trying to be kind, but it makes it so real.' She looked up at Jazz, her face agonised. 'He was everything to me, you know, everything.'

'I don't have any children, so I can only imagine. But, there are counsellors available to help…'

'God no!' Adele replied, visibly pulling herself together. She stood up. 'I don't need anyone patronising me or spouting psycho-babble. Of course I'll cope. What choice do I have?' she said simply. 'Now, I expect you want to get on.'

Jazz stood up, too, and followed Adele to the front door.

'You'll be in touch when you have any news?' Adele opened the front door.

'Of course. Goodbye, Mrs Cavendish.' Jazz turned and walked down the steps. The door closed on her abruptly.

Jazz drove carefully along the drive, away from the beautiful house in its spectacular setting and the desolate occupant within.

Adele Cavendish walked back across the hall and into the kitchen. She topped up her glass with gin and took a large swig. Then she pulled her mobile out of her handbag and dialled a number.

'It's me. She's been. Yes, it was terrible. When you see her, for God's sake, don't say anything. I just…well, I can hardly bear it.' She paused to listen for a moment. 'Thank you,' she said, 'I know you won't.'

She hung up and the fleeting ghost of a smile crossed her lips, disappearing almost immediately at the thought of the dreadful guilt she would have to endure for the rest of her life.

Chapter Five

The following morning, Jazz peered out of her window and saw the deserted Salthouse Road. Miles should have been here to collect her at seven thirty, a good half an hour ago. She'd got his voicemail when she'd rung his mobile, a fact that comforted her, as it probably meant he was somewhere nearby but couldn't get a signal. She'd left him a terse message. If he didn't turn up in the next ten minutes, she'd have to drive to St Stephen's in her Mini and get him to meet her there.

The first morning working with another constabulary was not the moment to tip up late.

Jazz smoothed a stray tendril of her thick auburn hair back into place. For the past seven months she'd left it to grow longer and hang in a curly mass round her shoulders. The old plastic clip she used now to twist it up was struggling to cope with its heaviness and felt uncomfortable digging into her scalp.

'Oh bugger it!' she muttered, as she removed the clip and let her hair fall back around her face. She smoothed down her suit, still crumpled from being stuffed in a box for seven months, and wished she'd had time to take it to the dry cleaner's. Just as she was collecting her car keys, a silver BMW pulled up outside.

'Thank God for that.' Jazz grabbed her briefcase and, slamming her front door behind her, she ran down the path to the waiting car.

'Where the hell have you been?' she asked DS Alistair Miles curtly as she climbed into the passenger seat.

'Isn't that what I should be saying to you?' Alistair smiled. 'I've only taken an hour's detour through the picturesque villages of Norfolk; you buggered off for over seven months. Good to see you, Ma'am.' He smiled again as he pulled out onto the road. 'Are we heading in the right direction?'

'Just keep going and I'll tell you when to turn.'

'How are you?' Miles glanced at his boss admiringly, struck afresh by her unusual beauty. There was something softer about her, the alabaster skin a few tones darker, setting off her green eyes, her long hair softening the high cheekbones and curvature of her face. 'You look fantastic.'

'Thanks,' said Jazz shortly.

'Not the same without you back at the ranch, though. Everyone sends their best. They were all green with envy that I was going on a country sojourn with you in charge. They want the low-down.'

'I'm sure they do.' She nodded. 'I took a leave of absence to sort my life out and here I am. And that's your lot, DS Miles, *capisce?*'

'Aye aye, Capitano, I do. So, how much do you know about the case?'

'It seems young Cavendish managed to swallow two aspirin tablets, even though he knew he was allergic to them. I interviewed his mother yesterday and she said as much.'

'Was he pissed?'

'The pathologist's report says not.'

'Drugs?'

'No.'

'Probably took them by mistake, then?'

'That, DS Miles, is why you are driving me through the wilds of Norfolk: to find out.'

'Gather it's a favour to the mate of the commissioner. Some schoolboy overdose wouldn't normally be our bag. Not that I care. Felt like I was on holiday driving up here this morning.'

'I'll ignore that last remark, DS Miles. However big or small the case, we're trained to give it our all.'

'Absolutely.' He grinned. 'So, how's life in the slow lane? All very Miss Marple round here.' Alistair indicated an idyllic row of cottages as they drove towards Foltesham.

'It's good, thank you.'

The closer Jazz got to the school, the faster her heart began to beat. She was glad of the comforting presence of her old DS. Alistair Miles and she had worked on numerous cases together. Always cheerful, Miles did not seem to begrudge Jazz her career trajectory, even though he was a few years older than she was.

He was the kind of policeman the force would be lost without:

solid, capable and reliable, but lacking the spark of imagination and flair that would gain him further promotion. Jazz knew she could always rely on him. She trusted his integrity and, most crucial of all, he made her laugh and had diffused many a tense moment with one of his armoury of silly or lewd jokes.

His baby face, blond hair and big blue eyes had set hearts a-fluttering amongst the office staff back at HQ, but Miles seemed oblivious to it all, rarely having a girlfriend and devoting himself to his work.

'They've booked me in to some hotel here,' Miles commented as they drove through Foltesham, a pretty Georgian town filled with quaint boutiques, art galleries and coffee shops. 'Do you think they have running water and electric light in this neck of the woods?'

'Cut out the superior urban act, Miles. It's not going to endear you to PC Plod of the North Norfolk Constabulary,' quipped Jazz.

'Who's being superior now?' Miles shot back. 'Anyway, nothing we can do is ever going to endear a couple of arrogant tossers from the CID to the local constabulary.'

'We'll do our best to be as professional and as courteous as we can,' said Jazz. 'Right, turn left here and pull into the car park.' Out of habit, she checked her reflection in the wing mirror. There was nothing that inspired confidence less than a female detective turning up with her mascara smudged, or lipstick on her teeth.

Miles brought the car to a halt in a visitor's space just in front of the main entrance.

The collection of austere red-brick buildings that comprised St Stephen's School were set around a well-manicured green. The school chapel, allegedly designed by Wren as a miniature version of St Paul's Cathedral, stood majestically beyond it, flanked by sports pitches on either side.

'Do you think that old dear hovering in reception is waiting for us?' Miles asked as he got out. 'Or perhaps she *is* Miss Marple and they've drafted her in.'

'Okay, enough,' said Jazz more sharply than she meant to. 'Let's go and find out, shall we?'

When Jenny brought Detective Inspector Hunter and her sergeant into his office, Robert Jones immediately had to reassess his mental image of the hulking male detective he'd been expecting. The tall, elegant woman in front of him looked more like a catwalk model than a policewoman.

She shook his hand firmly. 'DI Hunter, and this is DS Miles. Pleased to meet you. Is DS Roland here yet?'

'Yes, he arrived about ten minutes ago, so I took him across to the room I've set aside for you to use,' replied the headmaster.

'Right. Shall we follow suit?' Jazz suggested.

'I can take you across, yes, but as you might have been told, I've called the whole school together for assembly.'

'Good. Perhaps we can drop in on DS Roland beforehand? I should meet him before we address the school. He may have something to contribute,' said Jazz.

'Of course. Follow me.' Robert Jones indicated the door.

Detective Sergeant Roland was a nondescript man in his mid-forties. As she shook his hand, Jazz could feel the negative vibes emanating from him. And who could blame him? She wouldn't want her toes trodden on by some bigwigs from the Met CID either. However, she needed to get him on side so things could proceed as smoothly and as effectively as possible.

'DS Roland, it's good to meet you. Shall we talk on our way to assembly? Obviously I know a little about the case, but I gather you were actually there with the body in situ. I'll need you to take me through what you saw. Perhaps we could go and see where Charlie Cavendish died straight after assembly?' She turned to the headmaster.

'I'm going to address the staff and teachers very briefly, but if there's anything you'd like to add, please feel free,' said Robert Jones.

'Thank you.'

They entered the hall where the entire school was gathered waiting for them. Jazz felt a thousand eyes bore into her as she followed the headmaster to the front of the hall and up the steps onto the dais.

'Good morning, everyone,' he began. 'As I'm sure the school grapevine has already informed most of you, we're to have three detectives as our guests for the next few days. They are here to investigate the tragic death of Charlie Cavendish. I'm going to hand you over now to Detective Inspector Hunter of the CID who will talk you briefly through what will happen.'

Robert Jones turned to Jazz and she stepped forward and smiled.

'Good morning, everyone. I'm DI Hunter, and these are my colleagues, DS Roland and DS Miles. We hope to complete our investigation as speedily as possible. We'll be conducting interviews with both staff and pupils who had close contact with Charlie Cavendish and when I've spoken with Mr Jones, I'll pin a schedule on the noticeboard.'

Jazz paused and looked down at the sea of faces in front of her. 'I'm sure you're all aware of what happened to poor Charlie. At present, we're assuming it was a tragic accident, but we obviously need to be absolutely sure. Therefore, I would ask anyone who thinks he or she can throw any light on the events of that night to come to me. Any information given to myself and my colleagues will be treated with the utmost confidence, so please don't be afraid to come forward. The sooner you do, the faster we'll all be out of your hair and things can return to normal. DS Roland, is there anything you'd like to add?'

Jazz turned to him and he shook his head. 'Right, I'll thank you all in advance for your co-operation. Headmaster?'

'Thank you, Inspector Hunter. After assembly, can everyone please return immediately to their classes? Check the noticeboard regularly in case the Inspector wishes to see you.'

Jenny Colman, already feeling sick at the sight of the detectives, turned to follow suit. As she made her way slowly towards the exit, she caught sight of a familiar face on the other side of the hall.

Jenny hid behind a pillar, making sure her vantage point allowed her to see and not be seen. She studied the face. Yes, it was! She was sure of it. Even after twenty-five years, there was no mistaking those features. She waited until the hall was empty, then, her legs feeling weak beneath her, sat down heavily on a chair.

Jazz followed the headmaster out of the hall.

'Talk about a needle in a haystack,' murmured Miles. 'If there *is* something dodgy going on, it could be any one of that lot.'

'They just all happen to be in the same place, that's all. I'd guess there's more chance here than finding a hit-and-run driver in London, Miles.' Jazz stopped outside the hall and let Robert Jones and Roland walk ahead of them. 'Now, I want you to go and talk to our head, find out all you can about Charlie. I'm going across to his study with Roland.'

Jazz was surprised at how basic Fleat House was. She'd rather presumed that for the kind of exorbitant fees the parents were charged, a public school such as this would provide a better standard of accommodation than the austere, tatty building she'd just entered. She'd seen more luxurious prisons.

Waiting for them in the entrance hall was a woman. Jazz would have placed her in her mid-fifties. She was thin to the point of gauntness, her face lined beyond her years, her grey hair worn in a sensible bob. She wore no make-up, and her suit and shoes were unfussy and utilitarian. However, the woman's eyes were her redeeming feature: set wide apart, an unusual amber.

'Good morning. I'm Detective Inspector Hunter. I believe you've already met Detective Sergeant Roland?' Jazz said as she shook the woman's hand.

'Yes. Madelaine Smith, Fleat House matron.'

She spoke with an accent Jazz couldn't place.

'We'd like to see Charlie's study, if that's all right.'

'Of course. Would you like to follow me?'

'Don't think I'd fancy her bedside manner,' whispered Roland as they climbed the stairs behind her upright figure.

Matron showed them along the corridor and stood in front of the door to Charlie's study. She took a key out of her jacket pocket and unlocked it.

'I sent the cleaners in the day after Charlie died. His things are packed up ready for his parents to collect. I felt it was the least I could do under the circumstances. At the time, I didn't realise his death might be treated as suspicious.'

The woman did not speak defensively; it was a statement of fact. Jazz's heart sank. There would be nothing left to find.

'Will you need me further? I've got things to do.'

'No, Matron. We'll come and see you when we've finished here,' Jazz replied. 'Where will we find you?'

'I'll be in the house somewhere,' she answered unhelpfully, then turned and walked back down the corridor.

Roland opened the door to Charlie's study and stood aside to let Jazz enter first.

The room was immaculate. The sheets had been changed, washing away any possible clues to the last moments of Charlie's life. The smell of polish and disinfectant in the small room was powerful, made all the more so as the windows had obviously been sealed shut since.

Roland closed the door behind him and stood by it like a sentry.

Jazz picked her way through the boxes and perched gingerly on the end of the bed. She looked up at Roland.

'Well, this isn't much help, is it?'

Roland bristled. 'When I found the victim and Matron told me he was epileptic, I assumed, as she did, that he'd had a fit of some sort. He'd been foaming at the mouth, which the paramedics assured me was a symptom. We all thought the same until the results of the PM came in.'

Jazz shrugged in resignation. 'Nothing we can do about it now. What about forensic evidence? I assume the SOCOs were called?'

'No, Ma'am.' Roland was looking very uncomfortable now. 'Neither the school nor the paramedics nor I had any reason to believe a crime had been committed. I was only called because the headmaster wanted to cover his back. If the lad had been in his own home, we wouldn't have been involved. To all intents and purposes it was death by natural causes.'

'And it still may be misadventure at worst,' Jazz replied, trying to diffuse his defensiveness.

'My super gave me the impression you wouldn't be here at all if it hadn't been for the boy's father being so well connected.'

'Perhaps not, but we still have to establish whether or not Charlie took the tablets by mistake.'

'Well, he must have done,' Roland said. 'I mean, the alternative is murder. And who'd want to murder a schoolboy? We're hardly talking gang warfare here, are we? Foltesham's a quiet town and this school is full of decent middle-class kids.'

'Have you run the usual checks on Charlie Cavendish?'

'Course. Clean as a whistle. All he's got to his name is three points on his licence for speeding. He got a brand-new car from Dad on his seventeenth birthday and passed his test a few days later.' Roland rolled his eyes. 'The kids of today, eh? I had to save up for four years to buy my first banger.'

'Well, we know he wasn't short of money, that's for sure.' Jazz swept her eyes around the room. 'So, when you were called to the scene, where did you find him?'

'He was slumped on the floor near the door. As I said, he'd been foaming at the mouth and rigor had set in by then. He wasn't a pleasant sight.'

'Call the SOCOs in anyway. They might pick up something the cleaners missed.'

'I doubt it, but yes, I'll call them.'

Jazz could hear the antagonism in Roland's voice and knew it wasn't a good start to their working relationship. She stood up. 'I'm going to call DS Miles and ask him to help you sift through this lot.' She bent down and picked up a laptop from the top of one of the boxes and handed it to him. 'See what's on this. Call me if you find anything interesting. I'll text you with my number.'

Jazz left the room in silence. Walking along the corridor, she wondered if she'd been sent on a wild goose chase to keep a buddy of the commissioner happy. However much she wanted to make something of this case, from what she had seen so far, the chances of it being murder were slim.

Suddenly, the elite back-up she'd been provided on every case in London seemed a long way away. There, they had the manpower, computers, forensics, every available tool at her disposal. Miles might joke about Miss Marple, but that was exactly how she felt. How on earth was she meant to interview eight hundred pupils and two hundred staff with just two detectives to help her?

Maybe, she thought, suddenly angry, this was a soft-soap case, handed to her by Norton to keep her busy? To test her, even? Jazz reached for the mobile lodged in her breast pocket.

She dialled Norton's direct line, then immediately pressed the 'cancel' button. She leaned against a wall and cooled her hot cheeks against the cold stone.

She pictured Adele Cavendish's face, felt her desolation, and tried to concentrate on that.

There was no turning back now. Her role was to discover the truth.

However slim the odds, her duty was simply to look Adele in the eye and tell her for *certain* whether her son had been the casualty of a self-inflicted accident, or an innocent victim of something far more sinister.

Chapter Six

Hugh Daneman studied the sleeping pills in his hand. He felt this was the least painful way to die, and given the circumstances, there was a synchronicity that his aesthetic nature appreciated.

He lit the fire in the grate. It flared up then burned weakly. Everything in the small cottage he rented from the school *almost* functioned. But it had suited his needs for the past twenty years, and been the setting for small moments of happiness, so he looked on it fondly.

He'd gathered all his private papers together; they were strewn in a heap in front of the fire, ready for annihilation.

The thought of anyone poking through his personal belongings was untenable. He'd made sure all his affairs were in order, had even cleaned out his wardrobe and left only his best suits to be given away to charity.

He did not want anyone doubting *this* was a suicide.

Hugh took a slug of the large brandy he'd poured himself. Not being a regular drinker, he hoped it wouldn't take long to numb any last-minute doubts.

He picked up the papers from the floor and started to pile them on the fire. He smiled as the flames shot up the chimney; it was the best fire he'd ever seen here, and a pleasant last memory to take with him.

The bottle of temazepam pills were on the coffee table. A month's supply should surely do it. Hugh sat back down in his favourite chair and studied them. He'd contacted the school to say he was unwell with flu and wouldn't be in today. That should leave him plenty of time to die.

Hugh stared into the fire.

One mistake, after a lifetime of control…

Hugh sighed. He hadn't planned on ending his life quite so soon. But then, facing old age was a slow death in itself.

He opened the screw cap and shook the pills out onto the table.

At least his death would cause no one grief. He hoped the wishes in his will would be followed; it would be pleasant to think they would hold his funeral in the school chapel and that some of the children would attend.

But he knew, under the circumstances, that may not be possible.

Hugh dug in the pocket of his tweed trousers and took out his wallet. He carefully removed the photograph and studied it. It had once been in colour, but faded now to give it a sepia-like appearance.

He smiled at the familiar, much-loved face, and hoped he'd been wrong for most of his life and there *might* be a God after all; a God that could reunite them in death, after so many years apart.

If not, and he was about to face oblivion, it would surely be less painful than living the hollow life he'd endured these past forty years.

Hugh kissed the photograph one last time. Then he picked up three pills from the table and held the brandy glass aloft. He put them on his tongue and toasted the air.

'*Carpe diem* my darling!' he cried as he tasted the bitterness on his tongue, and swallowed.

By the time Jazz entered the lobby leading to Robert Jones's office, she felt back in control.

The headmaster's secretary was behind her desk, but she was not working. Like Jazz, she was listening to the male voice shouting from inside the head's office.

'What's going on in there?' Jazz asked, brow furrowed.

'It's David Millar. He's the father of one of our pupils. Been a few problems at home, what with the drink and his marriage breaking down. He seems to think his son is in trouble of some sort, but it's most likely the booze making him imagine it.'

'What's the boy's name?'

'Rory. He's only thirteen, bless him, and a little shrimp of a thing. Perhaps some of the older boys do give him a hard time, but what can you expect? Boys will be boys, won't they?' Jenny smiled weakly.

'Does his father think he's being bullied?'

Jenny shrugged. 'I've got no idea, but something's rattled his cage.'

The door opened and a man stormed out of the headmaster's office. He was flushed with anger and dressed as if he'd thrown on the first thing that fell out of his wardrobe. Jazz could read the desperation in his eyes.

'Christ! What do you have to do in this place to see your own child?!' Ignoring Jazz, he leaned over Jenny's desk. 'For God's sake, something is wrong with Rory. He's my son, I know him and he wouldn't have telephoned me like that unless he needed help. Why can't I see him?'

'Mr Millar.' Robert Jones was standing in the door of his office, looking flustered. 'As I've just said to you, I checked with Matron and she said Rory seemed fine at breakfast this morning. I really don't think it's beneficial to Rory to be dragged out of class, especially when you're in such a state of…agitation.'

'I just need to see him, to talk to him! Please let me see *my son!*'

'As I said, I'll make sure Rory calls you tonight. It's only a couple of days to the weekend and Rory will be at home.'

David Millar raised himself upright and turned to Jones. 'Yes, he will be at *home*, with his mother. Unfortunately, as you well know, I no longer live there and, strangely enough, am not welcome as a guest.'

Then the fight seemed to go out of him and his shoulders slumped forward wearily. 'Please, I beg you, get Rory to call me today.'

Jazz watched as David walked slowly out of the lobby.

'I do apologise, Inspector Hunter.' The head took out his handkerchief and wiped it across his forehead. 'Would you like to come through?'

'The boy is Rory Millar? Is that right?'

'Yes.' Robert closed his study door behind him and ushered Jazz to a seat. 'I do my best to meet parents' demands, but I think it's hardly in Rory's best interests to see his father so distressed. And, I regret, drunk.'

'Did Rory know Charlie Cavendish?'

'They were in Fleat House together, but Charlie was five years Rory's senior, so they would have had little to do with each other outside that. Now'—it was obvious the head wished to move on—'I think it might be best for you to start with Charlie's housemaster. Sebastian Frederiks was in day-to-day charge of Charlie and will be the best person to talk to to find out more about Charlie's circle of friends. And Fleat's house tutor, Hugh Daneman, who is also our Latin master, would be the other, but unfortunately he's off for a few days with the flu. Now'—the headmaster shuffled his papers on his desk in a pointed way—'I did talk to your DS Miles earlier and told him all I could about

Charlie. Is there anything else I can do for you?'

'Not at present, thank you, Mr Jones.' Jazz stood up. 'You've been most helpful.'

Miles was in the small classroom they'd been assigned, typing his notes up on his laptop.

'Hello there, how are you getting on?' he asked as he lifted his head from the screen.

'Just come and look at these, will you?' Jazz placed four small, round, white pills on the desk in front of her. 'Don't look too closely. From where you're standing, do they all look the same?'

Miles nodded. 'Absolutely.'

'Now look closer and you'll see that two of the pills are plain and two of them have numbers on them.'

'Zero seven two,' Miles read as he squinted at the tablets.

'Adele Cavendish, Charlie's mother, told me Charlie took two Epilim tablets each night just before he went to sleep. She was always worried Charlie would forget, so either Matron or the housemaster would come in every evening with the tablets and place them by his bed with a glass of water.'

'Yes?' questioned Miles.

'Now, I've just been on to the pathologist who did the PM and he's sure Charlie hadn't taken his two Epilim tablets just before he died. There wasn't enough of the substance in his bloodstream. The point is, if you had just arrived home from the pub and were getting ready for bed, would you notice that the two white pills you took every night of your life had a number on them? Or would you just grab them and swallow them back?'

'So you're saying that there's a possibility Charlie's epilepsy tablets were substituted?'

'Yes.' Jazz pointed to the two pills with the numbers on them. 'They are aspirin, and those'—she picked up a plain pill, then studied it—'are Epilim.'

They stared at the tablets in silence. Finally, Miles volunteered, 'I think it's almost certain he wouldn't have noticed the difference.'

'Plus, it would explain why, even though he knew they were deadly to him, Charlie took them. The pathologist estimated time of death as eleven thirty, only half an hour after Charlie signed back into Fleat

House. The reaction to the aspirin would have taken effect almost immediately. And if I'm right,' Jazz added ominously, 'I'm afraid we're looking at a murder investigation.'

Sebastian Frederiks, housemaster of Fleat House, had his living quarters just off the main lobby of the building. He used his sitting room to interview and entertain parents and children, and to host a variety of social evenings with the boys in his care.

To that end, it felt like a doctor's waiting room: functional, with a couple of dralon sofas, a few ancient chairs whose cushions needed restuffing, and a desk facing out onto the quad in front. But, as Jazz thought when she walked in, there was nothing to give an idea of Sebastian Frederiks's personal taste.

'How do you do, Inspector Hunter?' He offered his hand and gave hers a firm shake.

In his early forties, the housemaster had the body of a rugby player—Jazz knew from the list of teachers she had been given he was the head coach of the 1st XV—but he had the height to prevent his broadness from making him seem squat. He had blond hair, slowly greying at the temples, striking brown eyes and a set of slightly protruding white teeth.

'Do come in and sit down. Would you like some tea?'

'Why not?' said Jazz and sat down as Sebastian Frederiks ordered the tea from the telephone on his desk.

'So, terrible business this, isn't it? Never lost a boy in all my twenty years of teaching.' He came to sit down opposite her. 'How can I help you?' He spoke loudly, his physical and facial expressions exaggerated, as though he was used to shouting across far distances.

'You obviously had plenty of contact with Charlie. He'd been in your house for five years. I'd like you to describe him to me as best you can.'

Sebastian leaned forward and rubbed his hands together. 'When he first came, he was an arrogant little runt, but I think we managed to knock some of that out of him. And of course, he was one of my star rugby players, fly-half for the 1st XV. What the team will do without him, I really don't know.' He sighed, an elongated sound. 'Anyway, there we go.'

'Would it be possible to tell me who his closest friends were?'

'Of course. I've already made you a list.' Sebastian picked up an envelope from the coffee table and passed it to her. 'I presumed you'd want to know that kind of thing. I've listed his friends, his classmates and the boys who slept in the sixth-form corridor with him. Oh, and the odd girl he seemed to be friendly with over the past couple of years.'

'Well, that's very efficient of you, Mr Frederiks, thank you.' The tea arrived, brought by one of the boys.

'I'll be mother, shall I?' suggested Sebastian.

Jazz couldn't pinpoint why this man was irritating her.

'Thank you.' She took the proffered cup and sipped her tea. 'So, in your opinion, was Charlie a popular boy?'

'He was very much a leader and that generated plenty of respect, but some dislike too. He had his group of acolytes hanging around him, basking in his reflected glory—mostly the rugby types, to be fair. Then there were those who found him a little aggressive, rather full of himself, and they tended to steer clear.'

'He wasn't a prefect, I notice? Surely somebody with leadership qualities would be considered for a position such as that?'

Sebastian drained his cup. 'Perhaps the head didn't trust him not to abuse it,' he said carefully.

'I understand,' said Jazz, wishing she could become a little fonder of her victim than she was at present. 'Now, talk me through the night he died. Matron was off that evening. So, I presume you were here?'

Frederiks's ruddy complexion turned a deeper shade of red. 'Aaah, well, that's the thing, you see. As a matter of fact, I wasn't, no.'

'Where were you, then?'

'I was out,' he nodded. 'Yes, out.'

'So, if you were out and Matron was out, who was here in charge of the house that night?'

Frederiks leaned in closer to Jazz, assuming a confidential stance. 'You see, Inspector Hunter, it's all really rather embarrassing. The point is, I *should* have been here. It's a school rule that two members of staff must always be present in the house. I left our house tutor, Hugh Daneman, in charge alone for a few hours.' He shrugged. 'I had an urgent appointment to keep.'

'May I ask you where you were?'

'Er…no, not really, I'm afraid it's a private matter, but Mr Daneman can confirm I was back by midnight.'

'What time did you leave the house?'

'About seven thirty.'

'Then can I ask you who would have put Charlie Cavendish's Epilim tablets by his bed that night? You weren't here and Matron was out.'

'I did, before I left. It must have been about seven fifteen when I went to his room with the tablets.'

'And you placed them by his bed as normal, with a glass of water?'

'Yes, I did. Charlie was in his study at the time. He saw me do it, as a matter of fact. Not that it helps me now,' Frederiks acknowledged.

'How often would you visit the drugs cupboard to give out prescriptive and other drugs to the boys?' Jazz asked.

'When and if necessary,' Frederiks answered. 'Matron and I have a key each. We both record exactly what we have taken and the time, so there's no confusion.'

'And what about that night when both Matron and yourself were out?'

'I gave my bunch of keys to Mr Daneman, which would include those to the drugs cupboard.'

'Mr Frederiks, as you were presumably in a rush to leave the house and get out to your appointment, is there any chance at all that you could have mistaken two aspirin tablets for the Epilim?' Jazz pulled the four pills out of her pocket and put them on the table in front of him. 'As you can see, they're almost identical.'

Frederiks looked shaken. 'Inspector Hunter, I accept I made a mistake that night by leaving the house, but I can assure you I was most circumspect when it came to anything to do with the boys and their medicine, especially Charlie Cavendish. I was well aware he was allergic to aspirin. Besides, the analgesics were kept on a separate shelf to the prescriptive medicine, so there really is no chance I could have become confused.'

'Then, just out of interest, could you tell me which tablets are Epilim and which are aspirin?'

He squinted at the tablets and pointed to the two plain pills. 'Those are the Epilim. Those two with the numbers on them are aspirin.' He looked up at Jazz rather smugly. 'Okay?'

The fact you know the difference doesn't really help you, she thought.

'Yes. So, Mr Frederiks, you are unable to tell me exactly where you were on the night Charlie died?'

He nodded. 'Sorry and all that.'

'I have to point out it leaves you with no alibi, or witnesses to corroborate your story.'

The housemaster frowned. 'Surely I'm unlikely to need one? Besides, as I said earlier, Hugh Daneman will vouch for the fact I was out, then arrived here at midnight.'

'Is there a back entrance to Fleat House?' Jazz asked.

'What? Are you suggesting I went out and sneaked back in some other way to kill poor Charlie?' Frederiks's face was turning darker with anger.

'No, I'm simply asking you if there is a back entrance. Is there?'

'Yes, there is. I'll show you if you want. And there's the fire escape which runs from the top of the house to the bottom. Look, Inspector Hunter, let me make something clear once and for all: I above anyone am gutted about what has happened. Under the circumstances, I can't think of anyone less likely to hurt a hair on Charlie Cavendish's head.'

'What "circumstances", Mr Frederiks?'

He looked uncomfortable and some of his righteous anger dissipated. 'For the obvious ones, of course. I'm Charlie's housemaster, in direct *loco parentis*. The fact I wasn't here when Charlie died is something that will stay on my conscience for the rest of my life. And, as for my future teaching career, it's hardly going to do my reputation much good to have the death of one of my boys on my record, is it?'

'I think that's all for now. Thank you for your time.' Jazz popped the pills back in her pocket with the folded piece of paper Frederiks had given her, listing Charlie's friends. 'One more thing: Rory Millar, he's in this house, isn't he?'

'Yes, why do you ask?'

'I saw his father today, David Millar. He seemed to think his son was upset about something. How is he?'

'All the boys in the house have been unsettled by what has happened, Inspector Hunter. Rory has always been sensitive, so perhaps it's distressed him more than most,' Frederiks replied carefully. He stood up and ushered Jazz towards the door. 'If I can be of any further help, please let me know.' The false charm had returned.

'Yes, can you have Rory Millar present in your sitting room tomorrow morning at eight thirty? Thank you, Mr Frederiks, I'll see you tomorrow.'

As she left the building Jazz heard a loud bell ring and children started to pour out of the buildings around Chapel Lawn. She walked round Fleat House to find the back entrance. She turned the handle, but found it locked.

Jazz checked her watch as she walked back to the classroom and DS Miles. It was five thirty, time for a debrief and then home.

Detective Sergeant Roland was packing his briefcase and making to leave when Jazz arrived.

'Can you spare me two minutes to talk me through what Matron had to say when you interviewed her?' Jazz asked, perching on the edge of her desk.

'Of course, Ma'am.' Roland retrieved his notebook from his briefcase, checked the contents, then cleared his throat. 'As she may have told you earlier, she was not in the house on the night of the incident. It was her evening off.'

'Where was she?'

'I was just coming to that. She went to a choir concert in the chapel, which started at seven thirty and finished at nine. I saw the school chaplain as I was walking back across here and he corroborated the fact that he saw her entering the chapel, and then leaving. He stands by the door to meet and greet, you see,' he added.

'And did you ask her where she went after the concert?'

'Of course. She went into town and had supper alone at the Three Swans Hotel. I've confirmed that with the staff of the hotel, obviously. Then she says she walked back to school, arriving at Fleat House about half past ten. She went upstairs to her flat, located on the top floor. She said she heard nothing. Not that she would, her flat is at the opposite end of the corridor to his bedsit. But she was the one who found Charlie dead in his study the next morning and raised the alarm.'

'Thank you. Oh, and just before you go, can you give me directions as to how I find this road?' Jazz handed him a scrap of paper with an address on it.

'Of course, Ma'am. It's very close.' Roland scribbled the instructions down.

'Thanks. We'll see you here tomorrow at eight.'

'Goodnight, Ma'am.' Roland nodded at Miles and left the room.

'I've had enough, too.' Jazz sighed. 'What say you we have something to eat in town at the hotel you're staying in and chat through the facts?'

'Sounds good to me,' Miles nodded, closing his laptop and following Jazz out of the room. She locked it and put the key in her coat pocket.

'You know the big problem here? If I'm right and those aspirin were substituted for the Epilim, any number of people could have walked into Fleat House in those four hours and done the dirty deed. There's a security lock but the number is hardly a well-kept secret, what with eighty boys coming and going all day, not to mention staff. I checked earlier and there is a back entrance. Anyone could have got inside that way, too.'

'Like I said, needle in a haystack,' Miles commented as they headed towards the car.

'Sebastian Frederiks, the housemaster, says that he placed Charlie's tablets by his bed about seven fifteen, whilst Charlie was still in the room. We need to discover exactly what time Charlie left to meet his friends at the pub, but for now, let's assume sometime between seven thirty and eight. We know Charlie took the pills between eleven fifteen and eleven thirty. That leaves almost four hours during which the switch could have been made.'

Miles opened the passenger door for her and Jazz climbed inside.

'You seem pretty set on the idea that's how Charlie died.' He started the engine. 'Another thought: what if Charlie had bought some illegal substance, such as Es, at the pub that night? And the pusher had duped him by selling plain old aspirin instead?' Miles began to back the car out of the space.

'I find it very hard to believe there might be hard drugs being sold in a town such as this.'

'Who's being City-ist now, Ma'am? Drugs are everywhere. And especially in establishments where the kids have the money to pay for 'em.'

'Point taken,' Jazz acknowledged. 'But the way his mother had obviously drummed into Charlie that *any* unknown drugs could be fatal, never mind the fact that an epileptic shouldn't touch mind-altering substances, makes me doubt he'd take the risk.'

'Charlie was eighteen and, from what I've heard, liked a party. I don't think what Mummy says would have held much sway. Like all youngsters, I'm sure he had a taste for danger.'

'So say you're right,' Jazz mused, 'why would he wait until he got back to his room before he took the stuff? If there was drug abuse in his group of friends, it's a pack activity. Listen'—Jazz drew a piece of paper out of her pocket—'would you mind a quick pit stop before your pint? I want to visit Hugh Daneman, the Fleat tutor, see if he saw anyone coming or going out of Fleat House that night. Poor chap, it seems he's rather been dropped in it by Mr Frederiks absconding to a secret location.'

'Usually it's a case of being with someone they shouldn't be. Mind you, Frederiks is single, isn't he? Left or right to this tutor's place?'

'Er...left here, Roland says.' Jazz directed Miles down a narrow road. 'Frederiks is certainly hiding something. It all depends whether the "something" is relevant to the enquiry. Turn right here.' Jazz looked out of the window. 'There's number twenty-four; we're looking for thirty-six.'

They pulled up outside the terraced cottage and got out of the car. Jazz pushed open the gate, noting that the front garden was beautifully tended. She knocked sharply on the front door.

'He may not answer if he's upstairs sick in bed,' Miles suggested as Jazz knocked again.

'No, but I really would like to speak to him tonight if I can.' Jazz bent down, opened the letter box and peered inside. She saw a chair facing the fire and an arm hanging over it. 'He's in there, but he must be asleep.' She put her mouth to the opening and called, 'Mr Daneman, it's the police. Sorry to disturb you, but we need to speak to you. Mr Daneman?'

There was no response. She looked up quizzically at Miles.

'Maybe he's deaf?' he suggested.

Jazz put her eyes back to the letter box. Something about the way the arm hung, lifeless over the arm of the chair, told her it wasn't deafness preventing Hugh Daneman from answering the door.

She stood up and turned to her sergeant. 'He's not deaf. Break down the door, Miles. My guess is we have another dead body on our hands.'

Chapter Seven

Angelina Millar stirred her lamb casserole, then added some seasoning. She popped the pot back into the Aga and looked with satisfaction at the table, set for two, with a fresh bunch of early tulips in the centre to add a touch of spring.

She paused before she left the kitchen to make sure everything was ready, then went into the downstairs loo to check her make-up and her hair.

As always, she looked immaculate. Her pretty doll-like features stared back at her and she thought how lucky she was that a little mascara and a dab of lipstick were still enough to accentuate her big blue eyes and full lips.

Perhaps one day, she'd have to go down the Botox route, like so many of her girlfriends already had, but at present she knew she looked younger than her thirty-eight years.

She put her head round the drawing room door to make sure the fire was still burning merrily in the grate, then wandered back to the kitchen and decided to treat herself to a glass of wine while she waited. Julian had said he should arrive sometime after seven, so, seeing that everything was done, she felt she deserved a drink.

Angelina took her wine back into the drawing room and sat on a corner of the deep sofa, careful not to crease the cushion behind her. She straightened the pile of *House and Garden* magazines that lay on the highly polished coffee table and looked round the room with a feeling of pride.

Everyone who came to the house remarked on what a glorious room it was. Even though it was large, she'd managed to make it feel cosy and warm. In fact, she'd had so many compliments on the way she'd decorated the house, she'd decided she might try it professionally. She was going to take a part-time interior design course in the summer—not that she expected it could teach her anything about interiors she didn't already know, but because she felt it was important to potential customers that she'd had some kind of official training.

One of her girlfriends had already offered her a commission to do up a holiday cottage she'd just bought as an investment, and Angelina was looking forward to pottering around antique shops and choosing curtain material.

Especially now Rory was boarding during the week and Julian was never back home until later, if he stayed at all. It would give her something both enjoyable and financially rewarding to fill her days.

Angelina sipped her wine contentedly and allowed herself a smile at the way her life had worked out. A beautiful home, a child, and a wealthy, successful man to share her life with.

They needed to be circumspect at the moment. It would not be politic for either her reputation or Julian's career if others found out she'd been having an affair with a lawyer who might not have represented her, but had advised her over the difficult circumstances surrounding her divorce.

But even that had worked out well. Angelina had been on the verge of telling David she was leaving him to be with Julian, just as David had lost his job, and the plot, and attacked her.

She'd called Julian, terrified, after the police had taken David away. He had taken control.

He'd suggested Angelina charge David with assault. She'd been uncomfortable about it, given the fact that she understood why David was so furious that night, but as Julian had pointed out, it was a great reason to petition him for divorce and keep her reputation intact at the same time.

The talk in the social circles both she and Julian mixed in would not be of 'poor old David', left by a wife he adored for another man, but sympathy for Angelina, a battered wife, married to a violent alcoholic. And she, for her own and her son's protection, had no choice but to divorce him.

Angelina had been unsure when Julian had initially suggested it, but when David had turned up at the house the next morning and broken a window, she'd been genuinely frightened. Julian had mentioned the assault charge again, adding an ASBO to keep David away legally. By then, she'd had no qualms about asking her lawyer to action it.

Angelina had originally assumed that when she left David, she'd have to sacrifice her beloved home. Then Julian had come up with the suggestion that he take on the mortgage with her, put up the money from the sale of his current home to pay David off and move in.

She'd been enchanted by the idea. And dropping the assault charge in return for a quickie divorce had enabled Angelina's conscience to be salved. However much she wanted out of her marriage to David, giving him a police record for a crime he hadn't really committed was a low thing to do.

She felt sympathy for David, but not enough to keep her awake at night. He was one of life's losers and she was relieved she didn't have to drag him along on her coat tails any longer.

Now she had a man who was as ambitious as she was. He *wanted* the best of everything, to celebrate his achievements spending the money he made through all his hard work.

They'd already discussed having a big party to celebrate their partnership and Julian's fortieth birthday. Angelina had been on to marquee companies, caterers and band agents. Julian had given her carte blanche to spend his money and make a spectacular job of it. And she would have to go to London to buy a very special dress.

Yes, things had worked out perfectly for Angelina. There was only one fly in the ointment. And that was her son, Rory.

Angelina was a loving and devoted mother. She'd hated witnessing Rory's pain as he came to terms with his parents' divorce. She knew father and son had a special bond; she could recognise the similarities between them. When she'd told him Dad was never coming home again, Rory had cried all night.

Since then, he'd disappeared into his shell. When he was home from school at weekends, he rarely communicated with her about anything other than food and domestic arrangements.

She knew it was too soon to tell him about Julian's presence in her life. It had been hard, but manageable, what with weekly boarding and Rory staying with his father every two weeks.

Then, a few days ago, Julian had announced he thought it was time to tell Rory. He was fed up, he said, with creeping around like a furtive teenager. He wanted to move into the house that was costing him an arm and a leg on the mortgage, come clean with Rory and the world. He had booked all three of them on a half-term skiing holiday.

'Rory and I can bond on the slopes,' he'd announced.

Angelina shuddered at the thought of Rory, never sporty, being taught to ski by the athletic Julian.

However, she did agree Julian was right. Rory, fourteen in a couple of months, should be adult enough to cope.

This weekend, when Rory came home, she was going to broach the fact that her 'friend' was going to be joining them on the holiday.

Angelina heard the back door click and stood up. Julian was on time for once. She drained her wine glass and stood up, checking her appearance for a final time in the over-mantle mirror.

She heard footsteps across the flagstone floor in the hall coming in her direction. The door opened.

'Darling, I...' Angelina's hand shot to her mouth when she saw who had just walked into her drawing-room, leaving a trail of muddy footsteps across the duck-egg-blue carpet.

'Hello, Angie. I've come to see you about Rory.'

She was backing away as he approached her, but found herself wedged against the bookcase.

'Stop looking so terrified. I'm not here to hurt you. I just want us to have a chat about Rory. The bloody school won't let me see him and I'm worried sick.'

He was close enough for Angelina to smell the stench on his breath.

'Oh David, I thought you were on the wagon. You've been drinking.'

'Not enough to get me sloshed, unfortunately.' He moved away from her. 'Look, please stop treating me like an axeman. I'm not going to harm a hair on your head. Even though we're divorced, we do still have a child together. And he's in trouble of some kind.'

Angelina crept slowly towards the sofa and sat gingerly on the edge. David looked terrible. He'd obviously not shaved or washed for days and his hair, which had grown much longer in the past few months, hung greasily around his face.

'David, you know, you really can't just barge in here any more. It's not your house,' she began. 'Next time, please call me and then we can arrange to meet somewhere.'

'Angie, don't try that one. You rarely, if ever, return my calls and you certainly wouldn't be seen dead with me in a public place. What else was I expected to do? Let our child continue to suffer because his mother refuses to give me the time of day?'

She stayed silent.

'You haven't got a drink, have you?' he asked.

'David...I...'

He'd already left the room and came back with the bottle of wine Angelina had paid a small fortune for to accompany supper this evening. He took the cork out and sloshed the wine into a glass.

'I had to have a drink to work up the courage to get me here in the first place.' He lifted the glass to his lips and took a large gulp. 'Very nice too. You expecting company? I see the table's set for dinner *à deux*. Got a boyfriend, have you?'

'No...I, yes... Look, it's none of your business. Just say what you want to say, then leave.' Angelina glanced nervously at her watch.

'Rory called me from school a couple of days ago. He sounded very upset.'

'Really? He seemed fine when I saw him at the choir concert in chapel last Friday. He went straight off on Saturday morning for the Independent Schools Choir Festival, so I haven't had a chance to see him since. What did he say to you on the phone?'

'Something about nobody being there to protect him.' David took another slug of the wine and topped up his glass. 'I don't know what he meant, do you?'

'No. I've really no idea, David.' Angelina's brow furrowed in concern.

'I went to try and find him last Friday night but he wasn't there.'

'That's because he was singing in chapel, David.'

'Then I left messages for the head and that tosser of a housemaster at Fleat. No one returned my calls. So I went to the school again this morning and demanded to see Rory, but the bastard head refused. Jesus! I get so damned frustrated.' David drained his glass and refilled it.

Angelina thought how the head would have viewed David: drunk and aggressive, storming into the school and demanding to see his son.

'I'm going to call Fleat House as soon as you've left, check he's all right. And he's coming home in a day's time. I can talk to him then.'

'Please, Angie, could you not make the call now?'

'I'll do it as soon as you've left. And I promise to call you, really. Now, David, I—'

'The head said he'd ask Frederiks to make sure Rory phones me tonight, but, on past performance, I wouldn't bank on it.' David was pacing unsteadily. 'I know in my bones something's wrong. Promise you'll call?'

'Of course I will,' she answered gently. 'I promise.'

'Do you think he's been bullied?'

'I don't know. Maybe it could be to do with the death of that boy who died of an epileptic fit at the school?'

'I really don't know, but we must find out.' David stopped pacing, turned to stare at her. 'Look, I know how wrong things have gone, Angie, but at the very least, surely we owe it to Rory to try and communicate on some level?'

Angelina nodded. 'Yes.' She glanced at her watch again, then stood up, momentary harmony replaced with urgency. 'I'm expecting a guest any minute. I think it's best you leave.'

He looked at her sadly. 'Of course you do.' David suddenly crashed his glass onto the table. 'Don't fit in here looking like this, do I? Pissed, desperate... You never did like anything out of control, did you, Angie?'

'David, please, don't.'

'Don't *what*? Tell you the truth? What exactly was it I did wrong, Angie? I was kind, thoughtful, never unfaithful, I bought you the house of your dreams...'

'I think you should leave. I—'

'I loved you, tried to give you everything you wanted...' He walked to the mantelpiece and picked up a figurine. 'Do you remember me buying you this? It was our...sixth anniversary and I spent a fortune on it.' He put it back on the mantelpiece where it balanced precariously near the edge. 'All I ever wanted to do was to make you and Rory happy.'

Angelina heard a car pull into the drive. She stood up. 'David, you have to leave, *now!*'

'Okay, okay. I'm going, don't worry. Call me. Promise?'

'Yes.'

'Thanks. Just cos I've had to stop loving you, doesn't mean I don't still love my son.' David turned towards the door, but as he swung unsteadily round, the sleeve of his anorak caught the figurine on the mantelpiece and sent it crashing into the hearth below.

'Oh God, I...I'm so sorry...I...' David turned back and bent down to collect the pieces. 'I'll replace it...'

A pair of strong arms caught him by his elbows and brought him roughly to standing.

'What the HELL are you doing in my house! Threatening your ex-wife again? Using broken china as a weapon?' He was being dragged out of the room towards the door. 'You know what happened last time you tried to break in here?'

'Julian, really, it's all right. David came to see me about Rory. He hasn't threatened me and he was just about to leave when...'

But Julian was already out of the drawing room, manhandling the hapless David towards the front door. He opened it and threw David forcefully into the garden. David lost his balance and promptly fell into the rose bed just to the left of the entrance.

Panting with exertion, Julian swept a hand through his hair and straightened his suit as he watched David struggle to stand up.

'I swear to you, if I ever find you near this house again, I shall slap another ASBO on you so quickly your feet won't touch the ground. And as for your son, I shall make sure to tell him what a drunken lowlife his father is.'

The door slammed shut and David was left in the dark outside, his head spinning from alcohol and shock. There was blood trickling from one of his fingers, where he'd pricked it on a rose bush. He staggered down the drive towards the front gate, unable to stop the tears from running down his face.

'Oh God, oh God,' he muttered as he opened the door to his car.

He sank into the driver's seat and put his head in his hands.

Julian Holmes, the arrogant smarmy lawyer David had met several times at dinner parties, was shacked up with his ex-wife.

He was living in David's house, sleeping in David's bed and, worst of all, able to have unlimited access to his son. When David himself couldn't.

And... His alcohol-sodden mind searched for the connection that was there, just out of reach...

What if the person Rory seemed so frightened of was Julian?

David rested his throbbing head on the steering wheel and wondered if it was possible for things to get any worse.

Jazz was on her way home to her cottage, Miles driving her whilst she spoke on her mobile to Norton.

'The body has been removed and the pathologist is promising to put Mr Daneman to the top of the queue. We can't be sure until after the PM, but from what I saw, it was a straightforward case of suicide.'

'Do you need further back-up?' Norton asked.

'The Norwich SOCOs are coming to give Cavendish's study the once-over tomorrow morning. Not that there'll be much left to find.

The room has been cleaned since. They should have been called immediately after the incident.'

'No one was aware at that point it was anything other than an accident.'

'It just makes our job that bit harder, Sir. You know how crucial the first couple of days after a murder are.'

'Murder?'

'Sorry, Sir, jumping the gun there a little. But what with Hugh Daneman dead, it doesn't take a genius to work out there's something more to this than first met the eye.'

'Do you think the two deaths are linked?'

'It's one hell of a coincidence if they're not, but I won't speculate until I have some facts. And they're in pretty short supply just now. Anyway. I'll send the SOCOs straight over to Hugh Daneman's cottage once they've finished with Cavendish's study.'

'The big question is, how long can we keep this under wraps from the media? One death everyone so far assumes was accidental is troubling, but two will cause mass panic at the school and amongst the parents.'

'At least Daneman didn't die on the school premises.'

'No, but if there is something sinister going on, we can't have all those kids at risk, can we, Hunter?'

'No. We need to get the PM report back on Daneman as soon as we can.'

'Have you contacted the headmaster about Daneman?' asked Norton.

'Yes. I called him ten minutes ago. As you can imagine, he was very concerned. And that's putting it mildly. I'm seeing him first thing tomorrow morning.'

'Keep in touch, Hunter. Sorry to give you another death on your first day back on the job.'

Jazz could picture Norton smiling wryly. 'Didn't get home to paint the *Mona Lisa* after all, Sir.'

'No. Goodnight, then.'

'Night, Sir.'

Miles had come to a stop in front of her cottage. 'Thanks for the lift. I would invite you in for a cup of coffee, but I'm bushed.'

'You, Ma'am? Tired? Never.'

'I'm sure I'll get back in the swing shortly, but I'm for a bath and bed. Pick me up at seven tomorrow, will you?'

'Will do. I'm off to explore the fleshpots of Foltesham.' Miles winked at her as Jazz opened the passenger door.

'Perhaps you could explore the particular fleshpot Charlie and his St Stephen's cronies visited the night he died? Talk to the landlord, get some feedback.'

'Tough call, Ma'am. Might have to down a couple of pints to blend in.'

'Sure you'll cope. See you at seven. Night.'

Jazz lay in the bath, mulling over the events of the day.

What if Hugh Daneman, unusually alone and in charge of Fleat House, had either mistakenly, *or* intentionally, substituted Charlie's Epilim drugs with aspirin?

If she could find a motive, prove he *had* been the perpetrator, it was an open-and-shut case.

Jazz sighed as she stepped out of the bath and reached for a towel, her skin a mass of goosebumps as she ran across the unheated landing and into her bedroom.

When had she *ever* worked on an open-and-shut case?

But they must exist, surely?

She put on her dressing gown, went downstairs and saw her answering machine was flashing. There were messages from the plumber, the decorator and her father, wanting to hear how her first day back had gone.

She picked up the receiver and dialled her parents' number.

'Dad, it's me. Yup, good, but God, I'm tired. Found another corpse at five thirty, so things are hotting up.'

'What? In sleepy Norfolk? Oh well, all grist to the mill for you, darling. Pleased to be back?'

'I'll let you know in a few days' time. Tonight, I'm bushed.'

'I'm sure. Anyway, I for one think you've made the right decision. Could you make lunch here on Sunday, then you can tell your mother and I all about it?'

'I'd love to, but I'll need to see how the case is going.'

'Of course, but listen, I had a chap here to see me earlier today. He's called Jonathan Scott and he's doing his PhD, writing his thesis on crime in modern Britain. He'd heard my daughter was a DI on the university grapevine and wondered if he could interview you at some point in the next few days?'

'I'm going to be awfully busy, Dad.'

'I know. But how about you sparing an hour for him after you've enjoyed your mother's leg of lamb on Sunday? He's an awfully nice chap. Sure you'd like him.'

'You're not trying to set me up, are you?'

'Goodness, no. He's a few years younger than you anyway.'

'And he wouldn't fancy a shrivelled old maid anyway?'

'Exactly.'

'Thanks, Dad. I rely on you to do wonders for my morale. How are you feeling, by the way?'

'Chipper, as always.'

'Good. Well, barring this investigation running away with me between now and then, I'll be there for one on Sunday.'

'Look forward to it, darling. God bless.'

'Love to Mum. Night, Dad.'

Jazz put the phone down, switched off the lights and walked wearily up the stairs. As she climbed into bed, she realised that for the first time in seven months, she had not thought about her ex-husband all day.

Chapter Eight

Robert Jones was a strange colour. Jazz could see the beads of sweat on his temples.

'I'm most concerned, Inspector Hunter. Most concerned. One death that may have been accidental, we can just about cope with, but *two*...two is dangerous.'

'I understand, Mr Jones. It's a very unfortunate situation. If it's any comfort to you, we're pretty sure Mr Daneman committed suicide.'

'Well, I suppose that's something,' the head conceded.

'Obviously we can't confirm this until the post-mortem is completed,' added Jazz.

'No. So, perhaps it's just unlucky coincidence?'

'I'm afraid I can't answer that one at present. Tell me, did Mr Daneman and Charlie Cavendish get along?'

'Well...putting it simply, they were chalk and cheese. Charlie was not academic, liked being one of the lads and was noisy. Hugh, on the other hand, was a gentle soul, of the old school. He was a Latin scholar at Oxford when he was younger. He lived a quiet life surrounded by his books and did a lot of translation work for the British Library. I often wondered what he was doing here at St Stephen's, actually. He really was quite a renowned expert on fourteenth-century Latin manuscripts.'

'Was he a well-liked member of staff?'

'Oh, very much,' the headmaster replied. 'No one had a bad word for Hugh. He was such a kind man, and, if a little unworldly, made an excellent tutor for some of the younger boys, away from home for the first time. He'd provide a listening ear if they had a problem.'

'Did he have family?' Jazz asked.

'He was single. I don't think he'd ever married, actually. As for his extended family...' Robert Jones shrugged. 'I've no idea. He kept himself very much to himself. He didn't tend to socialise with the other members of staff.'

'Then we'll run a check through the computers and see if we can find next of kin.'

'I'm sorry I can't help you further on that score. Hugh really was an enigma on a personal level.'

'Had you noticed any changes in him recently?' Jazz probed. 'Did he seem depressed?'

'No, but then Hugh was never the type to show emotion. Anything could have been going on in that clever head of his, but no one here would have known quite what.'

'So, just going back on our conversation,' Jazz prompted, 'Charlie and Hugh didn't see eye to eye?'

'Hugh was Charlie's tutor when he first arrived, but we changed that arrangement within a few weeks. It was a case of rubbing each other up the wrong way. Charlie could be…overbearing and sometimes aggressive. Hugh, the eternal pacifist, was not capable of dealing with that personality type, so we handed him over to Sebastian Frederiks, which proved a far more effective relationship.'

'I see.' Jazz leaned in closer across the desk. 'Mr Jones, please answer me honestly here: was Charlie Cavendish renowned for being a bully?'

There was a pause, then a sigh before the headmaster replied, 'I suppose he had a certain reputation, yes. How intentional his behaviour was, I don't know, but he did give some of the younger boys a hard time, especially when they first arrived. He didn't like wimps, felt it was his duty to toughen them up. But I must reiterate, Inspector Hunter, we do not have a bullying problem in the school as a whole. We are on the lookout for it all the time. Charlie was an isolated case and he was admonished on several occasions.'

'So, he was a bully. He sounds like a difficult boy,' commented Jazz.

'He was one of our more challenging pupils, yes, but we can only try and deal with the raw material we are given. The fact is that Charlie had been indulged by his parents since the day he was born. He…struggled to grasp the concept of boundaries.'

'One more question.' Jazz placed a plastic wallet on the headmaster's desk. 'Do you recognise this person?'

He picked up the small photograph and squinted at it. 'Very faded, isn't it? But the face does look familiar.'

'We found it under the chair in which Hugh Daneman was found dead. He may have been holding it and it fell out of his hand when he became unconscious. So, you can't tell me who it is?'

'No.' Jones stared again at the cherubic face, long fair hair framing fine features. 'She's rather beautiful, isn't she?'

'Yes, and very young. I was half wondering whether it could be a child of Mr Daneman's, but you obviously have no knowledge of that?'

'No.' He handed the photograph back to her. 'Sorry.'

'Tell me, Mr Jones, can you think of any reason why Hugh Daneman would want to kill Charlie Cavendish?'

'What?! Hugh? Kill someone?' The head shook his head in disbelief. 'To be honest, Inspector, the idea is preposterous, absolutely preposterous! Besides, I understand you must investigate Charlie's death, but aren't we jumping the gun a little to suggest he was murdered?'

Jazz stood up. She looked down at Robert Jones and shook her head slowly. 'I'm afraid we can't rule it out. I've been through every possible way Charlie could have swallowed those tablets knowingly, when he was perfectly aware they might kill him. So, the facts are these: either he committed suicide, or someone substituted his Epilim pills with aspirin. And, if the latter is the case, that's murder in my book, Mr Jones.'

'It may have been suicide...' the head suggested weakly.

'You don't believe that, do you?'

He paused, before shaking his head defeatedly. 'No. No, I don't. I mean, one can never be certain, especially with teenagers, but knowing Charlie, I'd agree it was unlikely.'

'You say you think Hugh Daneman was incapable of murder?'

'Absolutely, in my opinion, yes.'

'Did you know he was alone in the house that Friday night?'

'No, Inspector, Matron was out but Sebastian Frederiks was there too.'

'No, he wasn't. According to Mr Frederiks himself, he had an appointment elsewhere, the details of which he is yet to give us.'

'Really?' The head looked at Jazz in astonishment. 'Are you sure of that?'

'I'm sure he told me he wasn't at Fleat House on Friday night between seven thirty and midnight, yes.'

'Frankly, I'm amazed. Sebastian Frederiks is the most dedicated housemaster we have. He lives for those boys *and* he knew the rules: that there must always be two members of staff on duty in the house at any one time. I can't believe he would blatantly put those in his care in danger. Or "sneak off" without telling me.'

'Perhaps you should ask him where he was, Mr Jones. He certainly had no answers for me.'

'I most certainly will.' He took a slug of water from a glass on his desk. 'Good God, this whole thing is turning into a nightmare!'

'Well, I suppose one could say that Frederiks's absence has only been discovered because of Charlie's death. But, rewinding slightly, it does mean Hugh Daneman had plenty of opportunity to go to his victim's study without being seen. And then took his own life rather than living with his guilt and the subsequent consequences of his crime.'

A small spark of hope appeared in the headmaster's eyes. 'Perhaps it could be a possibility.'

'You've just reiterated to me how preposterous it was to even suggest Daneman could commit murder.'

'As I said, I didn't know him well...hardly at all...I...well, however much I want a cut and dried solution to this mess,' Robert Jones sighed, 'I just can't see it. Hugh has dealt with a lot of difficult boys during his long career as a tutor at St Stephen's. I hardly think a clash of personalities would have incited him to kill.'

'Unless there was another reason that we're unaware of.'

Robert Jones clenched his hands together. 'I know of none. You're the detective, Inspector Hunter.' He sighed. 'How soon will you be informing the world of Hugh Daneman's death? You realise what mayhem it'll cause when the parents hear of this new incident, don't you? They'll wonder what the hell is going on here and I wouldn't blame them.'

'We won't be releasing any information to the press for the next couple of days, until we have the results of Mr Daneman's post-mortem. However, I want you to be aware it *is* possible there is a killer currently lurking in your midst.'

'But doubtful, surely?'

Jazz chose her words carefully. 'Mr Jones, this is your school. You are responsible for the overall well-being of your staff and pupils. I can only advise you of the information I gather as my investigation progresses, but ultimately, it's your decision to decide whether or not to close the school.'

'Well, surely, I need your advice? In your opinion, am I endangering lives if I don't do so? If we close, it would be the end of the school, you know, it really would.'

'If you want to keep the school open, what I suggest you do now is gather your staff together, and the prefects too, and inform them that Charlie's death is no longer looking like an accident. Adults are just as capable of panic as children, so try not to be alarmist. The chances are that even if Charlie *was* murdered, it was a personal vendetta and not the work of a serial killer.'

'Good God! You're scaring *me*, Inspector, let alone my staff.' Jones stood up and paced the small space behind his desk.

'Have the staff warn all the sixth-formers to lock their private studies before they go to sleep at night, and in the case of the younger boys and girls who share dorms, have a member of staff or a prefect sleep in with them. I'm also arranging for police officers to be on permanent patrol at the school.'

'Christ. St Stephen's is under siege! Do I tell them about Hugh's death?'

'Not as yet. As far as they're concerned, Mr Daneman is still at home, suffering from flu.' Jazz gave him a fleeting smile. 'Remember, it's in my interests as well to keep the school open. I don't want my suspects disappearing before I can get to the bottom of this. Thank you, Mr Jones. I'll keep you fully informed as things progress.'

Jazz left the head's office and walked across the quad to the incident room.

Miles was at his desk, yawning.

'Late night?'

'Yes. I went to that pub where the St Stephen's kids go and ended up chatting to the landlord until late.'

'Just chatting?' Jazz dropped her briefcase by her desk.

'Admittedly I kept him company in the beer department. Only had three but they must brew it stronger here than in London. I feel wiped out today.'

'All this fresh country air, DS Miles. Your lungs can't cope with it. So, what did the landlord have to say?'

'Nothing much of genuine interest. He asked the barmaid who'd been on duty that night and she remembers Charlie and his party coming in. He'd apparently had a brief fling with a friend of hers just before Christmas so she recognised him. The place was flooded with St

Stephen's sixth-formers as it's the only pub in town they're allowed to go to.'

Jazz took off her coat, sat at her desk and switched on her laptop. 'Did you ask whether there were any incidents of illegal substances changing hands on the premises?'

'Yes, not that he'd admit it if there were, obviously. He was understandably defensive when I asked him, said he'd never tolerated any kind of drugs on the premises. And I'd doubt it, personally. The pub has a good relationship with the school; they get the business, but keep an eye on the kids. I don't think the landlord would want to jeopardise that.'

'The point about drugs being a pack activity is a firm one. If Charlie had scored something illegal that night, I reckon he'd have taken it there and then. And been unconscious in a matter of minutes.'

'Unless he met a pusher after the pub. But the landlord said he didn't know of any dealers in Foltesham. But let's face it, Ma'am, kids get stuff all over the place these days. There are always some local lads in that pub. Any one of them could have had something on them they wanted to sell. But I doubt they'd do it in there.'

'Find out exactly who Charlie was with that night. Presumably he'd have left the school with his friends. Here.' Jazz handed Miles the list Sebastian Frederiks had given her. 'These are Charlie's closest cronies, according to his housemaster. Maybe some of them were with him at the pub that night. I'd like you to interview his classmates. We've heard from his teachers. Let's get a peers' perspective on Charlie Cavendish.'

'Okay,' nodded Miles. 'I'll put a notice on the board. Just one small point.' Miles indicated the stuffy room. 'Going to get a little difficult to breathe in here. Where should I see them?'

'Ask Frederiks if you can borrow his sitting room to conduct the interviews.'

'Okay.'

'Have you seen DS Roland, by the way? Thought we were meant to meet here at eight and it's now half past.'

'Yup. He went over to see the SOCOs in Cavendish's study about half an hour ago. Haven't seen him since. He was complaining of toothache. Not a happy chappy, by the looks of things.'

'I'm going over now so I'll catch him there. Shit!'

'What, Ma'am?'

'I've just automatically logged on to get into our files and realised there isn't even a phone socket in here, let alone broadband! Get on to someone and have them connect us up, will you, ASAP?'

'I'll do my best, but don't hold your breath.'

'I need to see what we've got on Hugh Daneman, if anything. Call HQ and tell them to email anything they find on him to me immediately. And search me out a telephone socket to use in the meantime, will you? I've got to go.'

Miles eyed her as she slammed her laptop shut. 'Makes you wonder how they did it in the days before technology, doesn't it, Ma'am?' His eyes were twinkling.

Walking towards the door, Jazz turned to him. 'Reckon Miss Marple saw it in the tealeaves. She certainly drank enough of the stuff. See you later.'

'I'll get you a couple of nice scones for your lunch, shall I?' Miles called as the door slammed behind her.

Jazz found the SOCOs in the entrance hall of Fleat House.

She shook hands and introduced herself to the head of the Norwich Scene of Crime Investigation unit.

'Shirley Adams.' The woman shook Jazz's hand firmly. 'Good to meet you, Ma'am.'

'Find anything?' Jazz asked her.

'Not a lot, I'm afraid.' Shirley shrugged. 'The study has been swept clean. Managed to find a couple of fingerprints, some hairs, the usual stuff. I'll pass these on to the lab and they'll be in touch as soon as they've analysed them.'

'You got my message about Hugh Daneman's house?' Jazz asked.

'Yes, we're going straight across there now.'

'Good.' Jazz fished in her pocket for the front door key and handed it to DS Roland, who was lurking uncomfortably behind Shirley. 'Roland'll let you in. I'll try and pop in later if I can.'

'I might have to go to the dentist after, Ma'am. Got chronic toothache,' said Roland.

'Ask Shirley to pull it out for you. Sure she's good at that,' Jazz smiled, but the joke fell flat and Roland glared at her. 'I'll see you back at the incident room later.'

'Yes, Ma'am.'

Jazz turned and found Matron standing behind her.

'Morning, Matron. I've come to see Rory Millar.'

'I know, but you can't see him now. He was very unwell in the night and he's just gone to sleep.'

'I see. What was wrong with him?'

'He has gastric flu. We'll see how he is when he wakes. If he's no better, I'll transfer him to the sanatorium and get the doctor to take a look. I'd guess it's all the upset. Poor little chap, he's had a difficult few months.'

Jazz watched Matron's eyes soften and re-evaluated her slightly.

'Well, maybe I could see him later, if he's feeling stronger. While I'm here, would you mind if we had a chat?'

'Of course. We can use Mr Frederiks's sitting room. He's out this morning training with the 1st XV.'

Jazz followed Matron into the sitting room. 'Please.' She indicated the sofa.

'Thank you.' Jazz settled herself and smiled. 'I know DS Miles had a word with you yesterday, so I won't go back over old ground. I just wanted to know your opinion on Charlie, what kind of boy you thought he was.'

Matron's lips visibly tightened. 'You really want to know?'

'Yes.'

'It doesn't make pleasant listening, and I'm aware one shouldn't speak ill of the dead.'

'No, but if it helps me to solve the mystery that surrounds Charlie's last night, then I'd appreciate your honesty.'

'All right then.' Matron's hands, resting on her knees, were knuckled balls of tension. 'The head should have expelled that boy long ago. Charlie had endless warnings last term to curb his behaviour, but it really made no difference. Boys like that, well... I know what I'd like to do with them.'

Two pale spots of colour had risen on Matron's otherwise chalk-white face.

'Would you like to elucidate?' Jazz asked.

'It's the same in every school: the staff are unable to control a certain group that make the rest of the boys' lives a misery. They claim they do, but make no effort to see what goes on behind closed doors.'

'Is that possible? To control bullying?'

'Of course it is! They should be expelled on the spot! Then our more vulnerable boys would not be crying into their pillows every night.

Believe me, I've heard them.'

'So, in your view, both Frederiks and the headmaster were not as tough on Charlie as you thought they should be?'

'I'd put it a little more forcefully than that.' Matron sniffed. 'Frederiks is a good housemaster. He cares about the boys. But he seemed to have a blind spot with Charlie Cavendish. He let him get away with murder.'

'Perhaps there was no proof of bullying,' suggested Jazz.

'Oh, there was proof,' Matron responded vehemently. 'I do accept that one of the problems staff have these days is that their hands are tied. I'm not suggesting a jolly good beating works in the long term, but at least it's a deterrent.'

'Yes.' Jazz found she agreed with her.

'I mean, take young Rory, for example. He suffers from migraines, which are almost certainly stress-induced. He was bullied consistently by Charlie and his gang of thugs. All because he's taking a little longer to grow up than some of his peers, or finds no pleasure in beating up another boy on the rugby pitch. You do know, Inspector, that Rory was locked in Fleat House cellar overnight by Cavendish a couple of weeks ago? Poor little mite was frightened out of his wits. And I don't blame him.'

'No, I didn't. But surely, Matron, if Mr Frederiks knew this had happened and knew Charlie was the perpetrator, he should have been dealt with accordingly?'

'As I said, Mr Frederiks is a good housemaster, but with that particular boy...his antics went unnoticed. As for the headmaster...' Matron bit her lip. 'Incompetent isn't the word.'

'So Charlie picked on Rory specifically?'

'Oh yes. He was an easy target. Most of these bullies, they're nothing but cowards underneath. They pick their prey carefully.'

Jazz sighed. 'Poor Rory. But it seems to be a problem in most schools.'

'It wouldn't be if these boys were rooted out and got rid of before they could do further damage. But it's all a numbers game. The head would prefer his sixty thousand for Charlie's attendance here, not to mention his uncle being a governor, than to help countless other pupils lead a safe and happy school life.'

'You're not suggesting Charlie endangered lives, are you?'

'Inspector Hunter, I'm not just talking about the *physical* effects of serial bullying. It's the mental and emotional scars that this behaviour can leave. Believe me, I know.'

'Were you bullied at school?'

'Me?' Matron smiled for the first time. 'No. I gave as good as I got.'

I can imagine, thought Jazz.

'I'm sure everything I'm saying is against "company" policy. If the head, and Frederiks, won't give you the truth, that's too bad, but I'm not going to lie to you about Cavendish and his aggressive behaviour.'

'Well, thank you for being honest. Tell me, how long have you been at St Stephen's?'

'I worked here very briefly earlier in my career, and began this stint at the start of the school year last September. My home is in Australia, but I was visiting relatives here in Norfolk—after a spell in the US—when this temporary job came up.' Matron shrugged. 'There was nothing particular to go back to Perth for, so I thought I'd extend my trip and work here in England.'

Jazz could now place the woman's accent as Antipodean.

'Mr Frederiks told me that the two of you have access to the drugs cupboard. You have a key each.'

'Yes, that's right.' She put a hand to her neck and drew out a chain with a small key on it. 'This is mine and I never take it off.'

'You didn't lend it to anyone on the night Charlie died?'

'Of course not! I know what boys are like these days. They'll use anything to give them a high.'

'We've received the results of the post-mortem. Charlie Cavendish died of anaphylactic shock, caused by swallowing aspirin, not an epileptic fit.'

Matron raised her eyebrows. 'The paramedics said, when they examined Charlie, that he had passed away from a fit. I agreed with them. I am a fully qualified and experienced nurse, you know.'

'I'm sure the symptoms were similar, but the PM was exhaustive. I now have to discover how Charlie came to swallow those two aspirin tablets. I'd like to see a copy of the drug sheet for that night, please.'

'Of course.' Matron nodded. 'You'll see everything is in perfect order. Shall I get it now?'

'If you would, thank you.'

She stood up, then paused and turned back. 'I hope the wrong diagnosis won't be seen as a blot against my name. He was long gone by the time I found him the next morning.'

'It won't. As you say, the paramedics came to the same conclusion.'

'Good.'

Jazz watched Matron leave the room. It was obvious, even if she was brusque, that she cared for the boys, especially the more vulnerable ones.

It was also obvious she'd hated Charlie Cavendish...

Matron returned and handed Jazz a sheet of paper.

'That's the sheet for last Friday. As I told your detective, I wasn't present in the house that night. Mr Daneman had Mr Frederiks's key. Very remiss of Mr Frederiks to leave him alone. And, I might add, unusual. From what I've seen in the past few months, apart from the determined way he's ignored Cavendish's behaviour, he's a dedicated housemaster.'

'He didn't tell you where he was?'

'No. And I would never pry. But it must have been an emergency for him to leave the house.'

'Well, he won't tell me.' Jazz folded the sheet and tucked it in her pocket to study later. 'Could you let me know whether Rory will be fit enough to see me this afternoon?' She handed Matron a card with her number on it.

'I doubt he will. Last thing the poor chap needs is to be interviewed by a police officer, if you don't mind me saying so.'

'I want to see him as soon as possible.' Jazz stood up. 'One last thing: you told Detective Sergeant Roland you were back in your room at about eleven last Friday night?' she asked as they walked towards the door.

'Yes, I was.'

'You didn't see or hear anything odd in the following hour?'

'No. I went straight to bed.'

'What time did you find Charlie the next morning?'

'I always walk along the sixth-form corridor, knocking on the boys' doors at six forty-five. Breakfast is at seven thirty. When I noticed Charlie was missing, I went to knock him up again. When he didn't reply, I went into his study and found him.' They'd reached the front entrance. She gave Jazz a brief smile. 'Will that be all?'

'For now, yes. Thank you for your help.'

Matron gave her a quick nod, turned and walked up the stairs.

Jenny Colman knocked on Robert Jones's door with his three o'clock cup of tea.

'Come,' said the voice, and Jenny opened the door.

Robert Jones was slumped at his desk, tie askew, misery etched on his face.

'Oh, Mr Jones, what is it?'

He shook his head as she put the tray on the desk.

'Nothing, Jenny, I'm just a little weary, and I've got a headache, that's all.'

'Can I get you an aspirin or…whoops!' She chuckled as she realised what she had said. 'Sorry, Mr Jones. Bit inappropriate under the circumstances.'

'Don't worry, Jenny. And no, I'll be fine.' He watched her pour the tea.

'Has something happened, Mr Jones? Not wishing to pry, but you do look awful.'

He had a sudden urge to confide in someone.

'Look, Jenny, can I trust you?'

'Mr Jones, I've worked for you for fourteen years and never a confidence has passed my lips. Of course you can. Might make it better if you tell me. You know what they say about a trouble shared?'

'Yes.' He took a deep breath. 'Hugh Daneman is dead.'

Jenny sat down in shocked silence. She opened her mouth to speak but nothing came out.

'I know, it's terrible news, and on the back of Charlie's death…' Robert shook his head. 'This could bring down the school.'

She sat there, biting her lip, willing herself not to cry in front of him.

'How?' It was a muffled sound, but all she could muster.

'He was found dead at home last night. The police think he committed suicide.'

Jenny put her head in her hands and sobbed. 'Why? Why would he do that? Not Hugh, not Hugh.'

Robert looked nonplussed. He had been expecting Jenny to dole out sympathy for *him* and his predicament.

'I'm sorry, Jenny, I didn't realise you'd be so upset. Did you know him well?'

Jenny nodded. 'Yes, I did. I've known him for nearly thirty-five years. I once cleaned for him before I came to work here.'

'Did you really?'

'Yes, and he was the kindest gentleman I've ever met. He wouldn't hurt a fly, he wouldn't!'

'Hush, Jenny! Please, this is a secret between you and me. You mustn't tell anyone.'

'No, I know, I won't, promise. Sorry, Mr Jones, it's the shock, that's all.'

'Of course,' he nodded. 'Look, why don't you go home early? You certainly stay later than you're paid to most nights anyway.'

'Thank you, Mr Jones. I think I will.'

'I'll see you tomorrow, then.'

Jenny was already heading towards the door.

'Are you sure you're going to be all right?' he asked.

'Yes. And I won't tell no one. Promise.'

Chapter Nine

Jenny put the key into the lock of her front door. Stepping inside the small entrance hall, she closed the door behind her and, legs finally giving way beneath her, she slid to the floor.

When she had finished crying, she picked herself up and staggered along the short corridor into the kitchen, where she slumped onto a chair. Even the sight of her smart new fitted units, the ones she'd saved up so hard to buy, couldn't help lift her.

'All these years of slaving, scrimping and saving every penny. And for what?' she asked desperately. 'What on earth is the bloody point?'

Jenny rose and walked slowly across to the kettle. She poured water into it and switched it on. Still in her coat, she wandered through the rooms of the tiny bungalow, which, as always, was as neat as a pin. Jenny searched in a pocket to find a tissue to wipe her running nose. She had worked all her life to be able finally to afford a small home of her own.

Jenny touched the soft dralon on the back of the sofa, still as immaculate as the day she'd bought it. She swept her eyes round the room, noting the big TV in the corner she'd bought outright only recently for a couple of hundred pounds, after years of renting one.

Everything in this bungalow had been paid for by *her*. Legs feeling wobbly again, Jenny perched on the arm of the sofa.

There had been male suitors over the years. Jenny knew she'd never been a beauty, but she'd certainly managed to attract men.

Perhaps the fact they knew her heart belonged elsewhere made the thrill of the chase more exciting. One suitor had been very persistent, couldn't understand why she had refused to accept his proposal of marriage.

She thought how life could have been so much easier if she had. She'd have shared the struggles and burdens of life, had a shoulder to cry on when things went wrong, but the petulant refusal to accept anyone other than the one man she had wanted made that an impossibility.

Jenny forgot about the boiled kettle and went across to the drinks trolley that sat under the window. Four bottles stood upright like sentries. She occasionally took a small sherry on a Sunday, but as guests rarely visited, the port, the brandy and the whisky, all Christmas gifts from Mr Jones, had remained untouched.

Knowing brandy was good for shock, Jenny unscrewed the top with her strong, capable hands. She poured a small amount into one of the glass tumblers that sat on the trolley in front of the bottles, and took a gulp.

The brandy burned her throat, its strength making her gag. But it felt good and comforting as it slid down into her stomach, so she took another.

She walked across to the inlaid mahogany sideboard, which had once been her mother's and was the only thing of real value she owned. She opened the left-hand drawer and felt at the back for the old brown envelope. The familiar roughness told her she'd found it. Sitting down on the sofa, she slid the contents out.

It had been the most important piece of deception she'd ever practised, the photograph providing years of comfort, enabling her to look at leisure at the greatest achievement of her life.

Jenny put the photograph back in the envelope.

And stared sorrowfully into the distance as she realised her last link with the past was gone.

Alistair Miles studied the louche group of fourteen young men and women sitting in front of him. Even though they were all in uniform, most of them looked as if they'd made a concerted effort to look scruffy and unkempt. There wasn't a neatly fastened tie or a polished shoe between the lot of them.

Christ, I sound like my father, Miles acknowledged to himself.

'Okay, boys and girls, thanks for your time. I'm sure you all know what this is about.' Miles perched on Sebastian Frederiks's desk and glanced at the sea of faces in front of him. 'Apparently, all of you were in the pub with Charlie on the night he died. Is that right?'

There was a general nod of agreement.

'Now, firstly, I want to say that anything you tell me will be treated in confidence. I'm not interested in personal misdemeanours and there will be no reporting back to authority figures on anything you tell me. I just want to find out a few things about Charlie and that night and I need you all to be honest. The first question is, do any of you know if Charlie ever used recreational drugs of any kind?'

There was a short silence and some nervous glances, before an attractive blonde girl piped up, 'No, he didn't.'

'And you are?'

'Emily Harris. I'm...I mean, I was Charlie's girlfriend.' Miles watched as she lowered her eyes and bit her lip, obviously struggling to control herself.

'I'm sorry, Emily. This must have been a horrible shock for you.'

She nodded silently.

'You say Charlie didn't use drugs? Are you sure of this?'

'Completely. He wasn't an idiot, Detective. He knew he had epilepsy and was putting his life at risk if he touched anything like that.'

'And were they...around?' Miles scanned the faces for a reaction.

'Look, Detective,' a male voice boomed from the back of the room, 'I don't think there is one of us here that could put their hand on their heart and say they've never tried illegal substances.'

There was an embarrassed murmur of tacit agreement.

'Who am I speaking to?'

The young man had a thick shock of dark hair, reaching almost to his shoulders. He wore no tie, substituting it with wooden beads strung on a piece of leather, and had a number of plaited cotton friendship bracelets wound round his wrists.

'Dud Simpson. I'm in Fleat. I was a good friend of Charlie's. We hung out together a lot. And I'd agree with Emily. I've known Charlie since we started here and I've never seen him touch anything like that.'

'Can I ask just where round here you'd obtain those "illegal substances"?'

'There's always someone who has something to sell.'

'At the pub?'

'Christ, no. At school.'

'But Charlie never partook?'

'Nope.' Dud shook his head. 'Mummy had drummed it into him. He could be a bit of an arsehole, Charlie, but he didn't need any medicinal help. It came naturally.'

A giggle spread through the room.

'So you were drinking with Charlie that night at the pub?'

Dud paused before nodding. 'Yup. I was there.'

'Come on, Dud,' another male voice interjected. 'Be honest: you and Charlie hadn't spoken for the past couple of months.'

'Why not? Fell out, did you?' suggested Miles.

A deep flush made its way up Dud's neck and onto his cheeks.

'Yeah, you could say that,' said the second pupil.

'Who are you?' Miles asked.

'James Arrowsmith. I'm in Fleat as well. You gonna tell the officer, Dud, or shall I?'

'For fuck's sake! Cheers, James,' Dud murmured. 'Look, it was nothing. Just a stupid argument.'

'He stole your girlfriend. You caught them snogging round the corner from the pub just before Christmas. You beat his brains in, said he was lucky you didn't finish him off. I was there to pick up the pieces, remember?'

The girl called Emily stood up, hand over her mouth. 'Sorry,' she gasped, then ran from the room.

The tension in the room was palpable.

'Okay.' Miles held up his hands. 'Let's move on. I want to know who left the school premises with Charlie last Friday to walk to the pub?'

'I did,' said James Arrowsmith. 'There was me, and Emily, and Stocky... You were there, right?'

A bulky, red-haired boy nodded. 'Yup.'

'How did he seem on that walk?'

'Cool. Same as always,' Stocky replied. 'Talking about how he couldn't wait to leave, his plans when he did.'

'So none of you would say he seemed depressed?'

'Charlie? Nope.' James Arrowsmith shook his head. 'He was the life and soul, always up for a laugh.'

'Not the type to want to take his own life, in your opinion?'

A number of the boys made clear their disbelief at the idea.

'You're not suggesting Charlie did himself in, are you?' Dud's deep voice rang across the room. Which became suddenly and unnervingly silent.

'No,' confirmed Miles.

'He died of an epileptic fit, right?' Stocky asked.

'No.'

'Jesus,' Dud breathed eventually. 'Then, can you tell us how he died?'

'Of anaphylactic shock, caused by aspirin tablets.'

'What?! How come? Charlie knew they could kill him,' James said.

'That's why it's important we establish how Charlie came to swallow them. Anyone got any ideas?'

'Well, he wouldn't have done if he'd known what they were, would he?' Dud shrugged.

'Quite,' agreed Miles. 'That's why I needed to know whether he was likely to have taken anything nefarious that night. Anything he scored could have actually been aspirin, substituted by a bent pusher.'

'Perhaps you slipped them into his beer, Dud,' quipped James.

'Sod off, Arrowsmith,' Dud replied nervously.

'So, is there anyone that you can think of who might have wanted to get rid of Charlie?'

'Apart from Dud, you mean?' James smirked.

Dud stood up. 'That's enough!'

'Oh, come on, only joking. But I'm sure Dud would agree with me, there were a few people who weren't fully paid-up members of the Charlie Cavendish fan club.' James crossed his arms.

'Anyone in particular stand out?' Miles addressed his question to Dud.

'Nope. I mean, lots of us thought he could be a tosser at times, but I don't think anyone hated him. Some of the younger boys were wary of him, though.'

'"Wary" of him?' Stocky raised his eyebrows. 'Petrified, more like.'

'I've heard he was a bully,' probed Miles. 'You'd agree, would you?'

'Would you agree, Dud?' Stocky asked him. 'You were his best mate and partner in crime before he stole your shag.'

'Just fuck off, you pillock!' Dud stood up, eyes blazing.

'All right, that's enough!' Miles raised his hand. 'You say the younger boys were wary of him?'

'Yeah, and too right,' muttered Dud. 'That kid with the blond hair, the one Charlie had decided to target...'

'Rory Millar?' Stocky said.

Dud nodded. 'We all know it was Charlie who locked him in the cellar overnight a couple of weeks ago. Poor kid. He was terrified. Mr Frederiks heard him shouting and let him out the next morning.'

'Did anyone 'fess up that they knew it was Charlie?' asked Miles.

'No. To be honest, even if we had, Mr Frederiks wouldn't have done anything. He thought Charlie, like, walked on water, which is odd, as he normally comes down like a ton of bricks on bullying. But Charlie could do no wrong. Got away with murder... Shit!' Dud blushed. 'Sorry.'

'I want to know who walked back to school with him that evening,' said Miles.

'Same as those that left with him,' answered James.

'Was he on good form?'

'Excellent.'

'What time did you get back?'

''Bout eleven. We signed in and Stocky 'n' me went to watch telly in the common room. Charlie said he was for an early night—he could never get up for chapel on a Saturday and was about to be gated if he missed again. We said goodnight at the bottom of the stairs, Charlie went up, and that was that.'

'Who sleeps next door to him?'

'Me,' replied Stocky, 'and Dud is on the other side. You didn't hear anything, did you?'

'Nothing.' Dud shook his head.

'Nor me,' shrugged Stocky. 'But neither of us came up until after midnight. Mr Daneman can confirm it, and Mr Frederiks. He came back just as we were going upstairs to bed.'

'You sure of the time?'

'Yeah, but you can check with Mr Daneman. He came in to chivvy us along, said he was for his bed too as Mr Frederiks was back.'

'Did you actually see Mr Frederiks before you went up?' Miles asked.

Dud looked at Stocky and shrugged. 'No, but why would Mr Daneman say he was back if he wasn't?'

'Okay,' nodded Miles. 'Anyone got anything else to add?'

There was silence.

'All right. Thanks for your time. If any of you think of anything about that night that strikes you as odd, even if it's a small detail, please come and see me, or Inspector Hunter, as soon as you can. Dud, can I have a quick word?'

The rest of the group left the room. Miles closed the door behind them and turned back to Dud.

'So, you and Charlie were best mates?'

'Yeah.'

'Until he stole Emily.'

Dud nodded silently.

'Then you knocked seven bells out of him when you found out.'

Dud looked up at him. 'Wouldn't you?'

'Probably. You knew he was allergic to aspirin?'

'Course. The whole year knew, and everyone in Fleat. It wasn't a secret.'

'Knowing Charlie so well, you're sure he wasn't depressed? I believe he'd had a fallout with his father just before he came back to school.'

'Christ, absolutely not.' Dud was adamant. 'Yeah, he was pissed off with his dad. He's a bit of a stick-in-the-mud, conventional type, and Charlie was a free spirit. They clashed. If anyone was depressed, it was me. I really liked Em, and Charlie knew I did too. It was like he stole her on purpose.'

'So there's nothing you can think of that could have happened in the days leading up to his death to shed some light on how he died?'

'Nope, sorry, Detective.' Dud shrugged. 'Charlie was the same as ever.'

'Okay, Dud. Thanks for your time.'

Dud stood up and walked to the door. Turning back, he said, 'I'm not under suspicion, am I?'

'Do you think you should be?'

'I can understand you guess I have a motive.'

'You do.'

'Yeah...but I'd have got over it eventually. Knowing Charlie, he might have binned Em next week. I didn't want him dead, not really. He was my best mate. I miss him.' Dud shrugged, opened the door and left the room.

'How did you get on?' Jazz looked up from her notes as Miles walked in.

'We can rule out any form of substance abuse. To a man and woman, Charlie's mates were adamant he didn't and wouldn't touch anything.'

'Okay. Anything else?'

'Fallout over a girlfriend with Dud, his best mate. The girlfriend ran out halfway through the proceedings. I'll go and hunt her down, have a word. She's pretty upset. And also, his mates confirmed Charlie was a bully. But Frederiks seemed to turn a blind eye, for some reason.'

'I know. Matron said. Any further info on the night in question?'

'According to those who walked back to school with him, Charlie was fine at eleven, which seems to be the last time anyone saw him alive. His neighbours on his floor were watching television downstairs so they heard nothing. According to the PM, Charlie was almost certainly dead by the time they arrived up in their studies.'

'So.' Jazz chewed on her pen. 'Looks as though I'm right about the Epilim substitution.'

'Yup. The problem is, Ma'am, everyone knew about Charlie's allergy. They therefore knew there was a very easy way to get rid of him.'

'Well, it worked like a charm. Okay. I've got to go across to Daneman's house, meet the SOCOs before they leave. Why don't you track down this girlfriend of Charlie's? I've spoken to Norton and I've got a rental car arriving here for you at three. Take that. With only two of us, we need the flexibility of separate transport.'

'Three, don't you mean?'

'Roland's still at the dentist. Wonder if it's official policy round here to bugger off early on a Friday?' Jazz sighed as she gathered her files into her briefcase. 'I'm going home afterwards to use my own phoneline, download this stuff on Daneman HQ have sent through. Throw me the keys to the car, will you?'

Miles did so. 'Talking of buggering off early, I wouldn't mind getting on the road sooner rather than later. Traffic'll be bad as it's Friday.'

'You're going back to London?'

'If that's okay with you. Soon as the rental's here. I can be back in a mere three hours if you need me.'

'I'll keep in touch. If nothing breaks beforehand, I'll see you here on Monday morning.'

'Righto. Have a good weekend.'

'And you. I'll catch you later.' Jazz nodded a goodbye as she left the room.

The SOCOs were just leaving as Jazz arrived at Daneman's cottage.

'Find anything?' she asked Shirley.

'Nothing of startling interest, but we've taken all the usual samples,' Shirley said, passing Jazz the key to the front door.

'Okay, thanks.'

'Bye, Ma'am.' Shirley nodded and climbed into her van.

Jazz put the key in the lock and reopened the door to Hugh Daneman's house. She'd always found it eerie going to the home of the deceased, who had only recently occupied it as a living, breathing person, and was now a lifeless corpse lying on a slab in a morgue.

Jazz wandered to the overflowing shelves crammed with old, leather-bound books. She pulled one out. It was in Latin and as she turned the yellowing pages, the distinctive, musty smell of old paper wafted to her nostrils.

She replaced the book, then wandered over to Hugh's leather-topped desk and pulled open the drawers.

Everything inside them was immaculately arranged. Stationary supplies: headed notepaper, pens, ink, pencils and rubbers lay with military precision within. It looked as if the drawers had been cleaned out recently. She'd been hoping to find an address book but there was none to be seen.

In the central drawer, there was a bunch of keys, and an envelope.

Jazz read the address on the label.

'Flat 4, 9 Sheffield Terrace, W8.'

She knew immediately where that was, in an upmarket residential area of Kensington.

Opening the envelope, she found the name and address of a London solicitor written in Hugh's immaculate italics.

It was as if this had been left here for her to find.

Taking herself up the narrow stairs, she went into the larger of the two bedrooms and found everything neat and tidy. She looked through the drawers, most of which were empty, and opened the wardrobe to find only three suits hanging inside.

As she wandered downstairs, Jazz was now sure Hugh Daneman had not only planned to take his own life, but had spent time beforehand tidying up his affairs. There was not a hint in this house of the usual common detritus that went hand in hand with being alive.

Jazz kneeled by the fire. It had obviously been substantial, as the pile of ash was large. Sifting through the grate, she found a number of small pieces of charred paper.

Looked like Daneman had lit a fire and burned anything he didn't want strangers to find.

She'd take a trip down to London first thing tomorrow morning.

Jazz left the house, the familiar feeling of wishing the walls could talk and tell her their secrets strong in her mind.

As she got into her car, her mobile phone rang.

'Roland here, Ma'am. I've just had a tooth out.' His voice was muffled.

'Oh dear.' Jazz gritted her own teeth to calm her irritation. 'Where are you now?'

'Outside the dentist in my car, awaiting instructions.'

'Go home, Roland. Take some painkillers and go to bed. But can you make sure you get a few of your boys down to the school? Plain-clothed, please, and low-key, so as not to alarm the inhabitants. Station an officer outside Fleat House. He's to check everyone coming in and out. I want someone there twenty-four seven.'

'Yes, Ma'am. Anything else?'

'No. I'll be in touch tomorrow. Hope your tooth sorts itself out.' Jazz knew she sounded insincere but couldn't help it.

'Thanks, Ma'am. Bye.'

She switched off her mobile and let out a small groan of frustration. She started the engine and pulled away from the kerb.

Turning her thoughts back to her two dead bodies, she mused on any possible connection as she drove through Foltesham towards the coast road. As she negotiated the narrow streets of Cley, Jazz was aware of a familiar figure getting out of a Mercedes estate on the other side of the road. Jazz slowed to a crawl and realised the woman was Adele Cavendish, Charlie's mother. Jazz watched as Adele unloaded a holdall and a couple of supermarket carrier bags from the boot, then disappeared out of sight down a narrow lane.

Recording the event as odd, Jazz picked up speed and headed for home.

Chapter Ten

The next morning, Jazz was in London by ten o'clock. She'd called Miles, conveniently back in London, who was meeting her at Daneman's Kensington flat.

Having not returned to the city since her flight from her career and her husband seven months ago, she'd felt a sense of trepidation as she'd driven along the Embankment, then past the Yard itself.

She felt so removed from it, from her old life, yet here she was in town, on CID business.

Miles was parked outside the flat in a custard-yellow Astra.

'Morning, Ma'am. Good journey?'

'Yes, fine.' She grabbed her briefcase and climbed out. 'Love the car,' she nodded. 'Very cool.'

'You mean my banana split? It was all the Foltesham rental people had left, apparently.'

'Particularly good for a spot of discreet tailing, I'd say,' she joked. 'Did you check the Land Registry to make sure Daneman owns this flat?'

'Yes, he took over the deeds from a Phyllida Daneman in nineteen sixty-nine. When I checked her out, seems she was his aunt, and that was the year she died. He obviously inherited the place. Couldn't find any living relatives on the records, though.'

'Our Hugh's turning out to be a bit of an enigma. I found the address of a solicitor in one of his drawers. I can only presume that's where his will is lodged. Jazz handed him a piece of paper. 'Get on to them first thing Monday, will you? Inform them of Hugh's death. It'll be interesting to see who he's left this to. Probably worth a fortune now.' Jazz stared up at the Edwardian red-bricked mansion block. 'Come on, let's go in.'

Daneman's flat was located on the first floor. As Jazz opened the door and stepped inside, she smelled old books again, and damp.

The curtains in the sitting room were closed and Jazz walked across the gloom to open them. Daylight flooded the spacious, but rather oppressive room.

It was painted a dull bottle green and a bookshelf lined the length of one wall. The other walls were covered with paintings hung randomly, with no attempt made at placing them to their best advantage.

'Obviously not a man interested in interior design,' commented Miles. 'Looks like this place hasn't been touched since he inherited it.'

'No.' Jazz walked over to the grand piano set in front of the long sash windows, which overlooked the narrow strip of communal gardens at the back of the block. A desk was set in the corner, piled with neat stacks of books. An old leather chair was placed by the antiquated gas fire.

'This is more a study than a comfortable sitting room.' She picked up a plastic wallet containing a photocopy of a Latin manuscript from the desk. 'I'd guess this is where Daneman did his translation work. Perhaps he came here during the long school holidays. Right, get started on his desk, will you?'

'Right you are, Ma'am.'

Jazz wandered down the corridor and saw the galley kitchen, its units so old they were back in fashion, the bathroom with its cracked iron bath, two trickles of green limescale indelibly etched into the enamel behind the taps. At the end of the corridor was a spartan bedroom containing a double bed with a tartan rug thrown across the bottom of it. An austere mahogany tallboy sat against the wall, a matching dressing table set under the window—a clothes brush being the only nod to vanity laid on the surface in front of the mirror.

Placed on the bedside table was a large photograph.

Jazz picked it up. She studied it, recognising it was of the same young girl in the faded photograph she had found in Hugh's cottage.

But this time, the features were much clearer. And whoever she was, she was beautiful. Curly blonde hair falling to just above her shoulders, blue eyes and an elegant aquiline nose set above rosebud lips. Jazz reckoned she must be in her late teens. She sat down on the bed, turned the frame over and removed the hardboard backing.

There, on the reverse of the photograph, was an inscription.

June 59
To my darling Hugh,

Carpe diem!
And we do!
All my love as always,
Cory x

She took the photograph carefully out of the frame, and walked back into the sitting room.

'Find anything?' Miles asked. He was on his knees surrounded by papers.

'Only this.' She handed him the photograph.

Miles studied it. 'The same girl. A lover perhaps?'

'I'd imagine so.' Jazz took an exhibit wallet from her briefcase and stowed it inside. 'There's an inscription on the back dated *fifty-nine*. Whoever she is, it all took place a long time ago.'

'He never married. I double-checked this morning. Perhaps the girl in the picture left him and he spent the rest of his life nursing a broken heart.'

'Perhaps. You found anything?' she asked.

'Nothing of interest so far. No personal letters, only work-related missives to various curators of libraries around the world. Daneman was obviously regarded as a serious authority.'

'If he was, why on earth was he working as a tutor in a little-known public school in a Norfolk backwater?' mused Jazz. 'At present, I can't get a hook on Daneman at all.'

'Perhaps he enjoyed the camaraderie of school life. He didn't need the money, that's for sure. There are invoices here for thousands of pounds, enough to keep a single man going very comfortably.'

'Any bank statements?'

'I've looked, but not found.'

'Okay,' Jazz sighed. 'I'll take the drawers under the bookcase.'

An hour later, Jazz re-closed the curtains and they left the flat. They'd sifted through every scrap of paper in the place, and found nothing pertaining to Daneman's will or his personal life.

'Spot of lunch, Ma'am?' asked Miles.

'I want to head straight back.'

'Sure you don't want to pop into the Yard on your way home? They'd all love to see you and you know who is on leave for the weekend. I checked the roster.'

'Er, thanks but no thanks.' Jazz smiled up at Miles wryly as she switched the engine on. 'I'll see you Monday. Bye.'

Jazz pulled out into the London traffic, feeling deflated and no wiser than when she'd arrived.

Angelina Millar put down the telephone and gave a small moue of displeasure. Matron had just called her to say Rory had a stomach bug and had been moved to the sanatorium. The doctor had been to see him and he was not unduly concerned, but felt Rory was too sick to come home at present.

Angelina was meant to be picking him up from school this morning for his weekly exeat. Matron had said Angelina could come and see him whenever she wanted over the weekend.

Which is very good of her, she thought crossly, considering he's my child.

She had been planning to have a nice cosy tea, try and find out if David's fears were founded on reality or alcohol. And then, later, broach the skiing holiday, prepare him gently for Julian's joining them on it.

But all this wouldn't be possible now. And next weekend he was with his father...

The thought of David and his last visit here made her stomach turn. Julian had assumed she'd been under threat from David. That was why he'd been so aggressive and manhandled him out of the house. But she felt awful about it.

Julian had been unrepentant, saying that the man could not just walk into what was now *his* home when he felt like it. He hoped by kicking him out David would get the message.

Angelina hadn't heard from David since. She knew she was meant to call him about Rory, but she couldn't face speaking to him.

Besides, if she *did* call David and told him Rory was sick, he'd probably go chasing off up to the school, upsetting Rory and causing mayhem.

On the other hand, she had promised...

Angelina's hand hovered over the phone. No. The best thing for Rory was to have a peaceful weekend in bed with no upsetting disturbances. David would just have to cope.

On the bright side, the advantage to having no Rory this weekend was that she could take Julian's breakfast upstairs, slip under the covers with him and tell him there was no need to decamp to the flat he was currently renting in Norwich.

As she warmed the croissant in the Aga and brewed some fresh coffee, Angelina looked down her list of 'things to do'. She'd gone on to a website last week, pretended she was Julian, so she could gain access to the St Stephen's class of '84. She'd left a message with a few of the names there in the hope that some of his old classmates would contact her and she could invite them to Julian's fortieth party as a surprise. She'd subtly found out from Julian who exactly in his year he'd been particularly friendly with.

Angelina carried the tray upstairs and into the bedroom. Julian was lying on his side, naked and still asleep. He was beautiful, his body fit and strong from sessions at the gym, his thick black hair a contrast against the bright white of the pillow.

She put the tray on the floor next to the bed, then took off her robe and slid under the covers next to him. His back was facing her, so she gently kissed the protruding knobbles of his spine, starting at his neck and moving slowly down to his coccyx. He murmured sleepily as a hand snaked round to the front of his body to caress him and feel his excitement.

Moaning slightly, he rolled over to face her.

'Morning, darling,' he murmured.

'Morning.' Angelina covered his face with kisses, finally finding his mouth and pressing her tongue inside. A hand reached for her small, neat breasts, the other slid down to find her buttocks and pull her closer to him.

Afterwards, Angelina lay in his arms, sated and content, thinking the passion she felt for Julian had never been there for David.

She reached for the breakfast tray and placed it on the bed.

'Good news, darling. Well, for *you*, anyway. Rory is ill, so he's in the san. Matron thinks it's better if he stays there for the weekend, rather than coming home here. I'll go and see him, but it means you and I can spend the weekend together.'

'Good God! You don't know what a pleasure it is when a man is told he can stay in his own home,' Julian replied sarcastically.

'Oh, I'm sorry. Coffee?'

'Yes.' Julian sat up and took the cup from her. 'Anyway, as our secret's out via your ex-husband, I vote we should take the plunge and be seen in Foltesham High Street together. "Come out" as an official couple. What do you think?'

'I suppose so,' she replied nervously.

Julian eyed her. 'Look, everyone will understand. Of course there'll be some gossip, this is a small community, and a lot of them haven't got anything more interesting to think about. The situation's getting ridiculous: arriving separately at dinner parties, then meeting up again here at home.'

Angelina sipped her coffee. 'The reason we've done it this way is for Rory. What if one of his friends mentions you at school, having heard from *his* parents?'

'There's far more chance of his father telling him, now he knows,' Julian replied irritably. 'And I'm afraid my patience has run out. For God's sake, your divorce came through weeks ago! Our relationship is hardly illegal and I'm sick to death of feeling it is. I'm going to shower.'

Angelina heard the shower door bang closed and realised that whatever she felt, it was a fait accompli, and Rory, like it or not, was going to have to be told.

Later, the two of them set off into Foltesham to run some errands. Angelina went to the fishmonger's to buy a side of salmon for supper, Julian to the off licence to buy some wine. They met by the pedestrian crossing in the centre of the high street, Angelina nervously glancing up and down to see if anyone they knew was watching.

Julian grabbed her hand and was about to pull her across the road when he saw who was standing on the other side.

'Hello there, you love birds!'

It was David.

'Come on, Julian, let's go.' Angelina tried to pull him back, but Julian insisted on stepping onto the crossing. They met David in the middle of the road. His eyes were bloodshot and he was unsteady on his feet.

'Hello, David, how are you?' Julian spoke politely as they tried to pass but David grabbed hold of the lapel of Julian's jacket.

'I'm shit, as you can see. And let me just tell you something. If you ever, *ever* touch a hair on my son's head, I'll *kill* you! Do you hear me?!'

'I do. Goodbye, David.' Julian wrenched himself away and walked towards the pavement with a horrified Angelina by his side.

'Did you hear me, you arrogant tosser?! I'LL KILL YOU!'

'The whole of Foltesham heard you, you prick,' Julian mumbled. 'Come on, leave him. He's drunk as a skunk, doesn't know what he's saying.'

Cars were beeping David, who was still standing in the middle of the road glaring at their receding figures.

Angelina arrived at the car, climbed inside and promptly burst into tears.

Julian patted her shoulder ineffectually. 'Come on now. He was drunk, that's all.'

'Oh God, how can we live here, Julian? I'm scared stiff every time I walk out of the house! Maybe we should move, maybe it's best.'

'Absolutely not. We will *not* be run out of town by a pathetic drunk. We have the law on our side.' Julian sighed as he pulled the Mercedes out of the parking space. 'I'm wondering whether I can get another restraining order placed on him. From the way he was today, seems like *I* might need protection as well. Anyway, we have plenty of witnesses to his threat. Just a pity he didn't attack me physically, then I really could have done something.'

'Please, Julian!' Angelina buried her face in her hands. 'Stop!'

'Sorry, but I really haven't done anything wrong and I'm sick to death of feeling I have. Don't cry, please. It'll sort itself out, you know.'

She nodded. 'It's just so hard at the moment, that's all. Could you drive to St Stephen's?' Angelina placed a hand on his arm. 'I want to go and see Rory.'

'Of course. Then I'll take you for lunch to that lovely pub in Itteringham. I think we could both do with a drink.'

Julian sat in the visitors' car park while Angelina went into the school to see Rory. He was mortified by David's public aggression, and very angry.

He looked out across Chapel Lawn, where he'd spent so much time on hot summer days as a pupil here, lazing on the grass with his friends.

Then he saw the figure, walking out of the dining room.

His knuckles tightened as he grasped the steering wheel. The colour drained from his face.

He watched as the figure passed not ten yards from him. His immediate instinct was to put his head down and hide. His palms were sweating, his heart racing as he watched the figure walk across Chapel Lawn and disappear inside one of the buildings.

He sat staring into space, his stomach churning. He hardly noticed Angelina climb into the car next to him.

'Rory was sleeping, so I didn't want to wake him. But he looked okay. I'll pop in again later.' Angelina waited for a response. 'Darling? Are you all right? Julian?'

He shook himself back to the present, turned to her and nodded.

'Yes.'

'You look as though you've just seen a ghost.'

She was right. He had.

'I'm fine.' He fumbled for the keys and turned the engine on.

'Probably delayed shock from earlier,' Angelina commented as they pulled out of the car park. 'Let's go and have some lunch and both calm down.'

'Yes.' He looked at her and smiled. 'And on second thoughts, maybe we should consider the idea of leaving here after all, making a new start somewhere nobody knows us.'

'Maybe,' nodded Angelina. 'Let's see how the holiday goes with Rory. It'll do us good to all have a break from here. Then we can see how we feel when we get back.'

He squeezed her hand. 'Yes, let's do that.'

Chapter Eleven

Jazz drove through the familiar Cambridge streets, negotiating the not-so-familiar one-way system.

She parked in the space reserved for her parents' car and walked past the Wolfson Building, an ugly, seventies blend of concrete and glass providing added accommodation for the students of Trinity College. Entering the arch that led to Trinity Great Court and nodding to the porter, she walked across the quad.

Perhaps it was because she had been brought up here that the mystique and beauty of the university had never touched her. But the few times she'd visited her parents since she'd come back from Italy, perhaps influenced by the beautiful architecture in Florence, she'd begun to see Cambridge in a different light.

Admittedly, with the rain beginning to drizzle onto the wet grass in the centre of the quad, the scene was not quite the Duomo in the soft autumn sun, but the gracious sandstone buildings, with their old mullioned windows surrounding her on every side, felt comfortingly safe.

Turning into one of the entrances, Jazz walked to her parents' rooms and knocked on the door. It was unusual for married lecturers to live in halls, but the ground-floor accommodation had provided the perfect solution to her father's physical limitations.

The university had been very supportive after the shooting, offering both her father and mother their old positions back at Trinity College. In the end, her father had never been able to take up the offer, being deemed too fragile by his doctors to take on the burden.

But it was Celestria, Jazz's mother, who provided for them both. She lectured in English and in the years since Tom had been disabled, she'd gone from strength to strength, recently publishing an acclaimed book criticising the dwindling use of correct grammar and punctuation in today's society. It had been an unexpected bestseller and would provide them with a nest egg for their retirement.

Which didn't mean Tom Hunter was idle. He filled in for the chaplain occasionally, taking services and giving the odd Theology lecture. He was also known by the students at Trinity to be a dependable, listening ear if they were in trouble.

The college had also been helpful in converting the rooms to make it easier for Tom to be self-sufficient, and he could zip out of the flat unaided in his electric wheelchair, giving both him and his wife a welcome feeling of independence.

They were the perfect example of two people who had adapted to adversity and made it work. Jazz was very proud of them both.

She knocked on the front door and pushed it open. 'It's me!'

'Jazz! For heaven's sake! Come on in.'

She walked through the hall into the small sitting room to see her father working at his overflowing desk.

Tom's face lit up with pleasure when he saw his daughter. He threw open his arms to embrace her.

'Hello, darling. Good to see you.'

She extricated herself and studied his elfin features. At only five foot six, he was four inches shorter than his wife and daughter. However, what Tom lacked in stature, he made up for with the force of his personality.

'How's the heart? Mum said you'd had some tests?'

'Ticking, as usual,' Tom said. 'I'm a good boy, Jazz, and I take my tablets every day. Really, I feel as well as I did twenty years ago. I wish everyone would stop fussing.'

'Dad, you had a serious heart attack on that operating table.'

'But I've survived,' he winked at her. 'For fourteen years, so far. Glass of wine for you?' Tom indicated the bottle placed on the coffee table.

'Lovely. Where's Mum?'

'Out at some drinks do at Kings. She'll be back any minute. Pour one for me as well, will you?'

'There you go.' Jazz handed him a glass and Tom wheeled himself into his usual position to the left of the fireplace. 'To you, darling. Congratulations.'

'Thank you. What for?'

'For making a brave decision and re-entering the fray.'

'Don't congratulate me yet. I'm still not convinced I've done the right thing. I wanted to paint, Dad.'

'I know, sweetheart. And yes, you may well have turned out to be the next Van Gogh. You're certainly talented, but I've always wondered whether the lifestyle would have suited you. You're very cerebral, darling, and sociable. You need constant stimulation and I find it hard picturing you alone in a garret, penniless and starving.'

'You mean I'd have cut off my ear, then *eaten* it,' she grinned.

'You *were* brought up to be practical.' Tom smiled, his eyes twinkling. 'At least your police career has had a point; not that art is pointless, you understand. But in spite of what you've always said about the ineptitude of the criminal justice system, for every four crooks you've lost, you've managed to put one away. In my book, that makes it worthwhile.'

'The glass half empty or half full scenario, you mean?'

'Exactly. And of course, the other point is, even though I joke about Norton having a soft spot for you, he does believe in you. He must do. He knows you're an asset he can't afford to lose.'

'Well, I just wish he could have made it a little clearer at the time.'

'Then perhaps your sabbatical won't have done you *or* him any harm. And remember, it's much harder to swallow your pride and stick your head over the parapet than it is to turn tail and run away to save face. Now, how about some more of that wine?'

'A small one, Dad. You know what the doctors say.'

'And *I* say it's red and renowned for lowering cholesterol, therefore it's medicinal.'

Jazz reluctantly topped up his glass.

'You know, darling, your mother and I weren't sure you'd made the right decision when you upped sticks and headed off to Hendon to become a bobby just a few months before getting your degree.'

'Yes, Dad.' Jazz rolled her eyes. 'I remember.'

'We thought you'd done it for all the wrong reasons.'

'We all know I did it because of what happened to you, Dad. Does that make it right or wrong?'

'Both,' said Tom. 'You're hot-headed, just like your old dad. You make decisions on the spur of the moment—'

'Which serves me well in my current profession.'

'Exactly. Which brings me neatly to my point: the good Lord rarely steers us wrong. Perhaps the shooting was all about getting you onto the right path.'

'Oh Dad, I'd prefer the wrong path and you healthy. But yes, I admit the past few days have been…challenging. And it's good to be back.'

'Especially without *him* around?'

'Yes.' Jazz's face became closed.

Tom knew not to pursue the conversation. He changed the subject. 'So, how's life in Salthouse?'

'I love it! The cottage is sorting itself out slowly, and by the summer I might even have a garden for you and Mum to come and sit in.'

'Sounds wonderful. I really miss a garden, but there's no space here, of course. Although, when your mother retires, who knows? We might come and join you and live in a seaside bungalow with all the other pensioners. I could start playing whist, your mother could join the WI and learn to knit.' There was the sound of a key in the door. 'Ah, here she comes.'

Often with mothers and daughters, there's a likeness that is noticeable but undefined. In the case of Celestria Hunter and her daughter, no one could have mistaken them for anything else. Jazz had inherited her mother's height, her fine features and thick auburn hair. At fifty-seven, Celestria was aging well. She looked barely older than she had fifteen years previously.

'Mum! How are you?' Jazz stood up and kissed her warmly.

'She's stressed and tired out from dealing with an old rogue like me,' Tom quipped as Celestria walked towards him. 'Don't ask if I've been doing too much, my angel, we'd only argue if I told you.'

'We never argue, darling. You do what you want and I let you.' Celestria massaged Tom's shoulders, then bent down to kiss the top of his head.

The easy intimacy and obvious adoration between the two of them always touched Jazz. Her mother could be forgiven for being bitter. Her life in the past few years had not been easy, practically, financially or emotionally.

That's what I want, thought Jazz, *for love to be enough.*

'Have you checked the joint, darling?' Celestria called as she went to hang up her coat.

'All is ready and waiting,' replied Tom.

'Perfect. Then let's eat.'

'So, this new case you're working on? Was it an accident, do you think?' Celestria and Jazz stood washing the plates.

'No, now I feel sure that it wasn't. And this other death just can't be unrelated, even though it's now confirmed as a suicide. The coroner called me this morning. A tummy full of sleeping pills, apparently.'

'Can you tell us who the dead man was?' Tom, busy putting clean plates away in a cupboard, looked up at Jazz, eyes alight with interest.

'A tutor at the school. He was an older chap, in his early seventies, and—'

'Enough of the "old", sweetheart. I'm in my mid-sixties, so not that far behind, and count myself as a young swinger, naturally.' Tom smiled. 'Anyway, pray, continue.'

'I'll rephrase that: he was of retirement age. I reckon the school had kept him on as he was a wonderful mentor to the boys. A bit like you, Dad. But I'm struggling to find a link between Charlie Cavendish and Hugh Daneman's deaths.'

'Hugh Daneman? The expert on fourteenth-century Latin manuscripts?'

'Yes, Dad. Why? Do you know him?'

'Well, I know *of* him, certainly. He has an excellent reputation in his field. He was at Oxford the same time as I was studying at Cambridge. I had a friend who knew him rather well. I'm pretty sure Hugh Daneman was famous for his wild parties.'

'Are you serious? Nothing that I've discovered so far would fit with him being a party animal.' Jazz chuckled. 'Everyone who knew him remarks on how quiet he was. Only interested in his books, apparently.'

'Jazz, it was the start of the Sixties when we were at university. And I can tell you, the things we got up to then would make your eyes water.'

'They certainly would,' remarked Celestria.

Tom nodded. 'Yes, I'm sure I'm right. Perhaps I even went to one of his parties, but I was so doped up in those days, I wouldn't remember.'

'Tom!' admonished Celestria.

'You know it was true, my darling. Anyway...' Tom scratched his head. 'I think he did a PhD like me, then taught Latin at Oxford. Couldn't tell you which college.'

'Go on, Dad,' urged Jazz. 'Anything you can remember will help me.'

'We-ell…if I remember rightly, and we're going back forty-odd years, there was some kind of scandal. He left Oxford under a cloud. I can't remember the exact reason, but I do know someone who can tell me. Want me to find out for you?'

'Do I?! Yes please, Dad. I've been stymied on Hugh Daneman for the past forty-eight hours. Can you call your friend as soon as possible?'

'Will do.' Tom smiled.

'So, darling, is it very different, hunting murderers in the sticks?' asked Celestria.

'Very,' nodded Jazz. 'I didn't even have a phone socket in our makeshift incident room, which means I couldn't access any data.'

'Oh dearie me.' Tom gave a look of mock horror. 'And no crimes were ever solved before computers arrived, were they?'

'Not as many, that's for sure. And certainly not as fast.' Jazz bristled.

'Only teasing you,' said Tom. 'I would have thought it was rather refreshing to have to rely a little more on your analytical powers and those great instincts of yours. As you know, my theory is that every murder is committed for four reasons: love, money, revenge or fear. All the great detectives have always had a superior understanding of human nature. And you do, darling. Don't be afraid to use your talent.'

'Have you finished lecturing your daughter, Tom, or shall I delay joining you so you can continue?' Celestria winked at Jazz as she brought through coffee and placed the tray on the table.

'Was I being patronising? I do apologise. It's old age, you see. You store up so much knowledge, but because you're so ancient, no one wants to hear it. I've always said Big G got it wrong: we should be born old and return to him a helpless, innocent baby.' Tom yawned.

'Time for your nap.' Celestria moved to the back of Tom's wheelchair.

'See? Just like a baby.' Tom's eyes twinkled. 'Can't I have coffee first?'

'No, you know the doctor says caffeine is bad for you.'

'Yes, Matron. See you later, darling.' Tom gave his daughter a small wave as Celestria pushed him through to the bedroom.

Jazz poured coffee for her mother and herself and sat nursing it, staring into the fireplace. Celestria came and sat down with her. Jazz noticed she looked distinctly weary.

They sat in companionable silence for a few minutes, sipping their coffee.

'How is he?' Jazz asked in a low voice.

Celestria sighed. 'As irascible as ever. We had a difficult day on Thursday. He had a bad attack of angina whilst I was out. The silly man didn't do the sensible thing and call the doctor. He waited for me to get home to see he was grey and obviously in pain. They whipped him into Papworth overnight. He was out the next morning, complaining how unattractive the nurses were.' Celestria allowed herself a small smile.

'Mum, why didn't you let me know?'

'Because you were starting your case and as soon as I established he wasn't in danger, there was nothing you could do anyway.'

'Oh Mum, it's such a difficult situation for you.'

'I don't mind caring for him in the slightest, you know that. The thing I dread is walking through the door one evening and finding him...' Celestria couldn't say the words. 'I really feel he should have someone here with him during the day. But I can't give up my job...if I did, we'd be homeless immediately.'

'Perhaps it's time to look at that bungalow on the coast Dad suggested. You have that money from your book tucked away.'

'Yes, I do.' Celestria sipped her coffee. 'And one day I'm sure that's what we'll do. But remember, darling, I'm only fifty-seven and that money is all we have. I really need to work here another three years so I can draw my full pension. As you know, Dad's one from the church is a pittance. Besides,' Celestria sighed, 'this place is what keeps your father alive. Not to mention me. I love my job. It stimulates me and keeps me sane. I think we'd both go mad in a retirement bungalow.'

'Yes, you probably would. But, Mum, you look exhausted. Working and caring for Dad is just too much for you. I think you're going to have to persuade him he needs someone in to help *you*. Threaten him with the retirement bungalow. That should do the trick,' Jazz smiled.

'Anyway, enough of me. You look good, Jazz. Being back at work obviously suits you.'

'I think it probably does,' Jazz nodded. She looked at her watch. 'I've got to be heading off to meet this chap Dad's set me up with.'

'Jonathan? He's awfully nice, really. You'll like him.'

'Rather off males in general just at present.' Jazz grimaced.

'Jazmine'—Celestria grabbed her daughter's hands—'don't become bitter, will you? I know you've been hurt, but there are some good chaps out there, really there are, darling.'

A quiet 'Mmnn,' was all Jazz could muster in reply.

'You're still young, young enough to start again, have a family if you wanted to. You won't give up on men completely, will you?'

'I'll try not to, promise. I know you're desperate to be a granny.' Jazz hugged her mother, who rolled her eyes.

'Hardly, not with that big baby I have asleep in the other room. This is about *you*.'

Jazz nodded. 'Anyway, Mum, I'll pop in on my way back and say goodbye.'

Chapter Twelve

David had woken up on Sunday morning still on the sofa, where he'd fallen asleep the night before. He groaned as he remembered the incident in Foltesham High Street yesterday.

He lay there, studying the cracks in the yellowing ceiling, berating himself for letting himself slip down the slope again.

He slid off the sofa and stumbled to the loo, whereupon he vomited the contents of his stomach into the pan.

He went to the cupboard in the kitchen and switched on the immersion heater. He needed a hot bath, a thorough shave and some decent food in his belly.

If that Julian arsehole was going to be a fixture in Angie's life, then he had no choice but to smarten up his act. He'd half expected the police to turn up on his doorstep last night and arrest him on some kind of trumped-up verbal abuse charge. As for Rory, if Julian was going to be his eventual stepfather, Jesus, David would have to mind his Ps and Qs or he could just imagine his visitation rights going smartly west.

He *had* to get his act together. For the sake of his son, if not himself.

Starting from now.

After a long bath, and running through the positive thought mantra that AA had taught him, David felt a little better. There was no doubt he needed to get out of this depressing dump of a house as soon as he could. A well-balanced person would suffer depression living here. And he had enough money to be able to rent something a lot better. He just hadn't got round to it yet.

He looked through the cupboards for something to eat and, finding nothing, drove off to the local Spar to buy some supplies.

An hour later, he was just about to tuck in to a hearty fry-up when there was a gentle knock on the front door. Terrified it might be the police, he peered through the kitchen window.

Another timid knock. Heart beating, David walked towards the front door. Gingerly, he opened the letter box and peered out. A pair of eyes stared back at him, making him jump.

'Rory! My God, you scared me to death!' David opened the door, and his son, dressed in pyjama bottoms, school jumper and trainers, fell into his arms.

'Dad, oh Dad!' Rory sobbed into his father's chest.

David stroked his son's tousled hair as he cried. 'Come on, old chap, it can't be that bad.'

'But it is! It is!'

David managed to steer Rory onto the sofa, then sat next to him with his arms around his thin shoulders. 'Is it Julian?'

Rory looked up at him questioningly. 'Who?'

'You know, Mummy's boyfriend. Has he been giving you a hard time?'

Rory shook his head. 'I didn't even know she had a boyfriend and I've never met anyone called Julian.'

'But...weren't you at home this weekend? I know he was there with Mummy. I saw them in town together yesterday.'

'No, Dad. I've been in the san since Friday. I've had a really bad tummy bug and the doctor said I couldn't go home.'

David's anger rose. 'Well, that's just peachy! Your mother didn't even bother to let me know you weren't home, let alone that you were sick. And she promised to ring me.' David made a mighty effort to push the anger down, for his son's sake. 'So what on earth are you doing here?'

Rory wiped his nose on the sleeve of his jumper. 'I've run away and I'm not going back. Please, Dad, don't make me! Please!'

'Okay, okay, calm down. You're not going anywhere at the moment. How on earth did you get here?'

'I walked. It was a very long way and... I don't feel so well.'

'I'm sure you don't. It's a good four miles to the school.' David felt his son's forehead. 'You feel a little hot. I'll get you some painkillers from the first aid box to take that temperature down.'

'NO!' Rory shouted. 'No tablets! That's what killed Charlie Cavendish.'

'I know, Rory, but he was allergic to one type of them. They're perfectly safe for other people, I promise.'

'Well, I don't want any,' said Rory stubbornly.

'Okay. I'll get you a drink of water instead.'

David walked into the kitchen, found a glass and filled it up with cold water. He handed it to his son, who was now slumped on the sofa, his eyes glazed with exhaustion.

'Come on, let's get this down you.' He held his son's head up and Rory drank it thirstily.

'That's nice,' he said as he rested his head against the arm of the sofa. 'Matron wouldn't let me drink much at school in case I threw it up. I'm so sleepy, Dad, so sleepy.'

'Okay, you get some rest and we'll talk later.'

David sat in the armchair and watched his son, pondering what he should do. There was no doubt that if Rory had run away, it could be any moment that the authorities came pounding on his door. He should call the school immediately, tell them Rory was safe, but after his drunken show in Foltesham yesterday, it was doubtful Angie and her boyfriend would allow Rory to stay with him.

He watched his son's breath rise and fall and saw he was sleeping peacefully.

He needed to make a fast decision.

Jumping up from his armchair, David ran upstairs and threw a few clothes into a bag. He collected the duvet from the bed and dragged that and the bag downstairs and outside to the car.

Returning into the house, he picked Rory up from the sofa and carried him to the car. Rory's eyes opened for a second as David laid him lengthways on the back seat and tucked the duvet round him.

'Where are we going, Dad?' he asked drowsily.

'On a little holiday, Rory, just you and me.'

When Angelina had received the call saying Rory was missing from school, Julian had refused to accompany her there.

'Better you go alone, darling. As you constantly point out, it's best if I don't meet Rory just yet.'

So Angelina drove hurriedly and alone to St Stephen's, heart in her mouth. The Fleat House matron was waiting for her, looking grim.

'Have you found him yet?' Angelina asked breathlessly.

'No. We have staff and the boarders searching the grounds, but being a Sunday afternoon, we're down on numbers.'

Angelina slumped into the nearest chair and put her hands to her face. 'Oh God, oh God, why would he have run away? What if someone's kidnapped him? What if—'

'Please calm yourself, Mrs Millar. The chances are that Rory is hiding somewhere in the school. For whatever reason, perhaps he wants to be alone. I know for a fact that this whole business with Charlie Cavendish upset him, and then the stomach bug, which gave him a high fever, has probably made him a little irrational. Have you contacted his father yet?'

'I've tried, but he isn't answering his mobile and he doesn't have a landline at the house.'

'Well, keep trying. I'm sure it's crossed your mind that Mr Millar has been eager to see his son recently. I've certainly taken a fair few calls from him.'

'No, that can't be.' Angelina shook her head. 'David didn't even know Rory was in the san. He thought he was at home with me.'

Matron eyed her. 'So, you're not in the habit of letting your ex-husband know when his child is unwell?'

'He was hardly at death's door, was he? Or that's what you told me, anyway,' Angelina snapped back guiltily. 'Besides, rather than criticising me, I'd like to know how you can explain losing a child in your care?'

'I'm matron of Fleat House, not the sanatorium, Mrs Millar. The matron in charge will be back to see you in a few minutes. She told me she looked in on Rory just before ten this morning and he was fast asleep. She left him and went to her office to complete some paperwork. Twenty minutes later, when she looked in again, he was gone.'

'But where? How? You must know something.'

'Remember, this isn't a prison. It would have been a simple matter of a couple of flights of stairs and out of the front door for Rory to gain his freedom.'

'Unless someone took him?'

'Well, now we've discounted your ex-husband, I very much doubt that.'

'Matron, I've heard there's a police investigation going on concerning the death of a child in Rory's house. What if there *is* a lunatic wandering around? What if he's got my Rory? Oh God! Where is he?!'

Angelina burst into tears.

'There, there, Mrs Millar, let's try and keep calm.' Matron patted her shoulder ineffectually. 'Come through to Mr Frederiks's study and I'll get you a cup of tea. I've contacted the head and he's on his way to see you. Please try not to worry. I'm sure Rory is fine.'

Two hours later, despite an extensive search, there was no sign of Rory. Angelina was frantic. Robert Jones had suggested she sit quietly in Frederiks's study, or go home until there was news, but she'd insisted on joining in the search.

Robert Jones stood at the entrance to Fleat House with Matron and watched as Angelina tore across the lawn and into the chapel, screaming Rory's name.

'The woman's hysterical. Is there anyone we can call to be with her?'

'She's tried contacting her ex-husband, and, I believe, her boyfriend, a Mr Forbes, but neither of them are answering her calls.' Matron sniffed.

Robert sighed. 'I've told her we have police officers on the premises assisting with the search.' He turned and stared at her. 'You don't think anything's happened to him, do you?'

Matron rounded on him. 'He was hardly happy here, was he? I wouldn't be surprised if he's run away, poor little shrimp.'

The headmaster paused. 'Was there a problem with Rory?'

Matron's eyes glinted. 'Oh, I think you know there was, Headmaster. I'd better be getting back to the other boys. Mr Frederiks has cut short his outing with the boys and is on his way back in the minibus.'

'I'm going to ask one of the officers to drive Mrs Millar home and stay with her there until there's news.'

'I'll go and fetch her from the chapel and stay with her until you do.'

Robert Jones hardly looked up as Matron walked across Chapel Lawn. The school, and his life, seemed to be slowly disintegrating about him.

Angelina sat in the passenger seat of her car and stared silently out of the window as the woman police constable drove to her house. She managed to indicate when to turn into her drive, then climbed wearily out of the car.

'Would you like me to come in with you, Mrs Millar?'

'No, my...partner is inside. I'll be fine. But thanks anyway.'

'We'll be in touch the minute there's some news. Try not to worry.'

Angelina didn't reply. She headed for the front door. It opened before she reached it. Julian stood there.

'Any news on Rory?'

Angelina shook her head wearily, fighting back the tears. 'I tried to call you to come down to the school and help me look for him.'

'I was busy. Sorry.'

She turned on him. 'What the hell do you mean you were "busy"?! My son has gone *missing*! He might be lying dead somewhere and you tell me you were *busy*! Christ!'

'Angelina, I—'

She moved past him and headed for the stairs. 'Leave me alone, Julian, just leave me alone!'

David arrived in the early evening, tired but triumphant, at the bed and breakfast just on the shore of Lake Windermere. He'd called the landlady on his way up to the Lake District, from a public phone box, just in case the police were already after them and could get hold of numbers dialled on his mobile. He asked if it was all right if he and his son moved their booking forward and arrived this afternoon.

As David and Rory took their bags up to their room, David was pleased as Mrs Birtwhistle, the landlady, had indicated they were the only guests.

'Well, what do you think of that view, old chap?' David put his hands on Rory's shoulders and steered him towards the window. It was dark and all they could see were the lights of the boats bobbing on the water a few hundred yards in front of them. 'Tomorrow, if you feel better, I'm going to take you climbing up Scafell Pike.' David pulled his son round to face him and hugged him close, stroking his matted blond hair.

Rory looked up at him, his blue eyes huge in his pale face. He smiled sadly. 'Yes, Dad, take me to the top of the world and never let me come down.'

Later, they ate a hearty supper of steak and kidney pudding in the deserted restaurant of the bed and breakfast. David was glad to see Rory finishing every morsel on his plate. The colour was returning to his cheeks, and he was obviously on the mend.

David was offered wine by Mrs Birtwhistle, but managed to refuse it. He did most of the talking, telling Rory of the times his own father had brought him here and how they had scaled the highest mountain in England.

After supper, they climbed the narrow stairs to their room. David tucked Rory up in one of the twin beds.

'Night, old chap.' He kissed his son, then gave him a hug. Rory clung on to him.

'Don't leave me, will you, Dad?'

'Of course I won't. I'm going to get into bed myself. We'll need all our energy if we're going to scale the Pike tomorrow.'

Rory reached out his hand and grabbed his father's. 'I'm glad I'm here, Dad. It's like an adventure, isn't it?'

'Yes, it is, just you and me.'

'I love you, Dad.'

'I love you too, old chap.'

David sat in the uncomfortable high-backed chair watching Rory as he fell asleep. Tears began to fall unchecked down his cheeks as love clutched like an iron glove around his heart.

David knew that by now, Angie must be frantic. And however much he wished to steal time alone with his son, he had to let her know Rory was safe.

He took his mobile out of his pocket and began to type a text message to his ex-wife.

Angelina let out a choked sob of relief and flew into Julian's study. 'He's all right! Rory's safe!' she cried.

Julian turned round from the computer screen and smiled tightly. 'Good news. Was he hiding in some particularly thick bush in the school grounds?'

'No, he's with his father. Apparently, Rory appeared on David's doorstep this morning. David said he's fine and just wants to spend some time with him alone.'

'I see. So, are they at that grim cottage of his?'

'No, David's taken him away somewhere for a few days.' Angelina hung on to the door for support. 'Oh God, I can't tell you what was going through my mind until David texted me. I must call the school.'

'Well...' Julian folded his arms and stared at her. 'I can tell you what's going through mine. Yesterday, your drunken, unstable ex-husband tried to assault me in the middle of the high street. He threatened to kill me.'

'Oh, for goodness' sake, Julian! He didn't mean it!'

'Who knows if he did or he didn't? And that's the point: I can understand your relief that Rory is ostensibly safe, but really, Angelina, do you think David, in his current frame of mind, is the right person to look after Rory?'

She looked at him quizzically. 'David might be an alcoholic, but he'd never harm a hair on Rory's head. He adores him.'

'Fine. Maybe he won't harm him, but I can give you a few uncomfortable scenarios which you should contemplate: firstly, David might get behind the wheel of a car drunk. Secondly, he may already have absconded abroad with Rory. Thirdly, do you know when David is going to hand Rory back, if ever?'

Angelina put her fingers to her temples and shook her head. 'Stop it, Julian, please! I can't take any more, really I can't. I have to believe Rory is safe with his father, I really do.'

Julian stood up and walked towards her. He opened his arms and pulled her into them. 'There, there. I'm sorry, darling. Of course I don't want to upset you. It's just the lawyer in me making me look on the bleakest side. I've seen too many children abducted by desperate parents. This situation with Rory sounds all too familiar.'

'Well, I'm going to text David back now and ask him to tell me exactly where they are and when they're coming home. I'm sure he will.'

'And if he doesn't?'

'He will.'

'Okay, but if David doesn't text back by tomorrow morning, letting you know exactly where he is, you'll have no option but to get the police involved. Now, go and telephone the school and let them know you've heard from David. I'll be with you in a moment. I'm just finishing something off.'

He gave her bottom a small tap and sent her out of the room, then turned back to the computer and continued writing his email. His usual calm composure undermined, he noticed his palms were sweating as he pressed 'send'.

Sighing heavily, he turned off the computer.

He hoped he'd get a response by tomorrow.

Never mind the kid… Julian Forbes had problems of his own.

Chapter Thirteen

Jazz walked across Trinity Great Court towards the porter's lodge.

Loitering under the arch with his back towards her was an unusually tall man.

Jazz walked up to him and tapped him on the shoulder.

'Hello, are you Jonathan?'

He swung round, startled. 'Yes. Sorry, I was assuming you would come in the other way.'

'My mother and father have their rooms just over there, on the Court. I went to see them for lunch.'

'Yes, I know. I mean, I know where your parents live. I should have thought.' Jonathan smiled then stuck out his hand awkwardly. 'Well, good to meet you, Inspector Hunter.'

'Jazz, please,' she smiled, thinking how pleasant it was to look up for a change. This man's stature made *her* feel petite.

She'd guess Jonathan was in his late twenties. His features were such that he could not be called traditionally handsome: his blue eyes were too close together, set above a long and hawk-like nose. His face was gaunt, his cheekbones like razors, giving him a hungry, bohemian look. But he was an attractive man, nevertheless.

'Shall we?' Jonathan indicated they should walk.

'Yes.'

Jonathan set off at a lick. Jazz struggled to keep in step with the pair of long legs that ate up the ground beneath them.

'It's very good of you to spare the time to see me.'

'Well, I'm not sure what help I can be, but I'll do my best.' Jazz smiled, following him down an alleyway.

He stopped in front of a pub Jazz knew well as a popular student watering hole.

'Okay to go in here?' He stared at her hard.

'Fine,' she nodded, and followed him through the door. The pub was empty and Jazz took a seat in the corner, whilst Jonathan went to the bar to order the drinks.

'White wine for you, not sure what it's like, though.' Jonathan put a glass on the table and sat down opposite her, cradling a pint in his large hands. 'Cheers.' He clinked his glass against hers.

'Cheers,' Jazz smiled back and took a sip. The wine erred on the side of vinegar. 'So, fire away and tell me what you want to know.'

'Right.' Jonathan drew a small tape recorder and a notebook out of one of his capacious coat pockets.

'You're recording this?'

'Yes, if you don't mind. I can just take notes if you prefer.'

'It depends on what you're going to ask me.'

'Nothing particularly outrageous. My dissertation, as your father might have told you, is on the state of the criminal justice system in the new millennium. I've prepared some questions for you.'

'I feel a little like one of my suspects when I haul them in for questioning.' Jazz indicated the recorder. 'Go on then. Do me good to see what it's like on the other side of the fence.'

'Okay.' Jonathan switched the recorder on.

'You're meant to caution me now, ask if I want a solicitor present.' She smiled at him.

'I suppose I should,' he nodded. 'Right, the first question I want to ask you is whether, in your position on the frontline of apprehending criminals, you're satisfied with the current justice system?'

Jazz bit her lip. 'Did my father tell you this is my pet subject?'

'No, but surely it must be the bane of every officer's life to spend months on an investigation, arrest the alleged perpetrator, then watch him walk free from the court on a technicality?'

There was a pause before Jazz replied. 'Jonathan, there are two ways I can do this. If you're naming me in your dissertation, then I would toe the party line. If you're not and we turn that thing off, I can give you a much more honest overview. Now, which would you prefer?'

Jonathan leaned across the table and switched off the tape. He smiled at her. 'Okay, shoot.'

Jazz began, cautiously at first, to tell him where she thought the problems lay. To her surprise, he responded knowledgeably, defending the system.

'It's not corruption that is its downfall, although I accept what you say about the abuse of power and personal ambition, but from what I've gleaned from others who I've interviewed, those that slip through the net are usually the result of a mixture of petty bureaucracy, inept lawyers for the prosecution—I mean, have you seen the new white paper the government has just issued, suggesting the CPS cuts barristers' fees?— so, of course, the best lawyers are going to play for the defence, and human fallibility.'

'Also, the system is clogged up with appeals,' Jazz added. 'Even when you get your suspect convicted, you never know when some smart-arse lawyer is going to appear with a trumped-up piece of evidence, sometimes material, but more often than not psychological.'

'The school of "it's not my fault I'm a murderer, my mother didn't breastfeed me as a baby", you mean?' Jonathan grimaced.

'Got it in one. Sorry, I may sound hard, but life *is* hard. No one has the perfect childhood or adolescence. We all have reasons why we might go out and murder someone in cold blood. Thank God most of us don't. But those who *do* have to take responsibility for their actions whatever the circumstances? They have to be punished for what they did.'

'Agreed. I understand you have personal experience, Jazz,' Jonathan said quietly. 'I know what happened to your father.'

Jazz loathed talking about it. The subject still conjured up vivid memories of the event. 'Yes. He was a good man, a vicar, trying to help a disadvantaged community. What did he get for his trouble? A bullet in the back. The gunman got two years and was out in six months. On the grounds of diminished responsibility. And then offended again three weeks later.'

'I'm sorry. I really don't know what to say.' Jonathan sighed. 'Do you mind me asking what he was doing in Hackney at the time? Thought he'd been a don lecturing on Theology here before that.'

'You're right. I was brought up in Cambridge until I was twelve. That's when Dad announced to his wife and daughter that he was fed up of teaching theology to a load of middle-class students. He wanted to go out there and practise what he preached. So he was ordained and we moved to Hackney. Going from my cosy grammar school here in Cambridge to an east London comprehensive was a culture shock. Toughened me up, though.'

'I'll bet. Christ, rather you than me.'

'It was hard, yes, but I admired Dad so much for what he was doing. And I learned all sorts of tricks along the way, things that have since stood me in good stead in my current career.'

'Such as?'

'We-ell, and this really is off the record, I might add.' Jazz smiled wryly. 'I can score anything you fancy by making one call: uppers, downers, blues, hash, Es, coke, heroin…'

'When do we leave?'

'Very funny.'

'I'm joking. Not into that stuff, never have been.'

'You would say that to a detective now, wouldn't you?' Jazz countered.

'No. I believe in telling the truth. And luckily for me, I've managed to avoid it. Honestly,' he reiterated.

'I didn't. For a while anyway. I tried everything. It was…*de rigueur* at my educational establishment. Bit like milk at break.'

'A rite of passage?'

'Yup. Something like that. Middle-class white girl…' Jazz sighed. 'I wanted to be accepted. And being on the "other side" has given me great insight. I understand what these kids have to go through just to grow up relatively unscathed.'

'So, what happened to your dad?'

'As usual, he got too emotionally involved. With his congregation, which grew from a few old biddies into three hundred whilst he was there. My dad's a very charismatic figure. And with one woman in particular, whose child was dying of leukaemia. She came to him for spiritual support, spent a lot of time at our house. Her old man, who was a renowned drug dealer, didn't like it, arrived one day at our house and shot him at point-blank range in our kitchen.'

'Shit,' Jonathan murmured.

'He was lucky to survive at all,' added Jazz. 'He had a heart attack on the operating table. He's very fragile, and becoming more so by the day.'

'But a fixture here in Cambridge, nevertheless. He's renowned in the university, for his wisdom, his kindness, and his filthy jokes.' Jonathan smiled, his eyes twinkling.

'He's a very special man,' murmured Jazz, 'and I love him to bits, for all his faults.'

'Trying to spread goodness isn't a fault, Jazz.'

'No, I know that. But living with a saint can be tough. My mother, especially, has been through a lot.'

'I'm sure. And you too, Jazz,' he said softly, his blue eyes fixed on hers.

'Anyway, enough of all that.' She felt herself blushing. 'Anything else you want to know? I need to be leaving.' The words came out more brusquely than she'd intended, but she felt uncomfortable.

'No, I don't think so. For now, anyway. I need to go home and write up my notes. If I need another meeting, would you be amenable?'

'I'm very busy at the moment.' She stood up.

Jonathan did likewise. 'On a case?'

'Yes.'

'Interesting?'

'Yes.' She was heading towards the door. 'Goodbye, Jonathan, hope I've been of some use.' She extended her hand towards him. He ignored it.

'Are you parked in Trinity?'

'Yes.'

'I'll walk with you. The house I share is in that direction.' Jonathan led the way out of the pub and onto the street.

Jazz walked silently, feeling unsettled and wondering how he'd managed to make her reveal far more than she'd intended.

They were back at the porter's lodge. Jonathan turned to her. 'Thank you for your time, Jazz. I really appreciate it.' He fixed her with his blue eyes for a second, then leaned down and kissed her on the cheek. 'Bye then.'

'Bye.'

Jazz walked briskly away from him, towards the safety of her parents' rooms. There was no time to ruminate, as she was met at the door by Celestria.

'Glad you're here, Jazz. Your father has refused to go to bed until you got back. He's been on the telephone to one of his old cronies about Hugh Daneman. Come in.'

'Jazz, my darling.' Her father looked pale but his eyes were alight. 'Found out the details on your cadaver for you. Celestria, the smallest of brandies for myself and our daughter to ease the story along.'

'Not for me, Dad. I have to drive home.' Jazz settled herself in the chair.

'And not for you either, Tom. You've already had your quota today.'

'Bugger quotas and get me a small brandy.'

Celestria looked at Jazz helplessly, then took a brandy bottle out of the cupboard, poured a tiny measure into a glass and handed it to Tom.

'Thank you, darling.' He took a sip. 'Now, this old chum of mine, Crispin Wentworth, was able to fill me in on Hugh Daneman. They were at Oxford together, and, having completed their PhDs, were both offered jobs as lecturers. I presume you knew Hugh was gay?'

'Not for sure, but the thought had crossed my mind. A man unmarried for all of his life...it has to be an option.'

'Well, let me assure you he was most definitely one hundred per cent homosexual. It takes one to know one and Crispin would know.' Tom smiled. 'At the time, there was some pretty racy stuff going on at Oxford, but as I said earlier, it was the start of the Sixties, so it was happening everywhere.'

'Terrible to be envious of what a good time your parents had when they were younger, but sometimes I am,' Jazz sighed. 'Anyway, go on, Dad.'

'Well, it seems Hugh Daneman did the unthinkable and fell in love with one of his students. Male, of course. Rather foolishly, he didn't hide it well enough from his elders and betters. They eventually got the drift loud and clear and he was dismissed forthwith.'

'I see. Do you know who the student was?'

Tom held up his hands. 'I'll get to that in a minute. Hugh then went abroad and Crispin lost track of him for a year or so. Next thing he knows, Hugh's working at St Stephen's as a Latin master.'

'I'm amazed they'd take him on, given the fact he'd been dismissed from Oxford for a relationship with a male student.'

'It may well have been hushed up. Things were in those days. Perhaps Hugh was to leave quietly and nothing more would be said. Police checks and extensive references weren't *de rigueur* like they are now. Anyway, somehow he tips up at St Stephen's.'

'So this young man Hugh fell in love with? Who was he?' Jazz asked.

'It's quite an interesting story. The student concerned was one Corin Conaught. He was renowned for his drink and drug abuse, but, according to Crispin, was a charismatic, beautiful and aristocratic young man. Rather like Bosie, Wilde's lover, I should imagine. He left a trail of both male and female hearts broken behind him.'

'He was bisexual?'

'Yes, but let me continue with my story before I lose track: Hugh Daneman fell head over heels in love with him. From what Crispin said, Corin was very fond of Hugh too and they were an "item" for quite some time, until Hugh was asked to leave.'

'I'm surprised it was such a scandal. As you say, anything went in the Sixties.'

'It *did* and it *didn't*. Any relationship between staff and pupil is forbidden to this day. Some things never change and that's one of them. And Corin came from a high-profile Catholic family. Corin's father, Ralph, Lord Conaught, died whilst his son was carousing at Oxford. Apparently Corin was told his father was about to shuffle off this mortal coil during a particularly debauched weekend of partying, and didn't even bother to go home to kiss Daddy goodbye. And I'm sure they would have got wind of their son's notorious relationship with Hugh Daneman. Subsequently, even though Corin was the eldest son, and heir to the Conaught Estate and the title, his father disinherited him and left everything to the spare, one Edward Conaught.'

'Dramatic stuff.' Jazz sighed.

'Yes, and as with all dramas, it has a poignant ending. Apparently Corin returned home from Oxford, having been sent down a few weeks after his father died. His younger brother, Edward, granted him a cottage on the estate. He spent the next five years drinking and injecting himself into an early grave. He died when he was twenty-six, poor chap.'

'Where is this estate?'

'Near you, actually; somewhere in Norfolk.'

'Really?'

'Yes.' Tom had a look of satisfaction on his face. 'So, does all this help, Ma'am?'

'Absolutely, Dad. It's fantastic. I have somewhere to go with this now. It also perhaps explains why Hugh Daneman suddenly appeared at St Stephen's: if the love of his life was living in Norfolk, then surely he might have followed?'

'Very possibly. Anyway, I hope that's given you something to work on.'

'It has, and please thank your friend Crispin for his help, too. Thank you so much, Dad.' Jazz stood up. 'I'd better be on my way. Bye, Mum.'

'Bye, darling.' Celestria kissed her. 'Let us know what happens.'

'I will.'

When she arrived at her car, Jazz opened the boot and retrieved her briefcase. She pulled out the wallet containing the photo she had found next to Hugh Daneman's bed in his London flat. She stared at the photograph, taking in the angelically beautiful face and the long, blond hair. She turned it over and read the inscription once more.

And realised the face was not, as she had first thought, female…

…but male.

Chapter Fourteen

'Morning, Ma'am. Good weekend?'

Miles was already at his desk when Jazz arrived at the school.

'Fine. You?' Jazz placed her briefcase on the desk, took out her laptop and plugged it in.

'Wild parties and a bed full of supermodels.' Miles grinned. 'Actually, I watched the cricket from the West Indies on Sky, trying to bask in some reflected sunshine. Now, the head requests an immediate audience. Apparently, this shambles of a school now boasts not only a dead pupil and a dead tutor, but also a missing child.'

Jazz looked up from her screen. 'Really? When? And why wasn't I informed?'

'Yesterday afternoon. And I presume no one contacted us because the child concerned appears to have been abducted by his father and the school probably thought it had nothing to do with the case. They had the local plods on site to help them search.'

'Who's the boy?'

'He didn't say, but the mother is with the head in his office. I said you'd go as soon as you came in.'

Jazz handed Miles a piece of paper. 'Can you get a number for this address? Give them a ring and say we want to visit this morning.'

'Right, Ma'am. Anything else?'

'Yes. Find out where the hell DS Roland has got to and why *he* didn't inform me immediately about this missing boy. And get Sebastian Frederiks to pay me a visit here in half an hour.' Jazz stood up and walked to the door, slamming it behind her as she left.

The head's secretary was sitting pale and wide-eyed behind her computer.

'They're waiting for you in there,' she said, nodding in the direction of the office.

'Thank you.' Jazz entered the room and found a pretty, petite woman sitting in front of Robert Jones's desk.

'Inspector Hunter, good morning. Thank you for coming. This is Mrs Millar, mother of the missing boy.'

'Who is...?'

'Rory Millar. Perhaps your sergeant filled you in on the situation?'

'Briefly. Hello, Mrs Millar.' Jazz shook the woman's hand. 'Could you tell me what's happened?'

'Yes, I'll do my best.' Angelina began to talk haltingly of the events of the past twenty-four hours.

Jazz listened until she had finished, then nodded.

'Right. So, in fact, your son isn't missing. He's with his father, but you don't know where.'

'I haven't received a reply to my text asking where they are and my...lawyer is concerned that due to my ex-husband's drink problem, and the fact he's suffered depression, it could be a case for the police. Is it, do you think?'

Jazz remembered David Millar, desperate and wild-eyed, outside this office. And Rory Millar himself, whom she was still to meet, whose name seemed to have a nasty habit of regularly cropping up.

'If he hasn't replied to your request to let you know where he's taken your son, then yes, there is some cause for concern. But equally, surely there's no reason to believe that Rory is in any danger, Mrs Millar? He's with his father, after all.'

Angelina's wide blue eyes indicated agreement. 'That's what I've said to my lawyer, but he insisted I came to see you this morning.'

'Have you any idea where your ex-husband might have taken Rory?'

'No. My lawyer was worried he might have taken him abroad, but that's impossible, as I have Rory's passport at home.'

'That doesn't necessarily mean he couldn't have obtained a duplicate for himself.'

'Really?' Angelina bit her lip. 'Oh dear.'

'I'll send out a general alert. Do you by any chance have a photograph of your son and your husband? We'll need one to scan onto the computer.'

'Yes, Juli...my lawyer, said you'd want one.' Angelina picked an envelope out of her handbag and handed it to Jazz. 'He will be all right, won't he?'

'I'm sure he'll be fine, but best if we try and find out where he is. Now, if there's nothing else, I'll get back to my desk. I'll pop in and brief you later, Mr Jones.'

Jazz smiled briefly at both of them and left the room.

Back behind her desk, Jazz slipped the photographs out of the envelope. The first one was of David Millar, obviously in the days before he took to the bottle and his life disintegrated. She put that to one side and stared at the photograph of Rory Millar. And caught her breath.

'Good God!' She whistled, then hunted through her briefcase to pull out the plastic wallet containing the photo of the young man she now knew to be Corin Conaught.

She put the photo of Rory next to it and called Miles over to take a look.

'Well?' she asked as he studied them.

'Wow! They must be related, surely?' Miles suggested.

'This is Corin Conaught, erstwhile lover of Hugh Daneman, and now deceased, and this is Rory Millar, the missing boy.'

'Hold on, are you saying Corin is a "he", not a "she"?'

'Yes. My dear old sleuthing pa managed to correct me. They are alike, aren't they?'

'Uncannily,' Miles agreed. 'Do you know if they are related?'

'Not yet, no. Rory's mum has only just handed me this photo. It could very well be coincidence. Photos can often be misleading. But I'd like to find Rory fast.' Jazz handed Miles the photos of Rory and his father. 'Scan these in and file a missing person's report.'

'Sure. We're expected at Conaught Hall at eleven. I spoke to Lord Conaught's housekeeper. She wasn't helpful, told me his lordship's an invalid and didn't like visitors.'

There was a knock on the door.

'Come.'

Sebastian Frederiks's false smile appeared as he leaned his face into the room. 'You wanted to see me?'

'Pull up a chair and sit down, Mr Frederiks.'

'Any news on poor old Rory?'

'No, not yet. So tell me, Mr Frederiks, why you did nothing to stop Charlie Cavendish's repeated bullying? And in particular, of Rory Millar?'

Sebastian raised an eyebrow. 'Who's been telling you this?

'That doesn't matter. I'd just like you to answer my question.'

He crossed his arms. 'You may have heard old Charlie was a bit of a bully with the younger boys…'

'Yes, time and again, Mr Frederiks. Are you telling me it wasn't true?'

'No, I'm not. But it was never malicious and I certainly don't feel Charlie specifically picked on young Rory Millar.'

'Really? So why was I told Cavendish had locked Rory in the cellar overnight? That sounds pretty specific to me.'

'Look here, there was no proof that it was Charlie,' Frederiks answered weakly.

'But the likelihood is that it was?'

'It may have been, yes. But Inspector, without proof, what could I do?'

Jazz sighed in frustration. 'You've been a teacher for twenty years, a housemaster for over eight. You must be experienced in dealing with many instances similar to this one. Even his mates knew it was him.' Jazz turned to Miles. 'Isn't that right?'

'Yes, Ma'am,' Miles nodded.

Frederiks was sweating profusely. 'Let me tell you, Inspector, I come down on my boys like a ton of bricks for any kind of bullying. But it's the same problem time and time again. The victim of the bully is so terrified of the repercussions, he won't admit he knows the perpetrator of the crime.'

'So Rory Millar didn't tell you it was Charlie Cavendish that had locked him in the cellar?'

'No. And how would he know anyway? He was on the other side of the door. However, I did realise young Rory was terrified. It was me that found him. I assumed it was more to do with this yarn in the house about the ghost of a boy who reputedly died down there. Rory would have naturally heard the story. He looked like a ghost himself when I let him out.'

'I'm amazed no one heard him before. He must have been shouting to get out. Poor kid,' Miles added.

'The boys sleep on the second and third floors and, as you know,

I'm in my wing on the side of the house. The point is, whether we should have heard him or not, we *didn't.*'

'You say he was very upset when he came out? Did you contact his parents?'

'Absolutely. This was the icing on the cake. Rory had been an unhappy young man for a while and was becoming more and more withdrawn. I'd put it down largely to the trauma of his parents' divorce, but when this happened, I obviously felt I had to speak to them. To wit, rather than worrying Mrs Millar, his mother, who can be overprotective and a little neurotic where her son is concerned, I decided to call Mr Millar instead. I spoke to him about Rory last week.'

'Under the circumstances, it sounds like Mrs Millar has every right to be neurotic about her son's welfare.' Jazz ground her teeth with irritation. 'So, did David Millar respond?'

'We had a little chat over the phone. I played it very low-key, no point in getting everyone overexcited. I suggested to Mr Millar it might be a good idea for him to have a chat with his son, see if he could prise out of him what was wrong. I subsequently asked Rory to give his father a call.'

'And did he?'

'I do remember seeing Rory on the house payphone…it was Thursday, yes, the day before Cavendish was found dead.'

'But you don't know it was David Millar on the other end of the line?'

Frederiks shrugged. 'No, I don't, but the thing was…actually…' He scratched his head.

'Yes, Mr Frederiks?'

'I've just thought of something. The day after I saw Rory on the payphone, which was the Friday that Charlie died, I went off for my meeting around seven thirty that evening. I was just pulling out of the school car park, when by coincidence I saw David Millar getting out of his car.'

'I see.'

'There were a lot of parents arriving for the concert in the chapel. Rory was in the choir, so it may have been that Millar was coming to listen to his son. But'—Frederiks shrugged again—'I've never seen him in chapel before.'

'I presume Mr Millar's car was gone by the time you arrived back at school that night?' Jazz probed.

'Of course. I've told you, it was midnight when I returned, or thereabouts. Look, Inspector, I'm not suggesting anything to you, but what if Rory *had* confided in his dad about his suspicion it was Cavendish who'd locked him in the cellar?'

'So you now admit Charlie *was* targeting him?' Jazz pressed.

'A lot of ribbing goes on between boys. Some can cope, some can't. The bottom line is that Rory couldn't. And yes,' Frederiks sighed, 'I accept I should have interceded before. And now he's run away…but…' Frederiks looked puzzled.

'What?'

'It doesn't fit, does it? I mean, if young Rory *had* been targeted by Charlie, surely he'd be ecstatic now he's no longer here? Why on earth would he run away?'

'We've no idea.' Jazz decided to change the subject, not wishing to speculate on aspects of the case with a possible suspect. 'Mr Frederiks, I need to ask you again where you were that Friday evening?'

'I really can't say.'

'Do you know it is an offence to withhold information relevant to a police enquiry?'

'Look, Inspector, I can only reiterate that where I was that Friday night is *not* relevant to your case.'

'Let me be the judge of that, Mr Frederiks. And I'd say it is. You were the person who's admitted he placed Charlie Cavendish's Epilim by his bedside before you left. We have no proof it wasn't you who substituted the tablets in the first place.'

'Then why on earth, if I had done it, would I have told you I had put the tablets there?'

'Because it was fact, and recorded on the drug sheet. And you may have thought Charlie's death would be uncontested; a simple case of an epileptic fit…'

'That *is* what we all thought, Inspector…'

'And that your actions would not be questioned…'

'Are you accusing me?' Frederiks stood up abruptly.

'No. Of course not. But I am advising you I think it would be sensible for you to tell us where you were that evening. The fact you won't only adds suspicion, rather than quashing it.'

Frederiks slumped down into the chair. 'I can't. I just can't.'

'Then I may have to caution and arrest you for perverting the course of justice. I have to presume you're protecting someone else, but let me warn you, at the same time you are risking your own integrity as a housemaster and the man who was directly responsible for Charlie Cavendish's safety. If you refuse to produce an alibi to corroborate the fact you were elsewhere, then I have no proof at all you were *not* here.' Jazz looked at her watch. 'Thank you for coming to see me.'

Frederiks nodded, stood and left the room without another word.

Jazz put on her coat and searched for her car keys.

'What do you think, Ma'am?' Miles peered at her over his laptop.

'He won't have the luxury of staying silent for long.' Jazz was rooting around in her briefcase. 'For the life of me I can't understand why he did nothing about Cavendish's well-known peccadillo for terrorising little boys but...bugger! Can't find what I've done with my keys. Can you drive me there? Let's chew a few things over on the way.'

The sun was just managing to appear from behind the clouds as Miles took the main road west out of Foltesham towards King's Lynn.

'What do *you* think of Frederiks?' she asked him.

'Put it this way: I wouldn't like to be under him in a ruck.' Miles grimaced. 'So, David Millar was at the school the night Charlie died. If Rory had pointed the finger at Charlie over the telephone, do you think Millar killed him as an act of revenge? And would David Millar have known about Charlie's reaction to aspirin?'

'All the boys in Fleat were warned of any allergy that affected their housemates, from peanuts to perfume,' Jazz said. 'Rory may well have mentioned it to his father, who knows? Whatever, we certainly need to find him. My instinct tells me Millar Junior is somehow involved in all this. And he's proving pretty elusive to get hold of.'

Miles grinned at her. 'Just like old times, Ma'am.'

'What do you mean?'

'Your instincts are usually right. The team trusted them implicitly.'

Jazz looked at him. 'Really?' She laughed. 'Well, if you want to know the truth, I've never felt further away than I do at the moment.'

'You'll get there, Ma'am, you always do.' He steered the car hard left. 'I think this is the entrance. The housekeeper said it was just after the garage.' Miles drove through a large pair of old wrought-iron gates, with a keeper's cottage on one side. The drive wound through open parkland, dotted with old oak trees. They passed a lake, shimmering in the weak sun, and finally arrived in front of the house.

'Blimey, awfully *Brideshead*,' Miles muttered, as he steered the car round the circular pond, a moss-covered fountain fashioned in the shape of a young boy blowing a horn placed at the centre.

'But ugly, don't you think? Late Victorian, I'd reckon,' Jazz said, looking up at the square, red-brick building. The many windows glinted blindly, the roof lined with gargoyles, their menacing faces now chipped and misshapen. 'Perfect setting for a gothic horror film.'

'Put it this way: the heating bills must be pretty steep,' Miles joked as they climbed the steps to the front door and Jazz pressed the bell. Above it was a rusted plaque stating *Tradesmen to the rear*.

The door opened and a middle-aged woman in a black dress appeared.

'Good morning. DI Hunter and DS Miles to see Lord Conaught,' said Jazz.

'Come this way, please.' The woman nodded as they stepped into an austere, lofty entrance hall, the ageing chequered marble floor stretching into the distance. Jazz shivered as she followed the woman out of the hall and along a maze of dark corridors. It was colder inside than out.

They stopped in front of a heavy oak door and the woman turned to them.

'I've explained to Lord Conaught that you wish to speak to him, but he's not a well man. He had a fall from his hunter a couple of years back and is in a wheelchair. Arthritis has set in and he suffers a lot of pain. He also had a family bereavement very recently,' added the woman.

'We won't be long, I promise,' said Jazz.

The woman nodded and knocked on the door.

'Come.'

The woman opened the door to let them in.

As she stepped inside, Jazz noticed the starkness of the rest of the house was in deep contrast to the cosy, oak-panelled room she now found herself in. There were colourful hunting cartoons lining the walls, a worn tartan carpet on the floor and a roaring fire burning merrily in the grate. On either side of the fireplace, books spilled untidily from floor-to-ceiling shelves. The room smelled of damp dog, a specimen of which was lying basking in the warmth in front of the fire.

Edward Conaught was sitting in a wheelchair to one side of the fireplace, a copy of the *Telegraph* placed on his knee. There was a table next to him, piled with dog-eared copies of *Country Life* and bottles of pills.

He smiled up at them wearily and stretched out his hand.

'Edward Conaught. Pleasure to meet you. Please sit down.'

He indicated the old sofa, covered in dog hairs, and turned his wheelchair around to face them.

'I've no idea why you should be calling on me. Not in any trouble, am I? Some hope, these days,' he chuckled.

'No, Lord Conaught, there's nothing to worry about.'

'Please, call me Edward. So tell me, how can I help you?'

'It's regarding your brother, Corin,' said Jazz.

Edward's face clouded. 'But he's dead. Has been for some forty years, poor chap.'

'Yes, we know, Sir,' said Miles. 'We're here about an old friend of Corin's, who has recently died. The coroner has confirmed it was suicide, but because we believe his death may be linked to a current murder investigation, we needed to speak to you about your brother.'

'I see.' Edward sighed. 'Who was the friend?'

'Hugh Daneman,' said Jazz.

'Right,' Edward nodded. 'Yes, they were…close friends.'

'Then the first question, Sir, has to be whether you were aware of an unusually intimate relationship between them.'

'Good Lord, yes. Of course I was, as were the whole family.' Edward stared at them. 'You could say Hugh Daneman was part of the reason why I ended up living in this mausoleum of a house and spending my life trying to keep the damned place going. Corin was my older brother. By rights, he should have inherited the estate. Did you know that?'

'Yes, Sir, we did,' Jazz replied kindly.

'Not that one can blame others for one's mistakes, but Corin's peccadillos certainly rebounded on me.' Edward Conaught sighed. 'Corin started experimenting with drugs and sex at Oxford. Subsequently, my father disinherited him just before he died.'

'So you remember Hugh Daneman from that time?'

'Oh yes. Hugh followed him around like a lovestruck child. Corin was obviously fond of Hugh, but I think, for Hugh, the relationship meant much more.'

'The information I've gathered suggests that Hugh was asked to leave his lecturing position at Oxford because of his unsuitable liaison with your brother,' added Jazz.

'It wouldn't surprise me. But what I do know is, whatever the nature of their relationship, when Corin was in trouble with drugs and drink, Hugh helped him through. He moved in with Corin, into the cottage I'd given him on the estate after he was sent down. Hugh did his utmost to nurse Corin through, but I'm afraid he was beyond help. He died after taking a lethal cocktail of heroin and alcohol. Poor chap, such a waste. He was only twenty-six.' Edward paused. 'One way and another, I sometimes wonder whether this family is cursed.'

'Why do you say that, Sir?' queried Miles.

'Well, another tragedy associated with this family occurred only last week. You say Daneman took his own life…was he depressed?'

'We don't know at present, but if I could ask you, Sir, to keep this information to yourself until we are surer of the circumstances, I'd be grateful.' Jazz smiled.

'Hugh was still working at St Stephen's.' It was not a question, but a statement.

'Yes, he was.'

Edward stared at her through grey, intelligent eyes. 'Are you not releasing this information because you believe it might have something to do with Charlie's death?'

'You've read about his death in the newspaper, have you, Sir?' asked Miles.

Edward Conaught gave a grim chuckle. 'Yes, but that's not the way I discovered he was dead. Charlie Cavendish is my nephew.'

'Your nephew?' Jazz was astounded.

'Of course. Sorry, Inspector, I presumed you knew, and that was why you were visiting today.'

'My apologies for my ignorance, and also my belated condolences,' Jazz spluttered, colour rising in her cheeks.

'Why on earth should you have known? Adele and Charlie are both "Cavendishes", due to that ghastly man she chose to marry. It's understandable you haven't yet had time to investigate Charlie's family tree. As a matter of fact, Adele is coming to see me this week. We have to discuss what on earth we're going to do with this damned place now Charlie's gone. He was our sole heir. There are no other living male relatives. Lot of them got wiped out in the Second World War and the ones who survived all had girls.'

'So, Adele is…'

'My sister, yes. Thirteen years younger than me, I might add, and fifteen years younger than Corin. She was only eleven when he died.'

'So why won't she inherit the estate?' Miles queried.

'I'm sure the Equal Opportunities Commission will one day rule that females can inherit titles and estates, but at present, *primogeniture* is the law. The heir has to be male. Therefore the Conaught line seems to have come to rather an abrupt end a few days ago.'

'I see, Sir.' Miles nodded.

'Your sister Adele, does she have a cottage in Cley?' asked Jazz.

'No. When she visits Norfolk she stays here, of course. There's plenty of room.' Edward smiled wryly. 'Why do you ask?'

'I saw her in Cley unloading some shopping a few days ago.'

'Really?' Probably on one of her charitable missions, food parcels to the elderly, or simply visiting a friend, although I'm surprised she didn't let me know she was here in Norfolk. However, I'm not my sister's keeper.'

'No,' Jazz replied shortly, as Edward looked set to continue.

'I suppose you are now thinking it does raise the question of why both Charlie, and Hugh Daneman, who, like it or not, had a connection to this family, should both be found dead within a few days of each other.'

'Yes, but the fact there is a connection gives me a new line of enquiry.'

'His mother told me Charlie died of anaphylactic shock. Is that true?' asked Edward.

'It is. We're currently doing our best to establish how he came to swallow the aspirin that killed him. Could you tell me, from an uncle's point of view, your opinion of him?'

Edward paused for thought. Finally he said, 'He was very like his father, for whom I had no time whatsoever. There. Does that answer your question?'

'Yes. But you were still prepared to hand over the Conaught Estate on your death?'

'My dear lady, can you imagine the generations of fathers who have looked at their heirs in despair? My father was relatively progressive; he decided to hand the estate to me rather than my elder brother, but he had a choice. The family name and lineage is more important than anything else in these situations. Even if I had little time for Charlie, who's to say he wouldn't grow into a fine master of the estate and have a set of strapping sons? Perhaps the place could have done with an injection of aggressive capitalism. We're in the new millennium after all. The responsibility made a man of me. It may have made one of Charlie, too.'

'Your mother? Is she still alive?' asked Jazz.

'Yes she is—although she's rather frail these days. She lives in the East Wing so I can keep an eye on her.'

'Would you mind if we visited her?'

Edward sighed. 'Adele and I haven't told her about Charlie's death. We feel it would upset her. And until we've decided what to do with the estate, we don't want her to worry.'

'I understand.' Jazz nodded. 'But I would like to see her, and soon.'

'Then let me prepare her, tell her the news myself. I'll also say you want to speak about an old friend of Corin's who has recently passed away. She'll like that. Corin always was her favourite child,' Edward added, an edge to his voice.

'I don't want to push you, but perhaps you could let us know when you have told her?'

Edward nodded. 'Give me a couple of days.'

'Of course,' said Jazz, standing up and shaking Edward's hand. Miles did the same.

'I feel I've hardly helped at all. And perhaps, if you do turn anything up, you'd kindly allow me to be party to it. History's my bag, you see. I've spent most of my time since my riding accident studying Conaught ancestors. It would be expedient to include the modern as well as the ancient members of the family in my book.'

'I'll keep you informed. Just one more question, Sir. Corin never had a child, did he?'

Edward raised an eyebrow in surprise. 'Not to my knowledge, no. Why?'

'No reason, Sir. Just making sure.'

'If he *had*, then I for one would be sleeping much easier in my bed about the future of the estate.' He sighed.

'Yes, I understand,' acknowledged Jazz.

'Well,' Edward nodded, 'good day to you both.'

The housekeeper showed them to the front door and they walked down the steps towards the car. Jazz turned back and surveyed the house. The sun had gone in, there was a chill wind and wet drizzle falling from the gathering clouds. At that moment Jazz could have sworn she saw a silhouette retreating from an upstairs window on the left-hand side of the house.

Jazz shivered involuntarily and stepped into the welcoming warmth of the car.

Chapter Fifteen

When Jazz arrived on Angelina Millar's doorstep twenty minutes later, the door was opened by a tall, immaculately dressed man. In his mid-thirties, he was classically handsome, with a chiselled jawline and a good head of neatly combed black hair.

'Can I help you?' he asked abruptly.

'Yes, Sir. I'm Detective Inspector Hunter. I've come to see Mrs Millar. This is her house, isn't it?'

'*Our* house, yes.' The man finally held out his hand. 'Julian Forbes. I'm Angelina's partner. I live here, too. Please come in. I sent Angelina up to bed for a rest, but I doubt if she's sleeping.' He ushered Jazz through the hall and into the drawing room. 'Wait here. I'll go and see if she's awake.' He nodded at Jazz and left the room.

Jazz wandered around, noting how pristine everything was.

It resembled a stage set; she could still smell new paint. There were carefully arranged photographs of the angelic Rory with his mother, but none, she noted, of his father.

Of course, if there was a new boyfriend on the scene, that must make life difficult.

She wondered how children of divorce coped when the photographs of one of their parents were removed from display and replaced with another, unloved and unknown face.

Jazz perched on the edge of one of the sofas, as Julian led Angelina into the room.

'Hello, Mrs Millar.'

Even exhausted, Angelina looked immaculate. Jazz thought what a perfect couple the two of them made.

'Is there any news?' Angelina's expression was held between dread of bad news and hope of good. Jazz had seen it so many times before.

'Not at present, no.'

'Oh.' Angelina's shoulders slumped, and she sat down next to Julian. He held her hand rather stiffly.

'I presume you haven't heard anything from either Rory or your husband?'

'No, nothing. Not a word. I...' Angelina bit her lip to stop herself crying. 'I've left so many messages on David's mobile, but he hasn't replied.'

'We're going to put a device on both your mobile and your home line, Mrs Millar. If it rings and it is your husband, then we need you to try and keep him talking. Then we can try and get a location through his phone.'

Angelina shook her head. 'He won't call, I know he won't. He's got Rory and he won't want to give him back.'

'Inspector Hunter, what are your boys doing about the situation at present?' Julian asked brusquely.

'We've put both of them on our missing person's file and the photographs Mrs Millar gave us have been sent out to every force in the country.'

'Well, that will really help.' Julian sniffed. 'For God's sake, hundreds of people go missing every day and the computers are swamped with pictures of missing persons. But we're talking abduction here, by a father who is mentally unstable and physically aggressive. We have no idea what he could do to that boy.' Julian squeezed Angelina's hand. 'Sorry, darling, but it has to be said.'

Jazz ignored Julian and turned her gaze to Angelina. 'Do you think your ex-husband is an aggressive man, capable of harming Rory?'

She looked at Jazz through agonised eyes. 'No,' she said finally. 'David may have a drink problem, but he adores his son, almost to the point of obsession.'

'You think he is obsessed with Rory?' Jazz pressed.

'No, sorry, I mean...he loves Rory to bits, like any normal father, and when we separated, it must have been very hard for him. It's my fault really. I should have realised how desperate he was.'

'Mrs Millar, did you know anything about Rory being bullied at school?'

Angelina looked up with her china blue eyes. 'No, nothing. At least, Rory didn't say anything to me.'

'And bullying goes on in every school, Angelina,' said Julian. 'It certainly did when I was at St Stephen's. You have to learn to live with it, not go crying to one's parents. Toughens you up for the future.'

'I'm glad to say that most schools these days wouldn't agree with you, Mr Forbes,' Jazz replied coldly, irritated at his insensitivity. 'It's their top priority and I'm sure the staff at St Stephen's are as aware of it as any other.'

'Oh, I'm sure. All I'm saying is that it's impossible to stamp it out completely. Boys will be boys.' Julian patted Angelina's hand. 'Rory almost certainly wouldn't have said anything to you, darling, so don't feel guilty that you didn't know.'

'But David might have known. That's why he came here last week, because he'd had a strange telephone call from Rory. He wanted to talk to me because he was concerned about him and...'

'I booted him out,' Julian said. 'He was very drunk, and I'm afraid I wasn't having him in my house. The next time I saw him, he stood in the middle of Foltesham and told me he'd kill me.'

'Darling, that's not quite right. He said he'd kill you if you ever touched a hair on Rory's head. He'd just found out about us. You can hardly blame him.'

'For goodness' sake, Angelina, you and David are divorced. It's no business of his any more what you do or who you choose to be with,' Julian snapped irritably.

'Mrs Millar, I was told today by Sebastian Frederiks that your son was being bullied by Charlie Cavendish, the boy that died. Have you ever heard Rory mention his name?' asked Jazz.

'No, never. Why hadn't Mr Frederiks told me? I'm Rory's mother!'

'I don't know,' said Jazz, not wishing to be drawn on Frederiks's reasoning. 'So, you had no idea your son had a problem at school?'

'Oh dear.' Angelina wrung her hands. 'He'd become so withdrawn lately. I'd put it down to the divorce. Poor Rory. Why on earth didn't he say something to me?'

'I'm afraid children often don't. Besides, you are entrusting your child to the care of what you expect will be responsible adults who will act *in loco parentis* and take appropriate action if necessary.'

'Absolutely,' agreed Julian. 'If anyone's to blame in this, it's the school.'

'But I'm his mother. I should have seen. David knew something was wrong. That's why he came here.' Angelina looked up at Julian, whose face was impassive.

Jazz decided to cut to the chase. 'Your ex-husband was seen by Mr

Frederiks on the night Charlie Cavendish died. He was parking his car in the school car park. There was a choir concert at the school chapel, which I believe your son was in. Did you yourself attend?'

'Yes, I did.'

'And did you see your ex-husband there?'

'No, I didn't. But the night David came to the house, he told me he'd been at the school looking for Rory.' She sighed heavily. 'This all seems completely surreal. Inspector, David was on the wagon up until a few days ago. He hadn't drunk in months and I know he was attending his AA meetings, because I'm friends with the wife of his GP. She has a child in Rory's year.'

'Darling, you've really no idea what David was doing. You've hardly seen him in the past few months and I don't think you are in a position to comment on his recent drinking habits. He was certainly legless when he came here.' Angelina didn't reply.

Julian addressed Jazz. 'So, Inspector, are you trying to suggest that David Millar had somehow found out Rory was being bullied by Charlie Cavendish and decided to take the law into his own hands?'

Jazz stared at him through cool amber eyes. 'Circumstances would suggest we can't rule it out as a possibility.'

'David? Kill someone?' Angelina had found her voice at last. She shook her head as if to clear it. 'This is ridiculous! He might have had a drink problem and been very upset because he lost his job, then his marriage and daily contact with his son, but that does not mean to say he's a murderer! Inspector Hunter, please, David's a gentle man, not a killer!'

'Darling.' Julian took Angelina's hands and faced her. 'Please, be honest with yourself. I can accept that when he's sober, David is a gentle man, but come on, look at what happened the night he lost his job? Not to mention the next morning when he was ranting and raving outside the house and breaking windows to gain access.' Julian turned to Jazz. 'I'm afraid Angelina had to issue a restraining order against her ex-husband a few months ago. He behaved violently towards her, and she was very frightened, weren't you?'

Angelina put her hand to her temple. 'But surely, *they* were extenuating circumstances?'

'Yes, I agree,' Julian soothed. 'The problem is, that the situation Inspector Hunter is discussing also indicates extenuating circumstances. You've already said how David was almost obsessively protective of

Rory. And realistically, it is possible that, with a bellyful of booze inside him, David may well have been capable of wanting this Charlie out of the way.'

Angelina stared at Julian in incredulity. 'I just can't believe...*no*!' She shook her head.

'Mrs Millar.' Jazz decided to break into what was becoming a two-way conversation with Julian in control. 'I know that this is a very difficult time and I'm sorry for exacerbating it. But I do think we will have to step up our search for Rory and your ex-husband. Have you any idea where David might have taken your son? Any special place that he had either visited or was planning to?'

'I know he was hoping to take Rory away for the half-term holiday and was cross when I said I wanted to take him skiing instead, but I didn't ask where, I'm afraid.'

'Was he fond of any particular part of the country? Anywhere he may have gone as a child?'

'He liked climbing a lot, I know that. He used to go with his father all over the place: Wales, Scotland, the Lakes... He always said he'd take Rory when he was old enough.' Angelina shrugged.

'What about his parents?'

'His father died some years ago, and his mother quite recently,' Angelina explained.

'Any close friends? Brothers or sisters he'd go to?'

'David was an only child. And no, he didn't really have any close friends. He was always a bit of a loner.'

'Besides,' Julian interjected, 'he'd realise friends and family would be the first place the police would look.'

'Mr Forbes, you're assuming David has actually run away with Rory. It may be he felt, quite understandably, that both of them needed some time together and he's every intention of returning soon.' Jazz turned to Angelina. 'Right, I think that's as much as I need to know for now.' She closed her notebook and stowed it in her briefcase. 'I'll let you know as soon as there's any news.'

Angelina nodded slowly. 'I just want my son back. You don't think he's in danger, do you, Inspector?'

'He's with his father, who, from everything you've told me, obviously adores him.' Jazz stood up. 'I'll have one of my officers call you when they've sorted out the tracers on your telephones. Don't get up. I'll see myself out.' She nodded a goodbye and left the room.

Miles was waiting for her in the car outside.

'Anything interesting?' he asked as he started the engine.

Jazz stared out of the window. 'We have a possible suspect. An emotionally unstable alcoholic, with a son whom he may well know has been bullied by our victim. And yet...'

'Yes?'

'It just doesn't feel right. I've met David Millar, albeit briefly. He was in a very distressed state. And actually, *because* he was very, very drunk at the time, I find it hard to believe he could conceive and carry out a premeditated murder.'

'Would he have known Charlie Cavendish was allergic to aspirin anyway?' asked Miles.

'Rory could have told him. It certainly wasn't a secret.' As Miles drove towards Foltesham, Jazz switched her mobile on to check for messages.

'That was Norton, wanting to know when we're announcing Hugh Daneman's death to the press. Any longer and it really will start to look suspicious.'

'In a wider context, it's not so unusual to hear of a lifelong schoolmaster topping himself when he's faced with retirement,' reasoned Miles.

'*Goodbye Mr Chips* and all that,' mused Jazz. 'I cried buckets watching that film.'

'Did you, Ma'am?' He stared at her. 'Find that hard to imagine.'

'Because I'm a hard-bitten, female copper without a heart, you mean?' Jazz raised an eyebrow and keyed in Norton's number on her mobile. 'Cheers.'

'Sorry, Ma'am.' Miles blushed. 'I suppose I just think of you as...one of the blokes, really. And blokes wouldn't cry at that kind of thing.' He swiftly changed the subject, knowing he was digging himself into a hole. 'By the way, I've spoken to Daneman's solicitor and yes, his practice does hold Hugh's will. He's going to contact the beneficiaries immediately, in line with procedure, and once he's done that, he'll release the details to us.'

'Good. First priority is to find Millar and his son. Hello, Sir, DI Hunter here. Do you have a moment to run through a few things?'

The weather had been fine as David and Rory had arrived at the of the Pike, having made a quick pit stop at a local shop to kit themselves out with boots and waterproofs. David paid by cash, knowing that if they were looking for him, they'd be checking his credit cards to see where he'd used them.

He hadn't thought yet about when he would return. He was seizing the moment, enjoying the fact that Rory had woken earlier with colour in his cheeks, knocked back a hearty breakfast and was now standing next to him, eyes shining with anticipation, as he looked up at the great mountain, the summit shrouded in a veil of cloud.

'Are we really going to make it right up to the top, Dad?'

'I should hope so, as long as the weather holds. Come on, let's get a move on.' David heaved the small rucksack onto Rory's shoulders and the larger one onto his own. 'It's half past ten already.'

They followed the other hardy souls through the stile, their feet crunching on pieces of flint, trying to avoid the hard sheep dung that littered the coarse grass.

'The slope's quite gentle to begin with, then towards the top it becomes far steeper. My goodness, it's worth it when you get there,' David said, beginning to stride out. 'We'll take it steadily, Rory, don't want you overdoing it after being sick.'

'Honestly, Dad, I'm much better today. I feel fine.'

'That's my boy.' David smiled and ruffled Rory's curls affectionately.

They walked in silence for the most part. Perhaps it was the fresh air, and the sight of his son beside him, but David's head felt clear for the first time in months. He felt some positive energy starting to trickle back into his veins. He hadn't touched alcohol for over twenty-four hours, his son still loved him and even though his marriage was over and his career may have stalled, surely he was still young enough to start again?

'Let's stop here and have a drink and a breather,' David said, indicating a small ledge with a wonderful view of the valley below. He helped his son off with his rucksack and they sat down side by side, swigging water from a bottle.

'See how far we've come already?'

'Yes.' Rory nodded. 'I feel safe up here, away from everything.'

David looked at his son, saw the fear in his eyes. 'Rory, when you called me on the payphone from school that day, you said you were scared of something. What was it?'

Rory shook his head. 'Nothing, Dad, really.'

'Rory, it's obvious something has upset you. I'm your father and you know you can tell me anything, however grim. Is it me and Mummy getting divorced?'

Rory didn't answer. He looked straight ahead.

'I know how hard it's been for you and I've been a bad father recently. But I promise you, I'm much better now and even if I can't be at home like I used to, I'm always going to be there for you.'

'Dad, it's not that.' Rory spoke wearily. 'It has been awful not having you at home, but...' he sighed, 'this is something a thousand times worse.'

'What? Worse than not being able to see your old dad every day?' David tried to lighten the atmosphere.

Rory tore silently at the grass around his feet.

David watched him, before finally saying, 'Come on then, old chap, spit it out. You've started so you'd better finish.'

Rory looked for a long time into the distance. He sighed deeply, then turned to his father.

'The thing is, Dad...shit! Can I whisper?'

'Don't think anyone's going to hear up here, but yes, if it makes you feel better.'

'Okay.' Rory took a deep breath, leaned towards his father and spoke quietly into his ear.

Chapter Sixteen

Jenny Colman had spent a sleepless night since the telephone call, but she knew she had to face her. Twenty-five years was a long time, so much water under the bridge. They said you could never escape from the past and this proved that you never could.

What with Charlie Cavendish being found dead, then the shock of Hugh dying, and now a face from the past reappearing, Jenny was feeling very vulnerable. It didn't help that Mr Jones, whom she'd adored from afar for years, looked as if he was about to have a nervous breakdown too.

At least that pretty lady inspector, who, with her lovely long, red-gold hair, reminded Jenny of a young Rita Hayworth, seemed to think, from what Mr Jones had said, that there was no foul play involved. Not that Jenny had ever expected anything else. Who would want to hurt Hugh? He'd never harm a fly, and what he had done for her when she was in trouble, well... Jenny would never forget his kindness and support in her moment of need.

Jenny had left work on time, stopped at the Spar to buy a bottle of wine, then rushed home to put the shepherd's pie in the oven. She'd decided it was best if they met in her bungalow. She knew she'd feel safer on her own territory.

It was sad, she thought, as she bustled around the kitchen, pulling out the table to accommodate the two of them and covering it with a patterned vinyl tablecloth, that she was frightened at the thought of having supper with the person who'd been her closest childhood friend.

She didn't know what to expect. Who Maddy *was* now.

So much had happened back then. And dredging up the past was never a good idea. Jenny had coped by tucking it safely away...for most of the time, anyway.

She went into her bedroom to powder her nose and apply a little lipstick. The doorbell rang and Jenny jumped. She took a deep, calming breath and walked to the front door.

The visitor stood there with a bottle of wine in her hand.

'Hello, Jen.' She smiled and offered her the bottle.

'Hello, Maddy. Come in.'

'What a nice little place you've got for yourself,' she said as Jenny ushered her into the tiny sitting room.

'Took a lot of saving to get it. Can I take your coat?'

'Thank you.' Madelaine took off her coat and Jenny hung it on a hook in the hall. 'Bet you were surprised to see me turning up as Matron at the school, weren't you?' She smiled at Jenny.

'I was gobsmacked, as the girls and boys all say,' said Jenny. 'And of course, I'd been off all last term, having my hip sorted. I've only been back at work since the beginning of this term so I hadn't seen you. Can't believe that's only a couple of weeks ago, can you? Seems like much longer, what with everything that's happened at the school.' Jenny knew she was gabbling nervously. 'Shall we have a drink?'

'I think we should. That wine is chilled. Shall I open it for you?'

'I can do it.' Jenny went to her drinks trolley and reached for the corkscrew and two glasses, hoping she'd start to feel less awkward once she'd had a drink. She opened the bottle, poured some wine out and handed a glass to Maddy.

'Cheers!' Madelaine reached out her glass to clink it against Jenny's. 'Here's to old friends.'

'Getting older by the day.' Jenny smiled, taking a large gulp.

'I bet you wondered what had happened to me,' said Madelaine.

'I did. To be honest, as the years went on, and I didn't hear from you, I thought you might be dead.'

'Charmed, I'm sure!' Madelaine raised her eyebrows. 'But you understand why I needed a clean break? After what happened...well, let's just say it took me a long time to get over it.'

'I'm not surprised. What happened was terrible, Maddy, terrible.' Jenny shuddered involuntarily. 'And are you? Over it, I mean?'

'No, but I also understand now that I never will be.' She shrugged. 'And somehow, that makes it better. Acceptance is the key. When I left Norfolk I was in a terrible state.'

'I remember,' Jenny said sombrely. 'When you upped and went, without even saying goodbye, I didn't know what to think.'

'I blamed myself, you see. I should have known how bad it was. I was *there* and I didn't stop it…' Madelaine stared off into the distance.

'No one knew how bad things were. How could you? It was one of them things that just got out of hand. So, where did you go when you left?'

'To Australia. I had a cousin in Perth who offered me a place to stay for a while. It wasn't a good time. I had a breakdown and ended up in the psychiatric wing of the local hospital. I was there for nine months. I had electro-shock treatment, the lot.'

'Ooh, Maddy, how awful. I wish I'd have known. I could have written to you or something.'

'I wouldn't have wanted you to then. I couldn't face thinking about the past or anything to do with it. I tried to commit suicide twice and the second time, I nearly made it.' She pulled up her sleeve and Jenny gasped at the ugly red scars across her wrist.

'Anyway, that's all in the past.' Madelaine pulled her sleeve down. 'When I came out of hospital, I decided I'd take a medical course myself and train to be a nurse. I moved to Sydney and worked in a hospital there, then I went across to the States.'

'How exciting. I've never been further than Yarmouth, let alone out of the country. You sound different too. Can't hear the Norfolk in you any more, my *lurve*.' Jenny grinned.

'No.' Madelaine drained her glass. 'What happened certainly led to me broadening my horizons, that's for sure. Anyway, enough about me. What have you been doing with yourself for all these years?'

'Nothing much, compared to you. I've been plodding along at St Stephen's, got promoted when the new head arrived fourteen years ago. I love my job, I really do. And that school's been very good to me. Shall we move into the kitchen? I should put the peas on if we're to eat before midnight.'

Madelaine followed Jenny into the pin-neat kitchen. She watched as Jenny bustled round preparing supper and half listened as she chattered.

'So I'm only a couple of years away from retirement now, then I have to decide what to do. I thought I might like to travel, as I never have, and at least being at the school such a long time means I get a good pension.'

'Maybe we should take off together, be an OAP version of Thelma and Louise, leave a trail of destruction behind us,' laughed Madelaine.

'Well, we were a bit of a pair at school, weren't we?' Jenny giggled. 'Always in trouble, the terrible twosome.' She put two plates on the table and they both sat down to eat.

'Our mums used to despair, didn't they? I mean, we didn't exactly have action in the wilds of Norfolk, not like the young folk have these days, but we found it, didn't we?'

'We certainly did! Do you remember Tommy Springfield? We both fancied him and he didn't stand a chance, poor lad! Do you remember we both made a pact to see who would be the first one to kiss him?' Jenny's eyes sparkled at the memory.

'I do. And...you won!'

'I did! But then you kissed him the night after and he thought he was Mr Big!'

'Bless him, he was a sweet boy.' Madelaine helped herself to more wine and refilled Jenny's glass, too.

'We did give our mums and dads the runaround, didn't we? But it was all good, innocent fun. What were we? Fifteen, sixteen?'

'Must have been. I met Jed when we went to that barn dance in Gately when I was almost seventeen.' Madelaine smiled.

'Yes, and you weren't half as much fun after you fell in love,' Jenny chided. 'Oh dear, he had some ugly friends and you were always trying to set me up with them.' Jenny went to the fridge to pull out the bottle of wine she had bought earlier.

'Well, we'd always said we wanted to have a joint wedding and bring up our babies next door to each other.' Madelaine sighed.

'It never really happened like that, did it?'

'No. Well, it all happened but in the wrong order.'

Jenny eyed her friend over her wine glass. 'Would you have married Jed if you hadn't got pregnant?'

Madelaine took another slug of her own wine and shrugged. 'Who knows? But I did, didn't I? Anyway, I hardly had to put up with him for very long. Shotgun wedding, then a shotgun through his groin the month after the baby was born.' She shook her head.

'And you never did get much compensation from the estate, did you?'

'A few hundred pounds. Enough for a good education.' Madelaine looked straight at Jenny and let out a hoarse laugh. 'Ironic really, isn't it?'

'I suppose it is, yes. Oh dear, it's all such a long time ago now.'

'I was only eighteen,' Madelaine mused. 'I can hardly remember what Jed looked like, or how I felt about him. I certainly didn't put him on a pedestal after he died, like some people I know.'

Jenny nodded ruefully as the comment hit home. 'I know.'

Madelaine leaned forward and patted her hand. 'You've never got over him, have you?'

Tears came spontaneously to Jenny's eyes. She wasn't used either to drink, or sympathy. 'No.'

'After all these years. Is he why you've never married?'

Jenny wiped her nose with the back of her hand. 'Maybe that, and…well, the right fellow never seems to have appeared. Apple pie?'

After pudding, they took their coffees into the sitting room. Jenny lit the gas fire, as the heating had gone off earlier. Relaxed now, they sat contemplatively together, both enjoying the familiarity of old friends.

'Do you ever go back to see the estate?' Madelaine asked finally.

'Never. My mum died ten years ago now and none of my brothers and sisters stayed. They're scattered across the country. I see my eldest sister at Christmas, but all her kids are gone now and have families of their own.' Jenny sighed. 'We're getting so old, Maddy.'

'I know. So much water under the bridge…'

'Anyway,' Jenny broke the moment, 'have you decided how long you'll stay at St Stephen's?'

'Until the matron I'm covering for returns from her maternity leave, if she does.'

'Don't you find it difficult, working there?' Jenny asked softly. 'It must bring back some memories.'

'Of course it does, but in a strange way, I find it comforting.' Madelaine smiled. 'I've been to visit him a few times.'

'Oh.' Jenny nodded, not knowing what else to say.

'Anyway'—Madelaine looked at her watch—'it's nearly eleven. I'd better be on my way. Up at six tomorrow, sorting out the boys.'

'They're a good bunch of kids, though, aren't they?' Jenny smiled. 'I always say, St Stephen's turns out polite, well-adjusted children.'

'Well, there's always a few bad apples in any school,' Maddy replied bleakly.

'Charlie Cavendish, you mean? He was in your house, wasn't he? You must have been interviewed by that Inspector Hunter. Did you tell her what a nasty piece of work he was?'

'Rest assured, I told her *exactly* what I thought of him.' Madelaine stood up and walked to the rack in the hall to pull down her coat. 'And now, of course, we have Rory Millar missing. Not surprised he's run away, with all the problems at school, and at home. His dad might be a drunk, but at least he isn't a bully. Poor little mite.'

'It's hard for single mothers, though, Maddy. You know that yourself. And Mrs Millar is devoted to Rory.'

'If she's so devoted, she should put her son first and be careful whom she chooses as a boyfriend.' Madelaine sniffed. 'Anyway, thank you for a lovely evening. Shall we do this again next week? Maybe go out for a meal in town? Or perhaps I could drive us to the Royal in Cromer?'

'Ooh my goodness, I've not been there for years. Since Harry Gurney took me. Remember him? He was a terrible kisser.' Jenny giggled in delight.

'I'm off next Tuesday night,' said Madelaine. 'Shall we go then?'

'I'd love to do that. Shall I see what's on?'

'Yes. I'll see you in the canteen in the meantime.' Madelaine hugged her old friend. 'It was worth coming back just to see you.'

'I'm so glad you did. I've worried about you for all these years, when I didn't hear from you. Seeing you in the hall that day was like seeing a ghost.'

Madelaine took Jenny's hands in hers. 'I'm real, I promise. Bye, Jen, probably see you at school tomorrow.'

Jenny shut the door and went into the kitchen to clear up from supper. Her heart was light with happiness at the return of her old friend. She finished the washing-up and secreted everything neatly in its rightful place. She made herself her usual hot chocolate, went to the bathroom, then climbed into bed. She sipped her hot chocolate thoughtfully.

Two simple country girls, and yet they'd both been through so much.

She'd wanted so badly to tell Maddy about Hugh's death, but she knew Mr Jones had entrusted her with a secret and she must keep it until it was public knowledge.

Poor, poor Hugh… Tears pricked the back of her eyes. She would miss him so much.

But then…what God took away, he also gave…

And perhaps Maddy had been sent back to her just at the right moment.

Thora Birtwhistle was worried. It was half past nine in the evening and the young lad and his father had still not returned to her bed and breakfast. She wouldn't normally worry about her guests staying out; a lot of them went for something to eat in town. But Mr Millar had made a point of saying before he left they'd definitely be back for supper. She'd told him she would have it ready for eight.

Now, the steak and kidney pudding was beginning to solidify in its own fat on the worktop in the kitchen and the vegetables sat, grey and soggy, in the saucepan.

Thora glanced out of the window and saw the rain battering against the pane. If it was bad down here, she knew only too well what it would be like up in the mountains. The two of them could have been caught in a squall, and the rain might well have turned to snow near the top.

These townies seemed to have no sense of the real danger that lay out there, hundreds of metres above sea level, especially in deep winter, when the weather could turn in an instant.

Thora had lost her husband, a Pennine man born and bred, on a night such as this, many years ago.

She sighed, wondering what to do. She knew they'd been headed for the Pike—she'd overheard the lad mention it at breakfast. He was only a shrimp of a thing, too, going off in his thin sweater.

Thora decided if they weren't back by eleven, she'd have to call mountain rescue and alert them.

Jazz had brought her computer and her paperwork home halfway through the afternoon. The school room was claustrophobic with three of them in it. Roland was still complaining of the pain of his missing tooth, and despite her best efforts, the man irritated the hell out of her.

When she arrived home, she realised that the scenario was going to be little better, as the plumber was upstairs installing the central heating system. Jazz shut all the doors, plugged in her computer into the one antiquated socket and tried to ignore the crashing and banging and the out of tune whistling from overhead.

Finally, she threw on her Barbour and wellies and went for a stomp across the marshes to clear her head. The sky was darkening and in the dusk the sea formed a grey uninviting eiderdown in front of her, menacingly encroaching on the land. Jazz shivered and retraced her steps home.

By the time she arrived, the plumber had gone and, despite the cold, she felt calmer. Making herself a cup of tea and lighting the fire, she took her case notes out of her briefcase.

She studied the drug sheet for the day of Charlie's death. Looking closer, she saw a word had been Tippexed out and written over.

10.45 Two paracetamol issued to Rory Millar.

There was a scribbled signature, which was illegible whichever way Jazz looked at it.

Rory Millar, again.

And what had been originally written under the word 'paracetamol'?

Jazz stared at it, scratched at it, turned the sheet over, but could not decipher the hidden script. She put it in an envelope to send to forensics. They'd have the Tippex off in a few seconds.

A thought came to her: what if 'aspirin' had been the original word?

And if Rory Millar *had* been issued with the brand of pills known to have killed Charlie Cavendish, was it possible that he had been involved? Or that someone wished it to seem as though he was...? Or protect him...?

Her ringing mobile broke into her thoughts.

'Inspector Hunter,' she answered abruptly.

'Jazz? It's me, Jonathan. Is this a bad time?'

'Er, no, it's fine. Fine,' she repeated, irritated at her train of thought being interrupted.

'Shall I call back another time?'

'No, it's okay.' Now she felt guilty. 'Sorry, I've been up to my eyes all day.'

'No problem. I'll make it brief. I was just wondering whether we could meet up either tomorrow or Wednesday? I've just got a few more questions I need to ask you. I'm running out of time to complete this damned thesis, so I thought I'd drive up to Norfolk. I know you're too busy to come here at present.'

'Right.' Her mind was still pondering the drug sheet.

'Well?'

'Well what?'

'Would you be able to? Meet up, that is? So I can pick your brains a little further?'

'Er...yes. I'm afraid you can't come here, though, as I've got the plumber putting in the central heating and the place is a tip. In fact, I'm half thinking of moving out myself.'

'Okay, you suggest somewhere. A pub maybe?'

'There's a good one on the coast in Cley called the Coach and Horses, which isn't too far from you. We could meet there.'

'Okay. Could you make tomorrow?'

'At the moment, yes. But I should warn you that I'm slap bang in the middle of a murder case at the moment and things are hotting up, so if something breaks, then...'

'I understand, but let's cross our fingers it won't and I'll see you tomorrow. At eight?'

'Yes, fine.'

'Thanks, Jazz, I really appreciate it.'

'Sure. See you then. Bye.' She ended the call, then sank back onto the sofa and let out a long sigh.

It was almost ten years since she had been in a position to enjoy any attention from men. When she'd been in Italy, she'd noticed the odd admiring glance, but she'd been closed, unresponsive to it.

She wandered into the kitchen to pour herself a glass of wine, then sat cross-legged in front of the fire, trying to stem the chill that still ran through her bones from the earlier walk.

As Jazz stared into the flames, she remembered what her mother had said about not becoming bitter. It was a tough call, after what had happened to her. How could she learn to trust again?

The truth was, she had trusted Patrick completely, absolutely. And worse, she had loved him.

What scared her now was that she *still* loved him. Even after what he had done to her, humiliating her in the worst possible way, after she had spent weeks and months telling her eminently logical self what a lowlife bastard he was, she still found herself waking in the night and reaching for him...

Maybe a distraction was the answer.

She found Jonathan attractive, and she was pretty sure he felt the same about her.

Would she sleep with him?

Jazz sipped her wine thoughtfully.

She had so many single, liberated girlfriends who didn't think twice about jumping into bed with a man they found attractive. There was no complexity, no thought of the future, just a few hours of mutually enjoyable pleasure.

But...even before Patrick, it had never been like that for her. However hard she'd tried, she'd found it impossible to separate sex from emotional commitment. Which meant, even though there had been no shortage of boyfriends, the number of *lovers* she'd had was a low, single figure.

Perhaps now, she had to grow up, take control, put what she knew were her deeply felt feelings to one side. If she wanted to sleep with Jonathan, or any other man she found attractive, why the hell shouldn't she?

Jazz shook her head. It was who she was. And it was doubtful she'd ever change.

Jazz smiled as she went into the kitchen to make herself a bowl of pasta. Maybe Miles was spot on with his Miss Marple analogy. Perhaps she was destined to be an old maid, solving crimes, but steering clear of emotional involvement.

She put Chopin on the CD player and ran over her notes and her schedule for tomorrow.

It was nearly midnight when her mobile rang.

'Norton here, Hunter. Your David Millar has just turned up with his son at a police station in Windermere. And he's confessed to the murder of Charlie Cavendish.'

Chapter Seventeen

When Jazz arrived at Foltesham police station at eight o'clock the next morning, David Millar was already waiting for her in the interview room.

'Hello, Mr Millar, we have met once before at St Stephen's.' She nodded at him as she sat down and removed her laptop from its case.

'Have we?' David Millar shook his head. 'I'm sorry, but I'm afraid I don't remember. I was probably drunk at the time.' He shrugged sadly.

'Mr Millar, you are entitled to have a solicitor present during this interview. And I would advise it.'

He shrugged again. 'What on earth for? I've already admitted to the crime.'

'All right.' Jazz pressed the start button on the tape recorder. 'Eight nineteen a.m. DI Hunter interviewing David Millar. He has declined to have a solicitor present. Mr Millar has already confessed to the murder of Charlie Cavendish on Friday the fifteenth of January, and I am conducting his first interview. All right, Mr Millar? Anything you want to say before we begin?'

David shook his head wearily.

'Mr Millar, last night you informed an officer in Windermere police station that on the night of Friday the fifteenth of January, you murdered Charlie Cavendish. Do you still stand by your admission?'

David Millar nodded. 'I do.'

'What I would like you to do now, Mr Millar, is run through exactly what happened that evening.'

'I'll do my best, but obviously, I was drunk at the time, so some of the details might be sketchy.'

'Take your time, Mr Millar,' Jazz nodded. She was far more used to interrogating a suspect with a view to obtaining a confession, rather than hearing the details of a crime retrospectively.

'Well, I knew my son Rory was being bullied by this boy at school,

Charlie Cavendish.'

'And who had told you this?'

'Well, Rory, of course.'

'Had anyone else mentioned the situation to you? For example, Sebastian Frederiks, Rory's housemaster?'

'He certainly alluded to the fact Rory was unhappy. Apparently, Rory got locked in the cellar overnight by this Charlie.'

'Really? Mr Frederiks told you it was Charlie, did he?'

'No. Rory told me.'

'I see. How could Rory have known for sure, Mr Millar? He was on the other side of the door at the time.'

'Look, Rory told me this Cavendish boy was making his life hell. That was all I needed to know. Okay, Inspector?'

'So, when did Rory confess to you that Charlie was bullying him?'

'I can't remember exactly, to be honest. Probably the day before I...killed Charlie.'

'Thursday the fourteenth of January,' Jazz said into the recorder. 'And this was on the school payphone?'

'Yes. And after his call, I got very drunk, to be honest. The next day, I tried to speak to Mr Frederiks, and the head, but no one would answer my calls. So I got in the car and drove to the school. I had to speak to someone. I didn't want another night going by with Rory being at risk.'

'What time was that?'

'Not sure.' David shook his head. 'But it was the evening.'

'So, when you drove to the school, was it with the intention of murdering Charlie Cavendish?'

'I was certainly mad enough to kill him, Inspector, but to be honest, I didn't have any fixed plan in my mind. When I got to Fleat, I was told by Mr Daneman that Sebastian Frederiks was out. And I couldn't see Rory because he was in a choir concert in chapel.'

'Can you try and remember what time you arrived at the school, Mr Millar? Approximately?'

'Around half past seven?' David shrugged. 'I remember the car park was packed and there were a lot of people heading towards the chapel.'

'Right, so, what did you do then?'

'Mr Daneman suggested I come back another time, but then he got caught up with a telephone call so...' David scratched his head. 'I decided to try and find this Cavendish fellow myself and give him a piece of my mind.'

'And did you see him?'

'No, I didn't. I went upstairs to the sixth-form corridor and found his room, but he wasn't there.'

'So what did you do next?'

'I hung around for a bit to see if Charlie might come back, but he didn't.'

'Mr Millar, did anyone else see you whilst you were in Fleat House? Either arriving or whilst you were searching for Charlie's room?' Jazz asked.

'Yes. I told you, Mr Daneman,' said David. 'Ask him, he'll confirm it.'

'Anyone else?'

'No. I think I passed a couple of boys on the stairs but I couldn't tell you who they were.'

'Surely, at around seven thirty on a Friday night, the lobby would have been a hive of activity? All the boys either coming in or out? Someone must have seen you.'

'Perhaps, yes. You could ask them.'

Jazz sighed, thinking it was unusual to hear a suspect actively searching for a witness to confirm his presence at a murder scene. 'So, Mr Millar, what did you do next?'

'I sat in Cavendish's room for a while, but when he didn't show, I realised he'd probably gone out for the night. I knew it was pointless hanging around. Then I saw the tablets by his bed and had an idea. I remembered what Rory had told me about Cavendish's allergy to aspirin. Being the drunk that I am, I always have some painkillers on me to help the headaches. It's a common myth that alcoholics don't get hangovers. Let me tell you, Inspector Hunter, they do. I pulled out the packet from my jacket, to see what they were. I usually grab the cheapest thing off the shelves, whether it be paracetamol, aspirin or ibuprofen. I'm not fussy.' David smiled sadly. 'Anyway, as luck—or should I qualify, luck for me—should have it, my current painkiller was aspirin.'

Jazz said nothing, waiting for him to continue.

'I took a couple of them out of the packet, put them next to Charlie's tablets and saw they were quite similar. So I decided to swap them over.'

'Were you aware that they would kill him, Mr Millar?'

'No, of course not! I had no idea how bad his allergy was. Just the thought of making him suffer for a few hours the way he'd made Rory suffer was enough for me. And to be honest, Inspector, I don't think I was sober enough to think it through logically. It was a spur of the moment thing. So I swapped the tablets and left.'

Jazz tapped her pen on the table. 'To go where?'

'Home, of course. I had some more to drink and slept where I fell. I woke up the next morning and remembered what I had done.'

'How did you feel?'

'Bloody awful, obviously. I realised that whatever Charlie Cavendish had done to Rory, that was no excuse for putting his life at risk. I drank some more to dull the pain, hoping against hope that at the very worst, Charlie had spent an uncomfortable night at the hospital having his stomach pumped.'

'When did you hear what had happened to him?'

'Rory must have called me sometime that afternoon to tell me Cavendish was dead.' David looked down at his hands. 'I can't remember any more of that day, to be honest.'

'And how did you feel when you realised you'd killed him?'

'Devastated. I couldn't believe I'd done such a stupid thing. I might be a drunk, but I'm not a murderer.'

'No one is until they commit the crime, Mr Millar,' Jazz said coldly. 'So, what were you doing in the headmaster's office a few days later when I saw you?'

David looked surprised she had to ask. 'I wanted to see Rory, of course. I still hadn't managed to see him.'

'I'm amazed you wanted to be anywhere near the school when you knew you'd murdered one of their pupils, Mr Millar.'

'I didn't think of it like that. I just wanted to see my son.'

'So, when did you decide you should confess?'

'Well, I've only sobered up in the past few days, whilst I was up in the Lakes with Rory. And it made me see what I needed to do. I couldn't live with the guilt. I needed to give myself up, whatever the consequences.'

'Why did you take Rory from school and disappear with him?'

'Hold on!' For the first time since the interview began, David seemed defensive. 'For a start off, I didn't "take" Rory. He turned up on my doorstep on Sunday. He wasn't feeling very well, I knew I had something to tell him, so I decided we should have a few days away so I could explain things to him. Besides,' David shrugged, 'I knew if I was going to confess, it was unlikely I'd be seeing him very much over the next few years. And I texted Angie when I arrived to let her know we were both fine.'

'Terminating the interview with Mr David Millar at eight forty-five a.m.' Jazz switched off the recorder. She rested her head on her palms and stared at David for a while.

'Mr Millar, I would like you to go back downstairs and try and think hard about the events of that night. I would also like you to think very carefully about why you've decided to confess to the murder of Charlie Cavendish.'

'I've told you, I can't live with the guilt. Isn't that enough?'

'A jury has still got to find you guilty in a court of law, Mr Millar,' Jazz reminded him.

'Well, surely if I've said I did it, that won't take long, will it?'

'The facts will still have to be put to them and you will have a defence lawyer. At the very least, a good counsel might lead to the lessening of your sentence.' Jazz pressed a buzzer and a constable appeared in the doorway. 'Could you take Mr Millar back down, please?' She stood up. 'I'll be back with you later.'

Jazz watched the door close, then rewound the tape and listened to the interview again. Then she picked up the receiver and dialled Angelina Millar's number.

Unable to sleep the night before, clockwatching as the hours ticked past slowly until four a.m., when she'd been told she could go and collect Rory from Foltesham police station, Angelina had left Julian asleep, had a bath, then paced the floors downstairs until it was time to make the short journey to retrieve her son.

There'd been an emotional reunion, after which she'd driven Rory home, tucked him up in bed, and lain next to him until he slept, stroking his soft blond curls with her fingers.

Rory was safe now, but it was the other news Inspector Hunter had imparted which had left her heart still racing.

At seven, she'd crept downstairs to make Julian a cup of coffee.

She placed it on his bedside table and gently shook him awake.

His eyes opened sleepily and she leaned forward to kiss him.

'Morning, darl—'

Angelina put a finger to his lips. 'Hush. Rory's here.'

Julian sat up. 'They found him?'

'Yes. He was in the Lakes, and driven back by the police through the night. I collected him at four this morning.'

'Why didn't you wake me? I'd have driven you. Is he all right?'

'He seems fine physically. Very tired, obviously, and…would it be okay if you made yourself scarce before he wakes up and finds you here? I really don't want him upset any further, especially until I find out what happened whilst he was away.'

Julian sighed. 'And there was me thinking you'd brought me a coffee out of love. Instead of which, it's a precursor to kicking me out of my own home.'

'Hardly, Julian. For goodness' sake, these are extraordinary circumstances. Please don't make me feel guilty.'

'Sorry, but all this cloak and dagger stuff is getting somewhat wearing.'

'I know and I'm sorry. Once everything is back to normal, I'll tell him, but surely even you can see this is hardly the best moment to announce your presence in my life. And his,' she said firmly.

'Yes, even I, insensitive bugger that I am, can see that.' Julian reached for his coffee and sipped it morosely.

'Look, there's something else I should tell you.' Angelina took a deep breath. 'Inspector Hunter told me David has confessed to the murder of Charlie Cavendish.'

'What?' Julian almost choked on his coffee.

'I know.' Angelina put her fingers to her temples. 'I just can't believe it.'

'Hate to say I told you so…'

'Then don't!' Angelina stood up from the bed. 'Christ! I can't cope, I really can't! Just get up and go, will you?!'

Forty minutes later, Julian appeared in the kitchen, looking immaculate in his suit, briefcase in hand. He came and kissed Angelina on the cheek.

'Sorry, darling. I really am. I know what strain you've been under.'

Angelina pulled away from his proffered embrace. 'No, you don't,' she muttered.

'Okay, I don't. I've never had a child.'

'No, you haven't.'

Julian didn't rise to the bait. 'Are you sure you'll be all right?'

'I'll be fine.'

'Sure? You look very pale.'

'Yes, I've said so, haven't I?' she replied irritably. 'Inspector Hunter has just called. She's coming round mid-morning. She wants to speak to Rory.'

'Then I should stay.'

'No, don't be silly. I can cope now Rory's safe.' Angelina gave him the ghost of a smile and tweaked his tie. 'Besides, it'll give me a chance to explain to Rory who you are.'

'What about tonight? Am I banished to my flat or can I come home and sleep in my own bed?'

'I'll call you later.'

'All right.' He kissed her on the top of her head. 'Any problems, ring me. I'll keep my mobile on all day.'

'I'm fine. David is locked up in a cell, so you don't have to worry about him either.'

Julian walked towards the door, stopped and turned round. 'I nearly forgot. I've just had an email from my secretary. I have a client who can only see me at seven this evening, so whatever, I'm going to be late. Bye, darling, take care.'

He blew her a kiss, and left by the kitchen door.

At eleven, Angelina opened the door to Inspector Hunter.

'Come in,' she said wearily.

'Thank you.'

Angelina led Jazz into the sitting room and ushered her to a sofa.

'How's Rory this morning?' Jazz asked.

'He only woke up twenty minutes ago. I took him breakfast in bed and he's just having a bath. He's quiet, but he seems unharmed.'

'He hasn't said anything about his father confessing to the murder of Charlie Cavendish, then?'

'No, nothing. And I haven't pushed it. I was just glad to get him home. He's going to have to deal with all that soon enough.' Angelina shook her head. 'This is a nightmare. And I feel responsible. If only I hadn't left David, had stood by him, then maybe none of this would have happened.'

'You do what you think is best at the time, Mrs Millar. You weren't to know what would happen.'

'David losing his job wasn't my fault, or his drinking problem, but my behaviour… Anyway, what's done is done. All I can do now is try and help Rory through the best I can.'

'I need to see him, Mrs Millar. Before we can proceed against your ex-husband, there are a few questions that we need Rory to answer.'

'Does it have to be now? Poor lamb, he's been through so much.'

'I'm afraid so. I'll be gentle, don't worry.'

Angelina's shoulders sagged. 'I'll go and see if he's out of the bath.' She stood up and left the room.

When Rory Millar walked in, his mother's protective hands on his shoulders, Jazz was once more struck by the likeness to the young man in Hugh Daneman's photograph. Both of them had the same aesthetic, feminine looks; Rory was yet to reach the stage of puberty that would rob him for a few years of his cherubic beauty. His pale skin was unmarked by acne, his ice-blue eyes dominated his face and his girlish, cupid-bow lips were still untouched by the kiss of a woman. His hair hung in still-damp golden curls, reaching almost to his shoulders.

He was taller than she'd imagined, thin of frame and narrow of hip. She could see a little of David in him, but nothing of his mother.

'Rory, this is Inspector Hunter. She's come to ask you a few questions. She knows you're very tired, so I'm sure she'll keep this short.'

Jazz stood up, smiled and reached out her hand for Rory to shake. He took her hand in his and she felt the iciness of his palm against her skin.

'Hello, Rory. It's good to meet you at last.'

'Thank you.' Rory sat down on the sofa opposite her.

'Mrs Millar, you couldn't by any chance find me a cup of coffee, could you? It's been a long morning and I'm desperate.' Jazz wanted Rory alone, if only for a few minutes.

'How rude of me not to offer. Of course. Will you be all right, Rory?' Angelina asked anxiously.

'Yes, Mother, I'll be fine.

Rory's voice had not broken yet. It had a strange, reedy quality to it.

'So, Rory, all this must have been a bit of an adventure. Did you realise your mother would be frantic when you disappeared?'

'No. At the time I was only thinking of myself. I'm sorry for all the trouble I've caused.'

He spoke slowly, precisely, in a quaint, old-fashioned manner.

'Rory, you went voluntarily to your father's house on Sunday, didn't you? Your dad didn't come to the school and take you by force?'

'Oh no. I ran away. Poor old Dad. I've got him into terrible trouble. All we wanted to do was to go on a little holiday together. He was trying to do something nice for me.'

'So why did you run away from school, Rory?'

'Because I wanted to see my dad.'

'No other reason?'

'No.'

'Rory, you were there when your father handed himself over to the police in Windermere and said he killed Charlie Cavendish. Do you think he did?'

Rory shrugged. 'Why would he say he did if he didn't? He must have done, I suppose.'

'And can you think of any reason why your dad would want to kill Charlie?'

Rory shrugged again. 'Perhaps.'

'Was Charlie a bully?'

'Yes.'

'And did he bully you?'

'Yes, but Charlie bullies…I mean, bullied everyone.'

'Did you tell your dad on the telephone that Charlie locked you in the trunk cellar one night?'

Rory's eyes searched around the room. 'I might have done.'

'Surely you can remember whether you did or you didn't?'

'Yes, I did tell my dad I was locked in the cellar, but I didn't know it was Charlie who'd locked me in. How could I know? I just heard the key turn.'

Jazz knew she was running out of coffee-making time and had to cut to the chase. 'Rory, where were you the night that Charlie Cavendish died?'

'I had a choir concert in the chapel and then I came back to the house and had cocoa.'

'Was it Mr Daneman who made it for you? I know that Mr Frederiks was out that night.'

For the first time, an expression of fear crossed Rory's impassive face. His hands clenched. 'Yes.'

'And then you went straight to bed?'

'Yes.'

'And you didn't see Charlie that night, or go anywhere near his room?'

'No. Why should I?'

'Rory? Are you all right, darling?' Angelina was standing at the door with the coffee. 'You look very pale. The inspector isn't upsetting you, is she?'

'No, Mum, but I think I'm a bit tired. Is it all right if I go and lie down?'

Angelina set the coffee tray down on the table and put her arms round her son.

'Of course it is.' She glanced at Jazz. 'He's exhausted. Can you come back later when he's feeling better?'

'Of course.' Jazz smiled. 'Oh, just one more thing Rory: on the Friday that Charlie died, were you given some painkillers for a headache?'

Rory stopped and turned in the doorway. 'I can't remember. Perhaps. I get a lot of headaches, you see.'

'Well, in the medicine logbook, it says you were issued with some tablets on that day. What would they have been and who usually gave them to you?'

'I don't know what they were. Just painkillers.' Rory shrugged.

'Did Mr Daneman give them to you?'

Rory nodded. 'Yes. Can I go now, Mum?' He rested his head against her shoulder.

'Of course you can, darling.' Angelina turned to Jazz. 'That's enough now. He's exhausted. Rory, pop upstairs and Mummy will come up when she's seen the inspector out.'

Rory nodded and silently left the room.

'I'll be on my way. I'm sorry to tire Rory, but the sooner we can collate the facts, the better,' Jazz stood up. 'Thank you, Mrs Millar.'

She followed Angelina to the front door. Angelina paused for a second before steeling herself to ask: 'I don't really want to know, but how...did David say he killed this boy?'

'He substituted Charlie's epilepsy drugs for a couple of aspirin tablets he apparently had in his pocket for hangovers. You may have known Charlie was allergic to them. Obviously David did.'

'What?' Angelina looked confused. 'David had aspirin in his pocket?'

'That's what he told me, yes.'

She shook her head. 'But that's impossible.'

'Why?'

'David would never go anywhere near aspirin, Inspector, let alone have them in his pocket! No.' Angelina shook her head vehemently. 'That just doesn't make sense.'

'Why not, Mrs Millar?' asked Jazz quietly.

'Simply because David is fatally allergic to aspirin, too.'

Chapter Eighteen

Jazz headed back to Foltesham police station. Miles was in the interview room, listening to the tape of David Millar's interview.

'Any joy with the boy?' he asked.

Jazz sat down heavily. She shook her head. 'No, not really. Angelina is protecting her cub like a tiger mother, as she should, but...' Jazz looked up at Miles. 'Guess what?'

'What?'

'Mrs Millar has just told me her ex-husband is fatally allergic to aspirin.'

'Really?' Miles raised an eyebrow. 'Well, I've just listened to the tape, and I've never heard a more unconvincing confession than Millar's. It's almost as if he's trying anything to make it hang together.'

'Well, his entire modus operandi for that night has just gone down the plug.' Jazz sighed. 'Either, the crime was one hundred per cent premeditated—Mrs Millar stated categorically that her ex wouldn't touch aspirin—or Millar is lying through his backside to protect someone.'

'On the tape, Millar says himself this was not premeditated, that the idea of swapping the tablets just "came" to him,' Miles said. 'Besides, if he was as pissed as he says he was, I'd say he was surely much more likely to find Charlie, then punch his lights out.'

'Whatever,' sighed Jazz. 'His entire confession has just been exploded.'

'I was up at the school earlier and none of the boys remember seeing him upstairs on the sixth-form corridor. Sandwich?' Miles pulled a plastic bag onto the table. 'Egg and cress or a BLT, Ma'am?'

'Neither, thanks. I'm not hungry,' said Jazz. 'Apparently, Millar did say he spoke to Hugh Daneman that night.'

'That's useful then.' Miles bit into his BLT.

Jazz was still musing. 'So, the question is: why is he lying? We know how much David Millar adores his son…and we know it was Rory who sought out his father on Sunday. What if he confessed to Daddy some involvement with Charlie's death during their trip?'

Miles studied his sandwich. 'And Daddy decides he must take the rap. We've seen that one before.'

'And Rory was issued with two painkillers at nine that night. The drug sheet records they were paracetamol tablets, but something written beneath it had been Tippexed out. I'm waiting to hear from forensics to see what.'

Miles aimed the empty sandwich wrapper at the bin, and missed. 'So, if by any chance we were to find the word "aspirin" has been Tippexed out and replaced with the word "paracetamol", Rory not only had the motive, he had the wherewithal.'

Jazz paused. 'It's a pretty big thing to accuse a thirteen-year-old boy of murder.'

'Yep, and, if he was involved, it also means someone in the school knows it and Tippexed the offending word out to protect him.'

'Unless he did it himself,' Jazz said quietly.

'The drug sheet is kept inside the medicine cabinet, which is locked at all times. The only people with the key are Frederiks, Matron and, of course, Hugh Daneman on that particular evening.'

'Why on earth did he have to top himself?' Jazz sighed.

'Maybe he was involved in some way with what happened.' Miles shrugged. 'We know Rory's motive, but why would an adult, for example Hugh Daneman, try to protect him?'

'Unfortunately, this is all supposition until forensics get back to us. Christ! This case is moving slowly.' Jazz tapped her pen irritably on the table.

'That's the sticks for you, Ma'am.' Miles grinned. 'Do us both good. We'll get back to London and appreciate what we have there.'

'You might, Miles, I certainly won't,' Jazz replied sharply.

He swiftly changed the subject. 'So, what was your instinct on Rory when you met him?'

'I didn't have a chance to get a feeling in the time I had. He was holding back on me, but that could have been for many different reasons. I'd mark him down as "odd", I suppose, but then most teenage boys are strange. It doesn't mean they're killers.'

'No,' agreed Miles, 'but your gut usually kicks in and tells you if there's more to it.'

'Think my "gut" got chock-full of pasta in Italy and needs a serious workout before it starts functioning again.'

'You haven't put on an ounce, Ma'am. Really.'

'I wasn't commenting on my waistline, Miles.' Jazz sighed. 'There's something I'm not getting here. Somewhere along the line, I know Hugh Daneman's suicide was no coincidence. Anyway, I called Isabella earlier this morning. She's on her way here now to assess Millar and his son. If anyone can get through to them, she can.' Isabella Sherriff was one of the Met's leading criminal psychologists.

'Wow, Issy has actually agreed to leave the smoke and come up to the wilds of Norfolk?' Miles whistled. 'You are honoured.'

'We go back a long way. And besides, Millar is presently in custody for murder. It's right up her street. I've booked her into your hotel, so you can take her for dinner tonight. She'll see Millar today and Rory tomorrow morning.'

'How are you going to get that one past Mummy Tiger?' enquired Miles.

'We can't lie about who Issy is, but we can frame it the right way. Issy also has experience counselling kids who have suffered trauma. That's Rory for sure. He needs an assessment, and that's why she'll be speaking to Rory. If anything comes out that's pertinent to the case, I'll make it clear to Angie that Issy will have to share it. But I'll also make it clear that Issy is one of London's finest psychologists—I reckon Angie Millar is the type of person who likes a bit of fuss made.'

'Don't include that last bit, boss,' Miles joked. 'I'm going back to the school to see our demon headmaster. I'd like you to have a quick chat with David Millar yourself; don't mention we know about his allergy to aspirin for the present, then wait here for Issy to arrive and tell her before she interviews him. She said she'd be here by three.'

'Right you are, Ma'am. I presume you'll be joining us for dinner tonight?'

Jazz picked up her briefcase. 'No. You're on your own, Miles. Sure you can cope. I'll be back here at five to hear the rundown from Issy. See you later.'

Robert Jones visibly calmed as Jazz informed him of David Millar's confession.

'Well, isn't that good news? Rory returned unharmed and a man in custody for Cavendish's murder. Perhaps we can get back to some degree of normality now.'

'It's good news Rory's back home and unharmed, but I doubt very much this is the end of the story as far as Charlie Cavendish's death is concerned.'

'But he's confessed! Surely it's an open and shut case?'

'I'm afraid there are gaping holes in his confession. A good defence counsel would shoot it down in flames and we'd be back to square one.'

'I see.' Jones sighed. 'So, what happens now?'

'We continue our investigation. Mr Jones, I want to ask you something: why, when Matron had made it absolutely plain to you on a number of occasions that Charlie Cavendish was a bully, and a danger to those he targeted, did you refrain from expelling him?'

The headmaster sighed. 'Charlie covered his tracks carefully.' He shifted uncomfortably in his chair.

'Mr Jones, I have no experience of running a school, but I do run a team and it's always been pretty obvious to me if one of my staff is behaving badly to another. Cavendish's name must have cropped up time and time again. So, can you please tell me why you chose to ignore his behaviour?'

'His father is a well-known and important barrister, his uncle on the board of governors...' Robert Jones's voice tailed off. 'What could I do?'

'Put the welfare of the pupils in your care first, perhaps?' Jazz replied icily. 'It's not my job to judge your ability as headmaster, but if Mrs Millar decides to take things further on behalf of her son, which she is perfectly entitled to do, either to the media, or legally, both your and the school's reputation are going to be severely tarnished.'

'Yes.' Robert paused. 'It's a serious error of judgement on my part, I agree.'

Jazz looked at her watch. 'I also wanted to let you know we're releasing details of Hugh Daneman's death to the press today. I suggest you gather the school together and tell them before they read about it elsewhere. You'll be glad to hear the coroner has concluded it was a straightforward suicide. And, at present, there's nothing to link his death to Charlie Cavendish's. You can make that clear to your staff and pupils.

I have to get back to Foltesham station and, in fact, that's where we'll be running our investigation from now on. But Detective Sergeant Roland and a couple of his men are on site if there are any problems.'

Jazz nodded at him as he sat, cowed, in his chair, then she left the room.

Sebastian Frederiks sat down at his desk and unlocked the drawer to his cabinet. He took out the envelope that had arrived this morning, and reread the letter:

Dear Mr Frederiks,

In reference to the estate of the late Hugh Ronald Daneman Esq.

We represent the late Mr Daneman and are currently acting as trustees as to the dispersal of his estate. I would request you contact me to make an appointment here at this office so that I can discuss the contents of his will, which do concern you. If you would kindly call us as soon as possible, we can get the matter settled to both yours and Mr Daneman's satisfaction.

May I take this opportunity to pass on my sincere condolences.

I look forward to hearing from you.

Yours faithfully,

Thomas Sanders

Solicitor

The letter had arrived that morning. Sebastian had been startled by its contents. Even though he'd been taught by Hugh as a pupil at St Stephen's and then subsequently worked with him as a fellow teacher for a number of years, he'd never been close to the old boy. If anything, he'd felt a certain distaste for Daneman's feyness. There had been no doubt he was gay, and politically correct or not, Sebastian had always struggled to empathise with homosexual predilections.

And to be honest, Sebastian had presumed the feeling was mutual.

There seemed little point speculating until he had seen the solicitor in a couple of days' time. If Daneman had left him something in his will, Sebastian would be surprised. He folded the letter, replaced it in its envelope, then studied the ring on his pinky finger. He sat back, sweeping a hand through his hair, feeling slightly breathless.

Now, there was no reason to remove it, ever again.

Isabella Sherriff was a lady of extravagant proportions. She dressed in voluminous silk kaftans, with scarves and beads adorning her neck, a magnificent mane of titian hair hanging to her waist.

At the Yard, she was nicknamed 'The Magpie', due to her passion for all things shiny. Every finger was covered in rings and her wrists clanked as she moved her arms, owing to the several layers of bangles.

Jazz admired Isabella for her individual sense of style. And her unmatched skill as a psychologist. Issy had rarely been proved wrong. Norton trusted her too, and her evidence in court had helped them nail a number of complex cases that could have gone either way.

As she walked into the interview room, she thought how Issy only needed a crystal ball to complete her 'look'.

'Darling!' Issy held out her arms to embrace Jazz. 'Let me look at you. My, my, the Norfolk air seems to be suiting you. You look wonderful!'

'Thanks, Issy. I'm so grateful for you coming. We're feeling like the troops in the last outpost in the desert just now. What started as a simple case seems to have grown far more complex.'

'Don't they always?' Issy smiled. 'Crime does take place outside the cities, even though that townie lot at HQ don't think it does. Awfully quaint this, isn't it?' Issy threw her arms open to indicate the interview room. 'I feel like I'm on the set of *Dixon of Dock Green.*'

'The local plods would argue that's because all the funding goes to the big cities,' Miles explained. 'You can understand their point. I know that this is only a sub-station, but the lack of equipment and low staffing levels are breathtaking.'

Issy reached over and chucked his cheek. 'Oh, my little bleeding heart. You're so cute when you're angry. I could just eat you. Couldn't you, Jazz?'

Miles blushed and Jazz, ignoring the comment, pulled out a chair and sat down.

'Right, presume you've seen our suspect?'

'Oh yes.' Issy balanced her ample frame on the small wooden chair. 'I talked to Mr Millar for forty-five minutes.'

'And?'

'As we know, one can never be one hundred per cent about these things, but I have to say I'd eat my Auntie Madge's extremely substantial bottom if he was our killer. I gave him the usual oral psychometric tests, plus my little box of trick questions and, in my considered opinion, David Millar is a non-aggressive, reactive individual whose modus operandi does not fit with any kind of premeditated murder.'

'What about the explanation that he was drunk?'

'Again, more likely to strike out, less likely to carry through a plan. No.' Issy shook her head. 'I don't buy it, don't buy it at all.'

'Even to defend his son?' Jazz pressed.

'There's no doubt his lad is the light of his life and I'll be interested to meet him tomorrow to give me the bigger picture. You know I'm not here to weigh up the technical side of the case, or the evidence. I'm here to tell you that in my professional opinion—even without the fact we know he's lying through his teeth about having some aspirin conveniently in his pocket—the scenario put forward by Millar does not fit. Poor bloke. Sounds as if he's had a dreadful time one way and another.'

'But the point still remains: why would he say he did it, if he didn't?' asked Jazz.

'I think you have two possible alternatives: number one, he's protecting someone, and that someone can only be his son, whom I shall be seeing tomorrow. The second, and equally valid alternative, is that it's a cry for help and attention. Goodness knows how many times I've seen that. A person at the end of his tether, desperate, confesses to something he didn't do in order to bring the spotlight upon himself. David Millar may not be a murderer, but that's not to say he hasn't lost his grip on reality. He's suffered loss and trauma and that may well have affected his state of mind. I'd have to talk to him some more to discover how deep that goes, but I'd certainly recommend some kind of counselling. I'd also suggest having another bash at interviewing him, telling him we know of his allergy to aspirin, and asking him why he's lying.'

'I'll go down to see him now. Thanks, Issy. By the way, talking of counsellors, that's the professional hat I'll need you to wear when you talk to Rory Millar. There's a possibility he's complicit in a murder and we need to find out what he knows, but we also need to tread carefully with the kid. He's been through a lot by all accounts. Play up your cuddly side with the mother, too, so she doesn't get spooked.'

'Darling, I can be whoever you wish me to be and play my part to perfection. Did I ever tell you my great-great-uncle trod the boards with Bernhardt? Acting's in the family. Now, where's the nearest hostelry?

I'm starving.'

'We've booked you into Miles's hotel in town and he's going to wine and dine you.'

'Wonderful.' Issy stood up and took Jazz by the shoulders. 'And what about you? Aren't you joining us?'

Jazz felt the heat rise to her cheeks. 'No, sorry, I'm afraid I can't.'

Issy smiled. 'Methinks our Jazmine has a hot date with a man. Would I be right?'

'I'm going out to supper with someone whom I'm helping research a thesis. I hardly know him.'

'But you will, sweetie, you will. Now, I must speak to Norton. I'll let you know the upshot.'

As Jazz left the room, she did wonder for a second if Issy really was psychic.

David was dozing when he heard the bolt of his cell door being pushed back. He felt exhausted. He could hardly remember the last time he'd had a decent night's sleep.

He opened his eyes and saw the beautiful lady detective looking down at him.

'Hello, Mr Millar, how are you feeling?'

David rubbed his eyes as the inspector sat down on the end of his narrow bunk. 'Groggy. Always happens when I come off the booze.'

'David,' Jazz began gently. 'We have a small problem with your confession.'

'Really? What?'

'Do you still stand by the fact this was not a premeditated murder? That you found the aspirin in the pocket of your jacket and acted on the spur of the moment?'

'Yes, absolutely.' David nodded.

'You see, Angelina told me this morning you are allergic to aspirin, too. So it's very doubtful you'd be using them as the painkiller of choice for yourself, isn't it?'

David's shoulders slumped forwards. 'Shit,' he mumbled.

'David, did you kill Charlie Cavendish?'

'I...'

'Is that a yes or a no?'

'The point is, Inspector, I may have done. You see, I honestly can't remember much about that night.'

'Do you remember stopping on the way to the school and buying some aspirin tablets with the intention of killing Charlie?'

'No...I...'

'David,' Jazz said quietly, 'who are you trying to protect?'

'No one! I...' He shook his head vehemently. 'No one.'

'Rory didn't tell you something whilst you were in the Lakes, did he? For example, that he'd mistakenly given Charlie some aspirin tablets himself?'

'God, no! Of course not! Listen, Inspector, Rory's the victim here.'

'The problem is, so is Charlie. And by making a confession that is so full of holes, you've actually made us all wonder whether it was done to protect Rory.'

'No, Inspector!' David looked genuinely frightened now. 'That really isn't the case. My son is innocent, he hasn't done anything. I...' David put his head in his hands and started to sob.

'You didn't go to the school with a packet of aspirin with the intention of murdering Charlie Cavendish, did you, David?'

He shook his head. 'No, I didn't. But really, the fact his father's a fuck-up who thinks he might have killed someone has nothing to do with Rory. Nothing at all. Please, leave him out of this. He's taken enough!'

Jazz put a comforting arm on his shoulder. 'I know. I'm going to send you home now, David. You need a good night's sleep. And then, tomorrow, when you're calmer, I'll come and see you at your house. Okay?'

'You're releasing me?'

'Not really. You came to us of your own free will and we haven't arrested you yet. One of the duty sergeants will run you home. I know your car's still in the Lakes. I'll be round tomorrow about eleven.' She stood up and turned to walk out of the cell.

'Really, this has nothing to do with Rory, Inspector.'

'As I said, we'll talk tomorrow. Goodbye, David.'

Jazz turned to face Issy, who was lurking in the corridor outside the cell. Issy gave a slight nod and a thumbs-up signal, then followed Jazz up the stairs.

'There you have it. As we thought, he's protecting his son,' she murmured in a low voice. 'Can't wait to meet young Rory. I've a strong feeling in my waters he might be able to shed some light on the whole affair. Especially when I tell him Daddy's been released without charge. Jazz?'

'Sorry, Issy, I was somewhere else for a moment. Tell Miles I'm at the Coach and Horses in Cley if he needs me. The signal on the coast can be dodgy.'

'I will.' Issy's eyes twinkled. 'And have a good time.'

Chapter Nineteen

'Is it all right if I disappear, Mr Forbes? It's past six and Steve's waiting for me outside the Forum. You'll need to answer the intercom when it buzzes to let your last client in.'

Julian looked up at Stacey. 'Of course, no problem. I'll see you tomorrow.'

'Night, Mr Forbes. Have a good evening.'

'Thanks, and you.' Stacey left his office but Julian's attention was already back on the file he was reading.

Twenty minutes later, he checked his watch and called Angelina.

'Hello, darling.'

'Hello.'

'How's Rory?'

'Tucked up on the sofa watching *The Simpsons*. He seems okay. A little quiet, but that's understandable. We have a counsellor from London coming to see him tomorrow morning. Do you think that's a good idea?'

'Being in the business has made me rather cynical about these kind of people. But I'm sure it can't do him any harm.'

'No.'

'Shall I come back tonight? I could arrive much later, when Rory is in bed,' he suggested tentatively. 'I'd like to try and make up for my callous behaviour this morning.'

There was a pause and in that pause, Julian had his answer. 'Okay, I'll go to the flat.'

'I'm sorry, darling, I just want Rory to recover from the shock of everything before he accidentally discovers a strange man in his mother's bed.'

There was a pause before Julian asked, 'When are you sending him back to school?'

'After all I've heard about that awful Charlie Cavendish and what he did to Rory, I can't bring myself to send him back. At present, I don't want to let him out of my sight.'

'Charlie can hardly be a problem to Rory now, can he?'

'No, I know, Julian, but…look.' Angelina sighed. 'We'll talk about it when I see you, but Rory won't be going anywhere this week.'

'I presume that means I'm gated in my flat for the present?'

'I'm sorry. I thought you understood I just have to put Rory first at the moment.'

'I understand, but that doesn't mean to say I have to like it, Angelina. So, I'm not going to see you for the next few days? I miss you.'

'Well…' Angelina's voice softened. 'Why don't I see if Rory is okay tomorrow and then get Lily, the babysitter he really likes, to come for a few hours in the evening? I can drive up to Norwich, meet you at the flat and we could stay in and get a takeaway?'

Julian did not feel in the mood to be won over.

'Maybe. Let me see what I'm doing. I'll ring you later.'

'Oh. Okay.'

It was obvious from her voice she was upset. But then, so was he.

'Better go. I have a client arriving any minute. Bye.'

Julian put the receiver down without waiting for her response. He knew he was behaving badly—it was obvious Angelina had to put Rory first. The problem was, would this always be the case?

In some ways it was a shame David Millar would go down for life. At least in the past, Angelina had managed to palm the kid off onto his father every other weekend. Now, especially if she did the mamby-pamby Mummy thing and sent him to a day school, they'd be stuck with him all the time.

Seeing he still had fifteen minutes before his client arrived, Julian logged on to check his emails.

He saw one of them was a reply to the message he had sent yesterday.

And his blood ran cold as he read it.

He heard the buzzer ring.

'Hello?'

The voice sounded muffled.

'Just push the door and come up to the second floor. I'll be waiting for you there.'

Julian logged out of his email and headed to reception to greet his client.

Having made sure one of Roland's boys would keep David Millar's cottage under surveillance for the night, just in case, Jazz had driven home.

She shivered uncontrollably as she stood in her underwear with her head under the kitchen sink tap, freezing water cascading over her shampooed hair.

She wrapped her hair in a towel and ran into the sitting room to huddle by the fire, teeth chattering.

The plumber had promised her she should have hot water and heating by tomorrow, but if she didn't, Jazz knew she'd have to decamp to a hotel. The temperature had dropped dramatically in the last two days and the heavy skies indicated snow was threatening. The entire upstairs had no electricity and her bedroom was like an ice box. Snuggling down under layers of quilts and reading by candlelight sounded romantic, but in reality, waking up in the middle of the night, needing the loo and groping round for a torch, then falling over toolboxes, to arrive back in bed so cold she couldn't get back to sleep, was not.

Jazz did her best to dry her thick curls with the heat from the fire, unable to stand the thought of rooting around for a dryer upstairs in the dark, and decided tonight she'd sleep on the sofa, where at least she'd be warm.

Pulling on a pair of jeans, a thick jumper and applying a little mascara and lipstick to her face, Jazz left the cottage and got into her car.

As she drove along the icy roads, Jazz realised she felt flustered and out of control. She thrived on order and routine—her father said it was because she was a true Virgo—and any kind of emotional chaos produced the butterflies fluttering in her tummy now.

She parked the car on the grass verge in front of the pub.

'Get a grip, woman! It's no biggie—only a meal in a pub,' she said out loud, and, taking a deep breath, she walked across the narrow lane to the front door.

Jonathan was sitting nursing a pint of beer by the fire. He smiled when he saw her, stood up and kissed her on both cheeks.

'How are you, Jazz? You look great,' he commented, his eyes sweeping over her long, jean-clad legs. 'Can I get you something to drink?'

'A glass of wine would be perfect.'

'Sure. You sit down and get warm by this fantastic fire. I'll bring the menus over, although the specials on the board look excellent.'

She watched him as he strode to the bar, towering over the other men already there. He looked different tonight somehow; more mature. Perhaps the university setting had coloured her memories of him, made her see him as a student still, when in fact he was only seven years younger than she.

'There we go.' Jonathan put the glass of wine in front of her, along with a menu, and sat down on the stool next to her, his long legs stretched out in front of him. 'Have a fast look. The kitchen closes at eight thirty and it's ten past now.'

Jazz chuckled. 'In London, most people wouldn't have arrived at the restaurant, let alone have it shut up shop.' She sipped her wine and looked up at the blackboard. 'It's an easy decision anyway. Cod and chips and mushy peas for me.'

'That makes two of us.' He smiled. 'When in Rome, although saying that, the cod caught from here has probably ended up in Scotland being vacuum packed and we're eating Norway's finest.'

'Probably, but it's the thought that counts.'

'Absolutely. And it's good to see a woman who obviously doesn't care about the calories...not that you need to, of course. I mean, you have a lovely figure, but...' The colour was rising to his cheeks. 'What I mean is, I resent taking a woman out for dinner when she spends all evening chasing a small piece of lettuce round her plate.'

'Well, it's not a problem you'll have tonight. I eat like the proverbial horse and I'm absolutely famished, so why don't you go and order before it's too late?'

Over the next fifteen minutes, Jazz relaxed. Jonathan had an ironic sense of humour that she shared and understood. The fish and chips were delicious and Jazz risked another small glass of wine.

'Right, I'm ready to answer those questions you have for me. By the way, sorry if I got on my high horse the other day.'

'You're passionate about what you do. That's hardly a fault. Don't even think about it.'

'It's passion or disillusionment, one or the other.' Jazz smiled. 'Two weeks ago I thought I'd left the force completely.'

Jonathan raised an eyebrow. 'Really? Why?'

'I was let down big time, both at work and at home. Anyway, it's too long and boring a diatribe to go into and I don't want to rake over the past anyway.'

'I understand. Your dad did say you'd recently got divorced.'

'Did he indeed?' Jazz raised an eyebrow. 'And what else did he tell you?'

'Bluntly, that it was the best decision you've ever made.'

'No. He never was a Patrick fan.'

'So I gathered. Are you happy about it?'

'No one's happy about failing, are they? And that's what divorce is admitting. But I'm certainly happy the whole thing is behind me, yes.'

'And you're back at work?'

'It seems I am, yes. Thought I was just doing my old boss a favour, but...' Jazz shrugged. 'We'll see how it goes.'

'Would have been a lot to throw away, surely? You've certainly climbed the career ladder, which must be tough for a female.'

'Not particularly. Anyway, just a plain old plod, me,' she smiled.

'Hardly plain,' he commented. 'And certainly better looking than Columbo.'

'I'll take that as a compliment, not an insult, I think!'

'I've always thought how much I'd like to work in a profession that really makes a difference to society, such as becoming a surgeon, or an inventor. I really admire you, Jazz. All I do is theorise on how things should be done.'

'As a matter of fact, my first love was not a helmet and a truncheon. I wanted to be an artist. Still do.'

'Your dad told me you'd studied History of Art.'

'My dear old daddy seems to have told you rather a lot about me.' Jazz frowned.

'Don't blame him. I admit to probing.' Jonathan grinned. 'Although it wasn't hard, as you are his favourite subject. Anyway, the great thing about having a natural talent is it never leaves you. I have none, as far as the arts are concerned. I can't paint a door frame, let alone a picture.'

'But you have the ability to think logically and clearly and translate those thoughts onto paper. That's your instrument of creation, surely?'

'I knew I liked you, Miss Hunter. What an elegant way of giving my paltry little life some meaning. Coffee?'

'I'd love some.' Jazz looked at her watch as Jonathan stood to go to the bar. 'Then I really must be making a move.'

'So, how's your current case going?' Jonathan asked as he put two coffees on the table and poured two heaped spoonfuls of sugar into his.

Jazz had spent ten years with a man who worked in the same job as her and understood the nuances and shorthand of the world they shared. Cases could be discussed openly without fear of an innocent slip of the tongue. She knew of many colleagues in the office with partners outside the force and how difficult they found it not to be able to share the minutiae of their day in case of a security breach.

This was new territory for her and she knew she must learn to tread carefully.

'More complicated than it first appeared, but then, that's normal,' she answered noncommittally.

'You're in Norfolk temporarily?' he asked.

'No, it's a permanent move. I love it here.'

'It's an amazingly raw county, no prettiness about it. Jazz.' Jonathan's hand moved across the table towards hers and grasped it. 'Look, this sounds slightly forward, but I've enjoyed tonight a lot. Can we do it again? I mean, I haven't got round to asking you those questions yet.'

'I...' Jazz felt disconcerted, not sure what to say, out of touch with the protocol of romance.

Before she could begin to formulate a reply, she noticed a horribly familiar figure enter the small bar. He was smiling broadly at her and heading towards their table.

'Jazz.' The familiar soft Irish burr assaulted her ears. Patrick. Her ex. He leaned down and kissed her on the cheek. 'You look wonderful!'

As his arms closed around her shoulders, she was aware of the familiar smell that, after ten years of intimacy, would mark him out to her instantly, even if she was blind.

She sat, not moving, waiting until he unwrapped his arms from around her shoulders and stood upright.

'And who is this fine fellow you have with you here?' He stared down at Jonathan, his eyes betraying the lie his lips had spoken.

'What the hell are you doing here?!'

'Ah, now, Jazz, don't be like that. I happened to be coming to Norwich on business, gave Issy a lift up as a matter of fact.'

'Issy?!' Jazz's throat constricted.

'It just worked out that way. I met up with Miles and our good shrink for supper.'

'What are you doing here then? In this pub?' she asked coldly.

'Ah, now, so sorry to interrupt your evening, but I'm after doing a favour for Norton. He wants to speak to you urgently. You weren't answering your mobile, but DS Miles knew where you were, so I decided to come personally to give you the message.'

Jazz didn't have the energy to reply. She saw Jonathan looking very uncomfortable.

'Better be on my way,' he said as he stood up. 'Those roads look icy to me.'

'They are, you take care now.' Patrick smirked.

'I will. Bye, Jazz, thanks for a pleasant evening.'

'Yes, thank you. I enjoyed it.' She kissed Jonathan warmly on the cheek.

'Jazz, will you not introduce us?' Patrick put a hand on Jonathan's shoulder.

You bastard...

Jazz gritted her teeth. 'Jonathan, meet Patrick Coughlin, my ex-husband.'

'Right. Bye, Jazz. Be in touch.' Jonathan then made a hasty, embarrassed exit from the pub.

'I'm off, too.' She tried to walk past Patrick but he held her firmly by the arm.

'Ah, now, Jazz, come on, there's no need for this, is there? Wouldn't it be possible for us to be civilised? To sit together and have a drink like the old friends we are?'

'We are not friends, Patrick, and we never will be again!'

He eyed her, then smiled slyly. 'My, my, from the way you're reacting anyone would think you still have feelings for me. If you didn't, you'd be able to sit with me and have a drink.'

Jazz sat down abruptly, hating him. 'One, then I'm going.'

'The usual?'

Jazz nodded, as her heartbeat sped up further, remembering the intimate knowledge he had of her.

He brought her back a cognac and put his whiskey down on the table.

'So, who was yer man?'

'A friend, that's all. Someone I'm helping with a thesis.'

'Looked to me as if he wanted to do a bit more than just have you help him. Fair play to him. Are you sleeping together?'

'Patrick, for God's sake! It's absolutely none of your business! I've only just met him.'

'Bit on the young side, isn't he?'

'Never seemed to stop you.' It was out of her mouth before she could stop herself.

'Touché.' Patrick took a gulp of his whiskey. 'Ah, really, it meant nothing, nothing at all.'

'Don't you dare give me that bullshit! I know you're lying. The affair went on for a year at least. The worst thing was, everyone in the office knew about it. Except your wife.'

'I admit I behaved badly, but—'

She could feel the heat rising in her cheeks. 'Badly?! Christ, Patrick, you behaved appallingly! Shagging her in your office with the blinds closed. Jesus! At least if you were going to indulge in infidelity, you could have kept it outside office hours.'

She could see the next-door table were enjoying the show but she was past caring.

'Jazz, I'm deeply, truly sorry.' He sighed. 'Perhaps we should have had this conversation a long time ago. I was there, waiting to apologise and explain, but you ran off into the sunset. Anyway, I'm sitting here in front of you now, admitting I acted like a total eejit and I'm awash with guilt for putting you through it. And even more sorry if my behaviour contributed to your departure from the Yard.'

She looked at him helplessly. 'How the hell could I stay?! As Princess Diana once said, three's a crowd in a marriage, and she didn't have to work in an office every day with Camilla…not to mention her husband.' Jazz shook her head as she drained her glass.

Patrick, for once, had no immediate riposte. He stared back at her silently.

'Anyway, what's done is done,' she continued. 'It's all in the past and frankly, I just want to move on. I can't believe you had the cheek to turn up here.'

'Jazz, I was desperate. I've been beside myself for months trying to find you. That solicitor of yours refused to give me any clue as to where you were hiding yourself.'

'I didn't want to see you then and I don't want to see you now.'

'You can't say I didn't play fair by agreeing to the quickie divorce. I could have refused to sign.'

'Want a medal, do you?' Jazz laughed bitterly. 'Patrick, you are so full of shit, you ooze. Correct me if I'm wrong, but perhaps you signed for your own benefit too? So you could be free to make a new life with Chrissie?'

'Want another?' he indicated her glass.

'Course not. I'm driving.'

'I'll drop you off.'

'No. I need my car in the morning. What did Norton want, by the way? You said he needed to speak to me urgently.'

'He didn't. I was lying to have an excuse to see you.'

'I'll shoot Miles for telling you where I was,' she muttered.

'Don't. I lied to him, too.' Patrick's hand reached across the table to rest on hers. 'I've missed you so much.'

She pulled it sharply away. 'What? You mean your sixteen-year-old has given you the heave-ho and you're lonely? Sorry.' Jazz checked herself. 'That's sinking to your level and I'm ashamed of myself. Actually, apart from the fact she shagged my husband, I liked Chrissie. She was bright and a bloody good DC.'

'If it makes you feel any better, she binned me a couple of months ago for a City trader fifteen years my junior and one hundred times wealthier. I'm on my tod now, so I am.'

Jazz forced a laugh. 'If you want me to commiserate with you, I can't. Obviously I'm thrilled and I hope you suffered terribly.'

'I have. But not over her. Over the fact that I was such an eejit to risk losing you.'

'Water off a duck's back, I'm afraid. You always were good with the charm, Patrick. Your Irish heritage and all that. Unfortunately, it just doesn't wash with me any more. Look, I really must go.' Jazz stood up.

'But we have things to talk about. I have your wages still sitting in our joint bank account. And your name on the deeds of our flat.'

'Your flat now, Patrick. You bought me out, remember? Send a cheque and any papers for signature to my solicitor.' He followed her outside, where flakes of snow were starting to fall heavily around them.

'Hard to imagine you as a country yokel,' Patrick joked as they walked to Jazz's car. 'You always thrived in the city.'

'It's amazing what you can get used to when you have to. Bye, Patrick. Safe journey back to the smoke.' Jazz bent to get into the car but Patrick caught her and pulled her into his arms.

'Jesus, I've missed you.' His hand stroked her hair. 'If you would ever even consider—'

Jazz pulled away abruptly. 'No, Patrick, it's over. Forever. Believe it.' She climbed behind the wheel and slammed the door. She started the engine and drove off as fast as she could, without glancing back.

That night, unable to sleep, Jazz sat on the windowsill of her sitting room watching the snowflakes fall against the pane and settle thickly on the ground. The humiliation she'd felt when she'd finally discovered the truth about Patrick, and realising the whole department already knew, washed over her again.

However, tonight, she was less angry with Patrick than she was with herself: for the stirring inside her when he'd taken her in his arms.

Chapter Twenty

Jenny Colman went through her usual morning routine. Whilst she ran the water for her bath, she made herself a strong cup of tea and poured her breakfast cereal into a bowl. After her bath, she sat in her dressing gown and ate her cereal. She stared out of the small kitchen window at the thick snow that had fallen last night and covered everything.

She went to her wardrobe and took out one of the three dresses she wore in rotation to go to work. She called them her 'uniform' and every January she went to Norwich on the bus to the sales and replaced them. She applied her make-up, then sprayed a little 'Blue Grass' onto her neck and wrists. Outside Jenny heard the footsteps of the postman coming up the little path to her front door.

'More bills,' she groaned, remembering as a child when the sound of the postman's footsteps had been exciting, especially on birthdays or Christmas. But now the postman just meant someone else wanting money.

The two envelopes plopped through the letter box and Jenny went to pick them up from the doormat. One was a circular for a local plumbing company, and the other...

Jenny studied the thick cream vellum envelope with her name typed neatly on the front. She saw it had a London postmark. She got her glasses, went into the lounge and sat down to open it, wondering who on earth could be writing to her from London.

She read the address at the top. It was from a firm of solicitors. She read through the letter twice, just to make sure she hadn't got it wrong.

When she had finished, she took off her glasses and stared into space.

A small bequest...

No. She mustn't get her hopes up. She read the letter again. The solicitor wanted her to go to London to see him.

She'd never been to London in her life. How would she get to the station? And then, when she got there, how would she know where to go?

Perhaps she would ask Maddy to come with her, or at least take her to Norwich and put her on the train.

Jenny tucked the envelope carefully in her handbag. She would ask Mr Jones when would be the best day, then organise for one of the girls in the bursar's office to come and fill in for her.

Then she would make the call.

As she put on her fleece-lined boots and left the bungalow, her footsteps careful in the slush on the pavements, Jenny smiled sadly.

Dear Hugh. Even if it was only a small memento, it was lovely of him to think of her.

When Jenny arrived in her small reception area, Mr Jones's door was open. He was reading the local paper and also had copies of *The Times* and the *Telegraph* on his desk.

She knocked peremptorily. 'Morning, Mr Jones. How are you today?'

'Come in, come in.' Robert waved her towards his desk. He indicated the front of the local paper.

Local Teacher Found Dead at Home

Jenny sighed. 'Oh dear, oh dear. What does it say?'

'Most of it's about Hugh and his eminence as a scholar, but they do mention Charlie's death, too. There's also a small article in both of these...' He indicated the two national papers.

'He must have been very well known for them two papers to write about him.'

'Yes.' Robert was obviously flustered. 'Can you organise coffee for myself and Inspector Hunter? She wants to see me and is due in any minute.'

'Of course, Mr Jones.' Jenny stood in the doorway, biting her lip, trying to work up the courage to say she needed a day off.

'Is there anything else?'

Jenny shook her head, knowing this wasn't the moment. 'No, Mr Jones. I'll get that coffee for you.'

Having given up on sleep at five, Jazz had left the cottage early for the relative warmth of the interview room at Foltesham police station.

At eight, Miles and Issy appeared, both looking slightly the worse for wear.

'Coffee, I need coffee,' Issy moaned.

Jazz ignored her. Issy slumped nonchalantly into a chair, but Jazz noticed Miles looking sheepish.

Eventually, Issy piped up: 'Did he find you?'

Jazz nodded. 'You told him where to look. Of course he did,' she answered sharply.

'Alistair, would you be a lamb and see if you can organise Auntie Issy some freshly ground coffee as penance for pouring all that wine down her throat last night?'

'Do my best, but I'm not sure if the coffee bean has made it yet to the furthest outposts of British security.'

'Thanks, my love.' Issy sat quietly, watching Jazz pretending to concentrate.

'You know he still loves you.'

Jazz slammed down the lid of her laptop and eyed Issy across the desk.

'Bully for him.'

'Oh, come on, Jazz, this is Issy you're talking to. I know how you felt about him. And probably still do.'

'No! Not any more. It's taken all this time to get to where I am, and I'm just not interested in reliving the past. Last night, thanks to you, I had to.'

'I'm sorry, Jazz, but I thought, at the very least, you two should talk. It's extremely unhealthy not to confront your demons.'

'Issy, I am not one of your head cases! How dare you interfere in my life!'

'No, you're my friend, Jazz. And I understand you. And care for you,' Issy said calmly. 'I also know your greatest weakness is your pride. Patrick humiliated you. And you turned tail and ran away, without even giving him a chance to explain himself.'

Jazz had been down this road before with Issy. And she wasn't interested.

'Look, let's drop it, okay? Patrick and I are divorced. It's over.'

'There's always the Liz Taylor and Richard Burton precedent…'

'Oh please, Issy! He slept with a colleague of both of ours, not just once, but many times. Apparently, it was a "love" thing, or so she told most of the office. They were making plans to be together long before I found out about it. And now she's dumped him, he's feeling the breeze of being alone, that's all.'

'Yes, I accept all that, but of course he didn't love her. I mean, Chrissie is a nice kid, but not a patch on you in the brains department. No, this was typical male behaviour, and it all comes down to lust: the excitement of a new body, the ego massage of having a younger woman after him and, let's face it, Patrick has an incredibly large…' Issy chuckled. 'Ego.'

'Absolutely. And you've just drawn your own conclusion. Patrick shouldn't ever have been married. Perhaps he's the kind of man who needs the permanent excitement that a wife could never give him. You know what a flirt he is. I'm positive Chrissie wasn't the first and it's just not up my street to be married to a serial philanderer.'

'No,' Issy sighed. 'Maybe you're right. Anyway, at least you have talked. God knows how he found out I was coming to Norfolk, but he insisted on offering me a lift.'

'You shouldn't have accepted, for my sake.'

'Sweetie, you know I hate public transport.' Issy sniffed.

'Sorry, but that's no excuse. Call yourself a friend? Huh! I nearly died of shock when he turned up at the pub last night. You might have warned me.'

'He made me swear I wouldn't tell you he was here. He knew you'd run. And so did I.' Issy smiled. 'Come on, Jazz, there must have been a small part of you that was glad Patrick turned up whilst you were being wined and dined by a prospective lover?'

Jazz was rendered speechless. She couldn't believe what Issy had done. Finally, she said, 'Are you telling me you set him up to find me? Christ, you had no idea whom I was meeting!'

Issy leaned forward. 'So can you honestly tell me that last night, when you saw Patrick, you felt nothing for him at all?'

Jazz could feel the colour rising to her cheeks. 'Enough! No more interfering from you, thanks. And I mean it, Issy!'

Issy shrugged. 'Okay. Sorry.'

Thankfully, Miles arrived with three mugs of coffee. 'Instant, I'm afraid. Best I could do.'

If he felt an atmosphere, Miles didn't comment.

'I'd better down my coffee and head off to the Millar household. Are you accompanying me, Jazz?' Issy asked sweetly.

She was still fuming. 'No. I have to go and see Mr Jones, the incompetent headmaster, and bring him up to date. The whole Hugh Daneman affair has come out in the papers today so he's probably on edge.' She turned to Miles. 'Once you've dropped Issy at the Millars', can you chase Hugh Daneman's solicitor? See if he'll release us details of the will.' Jazz packed her laptop in its case and stood up. 'I'll meet you back here at twelve so you can fill me in on Rory Millar.'

'I'm rather looking forward to it, actually. Strange adolescents are my current pet subject.' Issy smiled.

Jazz's mobile rang. 'Hunter here.'

'It's Roland, Ma'am. Got some bad news, I'm afraid.' He sounded nervous.

'What?'

'My sarge says Millar's gone AWOL.'

'Shit!' Jazz muttered under her breath. 'How? Where?'

'They're not sure. They were stationed across the road from his cottage, saw no one come in or out all night. At eight forty this morning, the postman arrived with a package for Millar, but had no joy getting an answer. Obviously my sarge was suspicious, went to check and found the back door unlocked and the house empty. Sorry, Ma'am, but you did ask us to maintain a discreet distance.'

'Right. We'd better find him then.'

'I'm on my way to his cottage now. And I'll send an alert out around the county. I'm sure we'll pick him up.'

'I hope so, Detective Sergeant Roland. Get back to me as soon as there's news. Oh, and have someone stationed outside Mrs Millar's house until he's found. Thanks.'

Jazz turned to Issy. 'I presume you got the gist of that conversation?'

'I did. Don't panic, Jazz. I'd reckon it was alcohol's siren call—poor bloke probably just wanted a drink and the cupboard was bare. Shouldn't think he's gone far.'

'I just hope you're right,' Jazz said grimly as she headed for the door. 'But I wasn't expecting it. And not a word to Angelina about her ex absconding, current whereabouts unknown. She'll have apoplexy, as will that arrogant lawyer boyfriend of hers.'

'Of course. Can I tell her about David being released? I'd like to see the reaction.'

'If you must. I'll see you later.'

Jazz climbed into her car to drive across to the school. She was still fuming with Issy. And concerned about Millar's disappearance. Last night's encounter, and the call from Roland, had rattled her frail confidence. To lose a suspect was one thing, to lose a suspect who'd already confessed to a murder and been released without charge was another.

What if she'd been wrong about him?

'Shit, shit!' Jazz thumped the steering wheel as she waited to turn right at the roundabout. Her thoughts turned to her time in Italy, when there was little more to think about other than which particular cafe she should wander down to in the evenings for a plate of delicious penne.

What the hell was she doing here?

But logically, Jazz knew she couldn't have run forever. Issy was right in the sense that she'd needed to come home to confront her past.

Jazz moved off the roundabout, comforting herself with the thought that she'd walked away before; she could walk away again.

The bright day had clouded over and more snow was threatening. The Met Office had issued a severe weather warning for the whole of the eastern region. Jazz made the decision that tonight she would stay with Miles at his hotel in town. Being snowed in at the cottage with no heating or electricity was not a sensible idea.

As she was driving along Foltesham High Street, her mobile rang. Pulling over in front of the newsagent's, Jazz answered it.

'Jazz?'

'Hi, Mum, how are you?'

'I'm...'

Jazz heard the catch in her mother's voice and knew something had happened. Her heart in her mouth, she asked, 'Is it Dad?'

'Yes.' Celestria choked back a sob. 'He collapsed an hour ago and they've rushed him to hospital. I'm there now. The doctors are with him, so I thought I'd better call you.'

'Oh Mum. How bad is it?'

'You know what these doctors are like, they don't tell you anything. They said they'll know more when they've run some tests, but they're pretty sure it was a heart attack.'

'Oh God.' Jazz swallowed hard. 'How bad?'

'Pretty serious, I think. Oh Jazz, he looks awful, I...'

'Mum, I'm coming now. Which hospital is he in?'

'Papworth, but really, Jazz, the weather is terrible here. It's snowing like billy-o. They're telling everybody not to drive unless they absolutely have to.'

'Well, it's not terrible here and I'm on my way now. Hold on, Mum, and tell Dad to as well.'

'Oh darling, I...thank you. He's in critical care. Please, drive sensibly.'

'I will. See you in an hour or so.'

Jazz let the mobile drop onto her lap and, feeling dizzy, rested her head on the wheel. This was the call she had dreaded for all of her adult life.

Come on, Jazz, she urged herself. *He's still alive, he'll pull through. He has to.*

There was a knock on the passenger window.

Jazz looked up and saw Patrick, *The Times* tucked under his arm, staring at her in concern. Before she could stop him, he'd opened the door and leaned inside.

'What is it, Jazz? What's happened?'

'Mum's just called. Dad's had a heart attack and is in critical care.'

'Jazz, I'm so sorry. Can I get in? It's freezing out here.'

She didn't stop him, hadn't the strength. As he climbed into the passenger seat, the smell of him and the bitter cold air comforted her and distressed her in equal measure.

He reached out a gloved hand and squeezed her arm. 'So now, I presume you're off to the hospital? Are you up to driving? The weather's going to be feckin' dreadful.'

Jazz nodded. 'I will be, of course. Sorry, I've only just taken the call.' She urged herself to find the strength to collect herself.

'Is it...very bad?'

'Mum didn't say much, but the fact she even called me says it is, yes. I'll be fine now, really.' She gave him a wan smile. 'I'd better get going.'

'Jazz, you look dreadful, you're in shock and there's just no way I'm going to let you drive through a blizzard.' Patrick was getting out of the passenger seat. 'Come on, move over, I'm driving. We'll drop your car back at the station as it's on the way anyway and pick mine up—I'd rather drive that in weather like this. We'll be there in no time.' He walked round the car and opened the driver's door. Jazz stared up at him, immobile. 'Jazz, my angel, for once in your life, just do as you are told without arguing. Because I'm a-standing here until you do.'

Patrick folded his arms as Jazz fought an inner battle she knew she'd lose. She nodded weakly.

'Okay. Thanks,' she said gruffly, and started to get out of the car. Her knees gave way and she held on to Patrick as he helped her round the car and gently into the seat.

'So now, where are we headed? Cambridge, I presume.'

'Yes.' Jazz watched as he threw his newspaper onto the back seat and started the engine. 'You really don't have to do this. I would have been fine.'

'I'm sure you would.' He smiled as he pulled away from the kerb. 'And I know I don't have to. Now then, haven't you got some calls to make?'

Jazz nodded.

'Will you be letting Norton know I'm going to be later back to London than expected?'

She frowned at him, then nodded again reluctantly.

'I'm sure if you explain, he'll be taking it on face value. We were man and wife for ten years, so we were. I'm after giving you a lift to see your sick father, not whisking you away on a romantic reconciliation.'

'I know. Sorry.' Jazz picked up her mobile and began to dial.

The weather held off and they made good progress until they reached Ely, where the snow began to fall thickly around them. Jazz sat quietly, staring out of the window, her heart racing at the thought of what she had to face. She'd tried her mother's mobile, but, as usual, it was switched off. In fact, Jazz doubted whether Celestria had even thought to take it to the hospital with her. She'd bought both of her parents a mobile for Christmas a couple of years ago thinking how useful they would be. Her father had taken to his like a duck to water and had even begun to text recently, but Celestria struggled to find the 'on' button and it had become a standing joke between them.

They came to a halt on the A14, a few miles outside Cambridge.

'Jesus, this looks bad.' Patrick sighed, leaning out of the window and looking at the traffic jam snaking ahead for as far as the eye could see, which wasn't far, due to the poor visibility. 'There must be a crash or a breakdown up ahead.' He turned to her. 'Time for blues and twos?'

'You shouldn't, Patri—'

'Let's go for it.' Patrick pulled over onto the hard shoulder, wound down the window and stuck the light on the top of the car. 'The worst that can happen is we both lose our jobs, but as you already quit, it's irrelevant.' He started to pick up speed. 'Besides, a matter of life and death, so it is.'

His words sent dread surging through her again.

The hard shoulder was clogged with broken-down cars and Patrick had to pull out, join the queue, edge past a stricken car and continue until they met the next one. It was a tense process and by the time they reached the next junction, where Patrick pulled off, Jazz's nerves were stretched to breaking.

'Jesus, Mary and Joseph! That was a nightmare. Where the hell are the authorities?!'

'In this car?' Jazz joked quietly, a ghost of a smile crossing her lips.

Patrick reached over and squeezed her hand, acknowledging the hard-won joke. 'And why does this godforsaken country fall to its knees at the first sign of bad weather?' He looked across at Jazz and saw how pale she was. He squeezed her hand again. 'Not far now.'

She smiled wanly, wondering if, now they were nearing the hospital, she'd have preferred to be stranded on the motorway rather than face what lay ahead.

Chapter Twenty-One

Angelina paced the kitchen, a third cup of coffee nursed in her cold hands. She stared at the winter wonderland outside, picked up the phone from the table and dialled Julian's mobile for the tenth time that morning.

Her call went straight through yet again to his voicemail. Angelina hung up. She'd already left three messages, one last night and two this morning.

She'd heard nothing back since they'd spoken on the phone the previous evening, and he'd said he'd call her back.

The thought running through her mind was a simple one: Julian was fed up with having to play second fiddle to Rory and had decided to make his feelings obvious by ignoring her calls.

Angelina bit her lip and sat down at the table. What was she meant to do? God, men could be so selfish! Was it her fault that Rory needed his mother, and peace and security to recover for a few days? The problem was, of course, that Julian didn't have his own children, so he couldn't understand the pure instinct of being a parent and needing to protect one's young.

And... Angelina allowed herself to be indulgent for a second. What about her? To have your child kidnapped, then discover your ex-husband might be a murderer was a pretty tough call, too.

She stood up, suddenly angry. If this was Julian's infantile way of punishing her, let him get on with it.

She heard the front doorbell ring. It was almost certainly the counsellor from London here to see Rory. She left the kitchen and walked across the hall to the front door.

A large lady wearing a wide-brimmed felt hat covered with snow stood on the doorstep.

'Isabella Sherriff, pleasure to meet you. You must be Angelina, Rory's mother.'

'Yes.' Angelina had a sudden urge to giggle. In the long velvet coat and hat, Isabella Sherriff reminded her of a snowman. 'Do come in.'

'Thanks.' Isabella shook herself first, dusting the snow off her shoulders and removing her hat. 'Thought I'd walk. Dumb idea.' Her eyes twinkled as she unbuttoned her sopping coat and Angelina warmed to her immediately.

'Why don't you give that to me and I'll put it on the Aga to dry?'

'Good idea. Think I'd better take off these boots as well, before I make a snowy trail through your lovely house.' Isabella hung on to the doorknob and removed her soaked boots, to reveal one red and one black sock. She smiled up at Angelina. 'Sorry about the footwear. This trip was pretty short notice and I didn't have much time to pack.'

'Don't worry.' Angelina led Issy across the hall and into the kitchen. Issy headed straight for the Aga and placed her hands on the warming plate.

'Think I can forget about making it back to London tonight.'

'Yes, the snow's really coming down now.' Angelina gazed absent-mindedly out of the window as she placed Issy's coat over the Aga rail. A sudden feeling of fear filled her. What if Julian had had an accident? Crashed in the snow on his way home to the flat last night?

'Would you mind?'

Angelina forced her mind back and stared at Issy, who was indicating the cafetière.

'Sorry. Of course, I'll make you a fresh one. That will have gone cold.'

Angelina filled the kettle and put it on to boil.

'How is Rory? May I call you Angelina?'

'Yes.'

'And call me Issy, everyone else does.'

'Rory didn't have a good night. I heard him crying out, but when I went in to see him, he was still asleep. He was having a nightmare. I sat on his bed stroking his forehead. I don't think he knew I was there.'

'Did you ask him this morning what the dream was about?'

'No. I didn't want to bring it up.'

'Nightmares are healthy things in any case, though not particularly pleasant. It's the subconscious mind working its way through problems or fears and trying to rationalise them, helping the person cope.'

'I see.'

Angelina didn't really. She was still thinking about Julian as she spooned the coffee into the glass jug.

'Strong as you like,' Issy indicated, sitting down in a chair at the table. 'Has Rory said much about his time with his father? What they talked about, for example?'

'I haven't wanted to bring David's name into the conversation. I thought it might only upset Rory further. How a child copes with the fact that his father is a murderer, I just don't know.' Angelina placed the cafetière, a mug and milk and sugar in front of Issy. 'Please, help yourself.'

Issy looked up at her. 'Just because someone confesses to the crime, that doesn't always mean to say they committed it. You were closer to David than anyone. What do you make of it?' She poured the hot coffee into her mug.

'I was amazed. And horrified. I told Inspector Hunter I just couldn't believe David would knowingly kill someone.'

'Even if he knew the person concerned had been responsible for hurting his son?'

'I can see him reacting, yes, but…' Angelina looked suspiciously at Issy. 'How come you know all this? I thought you were a child counsellor?'

'I am, but as the police will have explained I'm also a criminal psychologist. In that capacity, I interviewed Rory's father last night.' Issy sipped her coffee. 'God, that's good. The stuff I've been drinking at the police station is rank.'

'I just don't know what to believe any more.' Angelina rubbed her forehead in confusion. 'Does the inspector think David did it? I did tell her David was allergic to aspirin. He'd never have bought any for himself. The tablets would have killed him too.'

'She told me. As a matter of fact, Mr Millar was released last night.'

'Really?'

'Good news, though. Surely no one wants the father of their child to be on a murder charge.'

'No, I mean…what about his confession?'

'It didn't hold any water. I know you told the inspector you didn't think David was capable of murder.'

'That's right, but people change, don't they? And…well, what worries me most, to be honest, is if David has lost it and he did kill Charlie, even accidentally. You might not know it, but he did attack me once, and then he tried to break into the house to get me and—'

Issy reached out a comforting hand and placed it on Angelina's shoulder. 'Hush now. I understand this situation is stressful for you.'

'Yes, of course. Sorry for babbling. It's all been very distressing.'

'I understand. Now, why don't you go and find Rory so he and I can have a little chat and I can get out of your hair?'

Angelina went to find Rory, and Issy, despite the confidence she had in her instincts and experience, knew she would be an awful lot happier when David Millar was located. She sipped her good coffee and waited.

Rory was sitting on the windowsill in his bedroom watching the snow. 'The counsellor is here to see you, darling. She's very friendly and I think you'll like her.'

'Okay, Mummy.'

'When she's gone, I thought perhaps you and I could go and build a snowman in the garden.' She kissed the top of her son's blond head.

'No thank you. I prefer to stay warm inside.'

'Come on, let's get this over with.' Angelina took his hand and led him to the door.

'I don't have to talk for long, do I? I'm so tired at the moment,' Rory said as he followed his mother reluctantly down the stairs.

'No. And remember, this lady is here to help you.' Angelina put on a bright smile as she led him into the kitchen. 'Rory, this is Isabella Sherriff.'

Issy stood up and came to shake Rory's hand. 'Hello, Rory, call me Issy. What do you think of the snow? Looks like I should have brought my sleigh and my reindeer, doesn't it?'

Rory smiled weakly.

'Now, shall we stay in here where it's warm, or would you prefer us to sit somewhere else?' She looked questioningly at Angelina.

'Here is fine.' Angelina pulled out a chair for Rory and made to pull one out for herself, but Issy stopped her.

'Would you mind if Rory and I had a little chat by ourselves for a while? I promise I'll scream very loudly if Rory looks like he's going to beat me up.'

Rory smiled properly at that.

'Okay. I'll leave you both to it. Don't tire him, will you?'

'As long as he doesn't tire me.' Issy winked at Rory.

Satisfied Rory was okay, Angelina left the kitchen. She walked to the utility room to remove the clean load from the machine, then heard Julian's work line ring. She walked across the passage to Julian's study to pick it up.

'Hello?'

'Hello, Angelina, it's Stacey, Julian's secretary here. Could I have a quick word with Julian, do you think?'

'He's not here, Stacey. He stayed at the flat last night so I haven't seen him since yesterday morning.'

'Well, I've tried the flat number and his mobile and he's not answering that either. I thought he'd been with you at home last night, looked at the weather and thought better of trying to make it into Norwich.'

'No. Could he be out on an appointment? Or in court?' Angelina realised immediately it was a stupid question to ask. Julian's secretary was bound to know his movements.

'That's the thing. He had a ten thirty client meeting here. The lady is in reception and she's been waiting for twenty minutes. It's very unusual for Julian not to let me know if he's going to be late or needs to cancel.'

All sorts of terrible images were running through Angelina's head. 'Stacey, you don't think he's had a crash, do you? Should I call the hospitals?'

'Surely if he had, you'd have heard by now. Perhaps he's overslept or something,' Stacey offered unconvincingly, though they both knew that wasn't an option.

'Now I'm concerned he's collapsed at the flat,' said Angelina. 'I'd drive there now, but what with the weather, I'm worried I wouldn't make it. Besides, I've got Rory here with some police counsellor.'

'Well, the flat's not that far from here and I do know he keeps a spare set of keys in his desk drawer. If he hasn't turned up by lunchtime, do you want me to go and see if he's there?'

'I don't know.' Angelina bit her lip. 'Maybe we're being silly. Surely there must be an explanation?'

There was a pause at the other end of the line. 'I'll go at lunchtime, shall I?'

'Well, if you wouldn't mind. And let me know as soon as you can.'

'I will. I'd better get back to the client. I'll say Julian's been delayed by the snow and reschedule.'

'Ring me as soon as you get there. Thanks, Stacey.'

Angelina put the receiver back in its cradle. She held a hand to her mouth in anguish, her stomach churning.

Why, when only a few days ago, everything was perfect, was everything now going so horribly wrong?

Chapter Twenty-Two

Jazz had found Celestria sitting alone in the relatives' room situated just outside the critical care ward.

'Darling, I can't believe you made it! And so fast too.' She held out her arms to embrace her daughter.

'It felt like an eternity to me, Mum.' Jazz could feel her mother shaking against her. She sat in the chair, holding Celestria's hands in hers. 'Is there any news?'

'The consultant is coming to talk to me to tell me what's happening.' Celestria looked at her watch. 'The nurse told me that forty-five minutes ago.' She shrugged. 'One doesn't like to make a fuss, I know only too well what busy people they are.'

'How does Dad seem?' Jazz asked.

'I haven't been allowed in since I telephoned you. They've been doing all sorts of tests, wiring poor Tom up to bits of machinery… They said someone would come and tell me when I could go back in, but that hasn't happened either.' She squeezed her daughter's hand. 'Thank you so much for coming. I know how busy you are.'

'Mum, please don't thank me. I need to be here.'

'Would you like a coffee? There's a machine just along the corridor.'

'No thanks, Mum. I'm fine.'

'So, how was the journey?'

Jazz knew that under the circumstances, small talk was their only option.

'Awful, but luckily enough Pa—'

Before she could finish, the door opened and an attractive middle-aged man walked through it.

'Mrs Hunter?'

'Yes.'

'I'm Robert Carlisle, your husband's consultant.' He looked at Jazz. 'And this is?'

'Our daughter, Jazmine.'

'Okay.' Mr Carlisle pulled up a seat facing them and sat down.

'Has he had a heart attack?' Jazz asked, unable to contain herself any longer.

'Yes, I'm afraid he has.'

Jazz squeezed her mother's hand. 'How bad was it?'

'We're still running some tests to find out. He also has a chest infection. Had you noticed he'd been coughing recently, Mrs Hunter?'

'Yes, but he said it was nothing, that he was fine.'

'Don't blame yourself. It wasn't the chest infection that caused the heart attack, although it probably didn't help. The problem we have now is one of treatment. He's sustained two major organ failures, his heart and his lungs, which have filled up with fluid. This is due to the infection, but also due to his heart not pumping satisfactorily. His body isn't draining the fluid off in the way that it should.'

'Will he…be…?' Celestria couldn't finish the sentence.

'Mrs Hunter, your husband is a very sick man. We're doing everything we possibly can to help him. He's being put on a course of intravenous antibiotics to try and stem the infection, we are giving him drugs to help stabilise his heart and, this is what you might find most distressing, he's having to endure an air-tight mask which is forcing pure oxygen into his lungs to try and remove the fluid. It's unpleasant for him and not nice for you to look at. He won't be able to talk to you, just at the moment.'

There was silence as the two women processed the news. Eventually Jazz asked, 'What are his chances?'

'The next twenty-four hours are critical. We are obviously concerned that having had a major heart attack, he might have another one. Equally, his lungs may not clear. If you are asking me for a percentage,' Carlisle shrugged, 'I'd say he has around a thirty per cent chance of pulling through.'

Jazz nodded, willing herself not to cry.

'We'll do everything we can. And he seems like a fighter to me,' Carlisle smiled. 'Never underestimate the power of the human spirit. You can go and see him if you want, just for a short while. He's awake, which is a good sign. He knows he can't talk, so try not to encourage him.'

Celestria and Jazz stood up. Celestria held out her hand. 'Thank you, Mr Carlisle, I know Tom's in the best possible hands.'

'We do our best.' Carlisle nodded brusquely. 'Ring the bell and the nurse will let you in. If you'll excuse me, I need to check on another patient.'

'Of course.' They followed him out of the relatives' room and watched as he hurried off down the corridor. Jazz rang the bell at the entrance to the critical care ward. As they waited, Celestria grabbed Jazz's hand once more.

'Darling, we mustn't let him know how bad it is.'

'Mum, I'm sure he already knows.'

The door opened and a pretty Malaysian nurse came out.

'We're here to see Tom Hunter,' said Jazz.

The nurse nodded and they followed her through the door and into the strangely silent ward.

As they approached, Tom lifted a hand to acknowledge them. Jazz hung back as Celestria went to embrace her husband. She saw her whisper something in his ear and watched as his eyes lit up in pleasure. Celestria sat down on one side of the bed, holding Tom's hand, and Jazz approached her father on the other.

She kissed him on the top of his head, then bent down to whisper in his ear. 'Hello, Daddy. Don't laugh or I'll get told off, but you look like a baby elephant in that get-up.' She indicated the mask, with the plastic tube that stuck out at its centre over his nose, reminiscent of an elephant's trunk. She saw her father smile, and sat down on the other side of the bed opposite her mother.

'Trust you to get sick on the day we have the worst snowfall for years,' Celestria said, stroking Tom's hand. 'Your daughter had to ski here from Norfolk.'

'It's even bad on the coast at the moment, which is very unusual.' Jazz wondered at the banality of her comment. When all she wanted to say was, *Don't leave me, I need you and love you and it's breaking my heart to watch you suffer...*

Fifteen or so minutes later, Tom drifted off to sleep.

'Mum, I must find a loo. Will you be all right here for a few minutes?'

'Of course, darling.' Celestria was stroking her husband's forehead, a smile on her face as she watched him sleep. 'I know what he's like. He won't close his eyes and rest unless I'm here, making sure the doctors don't do anything he doesn't know about. Why don't you go and get yourself a coffee? Take a breather? I really am happy here.'

Jazz realised Celestria wanted to be by herself with Tom, maybe thinking she must savour every moment they had left.

'Okay, I'll be back up shortly.'

As Jazz left the ward, found the loo, then made her way through the maze of corridors that would perhaps lead her one day to the canteen, she shuddered at the smell of the place. As a police woman, she'd spent numerous hours in hospitals interviewing suspects, victims or witnesses, and had never been affected. Being a relative of a very sick patient was a different experience.

The canteen was deserted; perhaps some outpatients and visitors had been deterred by the terrible weather. She spotted Patrick reading his paper at a table by the window.

Jazz sank down into the seat opposite him, feeling completely drained.

'How is he?'

Jazz's face told the story.

He squeezed her hand hard, then stood up. 'Tell me about it after I've got you a coffee.'

'I'd like tea, please, and some water.'

'Anything to eat?'

'No thanks.' Jazz stared out of the window as the ceaseless flakes threatened to blank out the daylight. If the worst happened today, she knew she would hate snow forever.

'There, get that down you, girl. Good, strong builders' tea.' Patrick was back with a small stainless-steel pot and a utility cup and saucer, made for maximum use and minimum breakage.

Jazz poured the tea and took a sip. Patrick sat patiently watching her. Eventually she spoke. 'The consultant has said he has a thirty per cent chance of pulling through. He's very, very ill and the next twenty-four hours are crucial.'

'Have you seen him?'

'Yes, but he has this awful mask on, so he can't talk. Look, Patrick, it was so kind of you to drive me here but I'm obviously not going anywhere today and I don't want you hanging around.'

Patrick indicated the snow. 'Are you to be thinking I'm going anywhere, either? I've called in and nothing much is happening. Violent crime goes down in bad weather, as you know.'

'Aren't you working on a case at the moment?'

'Just closed one a couple of days ago. 'Twas very satisfactory. Got a pat on the back from the commissioner for it, actually.'

'Good for you.' Jazz wasn't interested. 'Well, you can't just hang around here all day.'

'I can do whatever I wish, so, and at present, I am quite content to sit here and read my paper. If I get really bored, I'll be going outside to make a snowman.' Patrick's eyes twinkled.

'I must go and phone Miles. No mobiles allowed inside.'

'Why don't you be giving me your mobile and I'll man it for you? I'll let them know you're going to be here for a while and pass on any messages they have for you?' Patrick leaned over the table and grasped her hands. 'Jazz, please, just forget about the case today and concentrate on your daddy. I swear I'll let you know if there's anything urgent.'

Jazz saw the sense in what he said and nodded. She delved in her bag to retrieve her mobile and handed it to him. 'For God's sake, don't disappear. That's my lifeline.'

'I won't, Jazz. Trust me.'

Jazz almost hit back with a caustic riposte, then decided this was not the moment.

'I'll be here waiting, okay?'

'Thanks, Patrick. I'd better be getting back.'

Rory had emerged a while back from his interview with Isabella, looking bright and relaxed. He'd gone up to his room to read.

'Do you think he's okay?' Angelina asked Issy as she took her coat off the Aga and handed it to her.

Issy nodded noncommittally. 'Yes, I think he's basically fine, but there does seem to be something worrying him. Can't quite get to the bottom of it yet, though. Interestingly, I don't think it has anything to do with his father. I'd say it was something to do with school.'

'Really? He didn't mention bullying, did he?'

'That was a line of enquiry I pursued but Rory was not receptive. He's a deep young man, plays his emotional cards close to his chest.'

'Yes he does, a bit like David used to until he lost it last year.'

Issy was buttoning her coat. 'Well, that's the problem with people who find it hard to express emotion. And men are always the worst. It's like a bubbling volcano: it's out of sight, getting hotter and hotter, until one day it can no longer contain itself, so it bursts in spectacular fashion.'

'Yes.' Angelina looked preoccupied.

'Are you all right, Mrs Millar?'

'Yes, I'm fine. I'm tired, that's all. Must be all the stress of the past few days.'

'You must take care of yourself.'

'And…Julian, my partner, seems to have gone AWOL. I'm sure he's fine but I haven't heard from him since last night and he hasn't arrived in his office yet, which is most unlike him.'

Issy raised her eyebrows. 'Men, eh? Totally unreliable. Try not to worry.'

'Yes.' Angelina nodded without conviction.

'Now, Mrs Millar, if this weather does continue to deteriorate, I reckon I'm going to be stranded here until tomorrow. Would you mind if I came to see Rory again? I think I gained his trust today and it might be he feels safe to open up to me a little more.'

'Of course,' Angelina replied automatically. Her mind was on Julian.

'I'll let myself out,' said Issy, heading for the kitchen door. 'Try not to fret about your partner. I'm sure he'll tip up soon with a perfectly reasonable excuse for driving you insane with worry. Goodbye, and thank you for the coffee.'

After Issy had gone, Angelina heated some tinned soup on the Aga and put some rolls in to warm. She set the table for herself and Rory, then decided to have a glass of wine to calm her nerves. Rory tripped into the kitchen and sat down as his mother put his bowl of soup in front of him.

'Eat it all up, Rory. You're far too skinny.'

'I'm like Dad, that's the way I'm made.' Rory picked up his spoon.

'Did Issy tell you the good news?'

'No, what?'

'That Dad has been released without charge.'

Rory froze, his soup spoon suspended in mid-air.

'But…if he said he did it, why won't they believe him?'

'I don't know the ins and outs, darling, but I'm sure they wouldn't have released him if they thought he had done it. Anyway, isn't it good news?'

Rory forced a nod. 'Yes, of course it is,' he said quietly.

Angelina stared at him. 'Rory, you don't look like it is. What's the matt—'

The shrill sound of the telephone stopped her in mid-sentence. She jumped up and grabbed the receiver. 'Hello?'

'Hello, Angelina, it's Stacey here. I'm calling you from Julian's flat.'

'And?'

'He's not here.'

'Oh.' Part of her was relieved Stacey had not found him in a pool of blood on the floor. 'Any sign that he's been there recently?'

'No. I checked the bed and it was immaculate, although he could have made it before he left this morning. There was no sign of a breakfast bowl or mug and his toothbrush is dry, too.'

'Stacey, I think you've been watching too many detective series on TV. You sound like a pro!' Angelina tried to make light of the situation.

'Well, it's only common sense,' she replied brusquely. 'What would you like me to do now?'

'Perhaps you could check his clothes are hanging in the wardrobe, just in case he's decided to go away without telling us.'

'I've done that as well, actually, although it's difficult to tell as I have no idea how many clothes he's got. But his wardrobe is certainly full and doesn't look as though it's been emptied.'

There was a silence as the two women tried to think what to do next.

'Well, I just don't understand,' Angelina said eventually. 'It's so out of character for Julian to do something like this. You know how he thrives on his rigid routine, Stacey. He's just not a spontaneous person.'

'I know.'

'Well, I think I'd better try ringing round the hospitals, just in case he had an accident and has suffered some kind of memory loss. You do hear that happens.'

'Yes, you do,' Stacey replied doubtfully. 'Okay, Angelina, I'll head back. It's blizzard conditions here and I think Mr Peters is going to shut the office for the afternoon. They've closed the courts as many of the jurors didn't make it in. Let me know if you hear from Julian and I'll obviously do the same. Try not to worry. I'm sure he'll turn up, like a bad penny, wondering what all the fuss was about.'

'Thanks, Stacey. I'll call you later.'

Angelina put the receiver down. She just didn't understand it. Something was wrong, she knew it.

She turned round to speak to Rory, but saw only his half-finished soup bowl and the empty chair on which he had been sitting a few seconds ago.

Jazz and Celestria sat on either side of Tom, like two guardian angels. Celestria had so far refused to break her vigil, grasping Tom's hand tightly in her own, as if by the sheer force of her love, she could keep her husband's frail heart pumping the precious life force around his body.

Jazz sat listening to the beeps and whirs of the machines keeping her father alive. The sounds became like a mantra in her head and if she concentrated on them, it took some of the pain away.

Tom had drifted in and out of sleep—as Celestria had said, seemingly comforted by their presence. Jazz watched her mother across the bed. Her eyes were drooping as she sat there and she was chalk white.

'Mum,' Jazz whispered.

Celestria jumped and her eyes opened wide with fear. Jazz realised she had been dozing.

'Mum, please will you take a break, and have something to eat and drink? The nurse has just said Dad's stable and I'll be here with him if he wakes up.'

Celestria looked at her watch and saw it was ten to five. She nodded. 'All right. I'll be in the canteen, if—'

'Yes, I know where you'll be, but we'll be fine, won't we, Daddy?' As Celestria took her hand away from Tom's, Jazz grasped his other hand in hers and held it tightly.

'I won't be long,' Celestria said softly. She cast a last fond glance at her husband, then walked towards the exit.

Jazz watched her father as he slept, then let her mind drift off to the case. She wondered how Issy had got on with Rory and whether they'd found David Millar yet.

She had to assume both her own and Issy's instincts were right and he was innocent. She tried to focus on the connection between Charlie and Hugh Daneman.

Charlie: Corin Conaught's nephew.

Hugh: Corin's—Cory's—supposed lover from many years ago.

Had Charlie known that Hugh had been close to the uncle who had died long before he was born?

Adele Cavendish, Charlie's mother, meeting with her brother Edward to discuss what they would do with the estate now that Charlie was gone and there were no direct heirs.

Was she missing something?

Perhaps Corin's mother could help shed some light on the subject. However, from the way Edward had described her, Emily Conaught sounded very frail. And as such, perhaps not a reliable source of information.

She felt a slight pressure on her hand and turned to see her father, his eyes wide open, smiling at her from beneath the mask.

She leaned forward and kissed him on the forehead. 'Hello, Daddy. Nice sleep?' she whispered in his ear.

He nodded slightly, then turned his head to the left looking for Celestria.

'I sent her off to get something to eat. She's had nothing all day. Are you feeling okay?'

Tom nodded slightly again, then looked as if he wanted to say something, and shook his head in frustration.

'Just keep calm, Daddy, you won't have this mask on for much longer. I have to say, you do look rather ridiculous in it. All you need now is a large pair of grey floppy ears.'

Tom rolled his eyes in agreement. He extricated his hand from Jazz's and made writing signs in the air.

'You want a pen and some paper?'

Tom gave the thumbs-up.

Jazz dug in her handbag for a pen and fished out her notebook. She placed the pen in one hand and the open notebook in the other. With effort, Tom managed to move the pen to the paper and began to write.

How is your mother?

Jazz read the quavery words and nodded. 'She's fine. Worried about you, obviously.'

Tom wrote again.

You will look after her for me?

Jazz choked back a sob. 'Oh Daddy, you know I will, but you'll be home soon to do it yourself.'

I'm not frightened.

Jazz was struggling to hold the tears back. She couldn't reply.

How is case going?

'Not well, to be honest. I'm still struggling to tie any of the strands together, but I'm sure there'll be a breakthrough. There usually is when I'm on my knees.'

Tom was scribbling away.

Look to the past for wisdom and the future for hope.

Jazz nodded. It was one of her father's favourite sayings.

I love you darling and I am v proud.

Tom's hands sank onto the bed, exhausted with the effort. He nodded slightly, then closed his eyes.

Jazz removed the notebook and pen from his hands. She studied his faint scrawl, the sight of its fragility tearing her apart. She grabbed her father's hand and stroked his forehead gently as he slept. *Please, God, I know he loves you but we love him and need him, too. Don't take him yet, not yet...*

Chapter Twenty-Three

Adele Cavendish zipped up the holdall, then dragged the two large suitcases to the top of the stairs. She walked back into the bedroom she'd shared with her husband for the past twenty years, then closed the wardrobe doors to hide the empty rails behind them.

She went to her bedside table and picked up the small framed photo of Charlie when he was a tiny baby and stuffed it into a side pocket of her holdall. She looked around the bedroom one last time, then shut the door behind her.

Heaving the first suitcase down the stairs, she left it at the bottom in the hall and went back for the other one.

Once the holdall and the suitcases were safely stowed in the back of her Volvo, Adele came back into the house and wandered around the silent downstairs rooms.

There was no doubt it was a beautiful house, but it wasn't a home, and hadn't been for many years. When Charlie was back for the holidays from school, it had been possible to rekindle the dead atmosphere. The friends he sometimes brought with him would see to it that laughter echoed through the rooms and Adele would feel useful again, feeding the boys with vast meals to stoke their growing bodies.

But now Charlie was gone. And was never coming back.

William came home on a Friday, then returned Sunday night to his flat in London; Adele could almost see by the way he ate his Sunday lunch at pace that he was desperate to return to town, leaving his wife to clear up the dishes and face another week alone.

She knew many other wives in the surrounding villages who were 'weekly widows', whose husbands also worked in London. They seemed unperturbed by their circumstances, knowing the quid pro quo of an absent husband was their expensive lifestyles. They forged friendships with each other, filling their days with school runs, yoga and long lunches.

William had always wanted her to be far more social than her retiring nature allowed. Being loud and ebullient himself, he liked nothing more than a raucous supper party, his table populated by successful and, Adele thought, completely shallow people.

She sometimes wondered why on earth he'd married her; she had always been a wallflower, preferring to listen rather than be listened to, but perhaps the cold hard truth of the matter was that the ruthlessly ambitious William had needed a certain level of social standing to complement his clever, quick mind and burgeoning career. And Adele, sister to a lord and an 'Honourable' herself, with a country estate on which to host a grand wedding for those he wanted to impress, had fitted the bill.

Of course, she'd been flattered by him wanting her; he'd been, and still was, a handsome, charismatic man. But as his career had proceeded steadily upwards, she had become less and less relevant to him.

As she walked into the kitchen to read the letter just one more time, Adele knew he had never really loved her.

She stared around the room in which she had spent so many hours trying to be a good wife and mother.

She'd often felt women's emancipation had completely passed her by. Her life had probably been no different from any character in an Austen novel. Like so many women before her, she'd been tricked into marriage by a charming, but heartless, rogue.

She'd stayed for one reason only: Charlie.

Adele reread the words she had written at six o'clock this morning.

Dear William,

I feel we no longer have a marriage, and haven't had for some considerable time. Now Charlie has gone, I can see no reason to stay and prolong the agony for either of us. I trust you will think it is for the best, too. No more pretending.

My solicitor will be in touch re: the divorce proceedings, but I will not be difficult. I will be moving back to Norfolk. I suggest we sell the house in Rutland, unless you want to keep it, in which case you could buy me out.

I would like our divorce to be as civilised and as fast as possible so we can both move on.

Thank you for the past twenty-five years. I will cherish the happy moments.

But thank you most of all for Charlie. He made everything worthwhile.
Adele

She folded the letter in three and pushed it into the envelope, knowing she had agonised over the wording enough. She took her pen from her handbag and wrote William's name on the front. As she carried it into the hall and laid it on top of the rest of the post, she wondered how he would react when he read it.

The one thing she could not imagine was that he would come chasing after her.

She walked to the front door, the fact she was leaving behind twenty-five years of marriage not causing her the pain it should.

Then suddenly remembering, she ran upstairs and along the corridor to Charlie's bedroom. Steeling herself to open the door, she walked quickly across to the bed and picked up the moth-eaten teddy that lay on the pillow. She ran down the stairs and opened the front door. Stepping out onto the snowy porch, she shut the door behind her without looking back.

Jazz glanced up at the clock. It was half past nine at night. Her father was sleeping peacefully. Celestria appeared at the door of the ward and gestured towards Jazz to join her. Once outside in the corridor, Jazz followed her mother into the relatives' room.

'Darling, I've just spoken to the critical care doctor and he says that Tom is not in any immediate danger. It's pointless both of us having no sleep tonight. If your father seems better tomorrow, you may well be heading back to work and you need some rest. I just had a word with Patrick and he's already found a hotel about half a mile away which you can walk to. If there's any problem, I'll call you.'

'Why don't you come with us?'

'I'm going to borrow a blanket and make do in here. I don't think the nurses are keen on having me on the ward all night, but at least if I'm here, I'm near him and can be there if he needs me.'

'Oh Mum, please come. You need sleep too.'

'Well, I doubt that even if I was staying at the Ritz I'd get any sleep tonight. Besides, if all goes well, you can come and relieve me tomorrow morning for a few hours.' Celestria took her daughter's hand. 'Really, it's where I want to be.'

'All right, but you promise you'll call if—'

'Of course. Now off you go downstairs. Patrick is waiting for you by the front entrance.'

'You know, it's sheer coincidence he's here. I—'

'Ssshh, I understand. And as your daddy would say, sometimes God moves in mysterious ways. I'm glad he's here for you. At least he understands. Now'—Celestria patted her hand—'go and try and get some sleep.'

Patrick was loitering just outside the entrance, smoking a cigarette. He smiled at her.

'Okay?'

Jazz nodded.

'The hotel doesn't look too grand, I'm afraid, but fair play, at least it's walkable. My car is after being buried under a foot of snow. At least it's stopped now. They're saying it'll thaw out by morning.' He held out his elbow. 'Shall we?'

The moon was shining bright and round, lighting up the snow that was shrouding everything in its glittery beauty.

'This way, and be careful, it's treacherous, so it is, especially in those shoes.' Patrick indicated the court shoes Jazz had worn for work this morning, anticipating a normal day.

The only sound was their footsteps crunching in the snow.

'Now this is real silence,' said Patrick as they made their way carefully across the car park and out of the entrance to the hospital grounds. 'It's incredible the way snow muffles any noise.'

'Patrick?'

Jazz needed to say it now. She took a deep breath.

'Thank you for being here. I really appreciate it.'

'No problem, really.'

Jazz's teeth were chattering, even in her wool coat. She stumbled slightly and Patrick grabbed her around the waist. 'Come on, it's not far now.'

The hotel was the kind of place that Jazz would not think of entering under any normal circumstances. She sat down in the small, ugly reception while Patrick checked them in and got the keys.

They mounted the stairs, covered in a worn patterned carpet.

'Here we are.' Patrick put the key in the lock and opened the door. Jazz walked through into the small but surprisingly pretty room. Patrick followed her and closed the door behind them.

'So now, shall I be running you a nice hot bath?' he suggested.

'Don't worry, I can do it. You go and get some sleep. You must be exhausted too.'

'Me? No! I've had a day off reading the paper and drinking tea. I'm grand altogether.'

'Well, anyway, thanks a lot.' She kissed him peremptorily on the cheek. 'Goodnight.'

She turned, walked into the bathroom and put the light on. Patrick stood in the doorway watching her as she put the plug in.

'Jazz, I'm afraid this was the only room they were having available. The place is heaving due to stranded commuters, so I'm afraid I'm in here with you. I'm prepared to sleep in the chair if that's what you'd be wanting.'

She turned abruptly to look up at him. 'You are joking?'

'No, I swear. Call down to reception and ask them.'

'Christ!' Jazz turned the water on full pelt.

'I'm sorry, really. I promise it isn't a ruse to be having my way with you, just the grand old British weather.'

When Jazz didn't reply, he shrugged. 'I understand. I'll be off to sleep in the car.'

He headed out of the bathroom. Jazz gave an inner scream of frustration, then followed him.

'Don't be ridiculous, Patrick! You'll freeze to death and then that'll be on my conscience too.' She glanced at the bed, which at least seemed to be a decent size. 'I'll cope, somehow,' she muttered, then turned back into the bathroom and slammed the door behind her.

Lying in the bath, letting the warm water unknot her aching shoulders and calm her frayed nerves, she closed her eyes and tried to be rational. Whatever had happened in the past, Patrick had been wonderful today, and it really wasn't his fault they were now in this predicament.

They were both grown-ups. Of course they could cope.

She reached for the thin towel, draped it round her and got out of the bath, realising that, just to top it all, she had nothing to sleep in. Putting her underwear back on and pulling the towel on top of that, she walked back into the bedroom.

Patrick was already in bed, his clothes draped over the chair. He was propped up with his hands behind his head, watching her.

She walked round to the opposite side of the bed, dropped the towel and dived hurriedly under the sheets.

Patrick chuckled. 'Jazz, I was after living with you for ten years. I've seen it all before.'

'But you don't live with me any more. We're divorced, remember?' She spoke grumpily, turning her back to him and making herself as comfortable as she could on the lumpy mattress.

'Do you realise we're in what this grand establishment refers to as the honeymoon suite? I pity any bride who begins married life in this bed,' Patrick remarked.

'It's fine, really. Thank you for finding it. Have you got my mobile?'

'Yes, it's right there on top of the chest of drawers. And before you ask, yes, it is switched on.'

'Thanks. I should call in but—'

'I called Miles earlier. There was nothing urgent to report, but he said he'd speak to you tomorrow morning to bring you up to date.'

'Which means they haven't found David Millar yet.'

'Who?'

'Just a suspect who's gone missing.'

'Oh.'

They lay there in silence for a while.

'Are you okay?' Patrick asked eventually.

'About what?'

'Your daddy?'

Jazz sighed. 'I can't quite process the fact that he's lying at death's door, just a stone's throw from here. I just have to believe he'll pull through. Anything else…well…I just can't go there.'

'Ah, sweetheart, I know so well how close the two of you are.'

Jazz nodded, the lump that had been lodged in her throat since this morning threatening to burst.

She felt a hand on her arm. 'Jazz, you have to believe he will pull through. If anybody can, he can. He's fought through today now, hasn't he? We know the first twenty-four hours are always the most critical.'

Jazz nodded, unable to speak.

'You know whatever happens, I'll be here for you if you need me.'

Jazz nodded, as the lump finally burst in her throat and the tears started to pour down her cheeks.

'He can't die, he can't. I need him, and so does Mum. He's being so brave, but I know he must be suffering terribly and that makes it worse.'

He kissed the top of her head. 'I know, Jazz, I know.'

'He's only sixty-five, for God's sake! He's not old! What about all those ninety-year-olds who live on for years in old people's homes? Why can't that be him? As long as he's alive, as long as Dad's alive...' She looked at Patrick. 'He will live, won't he?' she asked desperately.

'Course he will,' Patrick soothed. Then he reached down and kissed her forehead, then her nose, and then her lips.

His arms wrapped around her and he kissed her with urgency. His hands went to her breasts and she did not stop them, suddenly as hungry for him as he was for her.

She could hear herself breathing heavily as he rolled on top of her, and the next moment he was inside her.

He spoke to her, words of endearment, but she didn't hear him, didn't want to hear him as she felt seven months of abstinence build, sending her spiralling up and up until she exploded with him and he fell on top of her, panting with exertion.

She could feel his hot breath on her cheek. She closed her eyes, letting the feeling of calm that followed the storm fill her and prevent her brain from processing the ramifications of what she had just done.

'Oh my God...that was...amazing, just amazing,' Patrick murmured. 'I've missed you so much.'

Jazz remained silent in the darkness, not wanting to move on from the moment.

'I love you, Jazz. I truly do. I'm begging you to forgive me.'

Jazz stared into the blackness. 'Patrick, I forgave you a long time ago.'

Angelina had taken another Valium an hour ago, but it didn't seem to have affected the churning in her stomach or the abnormally fast beating of her heart.

Standing in the kitchen in her robe, she leaned over the sink looking out at the back garden, the spotlights illuminating the fairy-tale scene outside.

She padded across the kitchen, opened a cupboard and took out the brandy bottle. She poured herself a double, took the drink to the kitchen table and sat down. She took a large swig, the unfamiliar strength making her gag.

She checked her watch. It was nearly half past ten. Was it too late to call the police?

Then a thought struck her. Was it possible Julian's disappearance was connected with Rory? And to David's release?

Did David blame Julian in some way for what had happened?

Would he have gone to see him last night, after he was released?

Was he unstable enough to kill him?

Angelina gave a little cry of anguish.

Was she being ridiculous?

She stood up and paced round the kitchen.

No. Less than twenty-four hours ago, David was being held on suspicion of murder. A murder he had openly admitted to.

She shook her head. Here she was, considering seriously that her ex-husband had murdered her lover.

Angelina washed out her glass and left it to drain. She locked all the doors and went upstairs, going first to check on Rory, who was peacefully asleep.

She climbed into bed and reached for her book, trying to regain some semblance of normality, of her life before this nightmare had happened.

But she couldn't concentrate.

She put down the book and lay very still as she thought through all the possibilities.

Was it as simple as Julian having enough of the situation with Rory and David, and deciding to leave her? Perhaps, but that didn't explain why he would abandon his clients and work.

No.

Had some terrible accident befallen him in the dreadful weather? Was he lying somewhere in need of help, but unable to call?

Possibly.

Angelina reached for the mobile lying on the empty pillow beside her and dialled his number one more time.

No answer.

She reached to turn off the light. First thing tomorrow morning, if she had not heard from him, she would call the number Detective Inspector Hunter had given her when Rory had gone missing.

'Come in, Mr Frederiks. I hope the journey wasn't too strenuous? Robert Sanders.' The solicitor shook Sebastian's hand.

'Not at all. It's rather nice to come up to town once in a while. I did my teacher training in Wimbledon, as a matter of fact, and sometimes I wonder why I went back to Norfolk, but,' Sebastian shrugged, 'that was what fate decreed.'

'Do sit down.' Sanders indicated a chair in front of his partner's desk. 'Tea or coffee?'

'Coffee would be splendid, thank you.' Sebastian sat quietly, taking in the beautiful oak-panelled office with its huge Georgian windows overlooking Grosvenor Square. Sebastian was amazed a quiet schoolteacher such as Hugh could afford a practice as upmarket as this.

'So, Mr Frederiks, were you aware that Mr Daneman had left you a bequest in his will?'

'Absolutely not. I've known Hugh for over thirty years. He taught me as a pupil at St Stephen's, then when I joined the staff, we became fellow teachers.'

'Well.' Sanders picked up a heavy vellum sheet of paper and put on his reading glasses. 'Apart from his manuscripts, which are very valuable and have been left to the British Library, and one other bequest, he's left the rest of his estate to you.'

Sebastian gasped. 'To me? Why? Surely he has family that will be expecting to inherit?'

'No. It seems he had no other living relatives. The estate is not enormous, but it does comprise a flat in Kensington and some cash and insurance policies, which amount to a little over two hundred thousand pounds. Ah, Sophie, put the tray down on the desk and we'll help ourselves.'

Sebastian tried hard to suppress the surge of inevitable excitement. He watched the attractive young secretary place the tray on the desk, then leave.

'I'll pour, shall I? Milk and sugar?' Sanders asked.

'Thank you. Did, er, Hugh ever explain to you why he was leaving his estate to me?'

Mr Sanders passed Sebastian his coffee. 'No. Mine is not to question why. Though having known Hugh for over thirty years, I trust that his final wishes were as carefully thought through as the decisions he made in life.'

'Well, well.' Sebastian lifted the cup to his lips and slurped the hot coffee.

'As executor, I will be handling probate. If you wish, to keep it simple, I'd be happy to act for you too.'

'That's very kind of you, Mr Sanders. You say there's a flat in Kensington?'

'Yes. It may well be leasehold, with only a few years to run. Many flats were leasehold in the sixties, and the owners didn't bother to renew when they should, but if you wish, I can look into that for you, too.'

'If you would, Mr Sanders. I'm no expert on matters legal. I'm a simple schoolteacher who lives in a rented house.'

Mr Sanders took his glasses off his nose. 'Well, this must be manna from heaven for you.'

'Oh yes, indeed it is,' Sebastian replied disingenuously.

'Do you have a family of your own?'

'No. My parents are dead and I haven't yet managed to snare a female into starting my own dynasty.' Sebastian grinned.

'You were not adopted, as far as you know?'

Sebastian frowned. 'No. At least, if I was, my parents didn't tell me.'

'Mmn.' Sanders sipped his coffee slowly.

'Are you...suggesting that...?'

'Mr Frederiks, I'm suggesting nothing, that's not my place. But having been forty years in my current role, one usually finds a method behind the seeming madness of such a situation. Anyway, that, my dear chap, is down to you to find out. I can only oil the legal wheels, not the human ones. Now, I will, of course, set everything down in writing to you, but I'm afraid I did have to fit you in between clients today, so if you'll excuse me, I must say goodbye.'

Sebastian left the building in a daze. He headed straight for the nearest pub and downed a whisky to clear his head.

Had Sanders been trying to intimate that Hugh Daneman was...his father?

No! Surely not!

Everyone knew Hugh was an old queer. It just couldn't be.

Perhaps it was as simple as poor old Hugh having no one left in the world. Sebastian realised Hugh had always taken a fatherly interest in him, even when he'd been a youngster at school.

He took a taxi to Liverpool Street. Now that he was going to be a man of means, he could afford the odd luxury.

He daydreamed all the way home on the train, wondering if, now he had some funds, he would stay as housemaster at St Stephen's, or go off and travel the world...cricket in the West Indies, rugby in New Zealand...a whole raft of possibilities had opened up to him.

And what about her? What would she say when he told her? Would it mean he was finally in a position to offer her what she deserved?

Chapter Twenty-Four

Jazz woke abruptly at six o'clock. The oblivion of sleep left her instantly and she jumped out of bed to check her mobile, in case she'd missed a call.

There was nothing, but her heart was pounding and she wanted to get to the hospital and see her father. Patrick stirred as she dressed hurriedly and pulled her coat on.

'What time is it?' he enquired drowsily.

'Just gone six. I'm going to the hospital now.'

'Okay. Shall I be meeting you there?'

She peeped out of the window. 'The snow is melting fast. There'll be no problem about getting back to London now.'

'Jazz.' Patrick reached out his hand to her.

She ignored it. 'I have to go. I'll call you when I know how Dad is.'

Celestria smiled wearily as she entered the critical care ward.

'Hi, Mum.' Jazz bent down to give her sleeping father a kiss. 'How is he?'

'Good, he's good, Jazz. His vital signs are apparently much more stable, and he slept well.'

'Oh Mum, thank God!' She choked back a sob.

'Yes, thank God,' Celestria echoed. 'He's not out of the woods yet, but every hour counts. The nurse said they may take the mask off later and see if he can breathe by himself.'

'Why don't you go and get yourself some breakfast and I'll stay with him?'

'Yes, I will. I feel comfortable enough to leave him for a little while now.' Celestria indicated the weather outside. 'And the snow's thawing, so you should be able to get back to Norfolk without too much of a problem.'

'Mum, I'm staying until I know Dad is okay. End of story, all right?'

'Yes, of course, darling, of course. I won't be long.'

Jazz studied her father and thought that his colour was indeed better than yesterday. Then she blushed at the thought of him knowing what she had been doing whilst he was fighting for his life.

He'd never liked Patrick, always thought he was wrong for her, and being Tom, had made no bones about hiding it.

She stroked his hand gently, hating herself for needing *and* enjoying last night. She sighed, knowing there was no road back for her and Patrick. If anything, he wanted shooting for taking advantage of her while she was at her most vulnerable.

But the bottom line was, *she* had let him.

Jazz felt pressure on her hand and saw Tom's eyes were open.

A nurse appeared behind her, studying the monitors.

'Morning, Tom. Who's my star patient? You have done well.'

Jazz saw her father smile.

'So well that the doctor says you can take the mask off for ten minutes, as long as you promise not to chatter to your daughter too much.'

Tom nodded and the nurse gently removed the mask. She handed Jazz a cup containing some ice.

'Your father's mouth will be very dry. Give him these ice chips to suck.'

Jazz took an ice cube, moistened her father's cracked lips. Tom groaned in pleasure.

'Dad, you are doing so well.' Jazz tried to keep the emotion out of her voice.

'Can't believe I'm still here,' he rasped. 'Thought Big G wanted me up there.'

'No, Dad, we want you down here. Mum's gone to have some breakfast. That shows you how much better you must be. She hasn't left your side for the past eighteen hours.'

Tom's eyes filled with tears. 'Tell her I love her,' he whispered.

'You can tell her yourself when she comes back up. Try not to talk too much for now.'

Tom nodded and his eyes began to close again. The nurse appeared to put on the mask and Jazz sat quietly watching him.

When Celestria came back, Jazz told her what Tom had said.

'It's wonderful they removed that grotesque mask, even if for a few minutes. Patrick's downstairs in the canteen by the way. Waiting for instructions, as he put it.'

Jazz could feel herself blushing. 'Right. I'd better go and see him, tell him to go.'

'I think he's very happy to wait for you. He said he might take himself off around Cambridge for the morning.'

'There's no need for him to do that.' She stood up abruptly. 'Be back in a bit.'

Patrick was sitting at the same table as yesterday, looking bleary-eyed and drinking coffee.

'Can I be getting you something, Jazz?'

'No, I'm going straight back up to Dad. I just came to say I really don't need you to hang around here for the day. I'm not leaving until the consultant has been to see Dad and convinced me he's all right. I can always get DS Miles to come and collect me. Without the snow, it won't take long. But thanks very much for being there for me yesterday. I really appreciate it.'

Patrick looked up at her sadly. 'Jazz, can we not at least arrange a date to get together and talk about what happened last night? I might be sounding like a girl here, but it meant something to me, even if it didn't to you.'

'I'll call you later and let you know how Dad is. We can discuss it then.' She knew she was sounding cold and businesslike but it was the only way she could cope. She leaned forward and gave him a peck on the cheek. 'Thanks, Patrick, really.'

She turned from him and walked swiftly away, towards the entrance of the hospital. Even as she stepped outside into the fresh blast of cool air, she could feel the sweat on her palms and on her forehead.

Finding a bench, she sat down, took out her mobile and called Miles.

'How are things?' he asked immediately, in the tone of voice Jazz recognised as someone expecting bad news.

'Dad got through the night and he's a little better this morning.'

'That's fantastic! I'm so pleased for you.'

'Well, there's a way to go yet, and I'm not sure when I'll be back, but I'd like you to briefly update me on progress. Have you found Millar yet?'

'No luck so far. We're combing the city. To be honest, Ma'am, I wonder if he had a bellyful of booze, fell in a ditch somewhere and has frozen to death in this dreadful weather.'

'If that's the case, you'll find him today, now the snow's thawing. Have you managed to get a copy of Hugh Daneman's will?'

'Yes. I spoke to the solicitor in London and he faxed it through. It's quite a surprise. He's left everything, bar one other small bequest, to Sebastian Frederiks, the housemaster at St Stephen's.'

'Really?' Jazz knew she would have to process the information before it made sense.

'Not only that, but Daneman changed his will less than a month ago. Before that, more or less the whole estate had been left to the British Library. There is some money left to Jenny Colman, the headmaster's secretary. Do you want me to go and see Mr Frederiks? Try and find out more?'

'Absolutely. It could be coincidental Daneman changed the will so recently. Some people are obsessive about their wills and alter them all the time. Was the solicitor able to shed any light on the subject?'

'I asked him, of course, why he thought the will had been changed. He said he had no idea and it was none of his business to question these things. However, he did venture that in his professional opinion, there was usually a method behind the seeming madness. He had assumed Mr Frederiks was either a close friend or a relative of some kind.'

'Have forensics come back on the medical dispensary sheet?'

'Yes. And the drug that was Tippexed out was aspirin. You were right.'

'And how did Issy get on with young Rory yesterday?'

'It went well apparently. She's going back to see him again this morning and I know she's eager to speak to you about it when you have the chance. Rather fortuitous, this snow.'

'Really, why?'

There was a slight pause before Miles answered. 'Just that it's been good to have some company.'

'I'm going back up to the ward now, but as soon as I've seen the consultant, I'll know a little more about when I should be back and I'll call you then. I'd like you to come and collect me anyway. I'd like Issy to hang around a little longer so we can have a chat, but tell her I'll speak to her at lunchtime, whatever.'

'She's intending to stay the night here anyway.'

'Really? That surprises me. Thought Issy hated anything to do with the country. Must be your fatal charm, Miles. Speak later.'

Jazz was about to switch her mobile off and go back in when it rang. It was not a number she knew.

'DI Hunter.'

'Yes, hello, Inspector Hunter, it's Angelina Millar here. I am so sorry to bother you and it may be nothing but…my…er…partner, Julian, seems to have gone missing.'

All Jazz needed now was a neurotic woman whose boyfriend had done the dirty on her.

'Gone missing? Are you sure?'

'Yes. I haven't heard from him for two days now, since Tuesday evening. He didn't arrive at his office yesterday—he's a solicitor, you see, and his secretary hasn't heard a word from him. He's not answering his mobile and he isn't at his flat.'

'I see.' Jazz was eager to get back inside. 'I'm afraid I'm currently tied up, Mrs Millar, but if I give you my sergeant's number, perhaps he could help you. Have you got a pen and paper handy?'

'Yes.'

Jazz repeated Miles's number.

'Thank you, Inspector Hunter. You may think I'm being silly, and maybe I am, but it's so unlike Julian. He's so pedantic about arrangements, and as his secretary said, it's unheard of for Julian to not turn up to the office when he knew he had clients.'

'The snow yesterday was terrible. Have you contacted the hospitals?'

'Yes, and there is no one fitting his description that's been admitted anywhere in the area.'

'Well, call DS Miles and I'm sure he will be able to help you. I really must go now, Mrs Millar. Good luck.'

Jazz switched her mobile off before it could ring again and headed back into the hospital, her thoughts focussing only on her father.

Sebastian Frederiks was fast asleep when he heard his mobile ringing. His alarm had not yet gone off but the room was bathed in the soft white light that only reflected snow could give.

He reached for the light switch and turned it on, but not in time to take the call. He checked his watch. It was half past six. Jumping out of bed, he shivered in the cold room, surprised by it. The whole of Fleat House was usually unnaturally warm, overheated, rather like a hospital.

He wandered around, trying to locate his mobile. He found it in his jacket pocket and as he did so, it rang again to tell him he had a voice message. Dialling the number, Sebastian jumped back beneath the warmth of the duvet and listened.

'Hello, darling, it's me. I wanted to catch you before you started work. I'd like to see you tonight if you can make it. I'll be here all evening, so it doesn't matter what time. Call me when you can. I love you.'

Sebastian lay back on his pillows, pondering how he could extricate himself this evening. Being a housemaster was all-consuming. There was no time to have a life of any sort. He was on duty twenty-four hours a day during term time and now Hugh had gone, he didn't even have the back-up of a house tutor until someone else was appointed. James Cox, a sixth-former and head of house, was filling in at present, but Sebastian could hardly leave an eighteen-year-old pupil alone in charge.

He wished to God his inheritance would hurry up and come through and they could start to make plans for the future.

He still hadn't told her about it yet, wanting to save the news for a moment when they could spend some time together, enjoy it. No longer would he be the poor relation, and he wondered if that would change the dynamics at all.

The most important thing was that he would have the autonomy to make the necessary decisions for both of them, a position that a few days ago, he'd never have thought possible.

Sebastian allowed himself a smile. From a seemingly impossible situation, they were both now in a position to move forward.

The alarm clock went off, startling him. He leaned over and switched it off, threw back the duvet and headed for the shower.

He shouted in shocked protest as a freezing cold jet of water stunned his skin into a mass of goose pimples. Fiddling with the control, he saw it was already on the warmest setting. Stepping out and grabbing a towel, he waited outside the cubicle for a few seconds, testing the water with his fingertips to see if it became warmer.

It didn't.

'Bugger,' Sebastian groaned. There was obviously a problem with the system.

Dressing as fast as he could, Sebastian picked up his phone and dialled Bob in maintenance. Not surprised he was not yet in, he dialled Bob's home number and got his wife on the line.

Bob was obviously still in bed. His voice was groggy, but he promised he'd be there as soon as he could.

'Probably a burst pipe,' he muttered. 'It's starting to thaw this morning.'

Sebastian groaned. Seventy boys unable to take their morning showers, smelly and cold and complaining.

He dialled her number and she answered immediately.

'Hello, sweetheart, it's me. How are you?'

'I'm...' There was a pause whilst she thought about it. 'I'm good. Very good.'

'What are you doing here? I wasn't expecting you until the weekend.'

'No, but let's just say I had a sudden change of plan.'

'How long are you here for?'

'That's what I want to talk to you about tonight.'

'Okay. Listen, there's a small crisis here which I need to sort out. I'll have to call you later, but I'm hoping I should be able to get away around eight, only for an hour, I'm afraid, but it's better than nothing.' Sebastian paused. 'I have some news for you, actually.'

'Good news?'

'Yes, very good as it happens.'

'Well, I most certainly have news for you.' Sebastian could hear the smile in her voice.

'Let's say eight then, unless you hear from me. Gotta go now. Bye, sweetheart. See you later.'

Sebastian switched off his mobile, tucked it in his trouser pocket and went off to alert the three floors of dorms to Fleat House's lack of hot water.

'I'll be off to see young Rory, then,' said Issy, as Miles appeared in the reception of the hotel.

'I'll give you a lift there. I've just had Angelina Millar on to me. Apparently, her boyfriend has done a bunk.'

'Still not appeared then? She was very worried when I saw her yesterday.' Issy followed Miles out of the lobby and onto the street, which was slippery with melting snow, rivulets of water flooding down the road. 'Not having a lot of luck with the men in her life, is she? That's both her ex *and* her partner currently on the missing list. You don't think…?'

'I'd doubt it has anything to do with the case, can't see how it could, but I'd better go and have a word with her.' Miles opened the passenger door to allow Issy to step over the puddles and climb inside.

'Pretty odd, though, him disappearing when all of this has happened, isn't it?' Issy questioned as they drove off.

'It sure is, *if* he actually has. Wouldn't be my type, Mrs Millar. Bet she nags constantly, makes you pick your wet towels off the floor and irons your underpants and socks.'

'So what *is* your type, sweetie?' Issy's hand snaked onto Miles's thigh. He slapped it away gently.

'Behave! I'm behind the wheel!' Miles turned right and pulled into Angelina Millar's drive. 'How long will you be with Rory, do you reckon?'

'As long as it takes.' Issy shrugged.

Miles got out of the car and walked round to open the passenger door. 'I'll have a quick word with Mrs Millar, then I have to scoot off to St Stephen's. Can you make your own way back to the station?'

'I suppose so,' Issy sniffed. 'I do so hate walking.'

Miles tapped Issy lightly on her bottom. 'Some exercise'll do you good,' he teased as they walked towards the front door.

Issy rang the bell, to be greeted immediately by a pale Angelina.

'Come in,' she said dully. 'Rory is up in his bedroom.'

'Right. Shall I go and see him up there?'

Angelina nodded. 'If you want. It's the second door on the left.'

'See you later, Miles.' Issy shouted as she clomped up the stairs.

Angelina led Miles into the kitchen. She walked over to the Aga and automatically put the kettle on top of the hotplate.

'Coffee?'

'If you're making some.' DS Miles pulled out a kitchen chair and sat down. 'Any news?'

Angelina shook her head. 'Nothing. I've tried all his numbers and Stacey just called to say he's not at work again today and…' Her voice tailed off and she began to cry. 'Sorry, I haven't had much sleep in the past few days, one way and another.'

'No, I'm sure you haven't. But don't worry, we'll do our best to find Julian for you.' He smiled reassuringly as Angelina set a coffee cup in front of him. 'Thanks. Black is fine. So, could you tell me exactly where Julian was and at what time you last spoke to him?'

Angelina repeated their last conversation as accurately as she could.

'So'—Miles sipped his coffee—'Rory had never met Julian?'

'No. I felt it was best, under the circumstances, for Rory to get over the loss of his father not being at home before I introduced him to his stepfather to be.'

'So, you and Julian were going to get married?'

'We were going to announce our engagement in the summer at Julian's fortieth birthday party.' Tears once more pricked Angelina's eyes. 'I was so excited about it. I'd started contacting lots of Julian's old friends from St Stephen's and—'

'Your fiancé went to St Stephen's?'

'Yes. Coincidentally, he was in Fleat House, although Rory was down for it before I'd met Julian.'

'Right. So who were his old friends?'

Angelina listed the names, remembering them from the emails she'd sent on the website. 'And of course, Julian knew Sebastian Frederiks, who is now Rory's housemaster.' Angelina gave a thin smile. 'Small world.'

'In this county, it certainly seems to be. So how does Julian feel about becoming stepfather to a child he's never met?'

'I think he's nervous, obviously, having never had children of his own. But he always knew Rory was part of the deal. We have a skiing holiday booked for half-term for all three of us. Julian thought it might be a good way to bond with Rory.'

'And how did Julian feel about your ex-husband confessing to the murder of Charlie Cavendish?'

'He was shocked, as we all were.' Angelina shrugged. 'But not particularly surprised. He knew how unstable David was.'

'Does he know David's been released without charge?'

'Detective Miles, I haven't heard from him since Issy told me.'

'No, of course you haven't. Mrs Millar, the last time you saw Julian, did he do or say anything which gave you an indication that something was amiss?'

Angelina sighed. 'Not really, no. He wasn't particularly happy about having to stay at the flat, because Rory was here at home. I'd suggested I'd go and see him last night in Norwich and have a takeaway.'

'Can you give me the address of his flat, and a key? I'll arrange for someone to go and take a look,' said Miles.

'His secretary's already been and there was no sign that he'd gone away suddenly. Besides, it just isn't Julian to do a spur of the moment thing, let alone not contact his office. I've tried all the hospitals in the area and they have no one registered in the past two days fitting his description.' She looked at Miles forlornly. 'He has simply disappeared.'

'If you can give me a photograph, I'll add him to our missing persons file.'

'Is that all you can do?'

'As I said, we'll take a look at his flat, go to his office, but…' Miles shrugged. 'He's a grown man and he's only been missing for two days. Unless there's some evidence to suggest otherwise, we have to assume he has, for reasons best known to himself, decided to take himself off somewhere.'

'What about…' Angelina paused. 'My ex-husband? He hated Julian. We were in town a week or so ago and David threatened to kill Julian. There were lots of witnesses and…David was released on Tuesday night, and that's the last time I heard from Julian, and…'

'I take your point,' said Miles, cutting to the chase. 'But try not to worry. I doubt there's any connection. You yourself have said Mr Millar was not a violent man. Now, you'll have to excuse me, but I have another appointment.' Miles stood up. 'Try and keep calm. I'm sure there is a logical explanation for Julian's no-show.'

'I hope you are right. What with everything else, it just seems too much of a coincidence.' Angelina searched in her handbag for the key to Julian's flat and handed it to Miles.

'We'll do all we can to find him. Right, I'll be off. Issy's going to make her own way back to the station. I'll be in touch if there is any news.'

Angelina walked Miles to the front door. 'Thank you for coming.'

'No problem. Goodbye, Mrs Millar.'

Outside Miles took out his mobile to call DS Roland and find out if there was any news on David Millar.

Sebastian glanced up from the pile of paperwork on his desk as Bob, the caretaker, entered his study.

'Right, Mr Frederiks, that pipe is sorted. Just have to nip down to the cellar and restart the boiler, then we'll be on our way.' Bob's ruddy face was even redder than normal.

'Good. Have you got the key?'

'Yes, I do, thanks, Mr Frederiks.'

Bob left the room and walked down the back corridor. He unlocked the door to the cellar, switched on the light and clambered slowly down the uneven steps. The boys' trunks were stored in here, the perfect place to keep them warm and dry. As he reached the bottom step, Bob sniffed the air.

It wasn't overpowering, but he recognised the unpleasant aroma of decay.

'Darned rat got in here, most probably,' he mumbled to himself, his eyes sweeping the floor for tell-tale droppings. He looked behind the stack of trunks and could see nothing. He sniffed again. The smell was stronger here. Bending down, he used his nose to guide him. The smell seemed to be coming from one of the trunks, whose lid was not quite closed.

'Don't say the darned thing got in there. Poor lad'll have a fit when he comes to open it.'

Bob seized the brass lock and threw back the lid.

Sebastian Frederiks jumped at his desk as he heard the sound of a man's scream pierce the silence of the building.

Chapter Twenty-Five

Jazz and Celestria looked up nervously as Mr Carlisle sat down opposite them in the family room.

'Good news,' he smiled, 'Tom is responding to treatment. He's not home and dry yet by any means, but the fluid is draining off his lungs, his blood pressure is better, which means his heart is pumping more efficiently than yesterday. I'd say the prognosis is far more positive today and if he continues to respond, then we will have him out of critical care in a couple of days' time.'

Celestria squeezed her daughter's hand and smiled in relief. 'That's wonderful news, isn't it, darling?'

Jazz nodded. 'Absolutely.'

'Although I should warn you, if he does make it through, he will have to take excellent care of himself in the future. His heart muscle has been badly damaged by this second attack and considerably weakened. Therefore, as far as the long-term situation is concer—'

'Please, let's just get him through this and worry about the future when it happens,' Celestria cut in, eager to let nothing spoil the good news.

'Of course.' The consultant nodded. 'You're very sensible to take it day by day.'

'So he's no longer in immediate danger?' asked Jazz.

'When patients are as sick as Tom, there are no guarantees, but he's definitely moving in the right direction.' Carlisle stood up. 'I'll see you tomorrow.'

When he'd left the room, Jazz threw her arms around her mother. 'Oh God, I was so scared we were going to lose him.'

'Well, he's still here and fighting.' Celestria stroked her daughter's hair. 'And I think you'd better get back to Norfolk.'

'I'll go downstairs and check in with Miles, but unless I have to go,

I'd prefer to stay here.'

'If it's any help, my instinct tells me your father is going to cheat his maker yet again. Anyway, you go and make that call and I'll go and see Tom, tell him what a superstar his doctor thinks he is.' Celestria smiled and cupped her hands round her daughter's face as she planted a kiss on her forehead. 'What would I do without you, darling? Thank you for being here.'

'Don't be silly, Mum. I'll be back in a tick.'

Jazz hurried down the stairs and out of the hospital. Switching on her mobile, she saw she had a message from Miles.

The colour drained from her face as she listened to it.

Issy was enjoying a bowl of Angelina's excellent chicken soup when her mobile rang.

'Excuse me,' she said to Angelina, as she answered.

'Are you still at the Millar house?' It was Miles.

'Yes. I was just on my way back to the station.'

'Can you talk? Out of earshot?'

'Hold on just one second.' Issy could hear the tension in Miles's voice. She heaved herself out of her chair. 'Sorry, boss on the blower,' she mouthed to Angelina, then left the kitchen and walked into the drawing room. 'Okay, shoot.'

'Julian Forbes's body has just been discovered in a trunk in the cellar of Fleat House.'

Issy instinctively clapped a hand to her mouth. 'My God! Who found him?'

'The caretaker. He had to restart the boiler this morning. Piece of luck, actually. If there hadn't been a burst pipe, the body might have remained there until Easter, when the boys need their trunks to go home for the holidays.'

'How long has he been dead?'

'A couple of days, I'd say, but the SOCOs are on their way now.'

'Angelina is going to flip, poor love.'

'Tell me about it. Issy, I need a favour. Can you stay where you are for now? You're perfectly safe—we posted an officer outside the house when we knew Millar had done a bunk, but I don't want either Mrs Millar or Rory leaving the house just for the present. I've called Jazz and she's expected here in the next hour.'

'Angelina's ex turned up yet?'

'No. Could you make sure that all the doors are locked, just in case David Millar is on the rampage, and decides to give his ex-wife a visit?'

'I doubt he will, but yes.'

'I know you doubt it, Issy, but Millar was released at about the same time as Mrs Millar last heard from Julian Forbes. *And* he's been missing ever since.'

'As I really don't fancy eating my Auntie Madge's behind, I have to believe it's sheer coincidence,' Issy murmured. 'Especially as I have news on Rory.'

'I'll call you as soon as Jazz is back, but for the moment, say nothing.'

'I will make polite and interesting conversation as well as I can.'

'Thanks, sweetheart. Sorry to drag you into this.'

'It's okay. I'm going back to the city for some peace. Bye.'

Issy painted a smile on her face and walked slowly back into the kitchen.

Jazz had managed to catch Patrick just as he was about to get on the A14 back to London. He had picked her up outside the hospital and they had sped off to Norfolk.

Jazz had spent most of the journey on her mobile to Norton.

'Not a good situation, Hunter. I've dispatched extra SOCOs already, but you're obviously going to need more back-up to help you. You have one very experienced detective conveniently on the spot, so to speak. The point is, can you work with him?'

Jazz knew she was damned either way. If she said 'no', Norton would regard it as the height of unprofessionalism; 'yes', and she was doomed to working with Patrick until the case was solved.

She had no choice. 'Yes, Sir. Of course,' she answered brusquely.

'Good. I've contacted King's Lynn, and they're sending some officers along to you as we speak. They can at least provide a presence at the school.'

'I was just coming to that, Sir. Do I close it immediately? DS Miles has evacuated Fleat House, and the boys are being put up in other dorms for now. But the moment word gets out of this third death, which, from what Miles has told me is unquestionably murder, there'll be mass panic.'

'Get there first, then we'll take a view. Call me after you've been to the crime scene.'

'Will do, Sir.'

She closed her mobile and stared into the distance.

'You okay, there?' Patrick closed a hand over hers. Jazz moved it away.

'Yes, yes, I'm fine.'

'You're exhausted, Jazz, just remember that. Fair play to you, you've been through a difficult couple of days.'

'Really, I'll be fine,' she repeated curtly, her pride asserting itself. 'I can cope perfectly well.'

'I know you can, Jazz. And I accept working with me is the last thing you had on your mind.'

'Especially as you're now the senior officer, since your promotion,' Jazz muttered.

'Look now, I swear I won't step on your toes. Can you try and give me a briefing of where you are in the investigation?'

She gritted her teeth. 'I'll do my best.'

By the time they arrived in Foltesham, Patrick knew the nuts and bolts of the situation.

'From what you've just told me, I can't for the life of me see where the Julian Forbes connection comes in. Unless you and Issy got it wrong and David Millar really is after going berserk,' surmised Patrick.

Jazz opened her mouth to reply, but Patrick silenced her. 'No, Jazz, I'm not criticising you, so. Neither the facts nor the character analysis hang together, but fair play, he does have the motive, for both the boy Cavendish and his ex-wife's lover.'

'But even though that would tie in the deaths of both Charlie—Millar murdered him because he was bullying his son—and Julian—Millar hated him for being his wife's lover—that still leaves Hugh Daneman out of it.' Jazz sighed.

'I thought you said it was straightforward suicide? He doesn't have to be involved, so.'

'But there *is* a connection to Charlie; Hugh Daneman was the lover of his uncle many years ago.'

'Well, isn't that just sheer coincidence? Norfolk being such a small place and all?'

'Maybe, but I do need to follow it up. The mother of Daneman's dead lover is still alive. She's apparently very fragile, but maybe she can shed some light on what happened back then. And how it might be tied in to now.'

As Patrick turned into the school, Jazz could see the yellow police tape surrounding Fleat House.

'Right, let's go,' she said, and stepped out of the car. Before Jazz had taken more than a couple of steps, the headmaster was at her side.

'Thank God you are here! All hell has broken loose! The place is crawling with coppers, the boys are wondering what's going on and it's only a matter of time before they are on their mobiles to their parents. I know you'll need to close the school, evacuate the premises, then there's the press... My God, it'll finish us!'

Robert Jones was beside himself.

'I understand your panic, Headmaster. And it's not a good scenario,' Jazz agreed. 'We'll obviously need to talk, but first let me go and take a look at the crime scene, get an overview of what exactly has happened. This is DCI Coughlin, who's here to help us sort this situation out as fast as we can. Do you want to come across with us to Fleat House, Headmaster, or would you prefer to wait in your office?'

The head looked as though he was soon to keel over. 'No, no. I'll wait for you in my office.' Then he turned tail and almost ran back to the sanctuary of the main school building.

Jazz and Patrick walked across Chapel Lawn, still covered in heaps of melting snow.

DS Roland was waiting for them at the entrance of Fleat House, looking self-important.

'My men have sealed off the building and no one has been allowed in since we were called to the incident. The boys have been evacuated and only Mr Frederiks, the caretaker who found him and your DS Miles are waiting for you in Frederiks's study.'

'Thank you, Roland,' Jazz nodded. 'Any news on Millar?'

'Nothing, Ma'am. He seems to have vanished.'

'DCI Coughlin.' Patrick reached out his hand to DS Roland, who shook it nervously. 'Put every spare officer on it, Roland. We need to find him.'

Jazz led Patrick along the corridor to the study.

Miles, Sebastian Frederiks and an older man in a brown boiler suit were sitting tensely in the room.

'Morning, everyone,' said Jazz, then introduced Patrick to the caretaker and Frederiks.

'So, you found the body, Mr, er…?' asked Jazz.

'Bob Gilkes. Yes. There were a burst pipe and the boiler went off. I had to go down there to restart it, smelled something funny and…' The man swallowed. 'That's when I found it…*him.*'

'I heard Bob's scream, and ran down to the cellar to see what the problem was. And I was able to identify him,' Frederiks explained.

'He was a person known to you then?' Jazz asked.

'Coincidentally, yes, although I hadn't seen him for many years. He was in the year above me here at St Stephen's. I knew instantly it was Julian. Poor chap. I still can't quite believe it.' Frederiks shook his head.

'So you hadn't seen him for how long?'

'Maybe fifteen years?' He shrugged. 'We both moved on to university, then ended up for a while in London together. I saw him a couple of times for a pint, but then I came back to Norfolk and he stayed in London. I had heard he'd returned to Norfolk recently, but neither of us had made any particular effort to get together. You know how it is.'

Jazz saw Bob Gilkes was looking green around the gills. 'Bob, why don't you go home? Have a lie-down? Leave your telephone number with the detective on the door, in case we need to contact you again.'

'Thanks, missus.' Bob stood up gratefully.

'And as I'm sure DS Miles has already indicated, I want you to keep this discovery to yourself for now. We don't want to scare the pupils, or the staff, until we've figured out just what has happened down there.'

'O'course. I won't even tell my wife, I swear.'

'Thanks, Bob.'

Jazz waited until he left the room before she turned to Frederiks.

'Mr Frederiks, did you know that Julian was very soon to be Rory Millar's stepfather?'

Frederiks looked genuinely surprised. 'No, I didn't. I'd never seen him with Rory. I'd no idea that Mrs Millar even had a partner. Rory certainly never mentioned him.'

'Rory wasn't aware that his mother was in a relationship. Mrs Millar was very keen to see Rory had some time to get over the divorce before introducing Julian into the mix,' Jazz explained.

There was a knock on the door and DS Roland appeared. 'The SOCOs have arrived from London, Ma'am. They're unloading now.'

'Thank you. Tell them I'll be with them in five.' She nodded. Turning her attention back to Frederiks, she said, 'I hear you've just come into some money, Mr Frederiks.'

Sebastian raised an eyebrow and fiddled nervously with the gold signet ring which sat on his little finger. 'Yes. I didn't realise it was public knowledge.'

'It isn't, but, under the circumstances, we were interested as to who Mr Daneman had bequeathed his estate to. You were obviously close to him?'

Sebastian shrugged his shoulders. 'Not close enough to think he would leave me most of his estate. To be honest, I was very surprised, if pleasurably, of course.'

'You had no idea you were in the will, Mr Frederiks?' Patrick cut in.

'None, no.'

Patrick raised his eyebrows. 'I see.'

'Do you know Jenny Colman, Mr Frederiks?' Jazz asked.

'I know her, yes. But not intimately. She's worked here forever. Why?'

'She was the other beneficiary,' Jazz replied.

'That would make sense. They'd been friends from way back. If I remember rightly, Hugh got Jenny a job at the school originally.'

There was a further knock on the door. 'Sorry, Ma'am, SOCOs are waiting for you.'

'I'm coming now, Roland.' Jazz stood up. 'DS Miles, would you continue to take Mr Frederiks's statement? Patrick, are you coming with me?'

Patrick nodded and the two of them walked out of the room.

'Inspector Hunter?' Frederiks's voice halted her in her tracks. She turned round.

'You know, I didn't find Julian. Or, for that matter, put him there in the first place. And I didn't ask for the bequest from Hugh. It was a complete surprise. Ask the solicitor.'

'I know, Mr Frederiks. Sometimes life puts you in unfortunate circumstances, doesn't it?'

He nodded, comforted. 'Yes. Thank you, Inspector.'

Jazz and Patrick walked back along the corridor to find the SOCOs. Jazz was grateful Patrick had refrained from interfering whilst she conducted her interview.

'Little odd, isn't it, Daneman leaving the money to that fellow

Frederiks out of the blue?' he observed.

'When Miles spoke to the solicitor, he said Hugh had changed the will only recently in Frederiks's favour. We need to find out a little more about Frederiks's family background. Hello, Martin, thanks for coming.' Jazz went up to her favourite forensic officer with a smile and shook his hand. 'I'm glad it's you. This is turning into a bit of a nightmare. Shall we talk as we go?'

'Sure. I understand time is of the essence.' Martin Chapman nodded. 'Hello, Patrick, how's things?'

If Chapman was surprised to see DCI Coughlin in Norfolk with his ex-wife, he made no show of it.

'Grand altogether, Martin. Came to get a bit of fresh Norfolk air, and ended up with a stiff on my hands.'

'Any idea how he got down there?' Chapman asked Jazz as she unlocked the cellar door.

'None, I've only just arrived here myself.' Jazz walked carefully down the cellar steps. The familiar smell of rotting flesh filled her nostrils. Usually it didn't affect her, but she wobbled as she took the final step down. Patrick grabbed her to steady her.

'Careful there, Jazz.' He gripped her hand, and she understood he sympathised, that she'd been facing the prospect of death in an intensely personal way only a few hours ago.

She took her hand away, but gave him a brief smile. 'Thank you.'

'So, what have we here?'

Chapman was already peering into the trunk. 'Heavy bruising to the left and middle of the forehead—he took a serious bump somewhere along the way…gloves, please, Bonnetti.'

Bonnetti, Chapman's devoted assistant, struggled down the stairs with the forensic case, laid it on the cellar floor, opened it and passed a pair of gloves to his boss.

Jazz and Patrick stood side by side behind Chapman as he gently lifted the head of the dead man away from the side of the trunk. One of the reasons Jazz liked Chapman was because of the way he respected the physical remains of the human life that had recently departed. He handled his cadavers sensitively, unlike some forensics she had seen.

'Not much question as to how poor Julian met his maker. Look.'

Jazz and Patrick peered at the blood stains marking the side of the trunk behind Julian's head.

'A massive blow to the back of the head.' Chapman picked up one of Julian's hands. 'See, the palm is covered in scratches and has a layer of white dust on it.' Chapman checked the other palm, which was identically covered. He looked behind him at the steep cellar stairs. 'I'd say from the look of his hands and the bruising on his forehead, that he was hit from behind as he was walking down the stairs. He fell head-first. The dust on his palms looks like he reached out to break his fall, which would mean he was still conscious, if only for a few seconds, before he was hit again.' Chapman went back to examining the back of Julian's head. 'I'd say he was struck at least three or four times.'

Jazz swallowed, feeling nauseous in the confined space with its fetid air. 'With what? Any idea?'

'Something with a sharp edge, such as an axe, or perhaps a meat cleaver. This was a frenzied attack. Nasty.' He turned round, bent down and started to study the cellar floor, just a few feet in front of the stairs. 'Can you see, there are some bloodstains here, too? Looks like our murderer finished him off on the floor, then dragged his body into the trunk.'

'How long has he been dead, would you say?'

'Can't really tell until I've done the PM, because the heat in here is intense. The body has deteriorated faster than it would usually.'

'The boiler was off this morning for a few hours due to a burst pipe,' Jazz said. 'Julian's been missing since Tuesday evening.'

'Then at a guess I would say he died pretty soon after that; latest, early hours of Wednesday morning. Bonnetti, get the lads to bring a stretcher. Let's get Julian out of here and give him some dignity. I'll have a poke around down here, take some samples from the floor and the trunk, see if our murderer has left anything of himself behind.'

'Where are you taking him?' Jazz asked.

'I've already called the coroner in Norwich and Julian's going there. Doubt it'll be as state of the art as my own, but I'll get by, I'm sure.'

'How soon can you get back to me? We really have to move very fast on this one.'

'When I've finished here, I'll get straight onto it. I should have a report for you by tonight, but I'm not expecting much more than I've already told you as regards cause of death. If I pick up any juicy DNA samples, I'll let you know.'

'Thanks, Martin.'

'I think we're all done here.' As Patrick turned and began walking up the stairs Jazz crossed to the trunk and bent down to study the initials embossed on the front.

R.M.M.

There might be other boys in Fleat House with those initials, but Rory Millar would fit the first and last names.

'Thanks, Martin.' Jazz nodded at him and followed Patrick up the cellar steps.

Miles was waiting for them in the lobby. 'I've got Frederiks's statement, Ma'am. Did Martin Chapman have anything illuminating to say?'

'He thinks Julian died late Tuesday evening. And it's definitely murder,' Jazz said quietly. 'Patrick, would you go and see the headmaster, tell him what Martin has reported, preferably without sending him into a state of apoplexy. You can reassure him the school will be crawling with police officers and it's doubtful there will be another murder in the next twenty-four hours—'

'By which time the perpetrator will be safely under lock and key...' Patrick nodded. 'I'll do my best, but we're sailing close to the wind. If I was after being a parent, I, for one, wouldn't want my precious young'un anywhere near this place.'

'Luckily for us, Fleat House was deserted when Bob found the body, so only Frederiks heard him scream,' Miles said. 'The boys think they've been evacuated and the police are here because some old remains have been found under the cellar floor whilst the boiler was being fixed. They're all very excited and are speculating who it could be.'

Jazz frowned. 'Bit far-fetched, isn't it?'

'No, Ma'am, apparently not. Legend has it that Fleat House is haunted by a young boy. This boy was so miserable whilst he was here, he hanged himself from the iron hook in the cellar ceiling. The boys think it's him.'

'And did he? Hang himself?' asked Jazz.

'I don't know if the story is actually true or not.' Miles shrugged. 'Like all folklore, probably overexaggerated. I'll ask Frederiks, who, by the way, has asked if he can go across to the various dorms where they've put up his boys.'

'Yes. Tell him he can, but he's not to disappear from the school grounds. If he has a mobile, get the number.'

'Will do, Ma'am.'

'By the way, where was Matron when Julian's body was found?' Jazz asked.

'Don't know. I saw her earlier shepherding the boys out of the house, when the police were arriving.'

'Can you find her and take a statement?'

'Will do,' confirmed Miles. 'What about Issy? She's just called to say she's running out of small talk with Angelina Millar and wants to know when someone will arrive to relieve her. *And* she's bursting to talk to you about Rory.'

'Why don't you go on and get that over with now, Jazz?' said Patrick. 'Miles and I will cover things this end. I'm going to look into what's being done to find this Millar fellow.'

'Yes.' Jazz sighed. 'It would be nice to assure Angelina we know where he is when I tell her the sad news, but even so, I don't think Millar's our man.'

'To be fair, you'd be saying that anyway. You did release him without charge now, Jazz. If they find him, I'd like to interview him anyway, if I may,' Patrick said.

Jazz bristled. 'Of course. You're the senior officer. You can do as you wish. Would you speak to DS Roland and make sure his men continue to maintain a comfortingly high profile for the head? Right, I'll be off.' Jazz nodded grimly at them, and left the building to walk across Chapel Lawn to her car.

Patrick's inference had riled her, however ridiculous. At present she should be grateful for all the help she could get. But the old familiar feelings were lurking, ready to jump out and accost her. This was her case, she had taken it on in good faith, not thinking for an instant Patrick would become involved.

Part of the problem at the Yard had been that Patrick had seemed to take pleasure in undermining her, putting her down in front of both her team and their superiors. Towards the end of her time there, Jazz had felt that Patrick was one of the worst exponents of the chauvinism directed at her. But because he was her husband, she'd been unable to do anything about it.

It was interesting that his behaviour had not gone unnoticed by Norton. He'd mentioned it when he'd come to see her at the cottage last week.

Jazz started the engine, trying to put Patrick out of her thoughts and concentrate on the case. If there was one part of the job she hated, it was informing relatives of a death. Especially today, after the past twenty-four hours of thinking she was about to lose her father, she empathised even more with the way Angelina was going to feel.

She pulled out her mobile, dialled the hospital and asked to be put through to the critical care ward. The sweet nurse she had seen yesterday told her that Tom was continuing to progress, and if she called later, she might be able to speak to him.

Feeling reassured on that count, Jazz drove off towards the Millar house. Even though she was tired, her brain felt alert and the adrenalin was pumping, as it always did when the pressure was really on.

Two murders and one suicide, all three of which had a connection to Fleat House. Charlie, a pupil, Julian, an ex-pupil, and Hugh, the house tutor.

And Rory, too, Julian's stepson to be, whose trunk had almost certainly become Julian's temporary tomb.

What if Patrick was right and she had been taken in by David Millar's sad circumstances?

No. She must not let Patrick affect her confidence.

Jazz sighed. He'd got to her already.

Chapter Twenty-Six

Drawing up in front of Angelina's door, Jazz steeled herself.

Issy answered the door and raised her eyebrows. 'You took your time. I've been playing tiddly-winks and other fun games with Rory for the past two hours. She's in there.' Issy indicated the kitchen. 'I'll go and continue my nanny duties upstairs. Let me know when you've finished. I really need to talk to you ASAP,' she hissed.

'Thanks, Issy. Oh, and could you ask Rory what his middle name is, please?'

Jazz walked across the hall and opened the kitchen door. A pale Angelina was sat at the kitchen table, leafing listlessly through an interiors magazine. She stood up as Jazz came in, eyes bright with expectation. 'Have you found him, Inspector Hunter?'

Jazz nodded slowly. 'Sit down, Mrs Millar.'

Angelina searched Jazz's face for reassurance. When she could find none, fear flashed into her eyes. 'He's okay, isn't he? Please tell me he is? Has he had an accident in that dreadful snow? I knew something had happened to him, I knew it! Where is he? Oh God, Oh God!'

Jazz gently eased Angelina into the chair, then pulled one out for herself and sat close to her. She put her hands on top of Angelina's. 'I'm so sorry, Mrs Millar, there is no easy way to tell you, I'm afraid, but Julian is dead.'

'Dead? Dead? He can't be dead!' Angelina shook her head. 'No, he can't be…'

She was silent as she studied Jazz's face again. Then, as realisation began to sink in, her shoulders slumped forward and she muttered, 'How?'

'Mrs Millar, I'm so very sorry.' Jazz spoke softly. 'Julian's body was found in a trunk in the cellar of Fleat House a few hours ago.'

Angelina looked at Jazz in disbelief. 'How? Why?!'

'We don't know yet, but it's pretty obvious someone put him there. I'm so sorry to tell you this, but we think he was attacked from behind and fell down the cellar steps to his death. His body was then placed in a trunk.'

'You...you're saying he was...murdered?'

'Almost certainly, yes. I'm so dreadfully sorry, but it's better you know the truth immediately.'

Angelina was staring at Jazz unseeingly, her face a picture of horror. 'Julian, murdered?' she whispered. 'He had no enemies. Everyone loved him, respected him.'

'He was a lawyer, Mrs Millar. He's bound to have made some enemies amongst the local criminal fraternity, which is one route we have to explore...'

'He was found in the cellar at Fleat House... Charlie Cavendish was found dead there a couple of weeks ago, and the house tutor committed suicide...What on earth is going on in that place and why didn't you find out before Julian got murdered?!' Angelina was on her feet, tearing her hair in anguish and anger. 'Well, *where's* David?! He did it, he murdered Charlie and Julian! And now he's going to come and murder me and Rory! Julian died because you let David *go*!'

Angelina launched herself suddenly at Jazz, her small fists clenched together, lashing out like a child. Jazz grabbed her wrists easily as Angelina fought back in a frenzy of shock and anger.

'Mrs Millar, I understand what a shock this is for you...'

'No, you DON'T! Julian is dead! He's DEAD!'

All of Angelina's energy left her suddenly, and she slumped into Jazz's arms, sobbing. Jazz sat her down in the chair as gently as she could, and sat opposite her, helpless as she always was in these moments. Seeing the rawness and intimacy of another human being's suffering was never easy. She sat quietly, waiting.

Eventually, the sobs subsided. Angelina stood up and walked unsteadily across the kitchen to get a box of tissues from one of the work surfaces. She blew her nose and dried her eyes.

'Sorry, Inspector Hunter. I lost control for a minute.'

'Please don't worry. It's completely understandable. I'm probably the last person you want to be with right now. Can I call anyone for you?'

Angelina's eyes filled with tears once more. 'When you said that, I immediately thought you should call Julian, because he would be there for me, but then...' Angelina bit her lip in an effort to prevent the tears. 'I remembered...'

'What about your mother or father? You might want someone to help you with Rory just for a few days.'

'Oh God, Rory! Poor Rory. He never even knew Julian. He'll wonder why on earth his mother's so upset, and he's been through so much. What do I say to him, Inspector? Do I tell him?'

'Angelina, that's up to you to decide. Rory didn't know Julian, so the upside is at least he won't have to go through the bereavement process.'

'Yes. I'll call my mother. She and Rory are close.' Angelina nodded.

'Mrs Millar…Angelina, I know this is so hard for you, but could you cope with talking me through the last conversation you and Julian had on Tuesday night?'

Angelina was pacing, screwing sodden tissues into a ball with her hands. 'I don't know, I really don't.'

'You see, the more you can tell me about that night, the faster we might be able to find out who did this.'

'But there's nothing to tell.'

'Julian didn't seem in any way agitated or distressed when you spoke to him?'

'He wasn't happy I was asking him to stay in Norwich at his flat overnight because of Rory being at home. Oh God, would it have been different if I said he could come home? Would he be dead now? Is it my fault?!'

'No, of course not. We're pretty sure Julian didn't make it back to his flat either. Something, or someone, happened to stop him. Can you remember what time it was that you spoke to him?'

'Yes, it was around six forty-five. I only know because Rory was watching *The Simpsons*.'

'Does Julian often work late at the office?'

'Sometimes, but…oh yes, I remember. On the Tuesday morning, before he left…the last time I ever saw him…he said that even if he did come back here, he'd be late as he had a client seeing him at seven that evening.'

Jazz took her notepad from her handbag and began to scribble. 'Was that usual? To see clients out of office hours?'

'Yes, occasionally. Julian was very dedicated to his career and the people he looked after.' Angelina nodded. 'I'm sorry, Inspector, but I feel faint. I…I can't answer any more questions. I need to go and lie down.'

'That's a good idea, and thank you, Angelina. I know how hard it must have been for you, but what you've told me is very helpful. Shall I call the doctor to come and give you something to help you sleep?'

'No. The doctor prescribed some Valium when Rory went missing, when...when I didn't think things could get any worse.' Angelina shrugged sadly. 'They just did. Could you tell Rory Mummy's gone for a rest?'

'Of course. I think he and Issy have become firm friends. I'm sure we can persuade her to stay for a while longer until your mother gets here. Would you like me to call her for you?'

'No, I'll do it from my bedroom. It's going to be a shock for her, too. For everyone...' Angelina walked across to the door of the kitchen and hung on to the handle for support, her face suddenly a mask of fear. 'What about David? Do you know where he is? What if he does come here?'

'Please try not to worry, Mrs Millar. You have my word there'll be an officer sat outside twenty-four hours a day. You and Rory will be perfectly safe, I guarantee it.'

Jazz waited until Angelina had left the kitchen, then switched on her mobile. There was a message from Patrick to say David Millar had finally been picked up in Norwich, drunk, and was being driven back to Foltesham police station to sober up. Patrick was leaving St Stephen's and would meet her there.

Jazz left the kitchen and climbed the stairs to find Rory and Issy. They were sitting in Rory's bedroom, Issy trying to steer a car around a race track on Rory's PlayStation.

'Glad you're here. I've just gone down a one-way street and run over three mothers with prams. Is she okay?' Issy mouthed.

'Not good,' Jazz mouthed back. 'Hello, Rory, how are you?'

'Fine.' Rory's attention was focussed on getting Issy's car back up the one-way street.

'Rory,' said Issy, 'that thing we discussed, about Mr Daneman, I'd like you to tell Jazz here exactly what you told me.'

Rory turned to Issy with anxious eyes. 'Do I have to? I thought you said it was our secret?'

'Well, I'd like to let Jazz in on it, too. You see, it might help her solve the case. She won't tell anyone, will you, Jazz?'

'Of course not. I'm a police woman, Rory. It's my job to keep lots of secrets.'

'It's just that...' Rory looked to Issy for reassurance. 'It's very embarrassing, you see, and if any of the boys knew at school, then...' He sighed. '...they'd think I was even weirder than they do already.'

'I understand, Rory. And I promise I won't tell your friends,' Jazz said gently.

'She won't, honestly, Rory,' Issy encouraged. 'Now, tell Jazz exactly what happened that Friday evening when you went to see Mr Daneman to get some painkillers for your headache.'

'Well, you see'—Rory's eyes were lowered— 'my headache was very, very bad. It was just after I had sung in chapel. Matron wasn't in her flat, so I went down to Mr Frederiks's study to see if he could give me something for it. Mr Frederiks was out and Mr Daneman was there instead.'

'What time was this, Rory?' queried Jazz.

'I don't know exactly. About half past nine, I think. All the other Junior boys were in bed.'

'And what happened then?'

'Mr Daneman asked me to come in and sit down whilst he got the tablets for me. Then he came back and said he was just making some hot chocolate and would I like some, too. I said yes, I would, cos I was feeling a bit miserable.'

'Why, Rory?' Jazz asked, knowing the answer.

He shrugged his thin shoulders. 'The usual stuff, you know.'

'No, I don't,' Jazz urged. 'Tell me.'

'The other boys, bullying me, mostly.'

'Anyone in particular?'

Rory looked up at Jazz. 'None of the boys are very nice to me, but Charlie Cavendish was always picking on me. He'd done it that afternoon and I was upset.'

'Okay, so you and Mr Daneman have a cup of hot chocolate together. Did that help a bit?'

'Oh yes. Mr Daneman is...was...always great to me. He looked out for me. He knew what it was like, you see. He told me he got bullied at school, too, when he was a boy. We got on very well. He was my friend.' Rory shrugged.

'That's nice. It must have helped a lot.'

'It did. He asked me what was wrong and I told him about Charlie calling me a "fucking gay boy" in the changing rooms after rugby practice. Mr Daneman said that I had to ignore those types of comments, that it was Charlie's own insecurity that made him say things like that, and everyone knew he was a bully, and I sipped my hot chocolate and I felt better. Until...'

Rory's hands moved up and down his thighs agitatedly. 'Issy, do I have to?'

'Yes, sweetie, you do. I know this is going to help Jazz so much with sorting out what happened that night.'

Rory took a deep breath. 'Okay. Here goes: Mr Daneman came and sat next to me on the sofa. I was a bit tearful, so he put his arm around me, told me he'd speak to Charlie and make sure he'd leave me alone. Then...suddenly, he told me that he'd once known someone who looked very like me and he got hold of my face in his hands and he...' Rory gulped in some air from speaking so quickly.

'Go on, Rory, nearly there now,' Issy urged.

'Well, he...kissed me...on the lips...and...and tried to put his tongue in my mouth.' Rory's hand went instinctively to his face and he dragged his fingers across his lips, as if he was trying to wipe them clean. 'It was disgusting!'

Jazz nodded silently, looking at Issy, who raised her eyebrows.

'I'm sure it was. What did you do then?'

'I got away and ran out of the room and went upstairs to my dorm. I pulled the covers over my head and cried. Mr Daneman was my only friend, he did protect me and I knew I couldn't let him any more, that he was a dirty old man, and just as bad as the rest of them. And I knew I was completely on my own, that I couldn't trust anyone ever again. Except for...'

'Your dad?' offered Jazz.

Rory nodded. 'I rang him. I wanted to see him. When he didn't come, I ran away to find him.'

'Your dad tried very hard to find out what was going on and why you were so upset. I saw him, a few days later in Mr Jones's office, trying to get to see you.'

'And I suppose they wouldn't let him. Was he drunk?'

Jazz decided a white lie was in order. 'I don't know. But he was very upset he couldn't see you. So, when you went away with your dad to the Lake District, did you tell him what Mr Daneman had done?'

'Yes, I did. And he swore he wouldn't tell anyone. He hasn't, has he?' Rory looked at Issy and Jazz anxiously.

'No, he absolutely hasn't, promise,' Jazz replied. 'And just one last thing, did you actually take the tablets when Mr Daneman gave them to you?'

Rory paled. 'I think I did. But I can't remember.'

'Well, perhaps you could try. It's very important, Rory.'

'Yes, yes, I know.' Rory looked agitated. Issy mouthed 'enough'.

'Rory, you've been great.' Jazz smiled. 'And really helpful. If you do remember something, then here's my card.' Jazz handed it to him.

'Yes, thanks,' Rory said, pocketing it.

'Now, Mum isn't feeling too well, so she's having a lie-down. She's asked Granny to come and stay for a few days to look after you until she feels better. Issy, you can hang on a little longer until Granny arrives, can't you? I have to dash, I'm afraid.'

Issy's eyes said it all. 'And how long is Granny going to be?' she asked through clenched teeth.

Jazz drove round the corner to Foltesham police station, her mind buzzing with what Rory had told her.

Patrick was installed in the tiny interview room, sitting behind what *had* been Jazz's desk. Telling herself to stop being so petty, she nodded at him as she put her briefcase on the table.

'See you've managed to procure some proper coffee.'

'Yes, I sent a charming young constable out to get me some, so I did. There's one for you too.'

'Thanks.' Jazz raised her eyebrows. 'You can tell the Big Guns have entered the building. They never went out to get coffee for us.'

'You know me, Jazz, my natural Irish charm can work wonders,' Patrick grinned.

Jazz shuddered involuntarily at the thought.

'So now,' continued Patrick, 'how did you get on with poor Mrs Millar?'

'She's devastated, naturally. But Issy is a genius. She's managed to get Rory to open up about the night Charlie Cavendish died. She got him to tell me that Hugh Daneman had kissed him.'

'Jesus! I thought that kind of thing had been more or less stamped out, even in English public schools. Poor little fellow, probably be scarred for life now, and I dread to think how many other boys the dirty old bugger has done it to.' He grimaced.

'I think this is far more complex a set of circumstances. I doubt if

Hugh Daneman had *ever* done something like that before. But, for certain reasons, he was literally unable to stop himself. I think he was so ashamed that he decided to take his own life.' Jazz knew she was defending Hugh for unacceptable behaviour, but given the unique circumstances, she understood.

'Sorry, Jazz.' Patrick shook his head, reading her mind. 'There are no extenuating circumstances to excuse that behaviour, so.'

'I agree with you, but Rory just happened to be the spitting image of the young man that was the love of Hugh's life,' she explained. 'For a few seconds, he obviously lost control. And after that, how could he live with what he'd done? It would have come out one day. Rory told his father about it.'

'David Millar? The old soak downstairs? Christ,' expostulated Patrick, 'he was drunk when he came in here an hour ago. We're not going to get a decent word out of him until tomorrow morning. Well now'—Patrick tapped his fingers on the desk—'this is starting to fit together quite nicely. David Millar murders Charlie for bullying his son, Hugh Daneman tops himself for snogging Rory, then Millar murders Julian, the incumbent lover-cum-stepfather, in a jealous rage. All sounds grand to me.'

'I think it's a little more complex than that, Patrick,' Jazz replied as patiently as she could.

The exchange was bringing back memories of other cases in the past, on which they had fundamentally disagreed. Patrick used the 'broad-brush' factual approach, whereas Jazz had always seen the human detail. As a team, the two sets of skills could work well, but when one was trying to compete with the other, as so often had happened when they'd worked together, it was a recipe for disaster. Patrick had always wanted the case solved and fast. Jazz needed to follow her instincts and take her time, learning the stories of those involved, and exhausting every option before arriving at a conclusion.

'I believe Millar was almost certainly covering for his son when he came up with his trumped-up story of killing Charlie Cavendish,' she continued. 'Remember, his ex-wife has stated David was allergic to aspirin, too. There's just no way he'd have had some handy in his pocket.'

'Unless it *was* premeditated, and Millar had bought the tablets specifically before he arrived at the school. He might be lying to you. It's a possibility, Jazz, come on now.'

'Yes,' she agreed, 'it is. But the person who *did* have access to aspirin that night was Rory. Hugh Daneman put them into his hand. And when I asked Rory directly this afternoon whether he'd taken them himself, he said he "couldn't remember". I need Issy to speak to Rory again to try and get the story out of him.'

'You think a kid of thirteen did this?' Patrick whistled. 'Jesus, that's a nasty one. Anyway, when yer man downstairs comes to, I'll be giving him the once-over, that's for sure.'

Jazz gritted her teeth. 'You do that. But Issy agrees with me, too. Neither of us think it was Millar.'

'Well now, there is the small question of another body since you both last spoke to Millar. The fellow was even picked up in Norwich, close to the dead man's offices. You can't ignore the facts, Jazz.'

'I'm not. And to be honest, I don't want to waste any more time standing here and arguing about them. Where's Miles?'

'In Norwich at Forbes's office taking statements.'

'Right.' Jazz picked up her briefcase. 'I'm going to visit Corin Conaught's mother, see if she can shed more light on this relationship between her late son and Hugh Daneman. Then I'll head home and we'll meet back here tomorrow morning.'

'Surely you're wasting your time, Jazz? We know Daneman committed suicide. He's out of the murder loop; downstairs we have a suspect with a perfect motive...'

Jazz's good intentions abandoned her, as frustration welled up. 'I thought we agreed this is *my* investigation, not yours, Patrick. And until the time comes when we have made an arrest, it is my duty as commanding officer to continue to interview anyone who might be able to give me some further clue as to the reason why three men have died in the past week.' She eyed him. 'Unless, as senior officer, you're pulling rank and telling me not to?' Her eyes blazed with anger.

Patrick put his hands out in front of him in a calming gesture. 'To be sure, Jazz, I'm not, and have no intention of doing so. Now, so, off you go and I'll see you here tomorrow morning. Unless...you'd be wanting some company later?'

Suppressing a sudden urge to snort at the absurdity of Patrick's suggestion, Jazz said, 'I'm exhausted and I need some sleep. Goodnight, Patrick.' She walked quickly out of the police station and climbed into her car. Then she hit the steering wheel hard with a scream of frustration.

Chapter Twenty-Seven

Sebastian Frederiks stood outside Walsingham House, where twelve of his younger boys had been billeted whilst Fleat House was off limits, and pulled out his mobile. He dialled a number, and when the call was answered, spoke softly into the phone.

'Hello, darling, I'm not going to be able to get away tonight after all. All hell has broken loose here. Can I call you later? I might be able to make it tomorrow morning? Okay, love you, bye.'

He put the mobile back in his pocket and went in to his boys.

It was dark by the time Jazz arrived at the front door of Conaught Hall. There were no lights shining from any of the windows in the main house, though she could see a brightness coming from the smaller wing on the left-hand side. Getting no answer to her persistent ringing of the bell, she walked along the front of the house. Making her way round the side, she came to a door with a lamp lit above it, and rang the bell.

A few seconds later, she heard quiet footsteps on the other side of the door.

'Who's there?' The voice sounded fearful.

'Detective Inspector Hunter. And I'm looking for Lady Emily Conaught.'

There was a pause before the voice said, 'Why?'

'It's absolutely nothing to worry about. I wondered if she could help me on some family history, that's all. It's to do with a case we're investigating, involving a…friend of the family.'

The door was unlocked tentatively and Jazz saw a very elderly, but still beautiful, face appear behind it. 'Do you have identification? I'm sure you are who you say, but one can never be too careful these days.'

'Of course.' Jazz showed the woman her card. 'May I come in?'

'Yes.' The woman pulled back the door further, so Jazz could step inside.

'Thank you. And you are?'

'I am she. Emily Conaught. Pleased to make your acquaintance.'

Jazz noticed immediately the physical similarity between Adele Cavendish and her mother. They were both tall, elegant and handsome women. Emily was immaculately dressed in a tweed skirt and cashmere jumper, although Jazz noticed she was wearing slippers on her feet.

'Do follow me. I have the fire going in the sitting room.' Limping slightly, Emily led Jazz down a narrow corridor and into a cosy sitting room. The walls were hung with large oil paintings, which were too big in size to have been originally destined for this room. The television was on in one corner, and Emily immediately went to switch it off. 'So sorry, I wasn't expecting any visitors this evening. Do sit down,' she offered. 'Can I get you some tea?'

'That's very kind of you, but please, not on my account. I don't want to take up too much of your time. But I need some help piecing together the past.'

'My children are always commenting that's where I live most of the time, so you've come to the right person.' Emily smiled. 'How can I help?'

This lucid, spritely woman did not fit the image Edward Conaught had conjured up when he'd described his mother.

'As I'm sure you know by now, we don't think your grandson Charlie died by accident,' Jazz began.

Emily nodded slowly. 'Edward did indicate that was probably the case, but he didn't go into detail. He doesn't like to upset me, thinks I'm a frail old lady who couldn't possibly cope, when in fact I've suffered far more tragedy than he will ever know and I'm still here to tell the tale. Have you managed to discover who might have been the perpetrator of the crime?'

'We have a suspect, yes, but before I can draw any conclusions I need to discover a little more about his family background.' Jazz paused before saying, 'I'm sure it's been a very upsetting time for you.'

'Of course,' Emily nodded. 'I was distressed to hear of Charlie's death. But if you want me to be honest, I was never close to the boy, nor did I particularly like him. I suppose I should feel guilty,' she sighed.

'He was my grandson after all, but I'm afraid he reminded me far too much of his father, who I always thought was a pompous ass.'

Jazz tried not to let a smile reach her lips. 'Well, I'm sure at the very least, that you'd like to get to the bottom of why he died.'

'Of course. Forgive me, Inspector,' Emily checked herself, 'but speaking my mind is the one advantage of growing old. So, how can I help you?'

'Well, it isn't only Charlie who has died recently. A tutor at the school, Hugh Daneman, is also dead, but we're sure no foul play was involved. He took his own life.'

A shadow crossed Emily's face. 'Yes, I read his obituary in *The Times*. Such a gentle man, and I mean that in both senses of the word. If misguided.'

'Why misguided?'

'Surely, Inspector, you know about Hugh's sexuality? And the fact he was blindly in love with my son for most of his life?'

'I did know, yes. Lady Conaught—'

'Please. Emily will do.'

'Emily.' Jazz was pulling a plastic wallet out of her briefcase. 'Do you recognise this boy?' She handed it to Emily.

'Excuse me whilst I root around for my glasses.' Emily felt behind the cushions on the chair and produced them triumphantly. She put her glasses on and studied the photograph. Removing them, she looked at Jazz. 'Why of course, it's my son, Corin.'

'Actually,' continued Jazz, 'it isn't Corin. It's another young man called Rory Millar, a pupil at St Stephen's School.'

'My goodness me!' Emily looked genuinely amazed. 'The likeness is remarkable, especially when Corin was younger. Drink and drugs had ravaged him by the time he died. He looked fifty-six, not twenty-six, but there we go.' Emily handed the photograph back to Jazz.

'Thank you for that, Emily. You've just helped confirm one of my theories.' Jazz smiled. 'And now, perhaps you could tell me a little more about the relationship between Corin and Hugh?'

Emily sighed. 'Well, it was all rather tragic, really. Having spoken to Edward, you must know from him that Corin was wild. Goodness knows who he took after, as neither his father nor I were rebellious, but Corin *was*, right from the day he was born. Such a naughty little baby,' she chuckled, 'didn't much care for sleeping. Perhaps he felt he might miss something. Of course, going up to Oxford didn't help. To Corin, it was manna from heaven. He did absolutely no work, spent all his energies having a jolly good time, and experimenting with everything. And I mean everything.'

'And that's where he met Hugh?'

'Yes. Hugh was a don, yet not much older than his students. Fearfully bright chap.' Emily shook her head. 'Such a waste. He could have gone so far if he hadn't met my son.'

'They had a…liaison?'

'No need to be coy. I'm sure you know that already, Inspector Hunter,' Emily clucked. 'And when the powers that be at Oxford discovered it, Hugh was dismissed on the spot. My son was sent down not long after for all sorts of heinous crimes, including not appearing at lectures for an entire term.'

'Did Corin love Hugh, do you think?'

Emily paused in thought. Finally she said, 'In Corin's way, perhaps he did. When he was sent down, he came to live here on the estate. In a wink of an eye, Hugh was here in Norfolk, too, working as a teacher at St Stephen's. Hugh hung around Corin all the time. I rarely remember visiting Corin at his cottage when Hugh wasn't there. But if you're asking me whether it was an equal feeling between them, I would say without question, no.' She answered definitely. 'You see, Corin was not…how shall I put it…a full-time homosexual, and even if he had been, I doubt he could have been faithful to Hugh. No, he liked women as well. Which was what finally caused a problem between them.'

Jazz was surprised. 'Really? Corin fell in love with a woman?'

'No, my dear,' Emily chuckled. 'As I've just said, Corin was far too selfish to fall in love properly with anyone. But that did not mean to say he was averse to filling his baser needs. Anyway, Hugh came up to Corin's cottage one day and found him in bed. With a *woman.*' She raised her eyebrows. 'I mean, my dear, how could he hope to compete? Hugh arrived here at the house, and sought me out. He was devastated. I can tell you, it was a fairly strange task to comfort a young man in love with my son, who'd been usurped by a woman. But poor Hugh had no one else to turn to.'

'Did it destroy their relationship?' asked Jazz.

'Yes, at least for a while. Hugh stopped visiting, but Corin started to deteriorate and was drunk, or on drugs most of the time. He rang Hugh in his hour of need, and Hugh came scampering back to help him. Corin died soon after, of a heroin overdose. Hugh was the one who found him.'

'What a sad story,' Jazz mused. 'Corin was so young.'

'Yes. And to be honest with you, my dear, I don't think I ever got over losing Corin. First-born son and all that. There's an undeniable bond.' Emily shook her head. 'Interesting, isn't it? Most people spend their lives wanting to fall in love, and yet sometimes love can be so terribly destructive. It certainly destroyed Hugh. He was never the same from that moment on.'

Jazz thought for a moment before she asked her next question. 'Emily, you're quite sure that Hugh was fully homosexual? That he wouldn't have had a liaison with a woman? Like Corin did?'

'As sure as one can be about anything, yes,' replied Emily. 'Hugh loved my son. It was all-consuming. Why do you ask?'

'Hugh left his entire estate to a housemaster at St Stephen's. He'd changed his will only a few weeks before. This housemaster and he weren't particularly close, although they'd worked together for years and Hugh had taught this man as a boy.' Jazz shrugged. 'I suppose I was wondering whether there could be some...family connection? I have checked with the General Register Office and they're not officially related...' Jazz left the sentence hanging in mid-air, before she clarified it. 'I wondered if Hugh could have fathered a child. It would have been around the time that Corin died, approximately forty years or so ago.'

'No'—Emily shook her head—'*Hugh* didn't have a child. But...no...surely not?' she whispered to herself.

'What is it, Emily?' Jazz asked softly, as she read the confusion on the old lady's face.

'No, I'm sure it must be coincidence,' Emily muttered to herself. 'Because how on earth could Hugh...?'

'Could he what?'

'I'm sure I'm wrong, but I suppose there is a chance that...'

'I'm sorry, Emily, you've lost me.'

'Oh dear, oh dear.'

Jazz could see Emily was having a painful inner struggle. She waited patiently, saying nothing.

Finally, Emily looked at Jazz. 'Inspector, I've never told anyone of this, not even my late husband. Do you really think it is relevant to your enquiries?'

'I don't know until you tell me,' Jazz replied honestly. 'But if you think it might be, then please, go ahead.'

'Well, you see…the thing was…' Emily touched a long, bony finger to her brow. 'There *was* a child, Inspector. Corin's child. He never knew of it. He died before the baby was born. But Hugh *did* know of it.'

'I see. And how did you find out about this?'

Emily looked at Jazz again, her eyes troubled. 'It was Hugh. He came to me, a couple of months after Corin died, and told me about the expectant mother. Apparently, she'd appeared on his doorstep out of the blue, distraught. She was four months pregnant and didn't know what to do. Even though Hugh had every reason to hate her, he was very kind-hearted, and perhaps he felt in some way responsible for her *and* the trouble Corin had got her into.'

'Excuse me if I'm being tactless,' apologised Jazz, 'but under the circumstances you're describing, surely the best thing was for this girl to go off and have a termination?'

Emily smiled. 'My dear, I don't wish to pull rank age-wise, but forty years ago, abortion was only just legal, but not if you came from a Catholic background, as this girl did. And Norfolk was still coming out of the Dark Ages.'

'Yes, very different from now, I'm sure,' Jazz agreed, feeling uncomfortable. 'So, what did she do?'

'Well, Hugh came to me in confidence to ask my advice. Under the circumstances, he felt I should know. I, too, am Catholic, so I was certainly not going to condemn a life to death. But by the same token, there was no place in our family for Corin's illegitimate child, especially as the young lady in question was the daughter of one of the workers on our estate.' Emily sniffed. 'I suggested to Hugh that this girl go and have the baby quietly in one of the discreet homes that were set up for just that sort of thing, and then put it up for adoption. I also offered to pay, which the girl accepted. And that was the end of it, really. The girl did as I'd suggested and no more was said of it. In fact,' Emily mused, 'it's the first time I've spoken to anyone on the subject for forty years.'

'I apologise for reminding you of it now,' said Jazz. 'So you've no idea what happened to this baby?'

'Good God, no. He or she could be anywhere, Inspector Hunter. Or dead for all we know.'

'And this baby could have no idea who he or she really is?'

'Absolutely not. They were very careful about that sort of thing then.'

Jazz spoke slowly. 'But just say *Hugh* had found out who the child was?'

'I can't imagine how, but pray continue with your train of thought.'

'Let's go back a stage.' Jazz rubbed her forehead, as she tried to put the information into cohesive order. 'Edward told me Charlie was the only heir to the Conaught Estate. Now he's dead, there's no one else to inherit. Is that right?'

Emily nodded. 'We have an expert searching the family tree for a distant cousin, or branch of the Conaughts we may have forgotten. Otherwise, when Edward dies, the line is finished and the estate will be sold and the money left to charity.' She sighed. 'Over four hundred years... So very sad.'

'So, what if there *was* an heir, let's say, the son of Corin, your eldest child? I understand it would have to be a male.'

'But, Inspector, "he", if it *is* a "he", was born out of wedlock!' Emily responded, shocked. 'The child is illegitimate.'

'But still a direct blood heir. And with DNA tests, these days, this can be proved beyond all doubt. I'm pretty sure there've been some cases in the past few years where the courts have granted the illegitimate child his legal entitlement.'

'Well,' Emily replied stoutly, 'that closes the debate. Corin died forty years ago. It's not possible to prove any genetic inheritance. For goodness' sake, there's nothing of *him* left.'

'You kept nothing of his, Emily?'

'I kept some things from his childhood, photographs and whatnot, but nothing of him, Inspector.'

'Did you by any chance keep a baby book, detailing Corin's weight, his first smile, when his tooth came through, that kind of thing?'

'Yes, as a matter of fact, I did,' Emily nodded, 'but of what relevance is that?'

'If you can find it for me, I'll show you, shall I?' Jazz asked, mentally crossing her fingers. 'Do you know where it is?'

'Vaguely. I'd have to look.'

Jazz suspected Emily knew exactly where it was. 'Emily, if you could remember where that book might be, I'd be very grateful.'

Emily hesitated then nodded. 'All right. Won't be a tick.'

Jazz watched her leave the room. And prayed that she herself would be as sprightly an octogenarian as Emily one day. Which made her think immediately of her father. She lifted her mobile out of her bag and checked for messages. There was one from Miles, which she'd listen to later, but thankfully, none from the hospital.

Emily arrived triumphantly back in the sitting room. 'Found it!' She handed a carefully preserved, blue satin-quilted book to Jazz. 'Can't really see how it can help, but take a look anyway.'

'Thank you.' Jazz opened the book and began to scan the pages. She knew exactly what she was looking for. Heart in her mouth as she approached the last couple of pages, she gave a small mew of triumph, as there, stuck to the back page, was a small cellophane bag, containing a lock of white-blond hair.

She pointed to it. 'There. *This* is something of Corin, Emily. It'll provide his DNA, which, cross-checked with other samples, will give us ultimate proof.'

'The miracle of modern technology, eh? Emily looked at Jazz in concern. 'You think you know the identity of Corin's child, don't you?'

'It's nothing more than a hunch at present, Emily,' Jazz said. 'And I promise you'll be the first to know if it's confirmed.'

'I hardly know what to think.'

'Please try not to worry about it, Emily. After all, it could be a good thing, couldn't it?'

'Perhaps. I'm not sure.'

'No, but it might be that the Conaught line *could* continue after all.'

'In the most extraordinary way, but yes, I suppose you're right,' Emily conceded reluctantly.

Jazz watched the old lady's hands as her fingers weaved nervously in and out of her clasped hands. 'That's an interesting insignia on your signet ring.' Jazz was positive she'd seen the same ring recently, on someone else's finger.

'Yes. It dates back to Elizabethan times. The Conaughts are originally descended from the Dudley family—you'll have heard of the infamous Robert, possible lover of the Virgin Queen.' She stared down at the signet ring on her little finger. 'The crest—an acorn—was altered a couple of hundred years ago, to incorporate another insignia—a lark—when my husband's ancestor made a successful marriage to another great Norfolk family, whose seat was at Holkham.'

'Really? And only family members would be entitled to wear the ring?' Jazz probed.

'Yes. Odd you should mention it, actually, as Corin's ring was missing when we found the body. Sadly, we all assumed he'd probably pawned it to acquire some more heroin.'

'Really? So there's one ring missing?'

'Yes. Never bothered getting it replaced. No point really. Doubtful anyone will be wearing it in the future.'

'Well, let's wait and see, shall we?' Jazz stood up. 'Emily, thank you so much for your hospitality and all your help. I'll return this lock of hair to you in the next few days, and let you know the news as soon as I can. No, please don't get up. I'll see myself out.'

'Goodbye then, Inspector. Glad to have been of help.'

Jazz got to the door and stopped. 'Just one more question: do you happen to remember the name of the girl who was pregnant by Corin?'

'Well, of course I do,' Emily replied crossly. 'I'm not completely senile, whatever my son might say. She was the daughter of one of our employees. She was Corin's daily for a few months when he lived in the cottage. Her name was Jenny Colman.'

Outside the house, Jazz climbed into her car and paused to listen to the message from Miles, saying he'd been to Julian Forbes's office to interview Julian's colleagues and meet the SOCOs. There was nothing urgent to report, apparently, and he'd see her at the station tomorrow morning.

She dialled Martin Chapman's mobile number.

He answered on the first ring. 'Martin, where are you?'

'At the lab in Norwich.'

'I need one of your chaps to process and cross-check some DNA samples urgently.'

'Can it wait till I'm back in London?'

'No. I need it done now. If you give me the address of the lab, I'll get Miles to drive the sample across to you now.'

Martin did so and Jazz scribbled it down.

'Julian's car has just turned up here, so I'm going to be burning the midnight oil anyway, going over that. I'll see if I can persuade someone in the lab to process your DNA in the next twenty-four hours.'

'I need the results by tomorrow, Martin.'

'I'll do my best, but Patrick is demanding a full forensic report first thing in the morning. Otherwise, he says he'll have to close the school.'

'Does he, indeed?!' she snapped, then checked herself, cross for letting her anger slip out. 'Just do what you can, Martin. And I owe you dinner.'

'I'll take you up on that, Jazz.'

'Any news so far?'

'I'm working on it. I'll see you tomorrow morning with a full forensic report.'

'Look forward to it. Thanks, Martin, and bye.'

'Cheers.'

Jazz dialled Miles's number. He answered immediately.

'Yes, Ma'am?'

'Where are you?'

'At the hotel, just about to sit down for dinner.'

'Alone?'

'Er…no. Issy's here with me.'

Jazz smiled to herself as she heard the discomfort in his voice. 'Sorry to break up the *tête-à-tête*, but I need you to take something to the lab in Norwich for me. Can you meet me in the school car park in fifteen minutes?'

'Yes, Ma'am.'

'Where's Patrick?' she asked.

'Still at the station.'

'Okay, see you in fifteen.'

Jazz threw her mobile onto the seat and drove slowly along the tree-lined drive of the Conaught Estate.

She steeled herself to put aside the anger she felt at Patrick's meddling and tried to concentrate on the new information.

So, there was a child. And the mother was Jenny Colman—yet another connection to St Stephen's School.

Not Hugh Daneman's child but, in fact, a direct Conaught heir.

Hugh *must* have believed Sebastian Frederiks was Corin's child; it was the only explanation for the sudden *volte face* on his will. He would have regarded Corin's son as the closest thing to a relative he had.

And what if Hugh Daneman had told Frederiks who he was? Jazz let her thoughts run on…Frederiks would then have known he had a direct claim to the Conaught Estate, whose value in acreage alone must run into millions.

But Charlie Cavendish, as next direct heir to the estate, had been in the way. And maybe, mused Jazz, to be sure he had a clear path, and to avoid spending years, plus tens of thousands of pounds, as a court decided who in fact *was* the legal heir—a nephew or an illegitimate son—Frederiks had needed Charlie to be removed.

As Jazz turned right out of the drive and onto the road that would take her either home, or to St Stephen's, she realised how tired she was. The thought of bath and bed was hugely appealing. However, she would not be able to rest until she'd spoken to Frederiks. And double-checked, for her own satisfaction, the one thing Hugh Daneman had seen that had made him believe Sebastian was Corin's son.

Chapter Twenty-Eight

Having parked her car at St Stephen's, and given the envelope and address to a rather embarrassed Miles, Jazz went in search of Sebastian Frederiks.

She found him in the refectory, having his supper with a couple of the boys, who were trying to pump him for information on the reason for Fleat House being shut off by the police.

'Well, boys, here's the woman to tell you, the inspector herself.' Sebastian gave one of his best false smiles, as he picked up his empty plate and made to stand up.

In those few seconds, Jazz knew she had not been mistaken. The ring on his little finger *was* identical to Emily Conaught's.

'Actually, would you mind, boys?' Jazz indicated they should move. 'I'd like a few minutes to bring Mr Frederiks up to speed on what's been happening.'

'Have you found a dead body, Inspector? Was it the chap who hanged himself down there? That's the rumour,' said one of the boys.

'Get on with you, James,' Frederiks said amiably. 'I'll be over to Walsingham to tuck you all up in an hour.'

The boys moved away. Jazz was about to sit when Frederiks said, 'Would you mind if we talked as we walked? I haven't had time to pack my overnight bag. I'm going with the boys to Walsingham House and the police officer said he was about to lock up Fleat for the night.'

'Fine.'

They walked out of the refectory and made their way across Chapel Lawn. 'So, what's this story about the boy hanging himself in the cellar?' asked Jazz.

Sebastian shook his head. 'Nothing really, just a piece of St Stephen's history, that the boys like to turn into something more.'

'So, *did* a boy hang himself down there?'

Frederiks looked uncomfortable. 'Yes, he did. But it was all a long time ago.'

They'd arrived at the yellow police ticker-tape surrounding Fleat House. Jazz stepped under it and walked towards the entrance. Frederiks followed suit. There was a young constable pacing up and down outside, trying to keep warm.

'Evening, Ma'am.'

'Evening. I'll go in with Mr Frederiks, Constable.'

'As you like, Ma'am.'

They entered the dark, deserted building and Frederiks reached for the light switch. He shuddered as they passed the corridor leading to the cellar. 'What a day. Can't believe it, really. Poor old Julian. Have you any idea yet what's going on around here?'

'We're working on it, Mr Frederiks,' Jazz replied noncommittally as they arrived at the door leading to his flat.

'Won't be a jiffy, just collecting some stuff,' Frederiks said as he left her in the sitting room.

Jazz wandered around the room whilst she waited. On his desk, there was a large framed photograph of an older couple.

Frederiks arrived back carrying an open holdall. 'Are they your parents?' she asked, pointing to the photo on the desk.

'Yes.'

'Are they both still alive?'

'No, sadly not.'

'Did they die recently?'

'My father died fifteen years ago and my mum passed away a few months ago,' Frederiks replied.

'I see. Did you have brothers and sisters?'

'No, only me.'

'Did they live locally?'

'Yes...look, Inspector.' He frowned. 'I can't see what my family has to do with this. Can we leave it, please? I was close to my mum and I still miss her.'

'My apologies. And sorry to be a pain, but would it be possible to get me a glass of water? I'm terribly thirsty.'

'Okay,' Frederiks nodded, 'I can get you a glass from my bathroom, unless you want bottled and we'll have to go to the kitchens.'

'No, tap will do fine, thanks.'

Whilst Sebastian was fetching the water, Jazz walked to the holdall, took the item she wanted from the top of the pile of belongings and slipped it into her pocket.

Frederiks reappeared with a glass. 'Thank you.' Jazz sipped the tepid water. 'So, I presume you inherited everything when your mum died?'

'Yes, what there was left of it,' he confirmed. 'My mum was diagnosed with Alzheimer's ten years ago. She was only sixty. She spent her last seven years in a home. I had to sell her house to pay for her nursing costs. There wasn't a lot left over.'

'Did she leave you all her personal possessions?'

'Of course she did.' Frederiks was getting seriously irritated now. 'Why?'

'Mr Frederiks, sorry to ask this, but do you happen to know if you were adopted?'

'What?! No, I bloody wasn't! Or at least, if I was, my mum and dad made a damned good job of making sure I never knew. I'm sorry, Inspector, I'm a reasonable man, but these questions are really far too personal and unpleasant, and I don't see why I should have to answer them. I'm not under arrest, am I?'

'No, you are not, Mr Frederiks. Just one last question: can you tell me your date of birth?'

'The tenth of April 1965.'

'Right, that's all I need.' She nodded. 'Thank you for being so patient.'

Sebastian ran a hand through his hair in agitation. 'This is to do with the will, isn't it? Well, let me tell you I'm as much in the dark as you, but the fact Hugh decided to make me his beneficiary doesn't make me a criminal, does it? I'm starting to wish he bloody hadn't, to be honest!'

'Thanks for your help, Mr Frederiks. I'll leave you to round up your belongings. Let the constable know when you leave.'

Jazz stood up and walked out of Fleat House, reaching for her mobile as she headed across Chapel Lawn towards her car.

'Roland, Hunter here. Yes, it has been a hectic day. No, no news yet. I'd like a special eye kept on Sebastian Frederiks. Tell one of your officers to tail him. If at any time he leaves the school premises, make sure he's followed. And don't lose him, okay? Thanks. I'll see you tomorrow morning. Meanwhile, I'm on my mobile.'

Jazz then dialled Patrick, whose mobile was unusually switched off, then drove out onto the coast road heading for home. As she wound her way through the narrow streets of Cley, a memory came back to her. She made a mental note to pursue it tomorrow.

Arriving home, Jazz unlocked the front door and walked in to a blissfully warm cottage.

There was a note from the plumber saying he'd left the heating on continuously. He'd been worried about a burst pipe during the cold snap.

Jazz could have kissed him, whatever it had cost in oil.

She put her briefcase down, switched on her answerphone and went into the kitchen to fill the kettle as she listened. There were a number of messages from the builder, giving her excuses as to why he wasn't on site, and one from her mother, to say she'd allowed herself to leave the hospital for a night's sleep. And that her father looked as though he would be out of critical care tomorrow.

Climbing the stairs with a cup of cocoa in her hand, Jazz ran a deep and very hot bath and sank into it gratefully. Trying to run through the events of the past twenty-four hours, both personal and professional, then make sense of them, was not on the agenda tonight.

Fifteen minutes later, she was tucked up in bed. She dialled Patrick's mobile again and was irritated to find it was still switched off. She dialled Issy's mobile, also on voicemail, and left her a message, asking her to go back to see Rory first thing in the morning, to try and help him remember exactly *what* he'd done with the two aspirin he'd been given the night Charlie died.

Finally, she dialled Celestria and was answered on the second ring.

A tense voice answered, 'Hello?'

'Hi, Mum, only me.'

'Oh, thank goodness. I thought it might be the hospital.'

'Sorry to scare you. I only wanted to know how you and Dad were. I didn't wake you, did I?'

'No, I was just dozing. They told me to take a sleeping pill, but I'd worry I wouldn't hear the phone if it rang.'

'Take one, Mum. You need your rest too. How is he?'

'Much improved, darling, really. But as that rather patronising consultant says to me time and again, not out of the woods yet.'

'You must feel Dad's a lot better, if you were prepared to come home tonight.'

'He is, Jazmine, and if he carries on progressing without any setbacks, he should make it. He's an amazing man, your father,' she said, with a catch in her voice.

'I know. I'm hoping to be able to visit him on the weekend. I'd like to come tomorrow, but this case is at its zenith, and Patrick has been behaving true to form.' Jazz sighed.

'Oh dear. Didn't realise he was on the case. Sorry, darling.'

'He wasn't, but...oh...' Jazz yawned. 'It's a long story, Mum.'

'Poor old you. I'm sure that's the last thing you wanted.'

'Yes, but, in a strange way, it's done me good: helped me remember why I was so unhappy and why I left Patrick...flushed any lingering romantic thoughts away.'

'Well, don't be too hard on yourself, Jazz. We all remember the good times, and try and forget the bad. It's human nature and thank God for it.'

'Unless forgetting leads you down the wrong path again,' Jazz murmured.

'Patrick came up trumps for you yesterday, didn't he?' Celestria said gently. 'And when his ego isn't getting in the way and he isn't feeling threatened, I think he cares for you. That isn't to say that either of us ever thought he was right for you. And sometimes love can be terribly destructive.'

'Yes, I certainly agree with that.' Jazz yawned. 'Right, Mum, please promise to keep in touch with me. I'm going to be up to my eyes tomorrow, so I'd be so grateful if you could leave me a message to say Dad's okay.'

'Of course I will. Now, you get some sleep as well and good luck tomorrow.'

'Thanks, Mum. Night.'

'Night, darling. Sleep tight.'

As she sank gratefully under the duvet, Jazz lay in the darkness and thought of all the people today whose lives had not been enhanced by love, but destroyed.

Jazz tapped on Jenny Colman's front door at half past seven the following morning.

'Who is it?' Jenny called from inside.

'Inspector Hunter, Ms Colman. Sorry to bother you so early, but I wanted to catch you before you left for school. Can I come in?'

'Why yes, of course, Inspector.' Jenny looked flustered as she opened the door, then led Jazz into her tiny sitting room. 'I'm not in any trouble, am I?'

'No, none at all.' Jazz sat down on the sofa and Jenny perched nervously on the edge of the chair opposite. 'I just felt that it would be better to discuss this matter with you in private.'

'Oh Inspector, what on earth is it?' Jenny looked terrified.

'Well, I'll come straight to the point,' Jazz said gently. 'I went to visit Lady Emily Conaught last night. And she told me about you and Corin Conaught. *And* the baby you gave birth to forty years ago.'

Jenny looked as though she'd been slapped across the face. Her eyes welled up with tears and she sat silently, saying nothing.

'I'm sorry,' Jazz apologised. 'I know this must be a painful subject for you to talk about, but I'm afraid I need to know if Emily Conaught was right. And you were the mother of Corin's child?'

Jenny nodded numbly. She pulled a handkerchief out of her sleeve and dabbed her eyes.

'She also intimated you didn't find out you were pregnant until after Corin died?'

Again Jenny could only nod.

'And Hugh Daneman helped you?' Jazz asked.

'Yes, yes he did,' Jenny managed to whisper. 'He was ever so kind, I don't know what I'd have done without him at the time. He sorted me out, and afterwards, got me a job here at St Stephen's. I couldn't face going back home, see, not with Mum and Dad living and working on the Conaught Estate, and all.'

'No, I can imagine,' said Jazz quietly. 'So, the baby was adopted?'

'Yes.'

'Was it a boy or a girl?'

'A boy.' Jenny wiped her eyes. 'Yes, a lovely little boy.'

'Right.' Jazz felt a small surge of adrenalin run through her. 'Jenny, do you have any idea who adopted him?'

Jenny shook her head. 'No. They were very strict on all that, the nuns were. Thought it was better if us mums didn't know where they were going. And they were right. What would be the point? It wasn't going to get our babies back, was it?' Jenny blew her nose loudly. 'Worst day of my life, that, giving birth and a few hours later, my baby being gone. And still being so sore, and then the milk coming in, and the nuns binding you until it stopped… Sorry, Inspector, you don't want to know about that.'

'Jenny'—Jazz leaned forward as she spoke, deciding to test her theory—'did you, by any chance, give the nuns anything to pass on to your baby's new parents?'

'Oh no, they wouldn't have allowed anything like that.' She shook her head, but there was uncertainty in her eyes.

'Are you sure, Jenny?'

'Yes, yes, I didn't give the nuns nothing. Promise.'

Jazz tried again. 'All right then. I'll put it another way: did you, for example, manage to hide something on the baby? That might be found by the new parents, and perhaps kept for a day when the child was older and might want to discover his birth-right?'

Jenny put her hanky to her mouth and looked in horror at Jazz. 'How did you... Yes! Yes, I did! I did!' Jenny started to cry in earnest. 'I wanted my baby to know where he had come from! He was the son of a lord, even if Corin was dead, and his mother just some common scrubber that the Conaughts wanted rid of!' she sobbed.

'It's okay, Jenny, take your time.'

'I'm sorry, Inspector. You knowing everything has been a bit of a shock, that's all,' Jenny nodded. 'It's a secret I've kept to myself for so long, you see.'

'I do see, but the trouble is, I *don't* know everything. Please don't think I'm judging you, Jenny. I just need your help to put the pieces of this jigsaw together. And fast. So, if you feel up to continuing, could you tell me what it was that you hid on your baby before he was taken away?'

'Well, I...I gave him a ring, a signet ring, which had the Conaught family crest engraved on it. But I can't be in trouble for that, can I? I didn't steal it or nothing.'

'No, Jenny, I promise, you're not in trouble. Where on the baby did you hide it?'

'Well,' she snuffled, 'when the nuns left me to hold him for a few minutes just before he was about to be taken, they'd dressed him ready for his new mum and dad to come and collect.' Jenny smiled. 'He looked so sweet in his little hat and bootees, and so tiny. He had a nappy on him, under his Babygro, one of those old-fashioned terry towelling ones that no one uses any more. It had a big nappy pin holding it together. It was when I saw that that I had the idea. I took the ring out of my locker, undid the pin and slid the ring onto it. I closed the pin, tucking the ring into the folds of the nappy as best I could, and refastened his Babygro.' She smiled sadly. 'I've never known to this day whether the nuns found it before the baby was given to his new parents, or whether the new parents saw it, but got rid of it, not wanting anything to remind them their new baby wasn't theirs by birth.'

Despite herself, Jazz was finding it hard to swallow the lump in her *own* throat. 'Well, Jenny, if it's any consolation, I think it was a lovely thing to do, and I admire you for it. Really I do.'

'I'd have given anything to keep him.' Jenny smiled sadly. 'He was part of Corin. I loved him, you see. Always have, even though he died forty years ago. I think about him, and our little baby, every day of my life.'

Jazz instinctively reached forward and closed her hand over Jenny's. 'I can't imagine how awful it must have been for you.'

Jenny smiled sadly. 'Yes, it was, but I survived, didn't I? Just,' she added. 'At least I had Hugh. He understood. He loved Corin too. We had that in common, see.'

'I know he did.' Jazz nodded. 'Tell me, where did you get the ring from originally?'

'Oh, from Hugh,' Jenny admitted. 'He came to visit me a couple of times at the convent where I was sent. And the last time he came, before the baby was born, he drew a ring out of his pocket, said he wanted me to have it as a remembrance of Corin. I think he felt sorry for me. It was a nice thing to do.' Jenny smiled weakly.

'Yes, it was,' Jazz agreed. 'So, did you ever tell Hugh what you'd done with the ring?'

'Oh yes,' Jenny nodded. 'I thought he might think I'd lost it, or something, if I didn't. It was only right to tell him as he'd given it to me in the first place. Hugh said, like you, that it was a good thing to have done, but we agreed we had no idea what would happen to it in the future. Hugh said it didn't matter, that it was more about the gesture.' Tears came to Jenny's eyes again. 'Oh dear, I do miss him. He was the only one that knew, apart from my best friend, Maddy.'

'It sounds as though he was very kind to you.' Jazz smiled.

'He was.' Jenny nodded. 'And he's left me something in his will, bless him, although what with the goings-on at school, I still haven't got up to London to find out what it is.'

Jazz paused before she said, 'Jenny, have you heard who Hugh left the rest of his estate to?'

She shook her head. 'No, I haven't.'

'Well, he left it to Sebastian Frederiks.'

Jenny raised her eyebrows. 'Sebastian? That's odd. I remember Hugh telling me he'd never been very fond of him, as man or boy. Chalk and cheese they were, those two. But a good foil for each other at Fleat House.'

'What did *you* make of Sebastian, Jenny?'

She shrugged. 'I suppose I thought the same as Hugh, really. He was always a bit of a bully when he was a boy, and Hugh thought he was too physical as a housemaster. On the other hand, I suppose some of those lads need a strong hand.'

'So, do you have any idea why Hugh might have left everything to a man he had never particularly liked?'

Jenny shook her head. 'Not a clue, Inspector. If you want my opinion, it strikes me as downright odd, but it's not my place to say so. I'm sure Hugh had his reasons. He used to think everything through, never did anything on the spur of the moment, bless him.'

'Yes, from what I've heard of him, he seemed like a very careful man. So, what was it that made Hugh change his will in favour of Sebastian, I wonder?'

'As I said, I can't make head nor tail of it.'

'Unless...' Jazz knew she had to choose her words carefully. 'Jenny, what if Hugh had seen something...a...possession, of someone's recently that led him to think he'd identified your adopted baby?'

'I don't know what you mean, Inspector.' Jenny looked confused. 'How could he?'

'By the ring, Jenny,' Jazz said softly.

'You mean, the one I sent off with my baby all those years ago?'

'Yes.'

Jenny sat silently, staring at Jazz, who continued. 'Your son was born forty years ago?'

'He would turn forty this year,' Jenny confirmed.

'What month was he born?'

'April. April the fourth.'

'The fourth?' Jazz frowned. 'You're sure about that?'

'Excuse me, Inspector, for sounding rude, but it's not exactly a date I'd forget, now, is it?'

'No, of course it isn't. Jenny, thank you so much for your help.' Jazz rose from the sofa.

Jenny rose too and grabbed her arm. 'Please, Inspector, you can't leave me like this! I think you know who my son is, don't you? Please tell me. Please!'

Jazz saw the desperation on her face. 'Jenny, it would be very irresponsible of me to tell you something that might not be true.' She spoke as gently as she could. 'Let me check my facts and I promise you'll be the first to know. It might be coincidence.'

'That Hugh saw a man around the right age, wearing the ring I gave him as a baby?'

'There might be a lot of those rings…'

'No! The rings were only given to direct members of the Conaught family. I remember Hugh telling me there were no others in existence.'

'Then someone might have copied it,' Jazz suggested.

'For Pete's sake, why would they do that? It would mean nothing to anyone else.' Jenny shook her head. 'No, if Hugh found someone wearing that ring, he'd know if it was real or not. Oh dear.' Jenny sank down into the chair. 'I know who it is, I know who my son is. That's why Hugh left all his money to him, isn't it? Because he was Corin's son. And mine. Tell me, please, is Sebastian Frederiks my child? Is he?'

Jazz could see hysteria was setting in. She took Jenny's shaking hands in hers. 'I don't know yet. And that's the truth. Yes, Sebastian does wear a signet ring that was identical to the one Emily Conaught was wearing last night. And as he told me his mother died only a few months ago, she may well have left the ring to him in her will. Which would explain why he has only recently started wearing it. And yes, it is odd that Hugh changed his will in Sebastian's favour, but we mustn't make suppositions until we have absolute proof.'

'How can I *not* do that?!' Jenny wrenched her hands away from Jazz. 'I've known Sebastian since he was thirteen, and never thought for a moment he was my…' She bit her lip, unable to say the word. 'If anyone should know, I should, surely?'

'How could you, Jenny? Please try not to blame yourself. But, listen, the good news is that I *do* have a way to get proof: Lady Conaught has kept a lock of Corin's hair. It was in his baby book. If it matches a sample of Sebastian's hair, we'll know definitively if he is yours and Corin's child.'

'I did that too,' mumbled Jenny.

'Did what?'

Jenny stood up and went to the sideboard drawer. She searched at the back of it, brought out a tatty brown envelope and handed it to Jazz. 'Here. Take a look.'

Jazz took the contents out of the envelope. In a smaller envelope was a lock of white-gold hair and a black and white photograph. Tears sprang to her eyes, as she studied the blurred outline of Jenny's baby.

'Hugh lent me his Box Brownie, so I could take a photo,' Jenny explained. 'I had to do it quickly, so it's awful. I remember crying buckets when Hugh had it developed and gave it to me, because you can hardly see him.'

'And this is your baby's hair?'

'Yes. I snipped it off whilst no one was looking.'

'Jenny, would you trust me to take this away for a while? Obviously, the more material the geneticist has to cross-reference, the better chance we have of coming up with absolute proof.'

'Yes, I'm sure you'll take care of it.'

'I will. Thank you.' Jazz slipped the lock of hair into a plastic wallet and put it in her pocket. 'I'll be off now. Thank you so much for all your help.'

Jazz left the sitting room and made her way to the front door. Jenny followed her out.

'You know, the sad thing is I've spent all these years wondering what happened to my boy, where he is, who he's become, whether he would ever try to find me. And now, maybe, my son is a person who grew up under my nose, who I didn't much like as a boy and have no time for as a man.' Jenny sighed. 'Ironic, isn't it?'

'Well, let's just wait and see what the lab—'

'Oh dear! Oh dearie me!' Jenny's hand shot to her mouth suddenly.

'What is it, Jenny?' Jazz asked in concern.

'It's just clicked why you're so interested in Sebastian being Corin's son. It's because of Charlie and all, isn't it? You're thinking that if Sebastian had found out he was Corin's son, that he might have wanted to do away with Charlie and claim the—'

The doorbell rang.

'Oh dear, it's like Piccadilly Circus here this morning,' Jenny said as she opened the door. 'Hello, Maddy.'

Jazz came face to face with the Fleat House matron. 'Good morning,' she said, then turned back to Jenny. 'I'll be off now.'

'Thanks, Inspector, let me know, won't you?' asked Jenny. 'Good luck.'

The two women watched as Jazz made her way down the small path and disappeared out of sight.

'Are you coming in, Maddy?'

'No, I was just on my way back to the school. I had to drop some samples off at the doctor's in town for one of the boys. We think he might have glandular fever,' Maddy explained. 'You all right, my love? You look a bit pale.'

'Not surprising really, is it, with what's going on at school.' Jenny sighed. 'Hang on a tick. I'll get my coat and walk with you.'

Two minutes later, they left the bungalow to make the short walk back to the school.

'I just popped in to say sorry I had to cancel the other night. As I said, my car's in the garage. I was thinking maybe we could go to the cinema next week?' Maddy said.

'Yes, lovely,' Jenny said automatically, still thinking about what the inspector had told her.

'Not sure when my night off is yet,' Maddy added.

'No, well, one way and another, things are a bit chaotic, aren't they?'

'You could say that. Moving all those boys out of Fleat and into another house. I hope the police sort it all out soon and we can all get back to normality. What did the inspector want, by the way?'

'Oh, just some admin stuff. Nothing important. No one seems to know what's going on, do they?' Jenny sighed. 'So much trouble this term. It's not good for the school's reputation, is it?'

'No, it isn't, but until Mr Jones takes a stronger hand, nothing's ever going to improve.'

'Mr Jones does his best, you know,' Jenny defended her boss loyally. 'He has a lot of people to please. The governors, the parents, the children…talking of which, I haven't seen young Rory back at school yet.'

'No. I doubt he ever will come back, given what's happened to him. If I was his mum, I'd keep him safe and sound at home, watch over him. He's all she's got now *he's* gone, and he's a delicate little chap. Better at a day school, maybe.'

'Yes.' Jenny's mind was wandering to thoughts of her own long-lost son. 'Maybe…'

'You sure that detective was here asking you about admin? You seem a bit distracted.'

'Oh,' Jenny yawned, 'just tired, that's all. Trying to keep Mr Jones sane while all this is going on is a hard job. Although…' Jenny sighed. 'There is something I'd like to talk to you about, Maddy.' They came to a halt in front of the main building.

'Is there?'

'Yes,' Jenny nodded, thinking if she didn't tell someone what the inspector had said, she might explode.

'Listen, if you can, come over and see me at lunch break,' Maddy suggested. 'I'll be in my medical room, but we could pop up to my flat for a sandwich and a cup of coffee.'

'Will they let me into Fleat?' Jenny queried. 'Thought it was sealed off.'

'They're letting me use the medical room during the day. I'll meet you at the back entrance at one, shall I?'

'Righto,' Jenny nodded, 'I would like to talk to you. Thanks, Maddy, I'll see you later.' She waved to her friend and set off towards reception.

Chapter Twenty-Nine

Jazz arrived at Foltesham station to find Miles and Issy deep in conversation in the car park.

'Morning, Jazz, just off to see Rory,' Issy said.

'Good. Where's Patrick?'

'In with David Millar,' Miles replied.

Jazz frowned, wondering why he'd started interviewing him without her. She turned to Miles. 'Anything interesting come up at Julian Forbes's office last night?'

'Only that the seven o'clock appointment was with a Mr Smith. But it may be a false name. There was no telephone number or address registered in the diary. The secretary said she didn't remember taking the call, but she'd been off sick the week before and they had a temp in. I tried the agency yesterday but they'd closed for the day. I checked the client database and there are a hundred and thirty-two Smiths registered. It's a needle in a haystack job, Ma'am.'

'What about Forbes's computer? Anything there?'

'I've got a chap trying to hack in as we speak. It's the usual password problem, but he reckons he'll have it sorted in an hour or so. I'm off to the school to see the troops. Apparently, the press have turned up.' Miles raised his eyebrows. 'They don't know what's going on, apparently, but we can't keep a lid on the truth for long. I'll drop Issy on the way. See you later.'

Jazz felt a hand on her shoulder. It was Martin Chapman.

'Hello.'

'Morning, Martin.'

'Bye,' waved Issy, following Miles to his car and giving him a playful tap on the bottom as they walked towards it.

'Are those two...?' Martin let the question hang in the air. 'They were very touchy-feely when I joined them for a late brandy at the hotel last night.'

'As a highly trained police officer, I'd deduce from the suspects' joint behaviour that the odds are, yes.' Jazz smiled. 'Any news?'

'I've just given Patrick the full pathology and forensic reports.'

'Find anything?' she asked.

'I'll let you speak to Patrick about that,' he answered diplomatically.

'How about my DNA sample?'

'Someone's on the case.'

'Good.' Jazz pulled two plastic wallets from her pocket and handed them to Chapman. 'Here are two more for cross-referencing. One is a lock of hair from Baby X. At least one or both of the other samples should match it.'

Chapman looked at her questioningly. 'I presume this was obtained with the complete co-operation of its owner?'

'Of course.'

'And this hairbrush?' Chapman scratched his chin.

'No.' Admitted Jazz. 'I stole it from the top of a holdall while he wasn't looking.'

'Thought so,' Chapman sighed. 'Legally, you're stealing DNA, which is a criminal offence, and I should have refused to process it.'

'Martin, *please*. There was no other way. And I can't prove anything until I know whether that matches.'

'All right, all right, as it's you, Ma'am... But I insist that if this proves conclusive to your case, once you've made an arrest, we proceed with the usual DNA profile, so that he, and everyone else, is unaware you had prior knowledge. Okay?'

'Of course,' agreed Jazz. 'And I need them very, very urgently.'

Chapman raised his hands. 'Enough, already. I hear you, okay?'

'Fine. Sorry, and thanks, Martin.'

'Bye.' Chapman ambled away and Jazz made her way back inside. She walked towards the interview room, peered through the window and saw Patrick was alone, speaking on his mobile. He waved her in and indicated 'two minutes' as he finished his conversation.

'Yes, Sir, I will. I'll see you later.' He ended the call and smiled at Jazz. 'You okay? You look tired.'

'I'm fine,' she answered brusquely. 'I hear you've already interviewed David Millar.'

'So I have. He'd sobered up enough last night to talk, so I grilled him for a couple of hours, then, when I got the new information from

Chapman, gave him another go this morning.'

Jazz slammed her briefcase down on the table. 'Patrick! We'd agreed we'd interview him together!'

'Keep your hair on, Jazz. I thought I'd be doing you a favour. You were exhausted last night. I wanted to give you a good night's sleep without disturbing you and—'

'Patrick! This is *my* case! How dare you presume what I wanted?!'

'Look now, Jazz, surely it hardly matters who interviewed him? The good news is, we have our murderer under lock and key downstairs. I arrested David Millar ten minutes ago and charged him with the murders of Charlie Cavendish and Julian Forbes.'

Jazz stared at Patrick with a mixture of horror and disbelief.

'You've done *what*?!'

'Oh, come now, Jazz, you yourself had him arrested a few days ago.'

'No I didn't! I interviewed him when he'd walked into a police station to give himself up. He was here of his own free will. At no point did I *arrest* him.'

'Well, he told me last night he murdered Charlie Cavendish.'

Jazz put her hands on her hips and raised her eyebrows. 'Yup.' She nodded. 'When he was still half-cut and under pressure and—'

'New evidence has come to light this morning, so it has. Chapman found Millar's fingerprints all over the trunk in which Forbes's body was found. That's pretty conclusive, so.' Patrick looked suitably smug.

'Not if the trunk belonged to his son, then no it isn't!' she shouted. 'For Christ's sake, that was *Rory's* trunk! Of course his father, aka David Millar's fingerprints would be all over it! It proves nothing and it certainly wouldn't stand up in court. You know it wouldn't!'

Patrick said nothing. And Jazz realised he hadn't known about the trunk being Rory's.

'So.' Jazz tried to calm down. She paced up and down in front of Patrick's desk. 'Has Millar confessed to the murder of Julian Forbes?'

'No, not yet, but come on now, he admitted telling Julian he'd "kill him" a week ago or so…'

'If Julian ever laid a finger on Rory, which would be really quite hard, as he'd never even *met* the boy. Christ, Patrick!' Jazz finally flopped into a chair. 'I can't believe you didn't wait until I was here to make the arrest.'

'I'm sorry, Jazz, so I am, but everyone is keen on solving this as soon as possible. I've just spoken to the headmaster, who's mighty relieved an arrest has been made. Norton thinks we can probably control the media, keep it very low-key, a "domestic" incident that got out of hand and—'

'You really haven't hung around, have you?' Jazz stood up again. 'Letting everyone know of your trophy murderer? DCI Coughlin, sweeping in, clearing up his incompetent ex-wife's case in a matter of hours...'

'Ah, Jazz, let's face it'—Patrick leaned back in his chair, arms crossed—'you've always had a problem with me in the workplace. And now, of course, I'm after being promoted...'

'Excuse me!' Jazz leaned over the desk, arms akimbo. 'I have never had a problem! Ever! It's *you* that had the problem! Even Norton recognised it!'

'Did he indeed? Well now, he's never mentioned it to me, and, fair play, Jazz, if I do have a problem, it's got far more to do with Norton so obviously thinking the sun shines out of your backside, favouring you...' Patrick stood up and they eyed each other angrily across the desk.

'How *dare* you say that! He's not favoured me in any way whatsoever. I've got there by sheer hard work and—'

'That's not what everyone else in the department reckons.' Patrick smirked.

'You bastard!' Unable to stop herself, Jazz reached out and slapped Patrick across his cheek.

Joint shock stunned them both into silence.

'Shit! I'm sorry,' Jazz said eventually, as Patrick reached to touch his stinging cheek. 'I shouldn't have done that.'

Patrick shrugged. 'You always did have a rare temper. And I understand you're upset, what with your father, and all.'

'*No*, Patrick! This has nothing to do with me being "upset"! The bottom line here is that I'm in charge of this operation, and if anyone was going to make an arrest, it should have been *me*. The fact that you haven't given me the chance to interview Millar yet so I can ascertain the facts for myself...'

'Feel free.' Patrick shrugged, reaching down and shutting his laptop. 'He's all yours. Norton has asked me to drive straight back to London. Something's come up. I'm out of your hair as of now.'

He picked up his briefcase and searched in his pocket for his car keys. She watched him silently, seething with anger, as he walked towards the door. Hesitating, he stopped and turned round.

'Now so, Jazz, there was sufficient evidence to arrest Millar. And time is of the essence. The media have got ahold of something that's amiss at the school. They'll be gathering like a pack of vultures by now, so they will.'

'I'm sure,' she nodded, realising it was pointless to continue the argument.

He handed her a file. 'The PM is in there, as well as the forensic report. Down to you to extract a confession for Forbes's death, though I'm reckoning Millar'd go down, even if he doesn't confess. He said he spent the night of Forbes's murder on a park bench somewhere in Norwich.'

'Thanks.' She took the file from him.

Patrick reached out to open the door then stopped. 'Look, Jazz, surely what's just happened illustrates why our marriage didn't work?'

'You mean, you shagging Chrissie had nothing to do with it?' Jazz replied sarcastically, as she walked round the desk and slumped in the chair behind it.

'Well, that, too, of course,' Patrick nodded. 'What I'm saying is, Jazz, the other night was wonderful. When it was just you and me.'

Jazz concentrated on removing her laptop from its case. She did not look up at him as she spoke. 'Patrick, the other night, my father was dying and I was in no fit state to think straight about anything. You and me were a mistake, and it's my turn to apologise. Thanks anyway, for being there. I do appreciate it. But it's over. We're divorced. And that's an end to it.' She sighed wearily as she opened the computer. 'Safe journey back to London.'

'Jazz, I—'

Her mobile rang. She ignored Patrick and answered it. 'Hunter here.'

She watched Patrick out of the corner of her eye walk out of the room.

'Hello, Ma'am, Roland here.'

'Roland, everything all right?'

'I thought you might like to know that Frederiks left the school in his car about an hour ago. An officer tailed him to a cottage in Cley. He spent twenty minutes inside, then came out and drove back to the school. He's just arrived now.'

'Was he was meeting someone there?'

'The officer said Frederiks rang the bell and was let in to the cottage, but because the cottage is down the end of a narrow loke, he didn't get a look at who it was. Anyway, I'll give you the address.'

'Good. Thanks for letting me know, Roland. How many media have we got at the school at present?'

'I'd say ten or so, but you know what they're like; more are turning up as we speak.'

'Right. Have you seen Miles?'

'He's standing right next to me, Ma'am.'

'Can you tell him to drive back here to the station? I need to speak to him.'

'Very good, Ma'am.'

'Thanks, Roland. I'll be along to the school later. For now, hold the fort as best you can.'

Putting the mobile down on the desk, Jazz leaned back in the chair and stretched. The day had hardly begun and she felt exhausted. But her relief that Patrick had gone back to London knew no bounds.

She swept her hand through her long hair. There was a call she needed to make now, before she lost her confidence. Her hand hovered over the receiver as she ran through what she would say, then steeled herself to dial Norton's number.

'Morning, Sir, Hunter here.'

'Hunter, congratulations! Coughlin told me about Millar's arrest.' Norton sounded jovial. 'Good news, isn't it?'

'Yes, Sir.' Jazz knew she mustn't sound sour-grape-ish in any way. 'But at the time of the arrest, he was unable to discuss it with me.'

'I see. So, Hunter, come to the point, please.'

'The truth is, Sir, I'm not convinced Millar committed the crime. Until such time as I *am*, I'd like your permission to follow up other lines of enquiry.'

There was a pause on the line. Then Norton said, 'Coughlin told me there was incontrovertible forensic evidence. On top of which, this Millar has already admitted to killing Charlie Cavendish.'

'I'm afraid I'd have to disagree there, Sir, not that I'm doubting DCI Coughlin's judgement,' she added quickly. 'There was forensic evidence, yes, but its reliability in terms of upholding a conviction would be questionable. Having only arrived on the case yesterday, DCI Coughlin wasn't aware of all the facts.'

'Well, the *fact* remains there is a man currently in custody. At least the powers that be at the school are resting much easier, as I'm sure are

Mrs Millar and her son.' Norton responded curtly.

'Yes, Sir. I'm just not entirely convinced it's the *right* man.'

'I see.'

Jazz could hear Norton thinking.

Finally, he said, 'Putting it bluntly, Hunter, it's obvious that DCI Coughlin turning up as he did must have made it hard for you. Therefore, you have to give me your word that your need to continue with the investigation is based purely on professional reasons, not personal ones. Whoever arrested Millar is immaterial if he committed the crime.'

'I'm aware of that, Sir, and, despite what you might think, this has nothing to do with any situation between DCI Coughlin and myself. In my professional opinion, there are a number of leads which I've yet to follow up. I believe I would be compromising the integrity of the force if I didn't do so.'

She heard him sigh. 'All right. But I want Millar held whilst you do so. Twenty-four hours maximum, and then I'm pulling everyone off the case.'

'Thank you, Sir. I appreciate it. I'll call you when I have news.'

'You do that, Hunter. Good luck.'

'Thank you, Sir.'

Jazz put the receiver down in relief, glad *that* was over. She leaned over and switched on the tape recorder to listen to David Millar's interview. When she had finished, she asked the duty constable to bring Millar up from the cell to see her.

Jazz studied him as he sat down opposite her. Millar looked awful, his eyes bloodshot, his gaunt face tinged with grey.

'How are you?' she asked.

'How is anyone in my position?' He shrugged.

'I know you've already been interviewed by my colleague, so I won't go back over old ground, but there are a few questions I'd like to ask you.'

'Fire away, Inspector.'

'You say that on Tuesday night, the evening Julian Forbes was murdered, you left your house, walked to Foltesham, then took a taxi into Norwich and spent the evening drinking at a pub near Castle Mall.'

'I did, yes.'

'Can you remember which pub?'

David shook his head. 'I visited a few.'

'Then what did you do?'

'When they chucked me out at closing time, I found a bench and fell asleep.'

'When did you wake up?'

'Before dawn sometime. It had started to snow, and I'd sobered up and was freezing. I walked around trying to find a taxi, but no one would take me to Foltesham because of the weather. So I went to the Travelodge by the railway station and took a room there.'

'This was on Wednesday morning?'

David scratched his head. 'Yes, it must have been Wednesday. I slept most of the day, then went out to the pub again that night. Then I got back to my room and slept again, until the police banged on my door and drove me here.'

'So, on the night of Julian Forbes's murder, you slept on a bench somewhere in Norwich?'

'Yes.'

'Mr Millar,' Jazz sighed. 'You realise that information doesn't help you? There's unlikely to be anyone to corroborate your story.'

'I know.' David nodded. 'But what's the point anyway, even if someone *could*? Your colleague insisted that I would still have had time to visit Julian Forbes in his office at seven, persuade him to get in his car and drive at gun-point or knife-point to St Stephen's, do him in, then drive back again to Norwich in time to have a quick drink, then fall asleep on a park bench. And this morning, he told me my fingerprints were all over the trunk in which Julian was found.'

'Mr Millar, it was your son's trunk. It was *Rory's* trunk.' Jazz stressed the fact in an attempt to try and ignite even a basic level of fighting spirit in the man.

'Really?' David raised his eyebrows. 'I didn't know that.'

'So, you haven't admitted to killing Julian Forbes?'

'No.'

'And are you sticking to that statement?'

'Of course I am!'

Jazz tapped her pen on the desk. 'I only ask, as you continually seem to change your story on whether or not you murdered Charlie Cavendish.'

'I told you, Inspector, I *may* have done. I honestly can't remember.'

'And that's what you told Chief Inspector Coughlin? That you "can't remember"?'

'Yes.'

Jazz was silent for a while. Then she nodded. 'Okay, Mr Millar. Thank you.'

'Is that it? Aren't you going to give me the third degree like the other copper did?' David seemed surprised.

'No, that's all I need.' She pressed a buzzer and the constable came in. 'Take Mr Millar down to his cell, will you?'

'Yes, Ma'am.'

David stood up, walked to the door, then turned back to Jazz.

'I understand, you know. If I've admitted I killed Charlie Cavendish when I was pissed, why shouldn't I have done the same to my ex-wife's boyfriend? For all I know, I might have done. I was very drunk on Tuesday. And I've got the perfect motive. Julian was a tosser and I hated the thought of him bringing up Rory in my place. And I'm sure there were a few witnesses who heard me say I wanted to kill Julian in the middle of town a few days ago.' He shrugged. 'I'm stuffed, really, aren't I?'

'We'll speak later.' Jazz nodded, and watched him leave the room.

'Ma'am, DS Miles is outside. Do you want me to send him in?' asked the constable.

'Thank you.'

Jazz clicked off her mobile as Miles entered the room.

'You called?'

'Yes. Sit, Miles, please.' Jazz indicated a chair with her pen. 'Have you heard about the Millar arrest?' she asked.

'Not until Mr Jones told me at the school, no. Patrick didn't tell me. I felt like a chump, actually, not knowing,' Miles admitted.

'No comment.' Jazz sighed. 'I won't even waste my breath. Now, the bottom line is this: Patrick's hotfooted it back to London at Norton's request, and Norton has granted us twenty-four hours for further investigation before he cans the case and Millar is our man. So, I want to bring you up to speed fast on what I discovered yesterday. I'm not sure where it gets us. But if we can't come up with the truth, even if Millar's statement *is* full of holes, I reckon, with a good prosecution, he might go down for both murders.'

'Okay, Ma'am.' Miles sat down. 'Fire away.'

Ten minutes later, Miles knew all the facts. He used his fingers to rub his forehead in concentration. 'So, what you're saying is that, if Sebastian Frederiks had found out he was the true but illegitimate heir to the Conaught Estate, he might have got rid of Charlie to clear his path?'

'Yes.'

'But what about Julian Forbes? Why would Frederiks have wanted to murder him?'

'They were pupils at St Stephen's together, weren't they? I'm wondering whether there's a tie-in there. Frederiks did say they were friends, and had met up occasionally for a drink.' She slapped the top of the desk with her palms. 'We need to go back to the past.'

'Yes, Ma'am, I think you're right,' he agreed. 'The only common denominator to everything that's happened is the school. And more specifically, Fleat House.'

'Exactly,' Jazz nodded. 'I want to know more about this story of a boy hanging himself in the cellar; who and when it was, and what actually happened. Rory Millar was locked in there for the night a few weeks ago. It might be coincidence but...'

'We need to find an older member of staff who might know the story.'

'Precisely,' Jazz agreed. 'And the person who will probably know more than anyone is Jenny Colman, the headmaster's secretary. She's been there since the year dot. Poor woman. Bless her, she didn't look too happy when I indicated Frederiks just might be her long-lost son.'

'No. I can imagine.'

'I've got to wait on Martin Chapman and those DNA samples. If they come back a match, then I'm going to haul Frederiks in for questioning. If not,' Jazz sighed, 'I still want to know where he got that ring. Although, I do have a theory, actually...' Jazz's voice tailed off as she thought about it. 'Yes, I'll bet that's it.'

'You've lost me, Ma'am.'

'Sorry. I'll tell you later when I've confirmed my theory.'

'Okay. By the way, my chap's got in to Julian's computer. I'm going to have a session with it, see if that sheds any light. Is it all right if I work in here?'

'Feel free. I'm going to visit Angelina Millar, see how she is and try and find out a little more about her dead boyfriend. Call me if there's any news.'

'I will, Ma'am. And by the way, if it helps, Issy is still convinced that Millar is not a murderer.'

'Good. You know how much store I put on her opinion. How is she, by the way?' Jazz asked lightly.

'Oh...' Miles nodded. 'Fine. Yup. Just fine.'

'Mmm... For someone who hates the country, she seems to have settled in here quite well.'

Miles shifted uncomfortably, then changed the subject. 'Oh, by the way, Ma'am, Roland asked me to ask you whether there was any chance of you coming up to the school and making a statement? The place is beginning to swarm with journalists. They won't go away until we've given them something. And Jones is keen to get rid of them yesterday.'

'Tell them I'll hold a press conference at six p.m. tonight. Ask Jones to make the hall available so they can set up their gear. He'll have to hold on until then.'

'Will you tell them we've arrested and charged David Millar?' Miles asked.

Jazz sighed. 'No. I'll tell them he's helping us with our enquiries. We have twenty-four hours, that's all, before you're shipped back to London and I return to my quiet life in the country.'

'You can do it, Ma'am.' Miles smiled.

'Thanks. And this isn't about anything other than making sure the right man goes down for the crime. Okay?' Jazz stood up and eyed him.

'I know,' he nodded. 'Truthfully, I wasn't thinking anything else.'

'Good. I'm off. Let's hope Issy has worked her magic with Rory. See you later.'

'Good at magic is Issy,' Miles murmured under his breath as he watched Jazz leave the room.

'Just don't get hurt, will you?' Jazz murmured in reply, and shut the door behind her.

Chapter Thirty

Angelina looked tiny and fragile when she opened the door. As if the events of the past few days had physically diminished her.

'Hello, Angelina. How are you today?' Jazz asked as she followed her into the kitchen.

'How do you think?' Angelina slumped into a chair.

Jazz sat too. 'Is there anything I can do?'

Angelina shook her head, then looked up at her sadly. 'Bring Julian back to life?' She gave a feeble smile. 'That would do.'

Jazz reached for her small, cold hand. 'I'm so very sorry. I promise, we're doing our best to find out who did this to Julian and why. And I should warn you, the press have arrived at the school. They've got wind of something, as they always do. I've not yet made a statement naming Julian, but when I do later today, you might want to consider going to stay elsewhere. I'm afraid they're bound to doorstep you, and that's the last thing you and Rory need just now.'

Angelina nodded. She was hardly listening.

'And unfortunately, the other thing I need isn't pleasant: I'm going to have to ask you to come and formally identify Julian.'

Angelina put her head in her hands. 'Oh God, do I really? I've never seen a dead body.' She shook her head. 'Really, I don't think I can.'

'Perhaps we can contact his parents? I presume you've given them the news?'

'His mother's dead, but his father's abroad on holiday so no, he doesn't know yet. I could hardly leave him a message on his answering machine telling him his son's been murdered, could I?' she said desolately. 'I just asked him to ring me back.'

'Then I'm afraid it will have to be you. I'll come with you.'

Angelina nodded. 'If I have to, I have to. Julian would want me to be strong…' Tears came to her eyes. 'It'll bring it home to me, make it real. Because at the moment I can't believe it is.'

'No. Of course you can't,' Jazz said gently. 'Shall I make us some coffee?'

'Help yourself.' Angelina waved her arm in the direction of the Aga.

Jazz stood up and put the kettle on to boil. 'How's Rory?'

Angelina nodded. 'Fine. Your Issy has been a godsend in the past two days. She and Rory have really bonded. My mum's arriving this afternoon, so that'll help.'

'I really would suggest you think about going away, Angelina.' Jazz spooned some coffee, hot water and milk into two mugs and dumped a large teaspoon of sugar into the second. She took them back to the table. 'Try and drink this.'

'Thank you. No, I'm staying here, in our—*my*—house.' She bit her lip. 'Have you...?'

'Have we found anyone yet?' Jazz took a sip of her coffee. 'Well, your ex-husband is currently in custody, helping us with our enquiries. But he's not admitting to Julian's murder.'

Angelina said nothing, just stared into space.

'I'm afraid I need to ask you a couple of questions.'

'Go ahead.' Angelina shrugged listlessly.

'You don't happen to know if Julian knew anyone called Smith? Socially or professionally?'

'He might have done.'

'Did he keep an address book here at home?'

'Yes. It's in the drawer in his study.'

'Would you mind if I took a look at it?'

Angelina walked slowly to the study and came back with a leather-bound book. She handed it to Jazz.

'Thank you. Talking of people he knew, did Julian ever mention he knew Sebastian Frederiks?'

'Not really, no.'

'They were at school together.'

'Yes, I'd heard. But not in the same year.' Angelina's eyes looked dully at Jazz. 'Why?'

'No particular reason.' Jazz changed the subject. 'So, Julian had behaved perfectly normally in the past few weeks, had he? No unusual behaviour you can think of?'

Angelina shook her head. 'No. He was very happy. Work was going well, we were together...'

'So nothing seemed to be worrying him? Not the thought of finally meeting Rory and all that entailed?'

'No, although talking of Rory...' Angelina frowned. 'Actually, I've just thought of something.'

'What?'

'It's probably nothing, but last Saturday, I went to the school with Julian to see Rory, who was ill in the san. I went inside and Julian waited in the car. When I came back, I *do* remember Julian behaving strangely. He couldn't get out of the school fast enough. And the next day, when Rory went missing, Julian refused to come to the school with me to help look for him. It caused an argument, actually. I felt Julian wasn't supporting me.'

'I'm sure you did,' Jazz sympathised. 'Did you ask him why?'

'Of course.' Angelina nodded. 'He didn't give me an answer. But he looked...' Angelina paused, trying to find the word. '...frightened, I suppose. I remember commenting that he looked as though he'd seen a ghost when I arrived back at the car. He'd gone very pale.'

'Well, I wonder if he'd seen someone he didn't want to see whilst he was waiting for you? After all, it was his old school.'

'Perhaps.' Angelina shrugged. 'He didn't say he had, but we can't ask him now, can we?'

Jazz's mobile rang.

'Please excuse me,' she said as she answered it. 'Hunter here.'

'It's Martin Chapman. I've got the results of those samples you gave me.'

'Can I call you back in five, Martin?'

'Sure.'

Jazz ended the call. 'I need to go, but what you've just told me is very interesting. If I come back this afternoon around three, I can drive you to the morgue and perhaps we can talk some more. I'll just pop up to have a word with Issy, if that's okay? Don't get up, I'll see myself out.'

Angelina nodded. 'Thank you, Inspector.'

Jazz climbed the stairs and called Issy's name. She appeared from behind one of the bedroom doors.

'Any luck?' whispered Jazz.

'We're getting there, but it's slow going. I've told him Daddy is back in a cell. It might stir his conscience.'

'Do you want me to talk to him?'

'No, not at present. The kid's scared shitless and I'm still not sure why. Leave him to me for a while longer.'

'Okay, but I'm running out of time. And I've got to run. Keep in touch.'

'Will do.'

Jazz walked back down the stairs and swiftly through the hall to her car, dialling as she went.

'Martin. What news?' Her heart was pounding.

'The first thing is that the sample from the hairbrush does not match any of the other hair samples you gave me.'

Jazz's heart sank. 'Shit!'

'Sorry, Jazz. However, the other two samples *do* match. "Baby X" was directly related to "Sample A".'

'Right. Thanks, Martin.' Jazz bit her lip in disappointment.

'But listen, there *is* something interesting the lab technician found. He's cross-checking again to make sure, and I'll call you back when we know.'

'Can you tell me what it is?'

'Not until we've double-checked. Patience, please.'

'Of course, Martin, sorry. Speak later.' Jazz hit the steering wheel. 'Damn!'

She dialled reception at the school. Jenny Colman answered.

'Jenny, it's Inspector Hunter here. I thought you'd want to know the results as soon as possible.'

'Yes, yes.' Jenny sounded nervous and expectant.

'Sebastian Frederiks's DNA does not match Corin's, or the sample of hair you gave me. Which means he isn't your son.'

Jenny let out a sigh of relief. 'Oh my goodness! What I've learned from all this is that perhaps it's best not to know.'

'Yes. Well, my apologies for putting you through some hours of uncertainty, Jenny. Just a quick question. Can you remember a pupil called Julian Forbes?'

There was a pause on the line. Then Jenny said, 'Julian Forbes? Why do you ask?'

'I just wondered if you remembered him. He's the partner of Angelina Millar, Rory's mother.'

'Is he really? Well, I never knew that.'

'Do you remember him?'

'I…well yes, I do, but I didn't know him well.'

Jazz could hear the reticence in Jenny's voice.

'And one last thing: do you know anything about this tale that seems to be circulating the school, about the boy who was found hanged in the cellar?'

'No...I...not really, no,' Jenny replied cagily.

'Are you sure?'

'Yes. I mean, it did happen, but I don't really know much about it.'

'You mean, it happened during your time at the school?'

'Yes, but...Inspector Hunter, it's not my place to tell you. Mr Jones knows much more than me.'

'It was a suicide, was it?'

'Yes.'

'Can you remember the name of the boy?'

There was a pause on the line. Then Jenny said reluctantly, 'He was called Jamie.'

'Surname?' Jazz asked.

'Inspector, I think you should ask Mr Jones about this, really I do. I'd...prefer not to talk about it.'

Jazz could see she wasn't going to get anything further. 'Thanks for your help, Jenny. Can you tell Mr Jones I'll be along as soon as I can to see him?'

'I will, Inspector. My telephone's not stopped ringing all day. Thank you for calling. Goodbye.'

Jenny put the telephone down and stared into space. Why was the past coming back now? And why was the inspector interested in what had happened all those years ago? Not to mention Julian Forbes...

Did she know what had happened?

Jenny shifted uncomfortably in her chair. Was it wrong for her to have mentioned Jamie's name?

Surely not? After all, what had happened was a matter of public record...

But it wasn't for her to tell.

The curtains in the downstairs windows of the small cottage were still drawn when Jazz arrived in front of it. She knocked a couple of times to no response, then finally, she heard movement from inside.

'Who is it?' asked a familiar voice.

On hearing it, Jazz's theory was confirmed.

'Inspector Hunter. Can I have a word, Mrs Cavendish?'

The door was unlocked and Adele Cavendish stood on the threshold in front of her.

'How did you know I was here?'

'I saw you a few days ago, here in Cley, parked on the main street, unloading your shopping. May I come in?' Adele agreed reluctantly and led Jazz into a compact but cosy sitting room.

'So...' Adele made no move to offer Jazz a seat. 'Have you news about Charlie?'

'No, though I'm hoping to have very soon. But that's not why I'm here.'

Adele folded her arms defensively. 'Well, if you're not here about Charlie, what *do* you want?'

'I'm here, Mrs Cavendish, because I'd like you to tell me about your relationship with Sebastian Frederiks.'

Adele Cavendish put a hand to her brow and sighed heavily.

'Oh God. Sebastian said it would come out eventually.' Then she looked up at Jazz with a mixture of admiration and horror. 'How did you find out?'

'That hardly matters, Mrs Cavendish. And really, your personal life is not my business. However, you can understand how it would be remiss of me not to investigate any relationship between the mother of a victim and his housemaster. Shall we sit down?' Jazz suggested.

'Yes, of course.' Adele perched on the arm of the sofa and Jazz sank into an ancient chintz-covered chair.

'In your own time, Mrs Cavendish.'

Adele took a deep breath. 'It began very slowly, really. I got to know Sebastian because he was Charlie's housemaster. Charlie was always in one scrape or another, and in the first year Sebastian had reason to call me more often than perhaps he would other parents.'

'Was he sympathetic towards Charlie?'

'I wouldn't say overtly, but perhaps more importantly, he understood him. In short, he knew exactly how to handle him, which is more than his father ever did.'

'So, when did your relationship with Mr Frederiks start to change?'

Adele blushed. 'Well, he'd brought the boys for a sailing weekend on Rutland Water, very near where I live. William was away somewhere and I suggested to Charlie that he bring his eight friends round for supper on the Saturday night. Sebastian came too. They'd had a fantastic day on the water and were in very high spirits... It was the most fun I'd had in a long time...' Adele gave an ironic smile. 'I'm not as stuffy as I look, Inspector, but one ends up subjugating one's true self to fit in with one's life and spouse.'

Jazz nodded in agreement. She knew all about that.

'Anyway, I suppose we all had a little too much to drink. And Sebastian was making me laugh—he can be very witty when he wants to be—and I was clearing up in the kitchen whilst the boys were watching a DVD in the snug when Sebastian came in to help. We chatted away and...I realised he was actually *listening* to me.' She smiled fondly. 'He seemed to be interested in what I had to say. So, when it was time to take the boys back to the bed and breakfast, Sebastian suggested we should continue our conversation over dinner sometime, so he could repay my hospitality to him and the boys. I presumed he was just being polite. After all, he is seven years younger than me.'

'So, he called you?' Jazz prompted.

'Yes, he did, about three days later. He suggested lunch actually, said he felt it was more appropriate under the circumstances. I'd just bought this cottage, to give me somewhere to stay when I visited Norfolk to watch Charlie in rugby matches and other school events. I do so hate staying at the hall—it's like a morgue: so cold. So I was up here in Norfolk quite a bit putting things straight.'

Jazz cut to the chase. 'So the two of you became lovers?'

'Not straight away, Inspector.' Adele blushed. 'We were friends for a long time first. Remember, he was Charlie's housemaster and I was a married woman, hardly an appropriate relationship. I thought he was an attractive man; in fact, I think I had a bit of a crush on him, but I never supposed for a second that it was reciprocated. Then one day he told me it was.'

'How long ago was this?'

'Two years ago.' Adele sighed. 'Obviously, there was no alternative but to keep our relationship secret whilst Charlie was a pupil at the school. But we'd agreed that once Charlie left there was nothing to stop us being together. Sebastian was going to look for another position and I'd planned to leave William. We were planning a fresh start together.'

'You wanted to spend the rest of your life with him?'

'Yes.' Adele nodded. 'We like the same things, you see. We're both outdoor people, sporty. I may not look it now, but I was a demon netball shooter in my day. I used to ride and swim and...' Adele's voice tailed off. 'William was a city boy through and through. His idea of a day in the country was to find the nearest quaint pub and read the Sunday papers. Charlie's death has precipitated the situation. I left William a couple of days ago. We've agreed to divorce.' Adele shrugged. 'Easy really. There was nothing left to stay for.'

'I appreciate your candour, Mrs Cavendish,' Jazz said. 'Did you, at any point, give Sebastian a personal possession of yours...an item of jewellery, for example, as a...token of your affection?'

Adele looked surprised. 'Yes, I did. I gave him my signet ring, the one that bears my family crest. And he gave me this.' Adele held out the third finger on her left hand and showed Jazz a very pretty Russian wedding ring. 'Of course, Sebastian couldn't wear the ring in front of Charlie. He kept it in a drawer in his desk and wore it when we were together.'

'He's wearing it now, Adele. I've seen it,' Jazz confirmed. 'How long ago did you give it to him?'

'Around the beginning of November, I should think.' She rubbed her neck as if to remove the tension from it. 'Gosh, that seems a long time ago. Before my son died. When life was relatively normal.' She shook her head. 'You can imagine how difficult it's been for both of us since.'

'Tell me how,' Jazz encouraged.

Adele frowned. 'Surely, you don't need to ask, Inspector? My son died in Sebastian's care. Need I say more? He's wracked with guilt.'

'Except...he *wasn't* in Sebastian's care, Adele.' Jazz spoke slowly. 'Sebastian was inexplicably absent from the house the night Charlie died.'

'Exactly.' Adele sat bolt upright, staring at Jazz. Suddenly she put her head in her hands and rocked back and forwards. 'Don't you see that makes it all the more terrible?'

'What does?' Jazz asked gently, already knowing the reason.

Adele took her hands away from her face to reveal pain etched on it. 'The fact that, when my son was murdered, the man who should have been protecting him...was *here*...with *me*...'

Miles was still sitting at Jazz's desk when she returned to Foltesham police station.

She recounted her conversation with Adele as succinctly as she could.

'I think it explains why Hugh *thought* he was Corin's long-lost son. At some point, Hugh had seen Sebastian wearing the ring Adele gave him last November. Sebastian also looks the same age as Jenny's son would have been; plus Hugh knew Frederiks was brought up in Norfolk. Not to mention his blond hair and blue eyes, just like Corin's,' added Jazz.

'Yes, Ma'am, but where does it get us?'

'Well, it's doubtful Frederiks had a clue about why Hugh had left him the money.' Jazz rubbed her nose thoughtfully. 'I mean, if he had, it would have brought him to the painful conclusion that he's actually having an affair with his aunt.'

Miles grimaced. 'Yup. Nice one. Unless, of course, Frederiks and Mummy Cavendish were in this together...'

'Come on, Miles! Can you really believe Adele would plot to murder her own son?' Jazz shook her head. 'Highly unlikely, I suspect. Adele adored Charlie. But at least I can understand now why Frederiks turned a blind eye to Charlie and his *Flashman* style behaviour towards the younger boys. He wanted Charlie to like him. After all, he could have been his stepdaddy one day. No,' she sighed, 'I'm afraid we have to count Frederiks out...'

'Which brings us back to square one...'

'I'm off back to the school to speak to Mr Jones about this boy who died in the cellar,' Jazz continued. 'Jenny Colman said he was called Jamie, but she was very cagey. I want to know the whole story. My instinct tells me it has something to do with what's happened.'

'I'll carry on with Forbes's computer. I've done his business files and failed miserably to find any Smiths at all. I'm going to start on his personal stuff now,' Miles added.

'Fine. I'll also see Frederiks and lean on him to talk about this boy who was hanged in the cellar. And I'll ask him again about Julian Forbes. See you later.'

'Good luck, Ma'am.' Miles yawned—it had been a late one last night—then turned his attention back to Forbes's laptop and tried to concentrate on the job in hand.

Chapter Thirty-One

Issy watched Rory as he sketched a snowdrop which stood in a small vase on his bedroom desk.

'You draw beautifully, sweetie.'

'Thanks,' said Rory, concentrating on his sketch.

'Dad's back in the cell at Foltesham, by the way,' Issy said casually.

Rory's pencil only hesitated for a second. 'Really?'

'Yes. They seem to think he killed someone else, too.'

Rory's pencil hovered in mid-air. He turned to Issy, shock on his face. 'What?'

Issy nodded. 'I'm afraid so.'

'But...' Rory shook his head. 'That can't be.'

'Why not? If he says he killed Charlie, why shouldn't they think he killed someone else, too?'

'Because...because...'

Issy put her hands comfortingly on Rory's thin shoulders. 'I know, sweetie. It must be so hard for you.'

'No.' Rory shook his head. 'It's not hard for *me*.'

She felt his shoulders shaking beneath her hands, looked down and saw he was crying. 'Oh darling, it is, of course it is. Come here.' She kneeled down by his chair and opened her arms to hug him. He sobbed onto her shoulder as she stroked his hair. 'There, there, let it all out. Never hurts to have a good bawl, does it? You'll feel better afterwards, I promise.'

Rory's head moved so he could look her in the eye. 'No, I won't. I won't ever. You see, this is all my fault.'

'No, it's not, sweetie. You never expected your dad to go and kill Charlie when you told him about his bullying. You mustn't blame yourself. *He* took that decision, not you, and you're not responsible for his actions, really you aren't.'

'But I *am*, Issy, I am.'

'Why, Rory?' she urged. 'Tell me why.'

'Because…because…' Rory laid his head on Issy's knee, and closed his eyes with a sigh. 'It wasn't Dad that killed Charlie, it was *me.*'

'Jenny.' Robert Jones's grey face peered out of the office. 'Could you organise some coffee and bring it through?'

'Of course, Mr Jones. Won't be a tic.'

Jenny went to the small kitchenette and put on the kettle. She felt exhausted. The telephone had been ringing off the hook all morning, with the press getting wind of something going on at Fleat House. And what with the emotional rollercoaster in her *own* life… Jenny placed a cup, milk and sugar on a tray and took it through to Mr Jones's office.

'Thank you, Jenny.' Robert Jones poured milk and a heaped teaspoon of sugar into the cup, picked it up and slurped it noisily. 'Are you coping out there?'

'Just. But I don't know what to say to all these journalists. Do you know what's going on?'

He put the coffee cup down and sighed. 'Yes, I'm afraid I do; there's been another death.'

'Another death? Oh Mr Jones!'

Robert Jones sighed and shook his head wearily. 'I suppose it doesn't matter now if I tell you. The entire world will know in a few hours' time. A man's body was found in a trunk in the cellar of Fleat House yesterday. And it was obvious he'd been murdered.'

Jenny clapped a hand to her mouth. 'Mr Jones, oh my goodness! Do they know who he was?'

'He was identified as Julian Forbes, an ex-pupil of the school.'

Jenny opened her lips to speak, but nothing came out.

'Did you know Julian when he was a pupil here?' he asked.

She nodded numbly.

'Apparently, he was the live-in boyfriend of Angelina Millar, Rory Millar's mum.'

Jenny heard the telephone ringing next door. Somehow, she managed to find her voice. 'Excuse me, Mr Jones, I'd better go and answer that.'

'Of course. And not a word to anyone. DI Hunter is coming to give a press conference later. We'll all know more then.'

Jenny's breath felt tight as she walked back into her reception area to answer the call. Having dealt with it, she put the receiver down and stared into space.

A few minutes later, she stood up and went back into Mr Jones's office.

'Sorry, Mr Jones. I...did you say no one knew about Julian being dead up to now?'

'No one, apart from myself, the police, Sebastian Frederiks, and Bob, who found him, poor chap.'

'You're sure about that, are you?'

'Completely. We were all told by the police in no uncertain terms to say nothing. Why?'

Jenny shook her head. 'Oh, it doesn't matter.' She forced a smile and walked back to her desk.

Thoughts crowded in on her...thoughts she couldn't stop her brain processing, even though they were...

Stop it! she told herself. It's your imagination carrying you away.

But there was one thing she couldn't work out. However hard she tried.

'Hello, Jenny, how are you?'

Jenny looked up and saw Inspector Hunter standing in front of her desk.

'Oh, I'm...all right.'

'Good...good.' Inspector Hunter seemed as distracted as she was. She indicated Mr Jones's office. 'Is he in?'

'Yes.'

'Thanks, Jenny.' The inspector smiled and moved away towards the head's office.

'Inspector Hunter?'

She stopped and turned. 'Yes?'

'I... Well, the thing is...'

'What is it, Jenny?'

The words wouldn't come out. She didn't know how to say them. After all, she might be wrong and then, where would that leave her?

'It's nothing.' Jenny shook her head. 'Nothing.'

The inspector stared at her. 'Are you sure?'

Jenny nodded. 'Yes. I just...' She bit her lip. The inspector was so pretty and so kind, Jenny wanted to confide in her. 'I don't want to get anyone into trouble.'

'Why don't we have a chat when I've seen Mr Jones?'

'I'm going for my lunch break to see my friend in twenty minutes.'

'Well, I shouldn't be too long in there.' Jazz indicated the head's office. 'So we should have time. And Jenny, anything you say to me will go no further, you know that. And if there's something you—'

'Inspector Hunter! At last!' Robert Jones appeared at his door. 'The place is swarming with media. I've not a clue what to say to them and—'

She turned to Mr Jones. 'Let's go and talk about it, shall we? See you in a bit, Jenny.' The inspector smiled as she calmly marshalled Robert Jones back into his office and shut the door.

Jenny sighed. The question was: how could she find out what she needed to know without making trouble?

Perhaps the best thing was to go straight to the horse's mouth. Yes, that's what she should do. Jenny checked her watch, and, taking the receiver off the hook, picked up her handbag and left.

'I'd advise you not to go out of main reception at present. The vultures are waiting for tit-bits,' Jazz said, sitting down in the chair opposite the headmaster.

'Will they go away once you tell them at the press conference you have the murderer in custody?' the headmaster asked.

'After a while, yes,' Jazz responded noncommittally. 'Mr Jones, I need to ask you about this boy, Jamie, who died in the cellar of Fleat House. What do you know about it?'

He sighed. 'Inspector, it was way before my time. All I know is what everyone knows; the boy was thirteen, if I remember rightly. He hanged himself from a meat hook in the cellar.' Robert Jones shifted uncomfortably in his chair.

'Does anyone know why he took his own life?'

'You should be asking Jenny all these questions, she was here at the time, Inspector. Really, is this relevant?'

'Yes,' Jazz replied firmly, and waited for him to reply.

'Let me reiterate this was some ten years or so before my tenure...'

'So, some twenty-five years ago?'

'Yes, about that,' he agreed. 'And there was a lot of bullying going on at the time. Apparently this Jamie was subjected to some particularly cruel victimisation. I'd like to stress the police investigated his death and concluded there was no foul play.'

'And do you know who the boys were that carried out the bullying?'

'No, I don't.'

'So who would know?'

'Jenny? And Sebastian Frederiks, possibly. He's an ex-pupil.'

'Along with Julian Forbes?'

Robert Jones looked confused. 'Yes, but he can hardly help us now, can he? And why would any of this be relevant anyway? You're holding David Millar in custody. Your boss told me so this morning.'

Despite herself, Jazz bristled at the use of the word 'boss'. 'We are, but there are still some details I want explaining. For example, Rory Millar ended up in Fleat House cellar for the night, didn't he? Was that just coincidence, do you think?'

'Probably not. It's said that the boy haunts the cellar where he died. Whoever locked Rory in there knew what he was doing.'

'Charlie Cavendish, you mean?'

'Yes.' Robert Jones sighed. 'He paid his price for his misdemeanours, didn't he?'

Jazz ignored him. 'Any idea where Sebastian Frederiks might be?'

Jones checked his watch. 'Probably in the refectory, or in the changing rooms with the boys getting ready for rugby practice. Life must go on, though God knows what the boys are making of the television cameras outside. I only hope you can give them enough at the press conference to make them go away. Six o'clock, isn't it?'

Jazz was standing. 'Yes, I'll see you then. I'm on my mobile if you need me.' She nodded and left the room, her watch telling her it was only a matter of hours before she'd be naming David Millar as her chief suspect.

Jenny's desk was empty. She'd almost certainly gone for lunch. As Jazz left the building, her mobile rang.

'Issy here, Jazz.'

'Issy, any news?'

'Yes. Can you meet me back at the station?'

'Not just now. Tell me briefly.'

'Rory has just admitted his dad was covering for him. Apparently, Rory told him in the Lakes that he couldn't remember whether he swallowed the aspirin or not.'

Jazz kept on walking. 'Fine. But there must have been more to it than that.'

'There was. Apparently, Charlie Cavendish was using Rory as a lackey—getting him to clean his shoes, tidy up after him…you know the kind of thing.'

'I do, yes.'

'Well, the night Charlie died, Rory had been ordered by Charlie to go to his room before he arrived back from the pub, and switch his electric blanket on. So, after the distressing interlude with Hugh Daneman, Rory had to trudge upstairs to Charlie's room…'

'And he thought he might have left the aspirin there accidentally.'

'Exactly.'

'So, did he?' Jazz spied Frederiks marching across the rugby pitch and picked up speed, dodging a hack with a camera.

'Did he what?'

'Leave the pills in Charlie's room accidentally? Or on purpose? After all, Cavendish was making his life hell.'

'Well, Rory can remember Hugh Daneman handing him a glass of water. The chances are he took the aspirin before he got anywhere near Charlie's room. But what with the emotional trauma of Daneman's kiss, then Rory realising he was the last person to be in Charlie's room before he died, *and* the fact he'd had two aspirin in his hand only half an hour before, I think Rory's imagination worked overtime. It's called auto-suggestion, Jazz. Besides which, I doubt whether Rory was even beginning to think straight enough after what had just happened to him with Daneman to conceive an on-the-spot plot to murder Charlie.'

'But Issy, that puts Rory at the scene of the crime, with the means and it has to be a possibility… Issy? Hello?'

Jazz took her mobile from her ear and saw she'd lost the signal. 'Damn!' she muttered. Sebastian Frederiks was a few feet away from her.

'Mr Frederiks, can I have a word?' she called as she caught up with him.

'As long as it's not to question my parentage.' He carried on striding out. Jazz had to jog to keep up with him.

'Robert Jones said you might remember the pupils who were said to have been involved in the bullying of the boy who hanged himself in the cellar of Fleat.'

Frederiks stopped short and looked at her. 'That's ancient history, isn't it? What's it got to do with anything now?'

'Probably nothing, but if you can remember the boys' names, I'd be grateful.'

Sebastian looked wary. 'It was never proved, you know, and I wasn't even at the school when it happened. I arrived a few months after, in the Michaelmas term. But some of the boys said this Jamie was unstable, odd in the head. I don't think his death can be laid at anyone's door.'

'No, I understand, but I'd still like the names,' Jazz persisted.

He scratched his head. 'Look, remember this was all hearsay. I knew some of these chaps, they were ordinary human beings; boys like me who liked a joke.'

'Mr Frederiks, the names, please.'

'Okay, okay,' he nodded. 'There were four of them said to have been involved in the bullying, apparently. They'd arrived at the school, bonded and formed a "gang" of four. Adam Scott-Johnson, Freddie Astley, Harry Connor and...Julian Forbes.'

'Julian Forbes? Are you sure?'

'Yes. He became a mate later on. Fantastic fly-half. Poor chap, so sad he's gone.'

'Thank you, Mr Frederiks. You've told me all I need to know. Please excuse me, I have to get back to the station.'

Sebastian watched the inspector turn tail and walk swiftly across the pitch.

Walking into Foltesham station, Jazz went in search of Issy.

'She's popped out for a sandwich, Ma'am. She looked exhausted when she arrived back. Heard her news, I hear?'

'Yes, yes.' Jazz paced the small space, irritated Issy wasn't here. 'Where's Rory?'

'At home. Issy suggests you both go and see him this afternoon. But Ma'am, from what she said, Rory has done little more than get confused whilst he was in a state of high anxiety. Besides, how could we tie in Forbes's death? After all, we know Rory was at home with his mum on Tuesday night. There was one of our PCs sitting right outside her house.'

'I know, I know.' Jazz sank into a chair. 'Unless the deaths were unrelated, which, given there've been three in the past week, is statistically off the Richter scale of probability. I just spoke to Frederiks, who told me Julian Forbes was one of the supposed bullies responsible for the death of the boy who died in the cellar of Fleat...' She checked her watch. 'Shit! Two and a half hours until the press conference... I *know* David Millar didn't do this…it's something connected with the past but I just can't…'

'Tell me what Frederiks said exactly,' Miles said calmly. He was used to the high pitch his boss would reach when she was close to the truth.

'There was a gang of them…'

'Names?'

'Oh, Harry someone, Adam… I have them written down, but they weren't names I've come across before.'

'Hold on a moment, Ma'am.' Miles turned his attention back to the laptop, scrolled down and read the email in front of him. 'And Freddie, by any chance?'

'Yes.' Jazz stopped pacing and turned to him in surprise. 'Why?'

'I think you might be spot on about this being to do with the past. Look at this email. It was sent to Julian the night he died. Thought it was odd when I read it.'

Miles turned the screen towards her and Jazz began to read.

Dear Julian,

So good to hear from you after all these years. Glad you tracked me down. That 'School Reunion' website really works, doesn't it?

You asked if I'd heard about the rest of our gang of four. Sadly, I have to be the bearer of bad tidings, at least for two of them. Harry's wife contacted me last year to tell me he was dead. He'd moved to Sydney—did you know? And, by all accounts, was a very talented surgeon. Apparently he was found dead in the sluice room at his hospital. Don't know the details, but it wasn't accidental. Still haven't caught the perpetrator as far as I know.

And I heard only a couple of months ago that Freddie's no longer with us either. He died about three years ago in the States—a friend of a friend used to work with him at Goldman. Suicide apparently. He jumped out of his office window and was found dead on the pavement below. That's the high finance world for you—pressure's unbelievable. Only thirty-eight too; left behind a couple of kids. Blimey, it makes you humble. So, sadly, old mate, that leaves only the two of us.

I'm currently living in Provence, learning to turn grapes into wine. Off the City treadmill and onto a far more palatable one. On my second wife; two kids from the first and a baby on the way in three months with number two.

Love to come to your fortieth and will make arrangements nearer the time. Goes without saying it's a hop, skip and a jump from Norwich to Marseilles. Name the date and let's meet up.

Sorry to hear you saw 'Il Forgeron'. Not surprised you were shocked. I would

have been too.
Get in touch as soon as you can.
Adam

When Jazz had finished reading, she sat there in silence. Finally, she spoke: 'Harry, Freddie, Adam and Julian. The names of the boys whose continual bullying is said to have been the reason why Jamie hanged himself twenty-five years ago.'

'Harry, Freddie, Julian… All dead…' added Miles.

'Don't forget Charlie Cavendish, a renowned bully, too…'

Forgeron… The word was repeating itself inside her head…the answer just out of reach…

Sydney…the States…

Jazz pulled her notebook out of her briefcase, racing through the scribbled notes she had taken over the past week.

Then she found it.

'Of course,' she breathed.

'What?' Miles asked.

'*Il Forgeron…* Now I think I understand.'

Miles looked confused. 'Understand what?'

Jazz was already at the door. 'Julian saw his murderer recently. Angelina Millar told me he looked as though he'd seen a ghost when he drove her to school a few days ago. Someone who loved Jamie enough to kill those they believed were the cause of his death. And to put an end to anyone else guilty of the same crime. Email this Adam immediately. Get on to the Provence gendarmerie if necessary. Whatever it takes, track him down. And warn him.'

'Warn him of what, Ma'am?'

'*Il Forgeron.* Tell him he's next.'

Chapter Thirty-Two

Jenny was still not back at her desk when Jazz arrived.

She walked into Robert Jones's office and found him, head back, half asleep.

'Have you seen Jenny?' she asked abruptly.

'Yes, she's at her desk.'

'No, she isn't.'

'Then perhaps she's gone to the loo.'

'Mr Jones, it's really important I find her. When was the last time you saw her?'

'About an hour ago?'

'Right. May I borrow your phone?'

'Of course.'

'DS Roland, I need you to get as many men as possible into the school to look for Jenny Colman, the head's secretary. What? No, forget the media and start searching now. Let me know if you find her. Thanks.' Jazz put the receiver down and turned her attention to the head. 'I need a full list of employees at the school for the past twenty-five years *now*.'

'They'll be in the archive file in the bursar's office.' Robert Jones was on his feet, finally sensing the urgency. 'I'll show you where it is, shall I?'

They used the fire escape to leave the building and walked across Chapel Lawn and into Main Hall. Taking the steps two at a time, forcing Robert Jones to do the same, Jazz asked, 'I presume you take out thorough references on all the staff that come to work at the school?'

'Of course.' Jones stood panting in front of a door on the third floor. 'One can never be too careful these days.'

'Even on members of staff who may have been employed here before?'

'Yes, I…' Jones was sweating as he unlocked a large filing cabinet. 'Nineteen eighty-five?'

'We'll start with that, yes.' She could hardly contain her irritation at his pedantic slowness.

'Here we go.' Robert Jones took the ledger across to the desk and opened it.

'Thanks.' Jazz began to skim down the names.

'Can I help?'

Ignoring him, she turned over the pages in an agony of suspense. Then, finally, she found the one she was looking for. She smacked the book shut and gazed up at Robert Jones.

'Excuse me, Mr Jones, I've got to run.'

Jazz sprinted over to Fleat House, calling Roland as she went.

'Any sign of Jenny Colman yet?'

'No, Ma'am.'

'Have you been into Fleat?'

'Course not, Ma'am. Thought that was off limits. Didn't think you'd want my plods crawling all over it with their mucky…'

Jazz didn't bother to let him finish. As she arrived at the front of the house, she asked the PC if anyone had been inside.

'No, Ma'am, not for the past hour.'

'Thanks.' Jazz pushed the door open and walked swiftly along the corridor towards the stairs. Dialling Miles's number and getting no answer, she left him a message.

'Meet me at Fleat House urgently with back-up. Tell Roland to get his backside here too.'

Up the stairs she went, knowing exactly where she was heading, dreading she might be too late.

On the top floor, she ran towards the front door and found it locked.

'DAMN!' Trying every key on the Fleat House ring, none fitted. She stood back and launched herself at it, but to no avail.

Hammering on the door, she cried, 'Jenny, it's Inspector Hunter. Are you in there? Answer me if you can!'

Silence.

'Hello, Ma'am. How are things?' Miles appeared by her side with two burly constables.

'Break it down, boys,' she ordered. 'As fast as you can.'

The constables gave the door an almighty shove. At the fourth try, it opened.

'Thanks, chaps. There are certain occasions I remember I'm female,' Jazz quipped in relief as she walked through the door of the flat, Miles by her side.

She walked through the hall and into the small sitting room. Jenny was lying on the floor, unconscious. Jazz kneeled down and checked her pulse. She could feel a faint flickering.

'Call an ambulance, and tell Roland to station his men on every exit. No one comes in or out until I say so.'

Jazz stood up and walked into the bedroom. And, as she'd expected, found the wardrobes and drawers empty.

Miles joined her as Jazz sighed. 'Probably packed a day ago. I'd imagine she's gone to Norwich airport, or perhaps Stansted. They have flights to the South of France. Get on to the airport authorities. Give them a description, Miles. I'll see if the school has a passport photo in their records.'

'A description of who, Ma'am?' Miles frowned in confusion.

'Of Madelaine Smith, Miles. Matron of Fleat House. *And* the mother of Jamie Smith, the young man who hanged himself in the cellar twenty-five years ago. Or, as her victims preferred to call her, "The Blacksmith".'

Chapter Thirty-Three

Scotland Yard, London
One week later

Norton opened his door and welcomed Jazz inside.

'Come in and sit down. It's good to see you, DI Hunter.'

Jazz sat in the chair in front of his desk.

'Strange to be back?' he asked cryptically.

'Yes, but I've buried the ghosts, Sir.'

'Good, good,' he nodded. 'Now, I've obviously read your report on the case but I'd like you to talk me through it anyway. I have to live vicariously through my detectives now that I'm a sad old pen-pusher.' He smiled grimly and Jazz could see he meant it.

'Well, Sir, as you know, I was pretty sure David Millar didn't kill Charlie. None of it added up. I was convinced all along this was something to do with the past. And the only connection I could come up with for all three of the deaths was Fleat House. Once I'd heard the full story on Jamie Smith's suicide, then read the email Adam Scott-Johnson had sent Julian Forbes, things fell into place. I remembered when I'd first interviewed Madelaine Smith: she'd told me she'd once worked at the school many years ago. She also said she'd subsequently worked in the States and Australia. What she failed to mention was that her son had been a pupil at St Stephen's and had subsequently hanged himself.'

'So, who else knew her?'

'Poor Jenny Colman, of course. She knew,' said Jazz. 'They'd been friends from way back. And Hugh Daneman recognised her, so Jenny said. Certainly the headmaster didn't know. He produced glowing references from the file from her positions in Australia—notably at the same hospital where poor Freddie met his end—'

'You've been on to Sydney, I presume?' Norton interjected.

'Yes, and the Feds about Freddie Astley,' Jazz confirmed. 'Mrs Smith will never smell the scent of freedom again. She was picking off the "Gang of Four" one by one. Of course, her motive for the killings was perhaps the strongest of all: the love of a mother for a child.'

'Yes, it's a pretty solid motive as they go,' Norton agreed. 'So, she took a job in Norfolk with the intention of murdering Julian Forbes?'

'Yes. And I'm inclined to believe her when she says the temporary job coming up at St Stephen's was a coincidence. She was in Norfolk, looking for work, and an opportunity to get rid of Forbes, and there it was.' Jazz shrugged. 'She may well have seen it as ironic: it suited her needs perfectly, gave her somewhere to live and also the means to kill Julian in the very place where her own son had died. According to her, Julian was the ringleader of the gang. The one she blamed most for the bullying she thought led to her son's death'.

'And Charlie Cavendish was a victim of circumstance,' Norton suggested, 'in the sense that Smith watched Rory Millar being bullied mercilessly by him, in an exact replica of what happened to *her* own son twenty-five years ago. She felt she had to stop it.'

'Exactly,' Jazz agreed. 'The vigilante matron. Again, her motive for killing Charlie was solid. Smith was highly protective of Rory. One can understand why. His fragility reminded her of her own son, Jamie. That's why, when she saw on the medicine log Hugh Daneman had given Rory two aspirin, just after she herself had taken two from the medicine cabinet to kill Charlie, she decided to Tippex over the record and create a false one to avoid implicating Rory.'

'You say she walked into Forbes's office in Norwich that Tuesday night and somehow managed to persuade him to accompany her back to the school?'

Jazz nodded. 'He must have been terrified when she turned up. She'd been nicknamed "The Blacksmith" by the boys when she was Matron of Nelson House twenty-five years before, because of her name, nature and her jet-black hair.'

'She sounds terrifying,' admitted Norton. 'Had a matron like that myself when I was at school.'

'To be fair, I'm sure before her son died, she was a normal woman,' Jazz equivocated. 'And it didn't help that her husband had been fatally injured on a shoot on the Conaught Estate when Jamie was only a few months old. The small amount of compensation Smith got from the family enabled her to send her son to St Stephen's, where she presumed he'd stand a chance of a better future. Unfortunately,' she sighed, 'it turned out to be the opposite.'

Norton tutted. 'Yes, I remember the odd clever working-class boy on a bursary at my old school. I'm ashamed to say we gave them a rough time. The old British class system—never seems to disappear from our psyche. I'm sure that will have played a part in the boy's suicide, too.'

'However appalling, you're almost certainly right, Sir.'

'So, grief obviously sent the woman mad,' Norton concluded.

'Spot on, Sir. When I interviewed Adam a couple of days ago, he told me that after Jamie was found hanged, the "Gang of Four" were all paid a visit by Smith, and told that one day she'd make them pay for what they had done to her son. She left the school soon after, but Adam says none of them ever forgot her words.'

'It turned out to be no idle threat. Tell me about Jenny Colman,' Norton said. 'How is she?'

'Out of hospital and at home. She's doing well, considering. Still reeling from the shock of the woman she considered her best friend trying to murder her. Jenny had guessed. Thank God we got there in time. She's a lovely lady. Throughout adversity, she's put on a brave face, never blamed anyone for her misfortune. And...' Jazz smiled, 'there *is* one silver lining out of this cloud. Martin Chapman discovered something very interesting when he was comparing DNA samples.'

'He's discovered who her long-lost son is?'

'Yes,' Jazz nodded. 'By complete coincidence, Martin had seen a similar DNA pattern only the day before, during the course of the forensic examination at the crime scene. He cross-checked them and found they were identical.'

'May I ask who?' enquired Norton.

'Sir, as it's not relevant to the case, would you be offended if I didn't tell you? I feel both Jenny and her son should be the first to know,' Jazz explained.

'Of course.' Norton smiled at her. 'So, what was it Smith had said to her that made Jenny realise she might be involved?'

'Jenny said that Maddy, as she calls her, mentioned to her last Friday morning, which was the day after Forbes was found dead, that Rory was all Angelina Millar would have, and I quote, "now he's gone". At the time, the fact we'd found a body at all was still a secret, let alone that it was Julian Forbes. Jenny also couldn't understand how Smith knew about Angelina's relationship with Forbes. It couldn't have been Rory who told her. He didn't know. So when she heard the following day from Robert Jones it was Julian who had been murdered, and knowing more than anyone how Smith blamed him and his cohorts for her son's suicide, Jenny put two and two together.'

'So, before she spoke to you, she went to ask Maddy Smith to explain?'

'Yes. Smith told Jenny that Sebastian Frederiks had told her about Forbes dying, put her mind at rest, whilst making Jenny a cup of tea filled with antifreeze. Not enough, thank God, to do much damage but, really, Sir, this is the third case we've had. Can you not suggest to your friends in high places they should do something? It's readily available and if it doesn't kill, it leaves the victim wishing they *were* dead.'

'Rat poison and bleach are also readily available, Hunter.'

'But not as conveniently tasteless, Sir.'

'No. But the fact remains, most people want to have a car that starts in the morning, and a clean bathroom. They don't want to kill others.' Norton smiled. 'When you've left your soapbox, pray, do continue, Hunter.'

'Sorry, Sir. I know we see the tiny percentage of misuse and I have to keep it in perspective. Sometimes it's hard, that's all.'

'What's interesting, Hunter, is that *you* aren't hard. Yet. An empathetic, experienced officer is the best we can ever hope to offer the public. Make sure you keep it that way.'

Jazz realised she'd been given a back-handed compliment. 'Yes, Sir, I'll try.'

'Good. So, to continue...' Norton looked askance at her. 'I worry Mrs Smith sounds completely barking. Is she deemed mentally fit to stand trial?'

'Issy has been with her quite a lot, and says Smith is perfectly sane for someone *insane*, as she put it. She's shown no remorse whatsoever. She believes that justice has been done to avenge the death of her son. It won't be a long trial, that's for sure. Broadmoor's on the cards, I should think, Sir.'

'Well...' Norton closed the file on the desk in front of him. 'You got there eventually, Hunter. Congratulations. And before the press conference, too. I don't like to think of the consequences if you'd announced we'd arrested David Millar, only to discover later we were wrong.'

There was a moment's unspoken acknowledgement of who had almost caused such chaos.

'Now, leaving the case aside, I want to know how you are feeling about the future.'

'I haven't had a lot of time to think, Sir,' Jazz replied honestly.

'The thing is'—Norton picked up an envelope from his desk—'this is your letter of resignation. And I suggest that if you do wish to resign again, you put a little more thought and effort into its composition. I presume you're still determined not to come back to London?'

'Yes, Sir.'

Norton raised his hands in resignation. 'Well, I won't try and persuade you again, if your mind is made up. But whatever anyone may tell you, the Yard is where it happens, and where you, as a detective, get noticed in terms of future promotion.'

'I understand, Sir. But I'm not obsessed with career progression particularly, just in doing a good job. And being happy,' Jazz added.

Norton raised an eyebrow. 'And you think you're "happy" in Norfolk?'

'What little time I've had there, yes, I believe I am,' agreed Jazz.

'I'll make no bones about the fact I want you back here. However, if you are not staying with us, the commissioner would like to see you as soon as possible.'

'Really? Why?' Jazz asked nervously.

'To discuss how you could help him in his plans for setting up a Special Ops department in East Anglia. It'll cover Norfolk, Suffolk and parts of Cambridge and Lincolnshire,' Norton explained. 'To put it bluntly, the commissioner is sick of having his team here deployed all over the country. Especially as London becomes more and more in need of our services. There are three other regional departments currently being set up, which should cover the entire country, without the need to filch from us.'

'I see.' Jazz nodded. 'And what would the commissioner want me to do, exactly?'

'To head it up, of course. In the first instance, to recruit a small roving team that would liaise with the Serious Crimes Units in the regions mentioned above, and work with them in tandem. It's a specialised job, Hunter. You need excellent people skills and an ability to adapt to a hundred different situations. And I'd say you'd just had the perfect taster at St Stephen's.'

Jazz realised Norton had almost certainly known all about this new department when he'd come to see her a couple of weeks ago and offered her the St Stephen's case. He'd been testing her out. On one hand, she was irritated she'd been manipulated; on the other, she felt honoured they valued her highly enough to bother.

'Forgive me if this a surprise, Sir. I wasn't expecting it. Can I have a few days to think about it?'

'No longer than a couple of days, Hunter. I've stuck my neck out for you on this one. The commissioner is already nervous about your so-called "sabbatical" and has voiced his worry that you may disappear off into the deep blue yonder again. If you're going for this, I want us all to feel you are one hundred and ten per cent committed.'

'I understand, Sir. What about staff? Could I look to take some of my old colleagues with me?'

'A couple at the most,' warned Norton. 'I've lost enough of my troops in the past year one way and another. I presume you'd want Miles. He's been here for a long time now. Maybe he could do with a new challenge. Never felt we've quite brought out the best in him,' Norton mused. 'But you seem to. And maybe a change, plus a promotion might be the answer.'

Norton looked at his watch.

Jazz took it as the cue to take her leave. She stood up and offered her hand across the desk to Norton. 'Thank you, Sir, I really appreciate the faith you've shown in me. I'll be back to you by the end of the week, I promise.'

'Good. I hope the answer's in the affirmative.'

Jazz turned and walked towards the door. As she opened it, he said, 'Hunter?'

'Yes, Sir?'

'Don't let him win, will you?'

She smiled to herself. 'I'll try not to, Sir, I promise.'

Jazz drove along the A11 towards Norfolk, her mind ticking over.

Don't let him win...

They were powerful words, but she couldn't afford to make a decision based on anything other than what *she* wanted from the rest of her life.

She'd already made two major changes: divorcing Patrick and leaving London. And as her cottage began to take shape, she knew she was going to love living there.

But could she seriously see herself living without the adrenalin of her job? However frustrating and demoralising it sometimes was.

She was *good* at it, very good. And she *liked* the feeling. Perhaps without Patrick there to patronise her and strip her of her confidence, she might like it even more…

Jazz saw the sign for Cambridge and, on a whim, turned off and headed in the direction of the hospital.

Tom was down on a ward now, sitting up in bed, chatting to his next-door neighbour.

'Jazz, darling.' He threw open his arms to her and she hugged him, feeling his skeletal frame through his pyjamas. 'How's my favourite girl?'

'I'm good, Dad, very good.' She sat down in the chair next to him, studying his hollow cheeks and still grey pallor. His eyes, though, were clear and twinkling with life. 'How are you?'

'I'm alive, my ticker is still ticking, if rather erratically, so that doctor keeps telling me, and very glad to see you. Mum told me all about the case.' He reached for her hand and squeezed it. 'I'm terribly proud of you.'

'Thanks, Dad. Do you know when they'll let you out?'

'Next week sometime, if I behave myself and eat up my beta-blockers like a good boy. Can't wait actually.' Tom lowered his voice. 'They're all bloody senile in here, shout out in the middle of the night. Be far better at home with your mother, in my own little bed.'

'You are not to come out until the doctors say that you can, Dad,' Jazz chastised. 'It's not fair on Mum, apart from anything else. You know how she worries.'

'I do, but hospitals *make* you sick. They've been dropping like flies in here,' he whispered.

'I know, Dad, but you are still in the best place, really.'

'Anyway, enough of me. I want to hear about you. What's the next thing on the agenda?'

'The kitchen's nearly finished, I have a new bathroom suite, and the painter actually turned up yesterday.' Jazz gave a small clap of pleasure.

'Yes, yes, very nice,' agreed Tom. 'But I mean life-wise, darling.'

'Well,' said Jazz slowly, 'I've been asked if I want to meet the commissioner next week, with a view to heading up a new Special Ops department in East Anglia.'

Tom was impressed. 'That's rather an honour, isn't it?'

'Well, Norton would see it as a step down from working at the Yard, but I would be more or less autonomous.'

'No boss to kowtow to, because you'd be it,' acknowledged Tom.

'Yes. A big fish in a much smaller pond.'

'So.' Tom studied his nails. 'Have you decided yet?'

'No. I told him I wanted to think about it,' said Jazz. 'A few months ago I'd left the force and was going to do something completely different with my life. What do you think?'

He looked at her and smiled. 'You know, one of the things I've thought about in here is the fact that during your life, I may have influenced your decision-making process far too much. Because I'm too sure of my own advice, and…because I love you so very much.' He reached out his hand to her, tears forming in his eyes. 'Therefore, on this occasion, I'm going to keep shtum. You must do what you think is right. And that's all I can say.'

Jazz squeezed his hand, her own eyes welling with tears. 'Okay, Dad.'

'Whatever decision you make will be the right one. I know it will. Don't be afraid of failure, Jazz. Sometimes things go wrong, that's part of life. And it's also part of life to pick yourself up, dust yourself down and move on.'

'Yes, you're right. Thanks, Dad.'

'Jonathan popped in to see me the other night, by the way.' Tom raised an eyebrow.

'Did he?'

'Yes, he asked after you, sent his love and said to give him a buzz when you had a chance.'

'Dad, please, stop matchmaking. I'm not interested, really.'

'Jazz…' Tom tutted. 'One day you'll realise that the only thing which gets us through is love—be it for family, religion or art. The higher plane, as I like to think of it. Sorry, my darling, but you make a dreadful "island". You'll always want love in your life, I guarantee it.' He grinned. 'After all, you are my daughter.'

As Tom closed his eyes and drifted off into sleep, Jazz sat next to him and wondered how she could ever learn to cope without him.

David Millar was eating a solitary supper of baked beans on toast in his miserable kitchen. Since he'd been released a week ago, he'd spent a lot of time sleeping. It helped pass the time and meant he wasn't awake so he couldn't pour himself a drink.

The past two weeks seemed like a blur, but slowly his head was starting to clear and he was feeling a little better. His sponsor from AA had been round to see him and he was back on the programme. And this time, he was determined to kick it. He'd surrendered, admitted the booze had him beaten. There wasn't a fight any more, just a realisation that if he wanted to regain control of his life, take tentative steps to seeing it improve, he could never have another drink. Because he couldn't stop like other people. Because he was an alcoholic.

His mobile rang from the sitting room, and he ran to answer it.

'Hello?'

'David, it's Angie. How…how are you?'

'Oh, better for not being charged with a double murder, thanks.'

'Yes.' There was a pause before she said, 'You know, I never believed you did it. I told Inspector Hunter you couldn't have done it.'

'Cheers,' he replied coldly.

'And…I was wondering, if you were up to it, could Rory come to you on Thursday for the day? It's half-term, you see, and it's Julian's funeral. It would be better if he wasn't around.'

'Of course. As long as you trust me.'

'Are you…?'

'Yes, I'm sober. And you know that I've never been drunk in front of Rory on any occasion. I wouldn't and couldn't do that to him. Ever.'

There was a silence and Angelina said finally, 'I'm sorry, David. For everything.'

'Yes, well, no point raking over the past, is there?'

'No. But I was hoping we could at least be friends, for Rory's sake, if not ours.'

Eventually, David said, 'Angie, I loved you. All I wanted to do was to make you and Rory happy. And you completely screwed me over. So no, Angie, I can't see us ever becoming "friends".'

'No. Well, it's not been a good time for either of us, David.'

'Well, you seem to have come out of it considerably better than me. You have Rory and you now own the house outright, don't you? You're a wealthy woman, very eligible.'

He heard her choke back a sob. 'Do you really think I'm that much of a bitch?'

'Yes. Bring Rory over anytime on Thursday. I'll be here.'

As he put the phone down, there was a knock at the door.

'Shit! Who can that be?' he mumbled, as he went to open it.

'Oh, it's you,' he said, when he saw Inspector Hunter standing on the doorstep. 'You've not come to question me over the mysterious disappearance of a gnome from the neighbours' garden, have you? Because I didn't do it, honest, Officer.'

Jazz ignored the comment. She supposed he was entitled to his sarcasm. 'Can I come in?'

'I suppose so.' He opened the door wider so she could step inside and led her into the kitchen. 'Sorry about that, Inspector,' he sighed. 'I just spoke to Angie on the phone and it upset me.'

'I understand. Can I sit down?' Jazz asked, eyeing the dirty plates by the sink and the general domestic chaos.

'Suit yourself,' he shrugged. 'I'll stand.'

'Look, David, I can only apologise on behalf of my colleagues for your treatment. However, you must remember it was you who turned yourself in originally and confessed to the murder of Charlie Cavendish.'

'I know.' David ran a hand through his hair. 'Stupid thing to do really, but the thought of Rory being banged up for what was merely a mistake on his part made me feel I had to do something.'

'Well, he's very lucky to have a father who loves him so much he was prepared to go to prison for a crime he didn't commit. I admire you, David, I really do. Don't know whether I'd have had the guts to do the same thing in your shoes. But then,' Jazz smiled wryly, 'I know what prisons are like.'

'At the time, Inspector, it didn't seem like a bad alternative to the life I was living. I mean'—he waved his arms to indicate the room—'hardly Buckingham Palace, is it? Not compared to where my wife and son are living, anyway. That's all I wanted—a happy childhood for Rory.' He sighed.

'Did you have a happy childhood, David?' she asked.

'Very. It got a bit lonely sometimes, as I was the only one. I was adopted as a baby, you see. That's why I wanted Rory to have brothers and sisters, be part of a proper family.'

'Did you grow up in Norfolk?'

'I was here until I was two, then Dad got a job in Kent, so we moved there. But I've always loved Norfolk.' David managed a smile for the first time.

'Did your parents tell you you were adopted?'

'Oh yes,' he confirmed. 'They made no secret of it. And I know I was born locally. Maybe that's why I've always had an affinity with the place. Anyway,' David checked himself, 'you don't want to sit here listening to me and my dull past, Inspector. Is there anything else?'

'Actually, David, there is,' nodded Jazz. 'I've got something to tell you, and I really think you *should* sit down.'

Epilogue

One Month Later

When Jazz woke up and drew back her curtains, she saw blue sky and sunlight beyond the window for the first time in weeks. She opened the window and breathed in the smell of freshness that heralded spring.

Almost falling over herself to get outside and paint before the weather changed, Jazz threw on some clothes, grabbed her stool, easel and paints, and stomped across the road to the marshes.

Setting herself up at a good vantage point, and realising that the sunlight still flattered to deceive in terms of warmth, she spent a glorious couple of hours sketching the view. Normally, she'd take a much more surrealist perspective, but she wanted to paint this as accurately as possible, so she could hang it on the wall of her sitting room and remember it during the long, dark days of winter.

When she arrived back at the cottage, her fingers were icy and she couldn't feel her toes. She jumped in the bath to warm up, dressed in a pair of jeans and a jersey, then set about making a goat's cheese salad for lunch.

At one o'clock, she saw the car pull up outside.

She opened the door and waited for him to walk up the short path.

'DS Miles—Alistair—how are you?'

'I'm good, very good.' Miles kissed her warmly on both cheeks as she led him inside.

'Jazz, this is stunning.' He glanced around the sitting room, loving the freshness of the cream walls, the loose-covered cream sofa, coir matting on the floor and the thick gold curtains that hung at the windows.

'I'm glad you like it. Not too fussy, is it?' she asked in concern.

'Not at all. It's warm but elegant, unfussy but comfortable, a bit like its owner.' He smiled.

'Love the metaphor, Alistair. Drink?' Jazz offered, walking into the kitchen.

'A glass of wine would go down a treat. Forgotten how far this godforsaken part of the country is. Took me almost four hours—roadworks on the A11.' Miles followed her, noting the grey floor tiles and the clean white laminated kitchen units that set off the red Aga so well.

'You've performed miracles, Jazz, really,' he said admiringly. 'It's a fantastic mix of old and new.'

'That's what I was aiming for,' replied Jazz happily. 'And to try and brighten the place up a bit. Cottages can be so dark.'

Miles was looking at the large modern painting hung on the dove-coloured wall above the small kitchen table. It was painted in bold striking colours: confident blocks of white, grey and red that matched perfectly with the kitchen. 'Where did you get that?' he said, peering closer. 'It's an original, isn't it?'

'Well, it would be, as I painted it,' she smiled.

Miles looked awestruck. 'You?'

'Yes, me.'

'Is there no end to your talents, Ma'am?' he teased. 'That is seriously good. Cheers.'

'Cheers.' Jazz toasted him with a glass of water. Lately, she'd rather gone off alcohol. 'Let's go and sit down.' She led the way through to the sitting room where the fire was building nicely.

Miles sat down. 'This really is idyllic. You must be very happy here.'

'I am,' Jazz nodded. 'It's a perfect bachelor-girl retreat. And you're very honoured. You're my first official guest.'

'It's good to be back here, actually. When I left for London after the case, I felt claustrophobic for weeks.' He shrugged, 'I suppose you get used to it.'

'Perhaps I'll change, but I've no wish to return to London whatsoever,' said Jazz with feeling.

'So, fill me in on all the details post-case.' Miles settled himself back on the sofa. 'How was Jenny Colman when she met her son for the first time?'

'Emotional, obviously. As was David Millar. We've got Martin Chapman to thank for that. When he was checking Rory's trunk, he picked up David's DNA from the fingerprints, and a hair he found inside. He remembered it when he was checking the hair sample Jenny had taken from her baby. It was identical. He then crossed it with Corin Conaught's hair and hey presto!'

'Wow!' Miles replied in wonder. 'Sometimes I hate modern forensic practices—they seem to slow down or mess up a case—but on this occasion, it had a spectacular result.'

'It did. Jenny Colman has a new lease of life. And so does David.'

'What about the Conaught Estate?' questioned Miles. 'Will David have a legitimate claim as the direct, if illegitimate heir?'

'Absolutely. Despite her initial prejudice, Emily Conaught called to thank me a few days ago. David had been up to the house to meet her. He then took Rory with him, who of course, we both know, is the living image of his grandfather, Corin.'

'Hugh Daneman may have got the father wrong, but it's easy to understand why he was so fond of Rory,' Miles said gently.

'And died regretting his fondness,' Jazz sighed. 'However, the Conaughts have now got their bloodline back: David, and Rory. And Emily and Edward have already offered David a cottage on the estate. They're aware David has an alcohol problem, just like his father, and they want to keep an eye on him.'

'They do say it can be genetic,' Miles commented, holding out his wine glass for a top-up. 'Unlike me, my parents are teetotal. Does Angelina Millar know that the husband she dumped unceremoniously for being a loser will eventually be a lord of the realm and inherit one of the grandest estates in Norfolk?'

'Tee hee.' Jazz smiled. 'Can you imagine how she'll feel when she does? She'll be spitting! She's blown her chance to join the aristocracy and have half the county kowtowing to her. It's a social climber's dream. No doubt she'll try and worm her way back into David's affections. I hope he doesn't let her, after the way she treated him.'

'I'm so glad for David. He seemed like a genuinely nice bloke.'

'He is,' agreed Jazz. 'And, as Emily pointed out, as long as he keeps off the juice, he's got the business contacts to take the estate into the twenty-first century from his days in the City. Oh, I do like the occasional happy ending, makes this sometimes thankless job of ours seem worthwhile. Right, shall we eat?'

Jazz warmed some ciabatta, and they shared the salad companionably.

'What about Adele Cavendish and Sebastian Frederiks? I mean

really, the proceeds of Hugh Daneman's will should have gone to David Millar. Although I suppose he'll have plenty one day,' commented Miles.

'Mr Jones told me Frederiks has handed in his resignation. He and Adele are very much together apparently, and they want to make a fresh start.'

'Not surprised, after all that's happened. Give them both a chance to get over Charlie.'

'Well, at least this case, for a change, had a couple of silver linings.'

'Yes. And...umm...for me too, actually.'

Jazz saw the colour rise to Miles's cheeks.

'Oh yes? What?' Jazz knew already but she wanted to let him tell her.

'Me and Issy...well, we're,' Alistair shrugged, 'together, I suppose.'

'That's wonderful news, Alistair,' Jazz responded warmly. 'You know how I love Issy.'

'Seems I do too,' he said shyly. 'People've commented we make an odd couple, but I don't think we do. Yes, she's louder than I am, and there's no doubt she loves to mother me, but I rather like it.' Miles smiled. 'Don't know whether it'll last, but it's going well at the moment. And we're both very happy.'

'And that's all that matters. Coffee?' Jazz stood up and put the kettle to boil on the Aga.

'Thanks,' he nodded.

'The only thing I'd say, Alistair, is be very careful. I know you're not both coppers like Patrick and I, but you will end up working together at some point. Need I say that it proved a disaster for us and our relationship.'

'And dare *I* say that Issy is not an egocentric, arrogant jerk who wanted to prove his superiority over his more able wife at every opportunity?'

Jazz nodded graciously. 'You may.'

'Everyone knows he's an arsehole, Jazz. He's not well liked at the Yard. And you'll be pleased to know that word got around about the Millar debacle.' Miles shrugged innocently. 'I've no idea who could have spread the fact that he got a right ticking-off from Norton.'

'Thanks, Alistair.' Jazz patted his hand. 'You needn't worry. I'm over it. It's gone. Now, I've got something far more important I want to talk to you about. Let's go back in front of the fire and drink our coffee.'

Once Jazz had stoked the fire, she sat in front of it, as Miles settled himself on the sofa.

'Alistair, me inviting you here today was not only so you could boost my ego, and admire my interior design skills, but also to put an idea to you,' she began.

'If you want me to pose nude for one of your life sketches, then forget it,' he grinned. 'Other than that, fire away.'

'Well, I've been asked to set up a Special Ops branch here in East Anglia. I'm currently in the process of recruiting a team. And I'd like to know if you're interested in coming to join me as my second in command.'

Miles looked at her, speechless. Finally, he said, 'Sorry, Ma'am, I don't know what to say. I really don't.'

'Well, you could say you'll seriously consider it.' Jazz could not help but be disappointed at his reaction. 'We've worked together for five years very successfully. You'd be going up a scale in terms of pay, you'd have all your removal costs paid for, but I don't know how you might feel about leaving the Yard for a much more provincial scenario.'

Miles sighed and studied his hands. 'It's not the Yard I'd miss, Jazz, it's Issy. Damn!' Miles hit the arm of the sofa in frustration. 'A couple of months ago I'd have jumped at a new challenge, but now...' He shook his head. 'I just don't know.'

'I understand,' Jazz nodded. 'Why don't you have a chat with Issy and see what she says?'

'She'll say she doesn't "do" the country. You know what she's like. Which means I'd have to commute. Look, let me think about it, will you?'

'Of course. I want you, Alistair. Not in the biblical sense,' Jazz smiled, 'but I think we could head up a great team between us.'

'Thanks, Jazz. The feeling's mutual. And I like the idea of creating a department from scratch—no bad eggs already there to deal with—'

'I won't ask Patrick to apply then.'

'I'd suggest not.' Miles laughed. 'But there is one young woman DS who's been on secondment with us who's really impressed me. I think you'd like her too...'

'Give me her name,' Jazz said eagerly. 'Norton said I can't poach anyone from the department, but if she's on secondment, it doesn't count. And the more girls, the merrier. We can share lipsticks and swap gossip over the length of your lots' batons.'

Miles chuckled. 'Ma'am, it's so good to see your old sense of humour is coming back.'

Jazz frowned. 'Did you think it had gone?'

'You weren't your usual relaxed self, Jazz, no. Actually, when I think about it, not for a long time before you left,' he said honestly.

Jazz agreed with a sigh. 'You're right. But I'm feeling much more like me now.'

'I'm glad. I'd hate to think of that prat undermining you.'

'Rest assured, he hasn't.'

Miles checked his watch. 'I've got to get going, or I'll get stuck on the M25.'

'Use your siren, Alistair. Everyone does. Except me, of course.'

'Right.' He stood up and so did Jazz. 'I'll let you know as soon as I can. And thanks for lunch.'

'Anytime you're passing, which, if I have my way, might be quite often.' She kissed him on the cheek, and took one of his hands in his. 'Please consider it seriously, won't you?'

'Definitely. Bye, Jazz, take care.'

Jazz shut the door, then went to clear the lunch away. As she was pouring the remains of Miles's wine down the sink, she stared out at the marshes which sprawled in front of the cottage. The tide was rolling in, and in a few hours the intricate waterways and footpaths which snaked through the vast landscape would be completely hidden from view. Jazz smiled, pleased that her new home was both beautiful and emblematic.

As she watched the grey sea begin to distantly intrude upon the green of the marsh, her thoughts turned to Madelaine Smith, a woman as resolute as the tide in completing her task. Hers was a life motivated by a single, terrible purpose, fuelled by the pain and agony of the past.

Jazz's phone buzzed on the kitchen table, and she picked it up to read a text from Jonathan.

Leaving Cambs now. See you in an hour. X

Jazz had decided that, for now, she was happy to leave the past behind. She was only concerned with the future.

* * * *

Also from Lucinda Riley and Blue Box Press, discover *The Missing Sister*, *The Olive Tree*, *The Angel Tree*, and *The Butterfly Room*.

Acknowledgements

I am very grateful to Maria Rejt at Macmillan, whose enormous experience and knowledge of crime fiction assured us that *The Murders at Fleat House* would provide readers with the thrills and spills which Mum intended. Sincere thanks also go to the wonderful Lucy Hale and Jeremy Trevathan for continuing to champion Lucinda's work.

As mentioned in the foreword, this novel was written in 2006. At that time, I was thirteen years old, and I can't possibly begin to guess at who Mum would have wished to thank. Therefore, I will take this opportunity to acknowledge the author herself.

The true testament to Lucinda's indomitability is the fact that she wrote no fewer than five novels during her illness. What's more, through The Seven Sisters series, Mum rose to global stardom, and has become one of the world's most renowned storytellers.

The books, however, were always secondary to her family. Throughout her tragically short life, I do not believe that she ever, once, put herself first. In that, and all respects, Lucinda was the best Mum in the world. Her capacity to support, champion, console and motivate her four children was unparalleled.

Thankfully, her enduring wisdom means we all know the great secret to happiness, which Mum would impart to us often, and I feel duty-bound to share with you now:

Seize the day, live for the moment, and relish every second of life—even the hard parts.

Harry Whittaker

About Lucinda Riley

Lucinda Riley was born in Ireland and, after an early career as an actress in film, theatre and television, wrote her first book aged twenty-four. Her books have been translated into thirty-seven languages and sold forty million copies worldwide. She was a *Sunday Times* and *New York Times* number one bestseller.

Lucinda's The Seven Sisters series, which tells the story of adopted sisters and is inspired by the mythology of the famous star cluster, has become a global phenomenon. The series is a number one bestseller across the world and is currently in development with a major TV production company.

Though she brought up her four children mostly in Norfolk in England, in 2015 Lucinda fulfilled her dream of buying a remote farmhouse in West Cork, Ireland, which she always felt was her spiritual home, and indeed this was where her last five books were written. Lucinda was diagnosed with cancer in 2017 and died in June 2021.

On Behalf of Blue Box Press,

Liz Berry, M.J. Rose, and Jillian Stein would like to thank ~

Steve Berry
Doug Scofield
Benjamin Stein
Kim Guidroz
Social Butterfly PR
Ashley Wells
Asha Hossain
Chris Graham
Chelle Olson
Kasi Alexander
Jessica Saunders
Dylan Stockton
Richard Blake
and Simon Lipskar